Praise for *The Begotten*

"A full-bodied, absorbing tale that combines authentic historical detail with a universally appealing and gripping story that will have readers cheering on the Gifted as they race against time to decipher ancient prophecy and save the world from darkness. With crossover appeal for J.R.R. Tolkien and Madeleine L'Engle enthusiasts, this is recommended for all." —*Library Journal*

"Bergren's experience as a Christian historical-fiction author serves her well in this religious thriller, the first of a trilogy set in fourteenth-century Italy . . . [a] classic battle between good and evil." —*Publishers Weekly*

"Mysteries and miracles abound in *The Begotten,* a fourteenth-century Italian thriller with a fascinating cast of characters. The tender heart of Daria, the beautiful healer, gives the story emotional depth, while all around her spiritual and physical battles are waged between light and dark, life and death. *The Begotten* is the very definition of a page-turner."

—Liz Curtis Higgs, bestselling author of *Grace in Thine Eyes*

"Never has a novel been more timely than Lisa T. Bergren's *The Begotten.* While other books are distorting history and scriptural truth almost beyond recognition, Bergren has given us an amazing story—one that proposes a fantastic 'what if?' *and* remains true to the Spirit of God as well as medieval times. A wonderful read!"

—Angela Hunt, author of *Magdalene*

"Masterfully crafted from the heart of a modern-day word-artist, *The Begotten* will transport you to a world of medieval Italian mystery where truth and beauty break through the darkness and lead the way on a trail of wonder."

—Robin Jones Gunn, author of *Gardenias for Breakfast*

"An exhilarating religious historical thriller . . . delightful . . . action-packed . . . superb." —*Midwest Book Review*

Titles by Lisa T. Bergren

⚓ ⚓ ⚓

Novels of the Gifted

THE BEGOTTEN
THE BETRAYED

⚓ ⚓ ⚓

THE BRIDE
CHRISTMAS EVERY MORNING
THE CAPTAIN'S BRIDE
DEEP HARBOR
MIDNIGHT SUN

The Begotten

A Novel of the Gifted

LISA T. BERGREN

BERKLEY BOOKS, NEW YORK

THE BERKLEY PUBLISHING GROUP
Published by the Penguin Group
Penguin Group (USA) Inc.
375 Hudson Street, New York, New York 10014, USA
Penguin Group (Canada), 90 Eglinton Avenue East, Suite 700, Toronto, Ontario M4P 2Y3, Canada
(a division of Pearson Penguin Canada Inc.)
Penguin Books Ltd., 80 Strand, London WC2R 0RL, England
Penguin Group Ireland, 25 St. Stephen's Green, Dublin 2, Ireland (a division of Penguin Books Ltd.)
Penguin Group (Australia), 250 Camberwell Road, Camberwell, Victoria 3124, Australia
(a division of Pearson Australia Group Pty. Ltd.)
Penguin Books India Pvt. Ltd., 11 Community Centre, Panchsheel Park, New Delhi—110 017, India
Penguin Group (NZ), 67 Apollo Drive, Rosedale, North Shore 0745, Auckland, New Zealand
(a division of Pearson New Zealand Ltd.)
Penguin Books (South Africa) (Pty.) Ltd., 24 Sturdee Avenue, Rosebank, Johannesburg 2196, South Africa

Penguin Books Ltd., Registered Offices: 80 Strand, London WC2R 0RL, England

This is a work of fiction. Names, characters, places, and incidents either are the product of the author's imagination or are used fictitiously, and any resemblance to actual persons, living or dead, business establishments, events, or locales is entirely coincidental. The publisher does not have any control over and does not assume any responsibility for author or third party websites or their content.

PRINTING HISTORY
Berkley Praise hardcover edition / August 2006
Berkley trade paperback edition / September 2007

Berkley trade paperback ISBN: 978-0-425-21560-9

The Library of Congress has cataloged the Berkley Praise hardcover edition as follows:

Bergren, Lisa Tawn.
    The begotten : a novel of the Gifted / Lisa T. Bergren. — 1st ed.
        p. cm.
    ISBN 0-425-21016-2
    1. Bible. N.T. Epistles of Paul—Fiction. 2. Paul, the Apostle, Saint—Fiction. I. Title.

    PS3552.E71938B44 2006
    813'.54—dc22   2006009545

PRINTED IN THE UNITED STATES OF AMERICA

10 9 8 7 6 5 4 3 2

To Darren and Sarah, fellow travelers and seekers of the Word.
We are blessed by your friendship.

ACKNOWLEDGMENTS

My heartfelt thanks to my husband, Tim, my kids, my agent, Steve Laube, and my preliminary readers: Sarah Shonts, Pastor Bob Rognlien, Randy Ingermanson, Kathy Boyles, Alicia Miller, Pastor John and Hope Bergren, and Cheryl Crawford. Tim, Steve, Bob, Randy and Erik Wirsing, helped me hone my original concept for the series. Bill Myers spent an hour on the phone with me at the start, showing me how to do the research I needed in frightening, uncharted waters, by turning me back toward the rock-steady, grounding influence of Scripture; I was constantly thankful that I was surrounded by friends and family who prayed for me while I researched and wrote this project. Many laypeople allowed me to interview them in depth, prying and probing to find out more about their unique spiritual gifting; all preferred to remain anonymous but I acknowledge here that they helped me in innumerable ways. Piero Boeri, a ninety-year-old Italian I met on a plane from Montana, helped me with Italian via e-mail, and delighted me so much that I used both of his names for characters in this book.

I am also thankful for our tour guides, Dr. Caspar Pearson of ContextRome and Michael of Venicescapes. Thanks to my parents, who watched our kids, and my business partner, Rebecca, who let me leave my real job, so we could see some of these sites in Italy with our own eyes. The academic research librarians of AskColorado were very helpful, as were the local librarians of Colorado Springs. My editor, Denise Silvestro, her assistant, Katie Day, and the wonderful copyeditor, Amy Schneider, made substantial improvements upon the book. All errors that may still be contained within these pages are, of course, my own. Last but not least, my heartfelt thanks to Joel Fotinos, Leslie Gelbman, Lara Robbins, Craig Burke, Chris Mosley, Norman Lidofsky, and the rest of the sales force, the Noble Group, the pros at B&B Media, and everyone on the Berkley team.

Dear Reader,

A few facts to know before you join me on this adventure . . .

In the fourth century, church officials came together in Constantinople and agreed on common doctrine and works of the Holy Canon—those works deemed legitimate and worthy of being included in the Bible we know today. As had become custom, many books were reviewed and then set aside, due to questionable authorship or potential heresy. Heretical teachings were discussed and condemned.

Despite the fact that Saint Paul references earlier and other letters sent to the Corinthians (1 Cor. 5:9; 1 Cor. 5:11; 2 Cor. 10:10–11), no biblical historian has ever seen these work(s) and no further record or reference has been found to date. But they clearly existed.

In the eighth century, the Iconoclast movement gained momentum and ultimate power in the Eastern Church. Iconoclasts were vehemently against any graven images, including illumination—the ancient art of illustrating, gilding, and beautifying the Holy Scriptures along the margin and sometimes in the midst of the text. Some illuminists claimed to be divinely inspired, often adding illustrations that could be interpreted by only them. Others claimed they were prophetic. Thousands of books and manuscripts representing centuries of work were burned in the eighth century, and illuminists who refused to turn away from their craft were put to death. In Italy, the Western Church clung to the belief that icons were holy and blessed, something to be exalted rather than eradicated. Many illuminists made their way to Italy and beyond in that era to escape persecution or demolition of their works.

Join me in the eighth century now.

—Lisa T. Bergren

COUNTS
OF SAVOY

VISCONTI
FAMILY

PATRIARCHATE
OF TRENT

DELLA SCALA FAMILY

PATRIARCHATE
OF AQUILEIA

Como

Milano

Verona

REPUBLIC OF VENICE

venezia

GONZAGA FAMILY

ESTENSE FAMILY

REPUBLIC OF FLORENCE

MARQUISATE
OF SALUZZO

REPUBLIC
OF GENOA

REPUBLIC
OF PISA

Firenze

PAPAL
STATES

REPUBLIC
OF SIENA

Siena

Roma

Napoli

KINGDOM
OF NAPLES

ITALIA C.1350

KINGDOM
OF SICILY

PROLOGUE

Constantinople

The Year of Our Lord 731

"THIS way, Your Grace," whispered a monk ahead of him, gesturing toward a room bathed in shadows.

Bishop Claudiopolis Thomas turned the corner and paused a moment in the doorway, sensing everyone hesitating around him, neatly echoing the hesitation he felt inside. Before him, laid out on a table, with dusty streams of dusk light streaming through a narrow window and onto its pages, was the script.

The bishop willed his feet to move forward, but dread rushed through him like an inner robe slipping over his shoulders and down to his feet. What was this task before him? What evil laid in his midst?

Hiding a hard swallow behind a cough, he lifted his chin and placed one slippered foot before him. Monks moved to either side like the Red Sea before Moses. They were nothing, these men in drab gray robes who sought nothing of significance for themselves or their Lord. Mice, really. Rodents, feeding upon a molding cheese of the devil . . . If it weren't for men like himself, watching out for the children of God, they would all be swept away to Hades.

Reaching the front of the lambskin-covered manuscript, he nodded to his assistant. Taking a fabric-tipped stick from his robes, the plebe opened the cover of the book and turned to the first page. Touching it with his fingers would surely mean eternal damnation. The plebe carefully averted his eyes, looking not to the page, but to his master for guidance.

The bishop stared at the first page with hard eyes, praying for the will to withstand its siren call to admire, appreciate, draw him in. *For Thy will, Lord Jesus!* he cried silently. *For You alone, must I do this task!* Traveling the length of his emperor's territory, searching out the heretical works alongside other Iconoclasts, was becoming a burden almost too great to bear. He had burned paintings and ordered sculptures destroyed. *Like golden calves in the temple* . . . Now he had been called to seek out the illuminated manuscripts and cleanse the Word of God from graven images. This was his final task, his final endeavor.

He nodded, directing the plebe to turn another page. His knees and trembling hands threatened to betray him. Even a godly master like himself could feel the devil's temptation drawing him in. Could they all not sense it? The weak pope, Gregory III, had led them down this path . . . taught them to venerate the icons instead of cast them away. This script must be destroyed, along with its creator! The monk refused to recant, refused to change his ways. What choice did that leave the bishop?

"Your Grace," said a man from the dark corner, taking a tentative step forward. "I never allowed the evil one to enter these hallowed halls. My work . . . my work was meant as an act of worship. My paintings were divinely inspired."

The bishop stared hard at the man, and at the pubescent, dark-haired boy to his side, slightly behind the monk. A student in training, perhaps? The heresy already grew tentacles. He returned his eyes to the book, nodding toward the plebe. "Go to another section, please." The book was a complete Bible script, encompassing five or more years of work in a scriptorium. If only there had not been images, the careful, perfect writing could have been preserved for other students of Christ. But the artist had blasphemed the Holy, created work that could not have been divinely inspired unless it was for the dark lord and not his own.

Licking his lips, Thomas nodded once more. The plebe turned to yet another section, and Thomas sucked in his breath. He fought off a wave of dizziness, tried to clear his throat to speak.

The abbot rushed to his side. "Your Grace! Are you all right?"

Thomas could do nothing but stare at the Latin words at the top of the page. "You have blessed this project, man?"

The abbot, sweating now, stared down at what the bishop was reading. Slowly, he lifted his hand to his mouth and whispered, *"Deus Misereatur.* There must be some mistake."

"I can explain," said the priest behind them.

The bishop, never turning, raised one hand, fingers splayed. "We will not hear further words from a heretic. There is no way you can explain including an uncanonized letter in the Holy Writ."

The bishop dared to lean closer and read a few more lines. The cardinal would wish to know about this. Specifics.

A letter of a man masquerading as Paul, to the Corinthians, but not the first or second holy letters. A strange letter with haunting words. The bishop swallowed hard. He could not allow himself to be sucked in. He mustn't read heresy. The lies had a way of entering one's head and feeding upon a man's thoughts until it became truth. *Abyssus abyssum invocat . . . Abyssus abyssum invocat! Hell calls to hell!*

He glanced at the plebe, hoping the boy did not see the sweat upon his upper lip. Thomas refused to brush it off. "A bit more, please. I must know the breadth of heresy contained here."

Along the margin of a perfectly lettered page, was a gilt-enhanced painting of a woman, dark hair curling in lush tendrils along her neck, finger teasing at the nape, olive-shaped eyes of a seductress. . . .

"Goddess worship!" the bishop cried, slamming the bedamned book shut. If it hadn't been chained to the wall, he would have rushed it to the fires himself. "What madness has been allowed within these walls?" he thundered.

He whirled toward his guards. Outside, the hallway was lined by brown-robed priests who hastened out of view. Thomas whipped his head toward the abbot. "Out! Bring me the key at once! We must make haste and burn this treachery and its creator today! Satan has made his way into thy hallowed home, brothers. Today, we shall burn him out!"

The priest fell to his knees before the bishop. "I beg of you to understand, if you will give me but a moment to tell you—"

"Recant at once and make your boy understand the error of your ways."

"I will not. This is not heresy. It is where my Savior has led me—to use my gifts, to show the world what beauty and honor—"

"Recant!"

"I cannot," he said, clasping his hands before him. "I cannot turn away from what I know to be right and true. It took me a year to illuminate that particular letter. I stayed to the task because of a divine calling. Your lordship, if you will only—"

"You and your wretched work shall burn," Thomas said slowly, sorrowfully. He looked about to the brothers who still congregated in the hallway. "Quickly, before anyone else is swayed by the evil one's intentions."

The bishop turned back to the monk, squaring his shoulders, lifting his chin. "Brother, you were called by divine powers, indeed. You were fooled by the shadowed one into believing that you worked for your own cause! Foolish, foolish man. Recant now. This is your last warning."

He could see the fear that rushed into the balding man's face, could almost see the fires of the stake in his eyes. But then the monk became even more resolute. Slowly, he came up from his knees to stand before his master. What audacity! In the face of judgment? In the face of death? In Thomas's years of carrying out the emperor's edict ordering the destruction of all icons, this was a first.

"It was foreseen," the monk said simply. "I was foolish to try to avoid it. Do what you will, Your Grace. There is more at stake than my life. I give it, freely for the sake of the Master and all who follow him."

"What master?" the bishop asked, leaning forward, wanting to tear open the man's head and heart to see the darkness that must be quickly rotting him inside. "Who gave you this so-called vision? Permission to include it along the Holy Writ?"

"The Lord Jesus Christ and none other," the man said.

The bishop leaned back and slapped the monk hard across the face, sending the man reeling to the stone floor. "Blasphemy!" he whispered. "Blasphemy! You are no longer entitled to name our Lord in the presence of other holy men. You are hereby excommunicated from the Holy Church and sentenced to burn at the stake tonight, along with your wretched book. May your evil heart be condemned to hell and may the Holy Church be saved from parasites such as you."

He wheeled then, his fine robes cascading around him like a dancer's skirts. Over his shoulder, he said lowly, "Lock him in this room until nightfall. Let him stare at the bare space that once held his precious book; let him contemplate his downfall. Do not grant him last rites. He is no longer your brother. He is Satan in your midst."

The bishop paused at the door, waiting while everyone filed past him, staring at the monk and his dark-haired student.

"Please, sir, may I stay with him?"

"Nay, child. Come with me. You must not stay in his presence a minute longer."

"A word. I need a moment to say my farewell." His deep

brown eyes pleaded. Eyes of an innocent. He would soon be freed from his treacherous bonds. But he would need to feel an affinity to Thomas if the bishop were to win back his soul.

"Only a moment, child. I must speak in private with the abbot and then I will return for you." He eyed his two men nearest the door. "Lock them in and do not leave this hallway until I return."

⛋ ⛋ ⛋

THE boy looked to his master, the man he had assisted in the task of illuminating the letter this past year. He was not an instrument of the devil; he was not. The boy himself, though young, had witnessed the Holy Spirit in this very room, felt the warmth of the Presence, the brush of angel wings.

Hastily, he helped the old man to his feet and to the cot at the edge of the room, and as he did so, the elderly monk opened his fist and placed a slender knife into it. The monk closed the boy's fingers around it and looked into his eyes.

"Oh, my son, this was foreseen," the monk whispered, trying to smile. "We have spoken of this day. I will die but our cause shall not. There are others who will follow. You will be led to God's chosen ones." As he spoke, he caressed the boy's cheeks, like a father about to be separated from his son. He wiped away the boy's tears even as others streamed from his own. "Find your way to Roma and seek out my friend—he will guide your steps. Just as surely as God has guided my hand, the Lord will guide you too. Do not fear. It is imperative, child, that our work on the letter is not lost. Do you understand?"

The child nodded, wiping his nose.

"Good. Now go! Cut it out, quickly! Before he returns!"

The boy rushed over to the manuscript and turned to the letter, the letter that had brought the Holy One into this very room. He winced as he cut, frustrated that there was no time to properly slice the leather bonds and free the letter from the folds. He had just slid the pages under his robes and shut the cover for the last time when the abbot and bishop returned.

"Get away from that foul tool, boy!" the bishop shouted and the boy backed away in haste, hiding the knife among the folds of his robe. The abbot rushed to the wall and with trembling hands unlocked the chain that had held the book for years in this very room. Worth a year's wages, illuminated manuscripts were known to disappear, even from the center of a monastery, thus making locks necessary.

"Bring the boy," the bishop said, gesturing from the guards to the child.

But the monk's eyes held his as he was whisked away. "God is with you, my child. Never forget it. Always and forever, no matter what happens, *he is with you.*"

Unable to form any words through his tears, the boy simply nodded. The bishop placed a large hand on his shoulder, as if in comfort, but it only felt heavy upon him.

ʦ ʦ ʦ

Hours later, he watched as his master was tied to a stake and a great fire was set. Tears he thought were spent rose in his eyes, yet he refused to look away as the flames licked upward, as the heat made him step back.

The bishop threw his master's life's work, the book, into the fire at the priest's feet.

The priest glanced over at the boy, a quiet question in his eyes.

The boy patted his shirt in response, reassuring his master, feeling the sacred pages next to his skin. The boy shook his head in confusion; he could *hear* the priest, even though the old man's parched lips moved not. *Go, child. Go!*

The boy glanced over at the bishop, his face and grand robe dancing eerily in the heat waves between them. The bishop's eyes narrowed.

Go, child, go!

Looking at his master one last time, the boy turned and fled into the night.

THE GATHERING

Roma

CHAPTER ONE

The Year of Our Lord 1339

IN his six years as a knight of the Church, they had burned at the stake scores of sinners. As each died, Gianni de Capezzana could not determine whether any were any less saint than he. This one was different.

For the first time, Gianni longed to immediately put his adversary to death, to drown the chill emanating from the Sorcerer in the heat of flame. This one was coldly sinful, delighting in the dark power—Gianni could feel the force of it surrounding, threatening. He glanced backward, over his shoulder, to make sure his men were right behind him. As they passed, the men filled and lit occasional oil lamps among the loculi to show them their way out.

The lamps did little to dispel the dark shadows from the passageway of the ancient catacombs before them, but now was not the time for torches or even any more small lamps. If they did not surprise this group ahead . . . Surprise was their principal ally. They would simply have to risk the dark.

Cold sweat rolled down his neck and down between his shoulder blades. The death hallways were cool enough to ease the heat of his armor, but fear—a feeling rare to him—made him hot as fever. "It is only the stories, the foolish stories of the villagers," he muttered, as if mentoring a squire instead of himself. But his mouth was dry, making him want to pause, cough. He forced himself to take another step and then another, knowing if he stopped, he'd turn around and retreat.

It was dread. Different from the dread of battle—this fear filled his mind and soul. This was why he had been called to the Church, to do battle with evil, to hunt it down before it hunted the weak. But this . . . this threatened to overcome him. Over and over again he fought down the urge to turn and run. "*Deo iuvante.* May God give us his strength," he whispered, clenching his teeth. "Send your angels, Lord God. Be with us in this."

Sword in hand, his eyes scanned back and forth, briefly settling upon the loculi on either side, early Christian skeletons shelved like books in a scholar's library. The Romans had burned their dead. It had been the Greeks who had insisted on coffins and death crates, and the Christians who adopted the cheap burial grounds. The cardinal had spoken of this place, having seen early Church documents. But the abandoned catacombs had long been lost to the overgrown hills of Roma. Never did Gianni believe he would be within them! *Whatever happens to me here today, Lord God, do what thou wish with my bones. Just bring me into thy presence in heaven.*

Aeneas appeared at the doorway. "Up ahead," he whispered, casting a brief, curious eye about the room. But his mind was clearly on their adversary.

Gianni immediately turned and led the way Aeneas directed. Flickering light told him there was a torch ahead and he raised his hand to slow his company of knights. Their noise made him wince. There was no element of surprise possible, he realized, even with a stealthy approach. The stone caverns went on for miles, and carried sound just as far. Surely their approach was known by now, and if so, they were too late! "Charge!" he cried, in motion before the word fully left his lips, hearing his men follow after a moment's hesitation. They roared together, a great cacophony meant to send an enemy to quaking.

His company of twenty-four filled a large room, lit by one torch in the center, and stopped in stunned silence. The stone altar . . . the blood . . .

A knight behind him began to quietly retch.

Gianni raised his torch higher and slowly walked forward. He swallowed hard, forced himself to touch the pooling blood. It was fresh. This travesty had happened within the hour. He looked up and around the room, noting tunnels that led away, each equally cold and silent. *Horror ubique animos, simul ipsa silentia terrent,* he whispered, quoting Virgil. *Fear and silence everywhere present terrify the soul.*

He kneaded his temples with one hand, forcing himself not to be drawn into the fear. He must think! Their enemy was not far gone. He raised his torch again. "You men, light your torches. We must see where we are. What this place is."

Aeneas and the others lit their torches and the walls of their cavernous hall came alive with light. One man behind him gasped. Another fell to his knees.

Gianni lifted his torch higher, perusing the frescoes, reading the ancient Latin. "If you are searching for them, here lies united a host of the Blessed. The venerable sepulchers enclose their bodies, but the royal palace of Heaven has carried . . . Here lie the companions of Sixtus . . ."

Aeneas was reading alongside him. "Not Pope Sixtus."

Gianni looked about the room again and shook his head with grim fury. It was an ancient papal crypt. Six sarcophagi lined the room! His enemy had dared to do such evil here! Here, in the lost crypt of popes!

"Captain . . ." said a knight with a tremulous voice behind him.

Gianni turned. The knight stood in the center of the room, looking at the blood, pooled on the ground and atop the stone altar. It was then that Gianni saw it. It wasn't an altar, but another sarcophagus, ornately carved on the outside.

"They sacrificed him, right here, atop the pope's grave!" said the knight. Gianni walked toward him, dreading that he was right. What kind of man committed such sacrilegious acts? What kind of man dared to murder atop the monument of one of God's own?

"The boy's blood was put to good use, knight."

Gianni whirled, facing the dim outline of a man just ahead along a passageway, standing against him in cold defiance.

"You will die! You will face the wrath of God!" Gianni cried, rushing forward.

"Captain, wait! To whom do you speak?"

Gianni looked back in confusion to Aeneas. "There! Ahead! Come!" But when his eyes went back to where he'd seen the man, he noted five different passageways bleeding off the larger hall, and all lay empty. He swallowed the foul words that leapt to mind. "Did you not see him? Hear him?"

His fellow knight shook his head, brows furrowed in concern and fear.

"The Sorcerer? He spoke to me!"

"They cannot see me," the Sorcerer whispered in Gianni's right ear, and the knight whirled again, nearly nicking several of the closest men with his blade. They cried out, on alert with their leader, swords at the ready, but clearly confused by his actions.

"Captain," Aeneas said urgently, drawing near his left as was their habit, eyes scanning with him. "What is it?"

"He is here," Gianni said through gritted teeth, turning slowly, willing his eyes to see through the darkness.

"I was here," whispered the voice in his left ear, "but am no longer. You are too late."

CHAPTER TWO

PIERO knew her from the moment he first glimpsed her in the garden, even before he saw her guard with the family herald. A peacock as her family crest. But he would have known her instantly, even without it. After thirty years of waiting, seeking, watching, she was here.

Piero forced his eyes from her and walked to the wall, pretending to gaze out upon the city. But his thoughts were cascading back in time, to when he was a young man, a student. And to his teacher.

His teacher had taken him on a journey one day, out into the hills far beyond Roma's ancient walls. In the ruins of a small village, they made their way to the center, Piero biting back his question out of respect for his master, obediently following where he led.

The old man cast him a secretive glance and then entered an old Byzantine church, recognizable only by fragments of mosaic that likely covered the entire floor centuries before. Once, there might have been a ceiling, resplendent with gilt mosaics, or marble columns. But none of that remained. Only crumbling stone and mortar.

The teacher motioned him forward, to a side chapel with tall walls that remained largely unbroken. When he realized what he was seeing, Piero fell to his knees and then to his face.

A moment later, the teacher's hand rested on his shoulder. "You know what it is?"

"Surely this is the chapel of some saint."

"I agree," he said. "Although who, I have never been able to ascertain. Please, my son. Rise."

Piero drew upright, but remained on his knees, looking around in awe. There were biblical scenes in fresco as light and lively as if they had been painted but a week prior. There were Mark and Luke, John and Matthew. Jesus in numerous settings.

Piero sensed the teacher nodding and glanced his way. "Yes," the teacher said. "It is marvelous, is it not? There are many rooms in Italia such as this one, where the faithful met and worshipped, but this room is especially important to you."

"To . . . me?"

"To you." With some effort, he got down to his knees in front of Piero and brought his satchel closer. "I have looked for you for many years, my son. Your appearance in my seminary told me it has begun."

"What? What has begun?"

The teacher smiled and held up one finger. "Tell me what you see about us, among the frescoes."

"Christ, teaching beside the Galilee. Jesus again, as a boy, with the teachers in Jerusalem. There, at the Last Supper . . ."

"Yes. And who, who is that?" he said, pointing in the direction of a woman's figure. Behind her was a slave. The woman was standing over a child, one hand on the child's head, an herbal branch in her other hand. A healer?

"I know not. A saint? One of the mothers of our Church?"

"Hmm . . . possibly. Who is she reaching out toward?"

Piero's eyes ran down the length of the woman's elegant arm, past the herb that seemed to be pointing to the next figure. "A man, on a road. A monk, by the cut of his robe."

"Look closer."

Piero rose and went closer to the painting and then took a step back, spooked. He cast a tentative smile to the teacher. "It resembles me a bit."

But his teacher did not smile back. "And down the road, the road that monk travels. Who do you see?"

"A knight. Roman, by the cut of his dress."

"Do you see anything that ties these three figures together?"

Piero looked from one to the next. "A peacock. At each of their feet."

His mentor said nothing more about the frescoes, simply bent and unrolled a leather envelope that he had pulled from within his satchel. With arthritic hands, he untied the old leather bands. Piero found himself not wishing to draw closer, sure that he was about to know something terrible. Something wonderful, but mayhap too large for any normal man to take in. An irrational fear stole his breath.

"Come closer, my son. It is time you know of our divine secret."

cb cb cb

THE *divine secret.* And finally, he was no longer to share it alone. *She was here!*

But it had taken the friar weeks to approach her. Again and again, he questioned the leading of the Holy One, wondering if it was merely her likeness to the script and years of searching that made him assume she was the one. But she had come to the convent as if led to him. As the only man on the grounds, he stood out, and several times he had caught her staring at him. But it was not his shaved head that drew her eye. She felt it too. He was sure of it.

Walking with the abbess one day on their weekly visit, he saw her working in the garden, cultivating herbs, weeding. "Mother, who is that woman over there?"

The nun glanced over to the woman and then back to the path before them. "Lady Daria d'Angelo, Father, another noblewoman on pilgrimage."

"She carries much sorrow in her eyes."

"Broke her heart, he did," piped up a nun on the other side of the abbess. "Just as sure as their handfast."

The elderly nun frowned at the girl and shook her head. "Sister, again and again I've told you. You must learn to hold your tongue from gossip or you will never amount to anything as a woman of God."

Cowed, the girl stepped back and followed the two of them in silence.

"To whom was she handfasted?" Piero asked gently.

"Marco Adimari of Siena," the girl supplied helpfully. The abbess glanced back at her and her bright eyes fell again to the path.

Siena. It made sense. He had known he was to go to Siena, felt the pull of it many times. He had not known when. "She is a fine and beautiful woman. What reason would Adimari have had to break their handfast?"

"She is barren. Both families are in desperate need of an heir. Though they were fond of one another, they had no choice but to part. She came here to Roma on pilgrimage, hoping to find solace in the holy sites and direction for her life."

"And has she?" He gazed across the garden to the woman.

The abbess drew them to a halt and glanced up at him, curiosity alive in her eyes. "It is unusual for you to take interest in any of our guests, Father."

"Has she found solace?" he asked again gently.

"To a certain extent. She spends hours in the chapel and here, in the garden."

"It has been almost two months now," he said. "How long does she intend to remain within these walls?"

"I know not," she said with a shake of her head. "She refuses to speak of leaving, but she must go soon. Though just a woman, she is responsible for her family's businesses. If she fails to do so, distant cousins will step in."

"She has told you of this?"

"Nay. Her guardian in Siena, Vincenzo del Buco, sent me word a week past. And I must confess, her African makes many of the sisters ill at ease, with his silent, solitary ways, hovering over her. They whisper of their desires for him to depart. I do my best to hush them but—"

"I would imagine that nuns would be first to find comfort in silence and solitude. Mayhap I should have become a Benedictine rather than a Dominican." He tossed the nun a grin. "Who is he to her? Slave?"

"Freed slave. They were raised together, practically. He reads and writes as well as the lady. With no tongue, most assume he is dumb and frequently treat him as if he were deaf as well."

Father Piero had briefly greeted and observed the man these past weeks, always standing erect and alert at the edge of Daria's location, missing nothing. "You managed to learn a great deal from a man with no tongue."

"Yes," she said, glancing guiltily back at the young nun behind them. Gossip, no doubt.

They walked for a bit in silence. "He hardly appears to be a threat to our sisters here, in the convent. His manner is more guard-like than predatory."

"Yes, yes, it is Lady Daria he always watches over. It is as if he hopes to shield her from any harm again. But the harm has been done to her heart. Only our Lord can shield a woman in such matters."

"You said she has business to attend to in Siena. What business?"

The abbess paused for a moment, clearly thrown by his singular and obvious interest, let alone such an extended conversation.

For the two years since he had come to preside over the convent, their weekly talks had been no longer than five minutes of conversation, and almost entirely over the business of the convent or its holy women. Visitors were tolerated but largely ignored.

"The d'Angelos have headed the woolen guild for over a century, and she also does a significant trade in herbs, spices, even more in inks and parchment."

Piero threw her a quick glance. "She supplies Siena's illuminists?"

"Every one."

Piero laughed under his breath.

"And herbs? Spices, you said?"

"Herbs, spices, medicinals, yes."

Piero shook his head and laughed, ignoring the abbess's consternation and confusion. "She has no male kin?"

"No one but Baron del Buco—he treats her as a niece, of sorts. And as a member of the Mercanzia, it is he who leads her in matters of the guild. It is because of him that our lady has been able to hold on to her interests, even from afar."

"I see," Piero mused, moving away from the abbess to a point at the wall, where he could look out over the city. He leaned his arms out, supporting his body tentlike, and let his eyes scan the city's buildings.

She was here. He had to talk to her. The only question was how? And when?

Chapter Three

A week later, Lady Daria was again among the gardens, pruning and cultivating the plants and flowers. The nuns used the tender petals for flavoring food and water, and in liquids meant to soften the skin. As she worked, Father Piero drew near and kneeled in the herb garden to weed. "Lady d'Angelo," he greeted her with a nod.

"Father," she said with a demure nod back toward him. But her wide, olive-brown eyes did not leave his. "You intend to weed."

"I do."

"The nuns usually care for the gardens."

"Indeed. But at times, it is good for a man to contemplate the weeds in his own soil and take care to rout them out." He bent to pull weeds from between the straight rows of rosemary.

They worked in companionable silence for several minutes. Father Piero sensed, more than saw, Daria's man edge closer to them. But when he glanced up at the tall African, the man stared beyond him, as if watching the horizon.

"Why did you free him?" he asked, keeping his eyes on the ground before him.

"I did not free him. It was my father. Hasani chose to stay beside me. Have you been properly introduced?"

"We have shared a few words."

"He has few words in his mouth to share. But many more in his heart."

Father Piero's own heart was beating very quickly. He had not expected the woman to be so forthright, so free in her speech. Ladies of stature rarely spoke to men, and even more rarely to priests. He fought the desire to stare at her, to compare chin and long lithe neck to the illuminated page.

"You have words yourself, Father, that you wish to speak?" she asked quietly.

He glanced over his shoulder at her, and she stared boldly back at him. "I have seen you, gazing at me when you think I am not looking or aware. Hasani has seen you. What is it that you wish to say to me? Do you wish us gone from the convent? Have we overstayed our welcome?"

She was like a fortress preparing for battle . . . drawbridges pulled, men rising to their stations, arrows pulled to the bow. Father Piero sighed and gathered his cloth, spade, and knife. "I assure you, daughter, I have many words, holy words, to share with you. When the time is right. And nay, you have not outworn your welcome. Indeed, you may abide with us for as long as you deign necessary."

"I have met few priests who are uneager to share holy words."

She was brave, this one. Uncommon. He smiled, delighted by her strong spirit even though pain still seeped from her eyes. What was her role among the Gifted? How would others be drawn to her? He was eager to learn of it and fought the desire to drill her with questions, to allow his story to spill out before her and let her muddle through it alongside of him.

"There are holy words and there are holy hours, daughter. This is not the hour." He shielded his eyes and glanced up at Hasani, who still stared beyond them but clearly listened. He dropped his voice to a whisper. "But the hour is at hand. Take care to keep your lamp lit."

ᚪᚪ ᚪᚪ ᚪᚪ

Daria watched the curious, impish man go. He was unattractive, with an odd, conical-shaped head made more obvious because of shaving and no chin to speak of. Never had she met such an odd sort of priest. And yet she was unaccountably drawn to him, eager to hear more from him. It had been weeks and months since anyone had sparred with her, given her thoughts to chew on throughout her long, sleepless nights. Not since Marco . . .

She returned to her pruning with ferocity. "Do you sense danger from that priest?" she asked Hasani.

He gave her his customary grunt that meant *nay*.

"I am drawn to him. Not as a maid to a man, but from within. I get an odd sense about him. As if . . ." She shook her head. "Mayhap it's foolish, but I think I might invite him along with us, back to Siena. Perhaps he's the strength I have needed to return. A chaplain who will give me insight, direction. And if he's good enough to watch over the good sisters here, perhaps he's good enough to watch over our spiritual well-being."

This time Hasani nodded once.

The priest disappeared inside the amber, curved portico that led back to the kitchen. "If I could ever persuade him to leave his holy harem."

Hasani grunted his disapproval over her jest. And it was only then that Daria realized she was smiling for the first time in a very long time.

ᚪᚪ ᚪᚪ ᚪᚪ

"You actually saw him?" Cardinal Boeri asked, taking a gold-edged cup from a servant's tray.

"Nay. Not quite in full. His silhouette. No facial features."

"How tall?"

"My height, I'd wager, maybe seventeen, eighteen hands, maybe slightly taller. I am uncertain. Not as broad as me. But powerful."

The cardinal rose and set down his cup, then stepped down off the dais to pace with Gianni, as was his habit when he needed to think. He steepled his fingers before him, tipping index nails to lip, then motioned Gianni along. "He reminded you of no one you knew?"

"Nay, Your Grace. But he held himself as a lord. This was no serf. His diction, his carriage, was that of a man of means. An educated man. But it was terribly dark in the catacombs, and I saw little but his shadow."

The cardinal nodded, absorbing this information. "You have traveled with me for some distance and time, sir, and been in these noble halls far and wide during feast time. No man comes to mind that echoes this man's dark image?"

"Nay. Forgive me, your lordship. I have failed you."

"Nonsense, nonsense. This is a new adversary we fight, Gianni. It will require new tactics."

"I must confess he was like an apparition, a ghost. One moment here, the next there. None of my men heard his words. He whispered in my ear, and only mine."

Cardinal Boeri stopped and knit his hands beneath his rich crimson robes. He stared out the window, feeling the gentle morning breeze flow over his face. Gianni waited in silence, eager to hear the wise man's words, but respectfully waiting. Did he think the captain of his guard had gone mad? Gianni himself had wondered.

"With such evil in our midst, evil that dares to enter ancient papal chambers . . ." The cardinal shook his head as if pained. "We have no hope of restoring the papacy here in Roma with such madness about us. Word of it must not reach Avignon. And we must eradicate this evil—cleanse our city."

Gianni nodded once, leaving his head bowed.

"Tell me of the child."

Gianni fought to keep his voice neutral, militarily uniform in his report. He swallowed back the bile in his throat at the memory. "Male. Perhaps eight. Tied to a primitive stone altar. His . . . it was a horror."

"A reading among the remains?"

"Yes. They had spewed them across the stones like a divine map."

"And his heart?"

"It is as you feared, Cardinal."

The cardinal blanched slightly. They had heard of such dark happenings in other, more remote city-states, but not in Roma. He raised a pained hand to his head. "There is much work to be done with the faithful . . . to teach, to admonish, to share, to mold them into all that Christ called them to be. That task in itself is overwhelming, but to have to do battle with such powerful evil . . ." He again stared out the window, his dark eyes not really focusing on any of the buildings below them in the valley.

"You told me yourself, once, my lord, that our battle is not against flesh and blood. . . ."

"*Et potestates adversus mundi rectores tenebrarum harum contra spiritalia nequitiae in caelestibus,*" the cardinal finished in Latin.

"The powers of this dark world," Gianni said. "I feel as if we've merely encountered foot soldiers to date. This man, this Sorcerer, is the captain of a fearsome army."

"Nay, dear man. He is not a captain. I fear he is near to the prince of darkness himself. Who else would the fallen one send to our holy city? Who else could have such terrible power? The ability to whisper in your ear and yet not be seen? We must pray, Gianni, fast and pray over you and your men all night before you go hunting this one again."

"You are afraid?" Gianni said, eyes narrowing.

"I am respectful of uncharted, treacherous waters. Christ, our

Lord, will not allow any spirit close to us he does not wish us to face. Bring him to me and I will use faith as my shield, the Word as my sword. Together we will bring this man down, Gianni. We will bring him to holy judgment and God can confine him in the hellish prison he deserves. I want no other innocent harmed or misled."

They walked together down a hall, intermittently broken with sunlight streaming through narrow windows. "You never questioned me, my lord. Never asked me if I conjured up the whole thing in my mind."

"Nay."

They walked a few steps in silence. "Why not?" Gianni asked. "Could it not be that I am as mad as the hysterical women of the leper colony? That this holy work has addled my thinking?" ·

"Nay. I know you too well to believe it possible."

"But there is something else."

"Yes."

Gianni forced himself to remain silent.

The elderly cardinal paused again and faced him. His dark curly hair had become increasingly gray this last year. "I know that you have questioned my ways in the past."

"Nay, my lord. I have—"

He raised a slender hand. "Cease, Gianni. I know this is true. We have encountered things you did not understand, and yet you served us faithfully. Such devout service does not go unnoticed."

Gianni bowed his head. "I long only to serve, your lordship."

"All our battle on behalf of the Church, all the tedious trials, seeing justice done—and it *was* justice," he said, eyeing Gianni meaningfully. "It was all a proving ground. Our Lord God knew that this was ahead of us, my man." The cardinal placed his hand on Gianni's shoulder, and the knight was cast back to when he was a young squire leaving his village outside Siena, and his kindly and stooped grandfather reached up to place a hand of blessing upon his shoulder. "You had questions, and yet you served the Church faithfully. God will bless such faithfulness, my man. He will bless it. Come what may, believe in Jesus Christ as your Savior, and none can stand against you. None."

They parted and walked side by side in silence for a distance and then paused. "This is not a dream, Gianni. He is not an apparition. He is flesh and blood. But he is our spiritual adversary. Do not forget it. Go and prepare. We will fast this night."

"And tomorrow?"

"Tomorrow we hunt."

CHAPTER FOUR

"HAVE you hunted with the falcon long?" Father Piero asked, drawing near to the lady, who was outside the convent gates, among the olive trees of the orchard. Below them, down the valley, was a splendid view of Roma, with round, Castel Sant'Angelo guarding the winding, blue Fiume Tevere, and the tall, flat-topped Roman pines that marked the way to the sacred church of San Giovanni in Laterano.

The tall, black African guard watched him from the corner of his eye, allowing the priest passage without gesture. He never was far from Daria, an obviously devoted man.

Daria turned and studied the priest for a moment before turning back to the beautiful bird circling in the sky. "Three years. He was a gift from a friend when my father passed away."

"A rare bird, that one," Piero said, but his eyes were on the lady. She was delicate in features but with a steady, peaceful strength that emanated from within. Conscious that he was allowing his eyes to rest upon her, he turned to the sky. "From where did the trader bring him?"

"They say from near the Arctic. He was traded four or five times before he came to me in Siena. It's impossible to know for sure his lineage. But he is a prize."

"It must have been a dear friend indeed who would bestow such a prize upon a lady. A suitor, perhaps?"

Quick eyes met his a moment, wide orbs of golden brown with high, arched brows and long, lush lashes. Her visage as familiar to him as his own reflection. Surely this lady had had her pick of affairs of the heart!

"A suitor? Nay. A favored friend. Uncle, of sorts. My guardian, in some matters." There was more to that tale, he was sure of it. But he would allow it to rest for now.

"And your slave? Where did he come from?"

"Freed slave," she gently corrected. Daria bent down and picked several sprigs of violets, placing them in a basket that hung over her arm. "Hasani is of an East African nation, taken when he was but a boy. My father freed him when he became a man. He chose to stay with my family. We grew up together."

"He is mute?"

"In large part mute—by *choice*—but not deaf." Her tone grew louder as she spoke, obviously so that her friend would hear her irritation with him. Father Piero doubted it was much of a surprise.

Father Piero looked over to the man, who did not return his gaze. His eyes were on the horizon, studying like a sentry. His clothing was Roman, but his weapon was African or perhaps Turkish, a long, thin, curved blade at his side. "Illness or slaver?" he said lowly.

"You ask many questions, Father."

"I am curious. A student of life. Of human nature—at its best and its worst."

"Ahh. As am I." She paused to shade her eyes and find her falcon in the sky again, still circling. "A slaver took his tongue."

"Barbaric," Piero said. "Some day, the Lord will find his way into the hearts of all men and end such sorrow among us." Every day he saw slavers in the streets of Roma, driving the people of other nations—even others of the peninsula near Napoli—to market like sheep. Such grief to God!

"He speaks not at all?"

"Pride makes him refuse to try to even utter a sound."

Father Piero slid his eyes again to the tall, ebony man. She spoke of him more as a brother than a servant. "He communicates in other ways?"

"He speaks to me in grunts and gestures. Mostly long looks filled with meaning. He makes his thoughts known."

Father Piero laughed as Hasani boldly met his gaze and then, clearly bored, looked away again. "I can see that. That man can make more clear in a single look than my seminary instructors could in an hour's speech."

"You were schooled here in Roma?"

"Yes. By some of the finest within the Church. And some of the least fine."

Her gentle smile met his this time. "You are an odd sort of priest, willing to disparage others within."

"I am an honest sort of priest. There are men with the gift of teaching and there are others who should confine their efforts to prayer."

The falcon screeched, high ahead, still circling, and they both shielded their eyes to look up.

"Is he a birder or does he favor rabbits?"

"Bormeo? He favors rabbits, but if I have some time, I can get him back to pheasants and other birds."

Together, they watched as Bormeo paused just then, hovering in midair, then swept straight down to land on a poor, unsuspecting hare. He gave chase for a couple of steps, then landed and quickly ended the rabbit's life.

"He's done his duty. The cook will be happy." Daria flashed the priest a small smile as she pulled a long leather glove from her knapsack. "You are just in time, Father. I thrill to the hunt, but I'd rather not see my food until it is cleaned and roasted upon my trencher. How about I fetch my bird, and you the dinner?"

"Certainly, my lady." Together, they set off down the hill. "Your man, Hasani, will not assist you in these matters?" he asked gently.

"Hasani is in a foul mood. He is eager to return to Siena before St. John's Day and distressed that I wish to linger another week." They wove around the scrubby trees, breathing in the heavy summer scents of olive and eucalyptus.

"He must be bored here, guarding you in a convent."

"Yes," she said with a gentle laugh. "And truth be told, I am in agreement. It is soon time to return home. There is much to do in preparing for the feast, bringing in the harvest, seeing to our normal tasks. And yet the Lord asks my heart to tarry for a few days longer."

"You speak of the Lord with the intimacy of a nun."

She paused and pursed her lips, mulling over his words. "Perhaps they are molding me to think as they do. It is healing to think of being in the presence of God, day in, day out. Much more difficult to meditate on such holy matters in the city."

The air was dry and still, the heat of the day burning off the last of morning's dew. She was right. This convent outside Roma was a quiet, holy place, and Piero had enjoyed his time here among the holy women. But God was calling him onward too. . . .

Daria's long skirts snagged on an exposed olive tree root, and Piero paused to help her free herself.

"You are too long in the company of women," she said.

"Perhaps," he said, smiling in return, giving her a small shrug. "Or too long in a monk's robes, given to their own share of snags. But then I had seven sisters. It's always come naturally for me to be about females."

"*Had* seven sisters?" she gently inquired.

"Three died to a plague that came upon our small city when I was a boy. It also claimed my father, and soon the banker took our land, making it easier for me to follow my holy vocation. My grandfather funded my education with the last of his own funds. One sister married and went to Venezia—her husband is a merchant. The other three? I do not know. They may still be at home, old women attending my mother's grave or passed on to be with our Lord and Savior. It has been many years since the Lord called me from my home."

Daria had genuflected with him as he mentioned the sisters that might have died. She was clearly faithful, which pleased him immensely. Her faith was an affair of the heart, not merely the social contrivance of the wealthy. He could sense it.

She was the one. She had to be the one.

"Do you have any siblings, my lady?"

"Nay. I was the child of two who thought they would never be blessed with children. A gift, late in life, my father used to say."

"Like Abraham and Sarah?"

"Mama and Papa were not *that* old—"

And she was tutored in the Holy Scriptures!

"—but they were not young enough to fight off the illness that came to Siena three years past either."

"A coughing sickness?"

"Yes. And high fevers. My mother was gifted at ministering to the ill, often healing others with her tonics and salves." She gestured to the basket on her arm and Piero's heart skipped a beat. *A healer* . . . he fought to stay focused on the conversation at hand. "I am sorry for your loss."

"Thank you, Father. *Bormeo!*" she screeched, the *r* trilling off her tongue as if she were an old village grandmother chastising an errant son. "You know better than that. *Chit-chit.*" The bird ignored her lecturing, but at that last sound, he raised his head, white feathers about his beak and talons stained in blood. He hesitated, reluctant to leave his prey.

She muttered some furious Latin under her breath, eyes never leaving the falcon.

"Do you write Latin as easily as you speak it?" Piero asked.

"*Si, a Greco e Francese,*" she said. Again, that small, wise smile. "I know. An oddity, my learning such things. But my father was indulgent, my mother more brilliant than most men, and my tutor uncommonly willing. Hasani was even schooled along with me. We were among the most odd of Siena's noble households."

Piero smiled and shook his head. A woman and a slave with an education that few gentlemen attained! It was unheard of!

"*Chit-chit,*" she repeated, waving her arm, insisting. The bird complied then, stretching out great wings of gray and black and white, flapping them a few times to rise to her forearm. He set to preening the blood from his stunning white feathers.

"He's become lazy and swinish during our sojourn here. Unwilling to wait until I feed him his share, as is proper. I must return to Siena and school him in remembering that he is bird and I, mistress."

Mayhap this was why she had not yet married. Even beyond her barren state—men did not favor women who were too bright or strong-willed. It did not bode well for a marriage.

"You will return home soon, then?"

"Yes, Father. I plan to leave within the week. But I am seeking guidance on a matter that I believe you are already aware of. May we speak of it?"

Piero bent to gather together the long legs of the prairie rabbit and rose, then gestured ahead of them, to the path that led back to the convent. "Please, my daughter. Speak plainly. Because there is much I need to speak of with you."

CHAPTER FIVE

GIANNI de Capezzana loved the stately grandeur of being a knight of the Church. He had been a mercenary all his life; this job was as much a sense of fulfilling a divine call as it was a means to have a fresh straw mattress to sleep upon and a belly full of fresh meat. He rode in inspection before his men. All were adorned in red capes with bold, white, high tau crosses, and sat on the finest horses in Italia, with flags that would unfurl in the breeze before and behind them. Gianni's stomach was empty but his heart was full. After a night of fasting and prayer, he felt lean and sharp, ready for the battle before him. And these men before him were some of the finest fighting men in Roma, nay, any from Milano to Napoli. Twenty-four here. Another twenty-four on patrol. Twelve would remain at the Vatican, to protect the cardinal and other dignitaries and scholars. Yet another twelve were on a week's leave. By far, it was the largest group of men he had ever commanded.

"Captain, the men are ready," Aeneas said.

"*Si*. You are ready," he said lowly, meeting each man's gaze. "You are ready for your holy mission. You all saw for yourselves or heard how depraved this one is. He is a threat to the innocents. He is a threat to the holy ones we protect. And he must be stopped before any other children are sacrificed upon his heathen *altar*." He spat out the last word, wanting to vomit at the memory. The men cried out in agreement. Many of them had vowed vengeance, thinking of their own small children in villages about Roma. "Before he leads any others into this false faith—"

"Hear, hear!" the men roared.

"—a faith that will lead them all to hell!"

"Hear, hear!"

"Sir! Question, sir!"

"Ask it," Gianni said, waving at him.

"Sir, we have tracked many who practice the dark arts. But this one . . ." The young man cleared his throat uneasily. "Sir, is it true that we seek an apparition?"

Several men laughed at him but sobered when they saw Gianni's stern expression. Others crossed themselves.

"He is . . . different. I did not see his face. We did not find any clues about his identity in the catacombs. But the dwellers of our city, and those in the outlying villages, are bound to know of him. I am certain of it. Somewhere there are whispered secrets, rumors. Listen for word of a magician or holy man—anything suspicious—leads we may expose and follow until we find him. This man is evil, but he is still a man. Apparitions do not eviscerate children, leave footprints behind them. Evil men do. And our Lord will make us strong enough to face him. We will track him down and we will bring him to earthly justice. God will see that divine justice is done."

The cardinal appeared then, flanked by two bishops, to give the knight his blessing before they departed. Gianni met his kind eyes, grateful to know that the holy man would be constantly praying for them during their absence.

"We will separate into four groups," Gianni said. "We will spend the day canvassing the hills that surround our city, beginning at the catacomb entrance. Interview village leaders. Our Sorcerer was not alone—there were more than thirty people in the cavern last night. Someone will know something. Use gentle force, if necessary, to find out answers. But use *threat* of force more than a quick hand," he warned solemnly. "You are not to chase any trails that lead to this man without the rest of us with you. You are merely to find his tracks and determine where the Sorcerer headed. *Together*, we will hunt him down."

Gianni nodded to Cardinal Boeri and the old man moved forward, raising his hand with two fingers straight, thumb across ring finger in a gesture of blessing as all the men dismounted and knelt before him. "Men of God, I commission thee to go forward and do battle with our oldest of enemies, armed with the might of the Holy Spirit. . . ."

♣ ♣ ♣

It was puzzling, this thing invading her heart, taking over her thoughts. More and more her mind was preoccupied by what was happening about her, through her, rather than upon her ill-fated handfasting to Marco, her beloved, which had sent her scurrying to the convent two months past. He seemed like a dim memory now, in the midst of the troubling words and thinly veiled secrets Father Piero had shared earlier in the day. Could the holy man truly know such things?

I suspect you have a holy gift. I suspect your heart calls you to touch, to heal.

Could she have a gift? A holy gift of healing? He seemed so certain, so sure, as if God had told him all about her before they had even met. He cast eyes upon her that reminded her of her own father, the way he used to see through any guise, the way he knew her, through and through. She had spoken to no nun about her desire to follow in her mother's footsteps, how she had already begun ministering to the poor and ill of Siena. Only Hasani knew her secrets.

She walked along the path in the garden, approaching Hasani, who stood looking out upon the river and Roma. He glanced her way and then looked back out.

"We'll be on our way shortly," she said curtly, irritated by his pouting. "In plenty of time to see to the business at hand in Siena before we leave for the countryside. I need to tell you two things. I have asked Father Piero if he would consider coming to Siena with us as our new chaplain. We haven't had a priest at the manor since before Father died, and I think . . . I think it would be a comfort to me to have a piece of this place," she paused to gesture about, "at home."

Hasani studied her with wide, black eyes. There was no surprise within them. After a moment, he gave her one assenting nod.

"I am glad for your agreement." She paused for a moment, turned to walk away and then took a breath, paused and then took another quick breath. *Just get it out,* she thought. *Cease this frittering about and decide!*

"Hasani, do you remember my mother ever healing anyone? I mean beyond the herbs and baskets of foods we used to bring the people? Actually having a gift of . . . healing?"

Her friend, so tall and royal in stature, looked down and into her eyes for a long moment. He frowned slightly and shook his head quizzically, as if asking her what she was truly speaking of.

"I mean I . . ." Her voice trailed away. There were no logical words anyway. She looked out to the glittering river, to Roma's wall, a monstrous, snaking structure in constant disrepair. Even the Romans themselves had found it indefensible. It was too big; there were never enough men. Despite all appearances, those inside knew they were vulnerable. It was rather like what Daria felt at this moment. The priest's words rang true to her heart. The mysterious letter. The odd resemblance to her . . . If it had been anyone but Father Piero, she would have declared it madness and fled. She had not yet laid eyes on the scroll herself, but she knew already that this was no dark magic—this was like an earthquake under her feet. A mighty rumbling growing ever closer by the moment.

The priest said it was a calling, what she was feeling, as holy and sanctified as his own vocation. Daria blinked rapidly. It was all so odd. She wasn't sure she wanted to answer such a calling, know any more. It was a thrilling, dreadful secret. Her mind wanted peace; her heart called for normalcy, routine. But what was that routine at home in Siena? Without Marco, her entire life had been turned upside down. Mayhap this was a new path that God was opening for her. To settle into her mother's slippers. Mayhap that was all the mysterious letter meant—that she was to go and tend to, heal others, as her own mother had done before her.

"We were fairly young, Hasani, but I seem to remember—"

A scream shattered her reverie. Daria and Hasani shared one more quick glance and then they ran, Hasani quickly taking the lead and disappearing around the convent's south wall, in the direction of the olive press and winery. Daria's skirts held her back, and she gathered them in a fist in order to hasten her step.

When she rounded the corner, there were already four nuns beside the injured girl, Giovanna Maria. The old wooden press lever had broken, and the donkey stood to one side, a splintered end attached to his saddle. Somehow, Giovanna's hand had been caught under the giant stone wheel. She knelt before the press, her hand disappearing in a nightmarish, thin gap beneath the dial and blood quickly mixing with the fresh green oil by her wrist. The poor girl was not screaming any longer, but staring ahead as if in a trance, quiet tears slipping down her face.

Nuns cried out as they left the convent and discovered what had happened.

"What tragedy!" whispered one.

"Of all of us, not dear Giovanna!" cried another. "There will be no more of her fine lute. . . ."

"Hush, all of you," Daria admonished them, kneeling beside the slight girl and wrapping an arm about her shoulders. The nuns ignored her, going on about the state of the olive press and whose fault it was that a blacksmith had not been called to craft a proper lever—a flock of tittering, clucking chickens. Three of the more useful ones fell to their knees beside Giovanna, pleading in prayer with hands clasped and raised to the sky. One knelt beside the young girl, across from Daria, and stroked Giovanna's hair and kissed her scalp, trying to reassure her. Only one was beside Hasani, trying to roll back the heavy stone.

Daria leaned over Giovanna toward the other nun. "As soon as we roll back this stone, you pull her to safety."

"M'lady, they cannot move that stone. There is a divot, there, that the ass always has difficulty passing," the girl said.

"We will move the stone," Father Piero commanded, having just arrived on the scene. "You two, off your knees and to some earthly toil! You others, cease your mutterings and pray." They all waited a moment as the others joined them around the dais and Father Piero muttered a prayer. Daria could not make out the words, but added her own plea to God, willing the Lord's strength into their hands. *"Uno, due, tre!"* Father Piero called.

In a moment, the stone rolled out of the divot and Giovanna's friend had the girl in her arms, rocking her like a wet nurse with a babe. The nuns on their knees cried out in thanks, praying in Latin verses.

Father Piero gestured toward Daria impatiently. "Come. There is work for you to do."

"Me?"

He didn't wait for a response, and Hasani had already scooped up Giovanna Maria in his arms and rushed her inside the convent, following Father Piero's lead. Hasani, as a man and freed slave, had never been allowed farther than the kitchen, and had opted to sleep outside most nights. But this day he was led through one hallway and down another, until they reached the nuns' quarters.

"In there," the priest said, gesturing toward a straw tick and meager blanket.

ക ക ക

"I'LL fetch more blankets," said a nun.

Daria studied the girl, who stared vacantly upward, as if the shock of her injury were going to lead her to death. "You will be all right, Giovanna," she said, and a spike of heat ran down her arm. She would heal this child of God. She did have a gift. She knew it then, just as surely as that she was a d'Angelo of Siena. She had known it all along, deep within, but God had waited until Father Piero came into her life for her to know it as clearly as her own name.

She met Father Piero's eyes as he rushed back into the room and he was immediately becalmed. "You know now," he said.

"I . . . I know."

The room was filling up with nuns, all eager to help. "Abbess, Sister Estrea, Sister Rota, stay with us. Daria, do you need anything else?"

"Mm, yes. Someone please fetch us fresh linens, galangal, vervain, and foxglove. Gather it and yet keep it with you until we call for you. We will require it as soon as we've seen to Giovanna's immediate needs."

"Please, sisters," Father Piero said. "I beg this of you. Go and ask for divine healing for Giovanna this day. We will do so here too. Please, go to the chapel. Sister Angela, lead them all in prayer, concentrating on Giovanna's hand becoming fully restored."

The sisters looked at him in confusion. Never had they been asked to pray in such a manner. Piero raised his hands in frustration. *"Petite et dabitur vobis quaerite et invenietis pulsate et aperietur vobis. . . .* For everyone who asks, receives. Go! Ask! *Ask!"*

The nuns hurried away in a group, a bouncing sea of covered heads. There was no door to shut, but they were gone. Father Piero drew near to Giovanna's bed and then peered into Estrea and Rota's faces. "Sisters, I must ask you to make a sacred vow never to speak of this moment again. Word must not escape this convent about what you are about to see. The Lord is afoot, and we do not yet know what he intends to do. This is but the beginning."

Daria stared at him in confusion. Was he speaking about something he was about to do? How could he promise what was to come if it was her gift he spoke of and not his own? How could he know? But he did. And she did too. And when her eyes met Hasani's, she realized he knew it as well.

The abbess nodded regally, fear and wonder in her eyes.

"I promise," Estrea said, eyes wide.

"You have my word," Rota vowed. All three were older women, Daria's favorite nuns at the convent, full of life and hope and peace.

They all stared down at Giovanna, who was now gray in pallor, her eyes rolling backward. "It is too much," Rota said. "Too much for the poor girl. We're going to lose her to heaven."

"Nay," Daria said, suddenly finding her voice. "We will not."

Father Piero knelt beside Giovanna's head, praying quietly in Latin. The abbess knelt beside the girl's shoulder, on the opposite side of the bed. Rota and Estrea knelt at the foot of the bed, heads bowed. The air seemed full, as if on the brink of a lightning storm. There was the hint of an odd, sweet aroma in the room, as if they had entered an orange grove on the morn when all the blossoms opened at once . . . with a curious spice in the midst of it that reminded Daria of cloves. Hasani was the last to kneel, at Giovanna's feet, and then Piero gestured to Daria.

Daria stared at the girl's mangled left hand, blood seeping into the blanket beneath it, seeing her at the lute in the garden the day before yesterday, with lithe fingers flying over the strings, creating music worthy of heaven itself. Never again would she play. . . .

No, no, no. She must see Giovanna playing, must concentrate on seeing her play again! She began praying aloud, barely aware that she was uttering intimate, unheard-of prayers before holy women and a holy man of God. But it mattered not. This was what she was called to do. This was what she had to do! But how? With what words?

"Speak from your heart, m'lady," Piero said quietly. "As if our Lord were here in the room with us. There are no wrong words."

Daria studied him, frowning. Surely there was a prayer she should know. Was this not the priest's role? To pray? Her eyes went to him again and he gave her a gentle smile. "No wrong words," he repeated. "Simply begin and ask for the Lord's guidance. The words will come. They are almost unnecessary. It is our hearts that the Holy Spirit seeks."

Daria turned to Giovanna again. "Please, please, Lord Jesus. Heal your servant, Giovanna," Daria said, gently taking the nun's injured hand in her own. It appeared hopeless. The bones were crushed, her hand curiously flat and mashed, lying at odd angles to Daria's own. The skin was broken in a hundred places, with tendons and muscles and bones exposed. Daria felt curiously removed from the gore, her stomach calm. All she could see was Giovanna's hand upon the lute. . . .

"Heal her now. Lord God, Lord Jesus Christ, Lord on High, come and be present here. Enter her arteries and veins, enter her bones and tendons. Her muscles. Begin your healing work. Father God, heal her completely. Bring her back to completeness, mending every single bone. Let her use this moment and her music to serve you. Let her celebrate the glory of your might, Jesus. Let these nuns know that tonight, you drew nearer than ever before. You can do this. . . . You can do this, Father God. We ask you to do this. Come and be present. Come and be present in this room, Holy Spirit. Change our lives. Chase out our sin and make us worthy vessels of you, Lord. We are sinful, incomplete without you, Jesus. Cleanse us. Make us holy. Use us, Father. Use us."

Tears slipped down Daria's face as she pleaded with the Holy One. Dimly, she could hear the others sniffing through tears and muttered prayers begin to join hers. "Lord God, you are in this convent. You are in this room with us. Thank you for drawing near. Thank you for gracing us with your presence. Do a mighty work, here, Almighty One.

"You have the power to part oceans and tear down fortress walls. You knew Giovanna in her mother's womb, were present when she devoted her life to your service. Please, Lord God, heal her now."

For hours Daria prayed with the others, begging for God to intervene. Alternately, she would pause, and they would all hold their breath in silence, hearing the air hum as if listening to a rush of water in their ears. When Daria's voice failed her, when there were no words left to say, Father Piero entered in with prayers from the Scriptures or liturgy. The abbess added others. And Rota and Estrea moaned and cried their assent. At some point, Daria fell asleep, still praying in her dreams.

In the early morning hours, she awakened to the abbess's gentle touch on her shoulder. She had lit a candle and grinned in the ghostly, flickering light.

"What? What is it?" Daria asked, and her words awakened the others around Giovanna's bed. It was cool now, and she hurried to pull up Giovanna's blanket to her chin. It was then that her eyes fell upon the girl's hand.

Daria gasped and scrambled backward in awe and holy terror, then turned to lower her face on the cold stone floor, bowing again and again. "Praise you, Holy One. Praise you, Lord on High!" She wept, her tears choking her words, overwhelmed.

Because above her, resting on the bloody blanket, was Giovanna's battered and bruised—but perfectly formed, perfectly straight—hand.

CHAPTER SIX

HASANI had their belongings in trunks and everything in the wagon three days later. Father Piero had secured permission from the diocese to go and serve as the d'Angelo chaplain for up to three years in Siena. They were sending another priest to the convent, a man whom Piero suggested himself for the position. He knew the nuns would be in good hands with his old friend, a fine shepherd for any flock. But now he needed to fully disclose everything to Daria. She must know what he knew. It was beginning. Something terrible and wonderful. But it was beginning.

"My daughter," he said, opening up his arm to Daria and gesturing into his office. "I beg for a moment of your time before we depart for your home."

Hasani looked hesitant, and Piero knew then that he would need to be a part of this. "Please, dear man. Join us. I must speak with you both."

Daria broke away from Giovanna, from whom she had become inseparable in these last three wonderful days since her healing, and obediently followed his lead. Hasani canvassed the hallways before following, ever on the lookout, even while still in the midst of the convent. Did he sense the danger?

Finally the priest turned and ducked through the low doorway.

They watched carefully as Piero closed the door and turned the key in the lock—one of only three locking doors in the entire convent. "Before we depart, I must show you the actual letter. You must know all that I know now. Please . . ."

As Daria sat down in the lone chair and Hasani hovered over her, Father Piero went to the small chest he had packed with his own meager belongings and opened it. Three robes, an extra pair of shoes, and his Bible. But on top was the old, weathered lambskin that held the scroll. He took it in hand and studied Daria for a moment, wondering about the reaction to come. Would she be afraid? Would she not wish to continue this new trek together? "Father, thy will be done," he muttered, standing up and stifling a groan as old knees and hips made their discomfort known.

He sat down on the bedside nearest Daria and looked deep into her eyes and then Hasani's. "We have been drawn together for a reason. For what purpose, I do not yet know. But he has told me that this is the time. I share with you a secret that goes back hundreds of years, and a relic that is unknown to but a few men. It was passed along to me by an old priest when I was but a student, and to him from an old priest, and so on. Since I obtained it, I have not shown it to another soul."

"Why us? Why now?" Daria said.

Piero did not answer. Her fear mattered not. She needed to know. He untied the narrow leather strap and unrolled the soft lambskin to flatten it, then gently slipped out the delicate parchment sheets. They measured about the length of his hand, from tip of finger to wrist.

Daria's eyes scanned the first sheet. "Latin. It appears to be Scripture, although I am unfamiliar with . . . is it of the Vulgate? Do you think it is Pauline?"

Piero remained silent, studying her face, her wide, wise eyes, and waited.

"It is lovely. Some of the finest illumination I've ever seen! But what Scripture is this? I see reference to the Corinthians, but this is not either of the sacred letters to the Corinthians." Her eyes flowed over the end of the first page and then turned to the second.

Her hand went to her mouth and she stared at the page. With trembling fingers, she turned to the last page and gasped. She glanced up at him, and then back to the portrait of a priest upon a road, a priest with an elongated head. From over her shoulder, Hasani glanced at it quickly and then turned to the window.

Piero expected some accusing look from the African, as if he were up to some treachery, but the man was calm, as if he expected it all along. Piero nodded, putting it together; Hasani was one of them. With which gift? Daria rose, white-faced, and quickly set the letter upon his desk, backing away but unable to do anything but stare in its direction.

"What—what is that?" Daria asked. Her voice trembled.

"From what my teacher told me," Piero said, "possibly a portion of a lost letter of Saint Paul, or mayhap a scribe who followed him. Never canonized. Never presented to the Council, as far as I know. Perhaps unknown, other than this fragment."

"It is incomplete?"

"Yes. It appears to be the first portion. The last page ends midsentence. I do not know how much is missing."

"And these illuminations? How could this be?"

"Because of the content, I take it as prophecy. Daria, I told you that I suspected you had the gift of healing. In this script, the author speaks of spiritual gifts, much as Paul does in our first letter to the Corinthians. The illuminati of old, centuries ago, were gifted in their artistry, often illuminating the Scriptures with illustrations that were divinely inspired."

Hasani moved closer and hovered again over the last page, lifting it to Piero in question.

"I do not know where the rest of it lies. My master only had this portion to give to me, as the last three teachers had passed it along. Somewhere, somehow, the letter was divided, mayhap in the hopes that at least a portion of it would survive. I have it on good counsel that it was once in the eastern capital, but it has been centuries since it was last seen. There is some potential that it went to Venezia, when Constantinople was sacked of her relics, but it is only a guess. As you can imagine, it is difficult to inquire about it. But my sense is that we must try to find it soon."

Daria straightened and looked him in the eye. "We have connections with scriptoriums from Paris to Constantinople. Mayhap we can help find it. But tell us . . . of what does the letter speak? You said spiritual gifts—in what context?"

"You may read it for yourself, of course, when we have more time. But suffice it to say that the letter is prophetic in tone, more like John than Paul but using phrases that are uniquely Pauline . . . it speaks of a gathering. Not just of us here in this room, but others too. I assume we may meet them soon, or perhaps they will join us. They are part of the Gifted, as are you."

Daria looked at him quickly. "The Gifted?"

Piero rose and paced. "The author of this letter speaks of the spiritual gifts in Corinthians, but in this letter, he speaks of a time coming when a group of people will be brought together, to show the world the power of God through the power of Christ through his devoted people. He refers to these people as the Gifted—specifically noting these gifts: wisdom, which I believe is my own gift; healing, which has already been shown as your own; faith; visions; discernment; miraculous powers; prophecy." He held up seven fingers. "Through the Gifted, the people are to know of God's great love for them."

He paused to pace back and forth. "If this is of Santo Paulo, his tone is prophetic, visionary, more so than any of his other writings. Perhaps that is why this letter was never presented to the Council and appears to be forgotten. As I said, it may not even be his, but someone who emulated his style, his method of speech, like so many did in the days of old."

"And if it is unworthy of canonization? Should we even read it? Let alone try to find more of it?"

"Our Lord leads in many ways, at times in ways contrary to current culture. Look at how he healed on the Sabbath. He constantly was at odds with the Sanhedrin, Pharisees. Why can he not work in such ways today, during our lifetimes?"

"You are a Dominican! Sworn to weed out heresy, to hold to the truth."

Piero crossed his arms. "Exactly. God knew we would give the letter the most thorough of examinations." He tapped the letter. "This is not any Scripture as we know it. But it says nothing that we would label heretical."

Daria let out a humorless laugh. "Nay. It only speaks of things that would threaten the Church—power from within the people. The power of Christ within." Her eyes fell again to the letter. "And these illustrations? The one with such an eerie resemblance to you? The other to me?" Daria asked in a low tone.

He shifted the pages so the second was on top. "Your likeness appears beside words of healing power. Of the Gifted healing and doing mighty works in Christ's name, winning many to the faith. I must be honest—I expected a man. But it is a woman the illuminist chose to draw beside the verses, Daria. You. Hundreds of years before you were born. You."

"And the words beside your likeness?"

"They speak of wisdom." Piero came to rest before her, eager now in his excitement to share this with others. To no longer be alone in carrying this great secret, this sacred knowledge. "You coming to the convent, your gift of healing, me the keeper of this script, the abbot here . . . It is no accident or coincidence, Daria. It has begun."

Hasani grunted a question, lifting his chin in careful observance.

"What? I know not, fully. Only that I am to go with you to Siena. And that our lives have just taken a profound turn."

♛ ♛ ♛

"CAPTAIN, there!" Gianni followed the direction of Aeneas's pointed finger, down the mountainside toward a narrow canyon that eventually fed into a dry riverbed that extended to the sparkling, aquamarine sea. They had picked up the Sorcerer's trail on the western side and had been tracking him and his companions for days, just a half day ahead of their group at any time. The Sorcerer drove on relentlessly, barely needing sleep, it seemed.

There appeared to be no reason for the man's curving trail other than to attempt to shake them from it. He was almost successful. But now, now he was within sight again, and soon enough he would be in their custody. That morn, Gianni had sent a messenger back to collect the other troops and have them rejoin their contingent so they could close in on the Sorcerer as planned. Could they keep track of their enemy while they awaited their companions?

Gianni watched the three on horses pull up, then turn in their saddles and gaze upward to the top of the hill as if they had heard Aeneas call out. They were still too far off to see clearly, and, as they were cloaked in long, flowing capes, Gianni could not determine hair color or even if all three were male or female.

"Could they have heard me?" Aeneas said. "It's as if—"

"Impossible," Gianni interrupted. But he found it eerily coincidental. Grimly, he watched as the three disappeared back into and around a bend in the riverbed.

Gianni dug his heels into his horse's flanks, heading down the hill, disobeying his own order to wait for the entire contingent before attempting to intercept the Sorcerer. But he could not let this man escape. Not after what they had seen in that cavern . . .

"Captain!" Aeneas called, trying to pull him back, give him a moment's pause. But he was not stopping. He had to capture this man and hand him over to the cardinal before the Sorcerer misled another, injured another, murdered another.

❧ ❧ ❧

BORMEO rested on Daria's leather-gloved forearm as they rode away from the convent. All three of them were on horses, and Hasani pulled another horse, which drew the wagon. As they rode down through the olive grove, the high, clear notes of Giovanna's lute followed them, and Daria and Piero shared the first smile since he had shown them his shocking secret.

Daria's mind was racing as the sweet notes settled into their ears. Just what was happening to her? What was ahead? And what on earth had happened behind? She shook her head and gave Bormeo permission to fly. "*Titt-titt,*" she whispered, untying the leather strap from his ankle and tossing him into the air to give him a start.

Thinking of Giovanna, how God had known her in her mother's womb and had seen the day she would be healed, the day Daria would discover her gifting, cast her mind to her own creation, her own calling. Her hand went to her belly, wondering over the promise that God had made her last night as she prayed. She would not always be alone. She would have a child. And yet her belly remained flat, her menses had come and gone since she had left Marco's side, and it was unlikely that she would ever be handfasted again. Still, she felt assured, becalmed, even in the midst of such swirling doubt and questions.

Piero drew beside her when the road widened. After a few paces in silence, he said, "The Lord will show us what we need to know, as we need to know it. We must center our hearts in prayer and focus on what He wants us to do. It may be nothing more than what we presently see before us."

"Or it may be much more," she said.

"Yes, yes. Much more."

"What about you, Father? What does it mean for you to have the gift of wisdom?"

He wagged his head back and forth as if weighing thoughts on either side. "Mayhap I am here to help guide all who join us. Help you explore your gifting, understand it. Make sure none of us fall from the path."

It made sense to Daria. She had been glad to offer Father Piero the position of family chaplain, and was even more grateful for his presence now. There was a comforting, divine order to it. But she had so many questions . . . if only she had had time to read the entire letter . . .

"You asked the sisters not to speak of what happened to Giovanna. The other sisters believe it was our combined prayers that healed her."

"Mayhap it was. A miracle, regardless of how it actually occurred."

"But you were afraid."

"Yes. If your gifting is as powerful as I think it is, there will soon be much to contend with."

"Such as?"

"Crowds. People clamoring for healing. You know how the people are. They flock to anything near the hand of God. Think of the Scriptures—how Jesus and his disciples were hounded."

"But if I am a healer, why not heal? If this is a divine gift, why not allow God to work?"

"Oh, my daughter, I do not intend to chain the Holy One. We will allow him to work. But I don't want any of us confined before we fully explore what he might have in store. And . . ."

Hasani grunted behind them, lifting his chin, listening in.

"And . . ." Daria encouraged.

"And there are those who will not smile upon your gift, especially if others join us. Together, the Gifted could be a spiritual force of some note." Father Piero spoke to both of them, making sure Hasani could hear.

"The Inquisition. You are afraid of the Church itself! That is why you swore the sisters to secrecy."

Father Piero sighed. "The Church is changing. But there are those who fear change. They fear the people becoming too powerful. Some fear that the people will pervert the Gospel, send us on a path that will lead to the end. Others fear that any power held outside the Church is a power that must be contained, curtailed, manipulated, or destroyed. Many would see our letter as containing heresies; although it is not there, they would read a threat to their power as heretical, act before they thought and prayed. Many would see your gift, especially, as witchcraft."

"This is not witchcraft. It is God moving through us. Not us wishing to be God."

"And he will protect you because of it. As long as we focus on him, as long as we do our best to serve only him, there can be none against us. But that does not mean that there shan't be those who try."

"You know of still others? As if the Church is not enough as an adversary?" Daria's heart sank. This was too big. The thoughts too impossible to absorb. Surely this was a dream. . . .

"Daria, good always battles with evil."

She nodded, desperately trying to get hold of his words, but feeling more and more lost.

"I have said too much. You are afraid. We will speak of it more when you are ready."

"Nay. We must know what might lie ahead. . . ." But her words sounded feeble in her own ears.

"There will be others, Daria. The time is now. In our lifetimes, or in the next few years, or even in the next few months, I expect others among the Gifted to draw near to us. Together, we will become stronger, build one another up. But as we become stronger, we will draw more attention. We can remain cloaked for a time. But we will want to control when and where we come into the open."

"I know Bishop Benedicto, of Siena. He is a good man, kind and honest. We could go to him. Tell him of this great secret. Win his heart to our cause and seek his counsel on what it may be in the first place."

"Perhaps, at some point. We must seek God's direction first. Then, if he gives us confirmation, go to your bishop."

"You are an odd sort of priest. No Church sanction? No priest has ever counseled me to go to God first. Always God through the Church."

"You are an odd sort of woman," he returned, making her smile. "We have entered a strange time, Daria. Things are changing— everything is changing. Right now. It is important that we constantly seek divine counsel, but that we prepare for changes like we've never seen before. We must prepare our minds and hearts. If the time of the Gifted has come, if the letter is divinely inspired, we are on the threshold of change."

Daria fell back and spoke in soft undertones to Hasani. Piero heard the African grunt a few times. "The others, in the letter . . . ?" Daria spoke up.

"Yes," Piero said, turning in his saddle toward them as his horse kept walking forward over the old Roman road that led out of Roma and toward Siena. He remained quiet as they passed four pilgrims on the road home.

"Tell us again of their gifting," Daria asked, when they had at last outdistanced the pilgrims' hearing.

"It says God will raise up among us the Gifted—those with profound and God-given powers to combat evil, to change the world for Christ." He took a deep breath and blew out his cheeks, held it, and then exhaled, as if suddenly absorbing the burden of what was ahead himself. "A prophet. A wise man, those with profound faith, a healer, one who sees visions, and still another with miraculous powers. One with discernment—"

"You?"

He blew out his cheeks and exhaled. "What I see in the description is one who can actually discern good from evil. Something beyond my own gifting." He eyed Hasani and then shrugged his shoulders. "There are many things left *unsaid* in the letter."

"And you think we will meet the others soon?"

"Possibly. Or we may wait for years. We do not have the complete letter. That is why I think we must try to find the rest of it."

Daria shared a glance with Hasani and suddenly felt what he had been feeling for weeks. A longing for home, for the familiar, for protection. Because suddenly she was very afraid. And the only thing that might bring her peace about the unknown would be to surround herself with the known.

⳨ ⳨ ⳨

THE three on horses were impossibly fast. Gianni's Spanish horses were some of the finest in any city of the Great Peninsula, but they were having difficulty keeping up with the trio they pursued. Just before the narrow canyon gave way to the riverbed, an old stone archway formed a natural bridge over a chasm that reached deep into the mountainside.

His men pulled up beside him, all panting for air in tandem with their belaboring horses. Gianni waved up the canyon. "This man knows this country well. Had he headed north on our track at the top, he would've hit the canyon."

"No way to cross but around. And this is faster than the eastern route," Aeneas said.

"I've heard tell of this old stone archway, but never seen it for myself," Salvatore said.

"He's wily and smart," Gianni said. "He thinks he can circle back to Roma from here and lose us. But we're right behind him. Water the horses and let's be on with it. He shall not enter our city again unless in our custody."

"Captain, do you not wish to wait on the rest of our contingent?"

"Nay. We cannot afford to let this man slip away."

"But you said—"

"I said nay! We head out in five minutes' time. Water the horses!"

He knew it was potentially foolish, but turned before the men could see the concern in his eyes. He knelt beside the tracks in the sandy soil. A man on the lead horse. And either women or very small men on the two behind him. Who were they? What sort of people fell into such darkness? Witchcraft was a mainstay of peasants, not the wealthy. But these three were on some of the finest horseflesh available. And rode as nobility. Yes, this was a whole new breed of adversary. And God had set him, Gianni, upon their trail. God on High would give his men the strength to waylay them.

"Mount up!" he called, taking a long drink from his skin and then bending to refill it in the river, as his men had already done. He placed a foot in a stirrup and easily swung up into the saddle, pushing his horse into an immediate gallop.

They would capture this Sorcerer and his followers. By nightfall, they would apprehend them. And tomorrow Gianni and his men would celebrate over a fine, Church-furnished dinner of roasted pheasant and then give thanks to God during midnight mass at San Giovanni. Another enemy of God was about to be vanquished.

CHAPTER SEVEN

DARIA's troop was two days' travel out of Roma, three hours distant from where they would take their night's rest, when Hasani spotted the trio below them, winding in and out of a dense forest of eucalyptus and cypress. The trees would soon give way to the first oaks, which would then give way to sweet chestnut and beech as they entered Toscana. They could hear the hammering sound of rock on metal and paused to see if they could make out what they were doing. No one traveled this land unless they were on the old Roman road.

"Strange," Daria said.

"Indeed," Father Piero said. At one point they could see all three travelers in a clearing, circling about on horses, talking. Two carried archer's bows upon their backs.

Hasani grunted, disturbed by what he saw, perhaps concerned they were highwaymen, robbers who might attack.

Still, Daria stared downward.

That was when the leader looked up, obviously spotted them, then ducked, pulling his hood down over his head and galloping deeper into the trees. They heard pounding again from the trees far below them.

"Look. Over there," Father Piero said. Just entering the forest, below them and to the left, was a group of six knights. Knights of the Church, judging by the tau cross that decorated mantles and flag.

"Impossible," she said, with a humorless laugh. "We are already encountering the Inquisition?" she quipped. She was not truly afraid. While the Inquisition held sway elsewhere, it had not yet made much headway in Italia.

"It is not us they chase," Father Piero said calmly. "It is those unfortunates below."

ఈ ఈ ఈ

"CAPTAIN," Aeneas called, and all five pulled to a stop beside him.

Gianni stared at the upside-down cross. "They taunt us."

"There's another," said a guard to his left. "Up ahead."

They rode deeper into the eucalyptus grove, slowing to a walk, ducking low branches and winding around trees. Between the sun dropping low in the sky and the dense forest, odd shadows were all about them.

"Could they be laying a trap?"

"I doubt it. They wish to escape." They came across a third cross. "These are meant as a fear tactic."

"Or a warning," said another guard.

"We are knights of the Church," Gianni said, willing courage into his men. "Evil men may try to frighten us, but it is they who should take heed."

The two arrows came then, from opposite directions, from unseen archers. They sliced through the neck of a guard on Gianni's left and another to his right. Both men wavered in their saddles and fell as one to the ground.

Gianni was in instant motion, pulling out his sword and screaming, "Ambush!" as he urged his horse forward. The trees made it difficult to move quickly and the arrows came as fast as a

Saracen's scouts. One narrowly missed his head and struck the horseman to his left in the shoulder, taking Aeneas down, screaming in pain. *Their arrows are piercing chain mail,* Gianni thought. *What sort of enemy is this?*

He circled around to help his fallen comrade and leapt to the ground from his still-moving horse. But just as he got the man's good arm around his shoulder, an arrow came singing through the trees, just over a chest-high branch before them. Gianni was too late in dodging. As he came down heavily upon his friend, too much weight cast to land otherwise, he spotted the arrow lodged through Aeneas's throat, watched as his friend's eyes grew wide with fear and he gurgled his last breath.

With a roar, Gianni rose, picked up his sword and circled, madly searching for his assailants. Up ahead, he heard another man's cry. "May God have mercy on your souls!" Gianni screamed. "Because there will be vengeance here today! You may not cut down a knight of the Church without paying a divine penance! Show yourselves! Show yourselves! Face me as men!"

Two arrows came at him from opposite directions, one directly after the other. One struck his leg in the side, between the two leg plates of his armor at the ankle. And as he raised his arms in anguish, stumbling backward, fighting not to cry out at the pain, the other caught him in the side, between front and back armor.

He fell to the ground, gasping for breath, concentrating every moment on not crying out. He refused to end his life mewling like a lost child. He would finish as a proud knight, a man God would commend in heaven.

Fury at their assailants kept him focused for a few long minutes; righteous anger that they would dare to attack an army of God kept the pain at bay. But then the pain, the breath-stealing pain, swept through him all at once. His wounds were mortal. He would die here in this grove along with his squad of men and the Sorcerer would escape. He rolled to his side, hearing his faltering heart beat in odd time to the dull thuds of departing hoofbeats. Their assailants were escaping, fleeing this death scene. He tried to concentrate on the desire to get up, to give chase, but with one halfhearted attempt up, he fell back, panting for breath.

High above, a curious white bird circled. More white than a peregrine falcon—one like Gianni had never seen. It disappeared behind tree branches and then reappeared, like an apparition, a heavenly sentinel.

A sign from God. He was coming for Gianni.

This was the end.

cb cb cb

"My lady, wait," Father Piero cried, as Daria descended down the hill. "No! You mustn't!"

They had watched, or rather heard, the knights cut down in the forest below them. In three minutes, the battle—or lack of it—was over. None of the six knights had emerged from the grove. Only the three they pursued.

"The robbers are gone!" she shouted from partway down the hill, waving northward to the trio who raced up the hill and then disappeared over the crest without a look back. "There may be some yet alive!"

Hasani cried out in warning too, but had to pause to untie the wagon horse's reins from his saddle before trying to intercept her. In his haste, the reins became even more entangled. Frustrated, he dismounted and rushed down the hillside after his lady, sword drawn. Father Piero was just ahead of him.

Daria paused, intending to wait for them to reach her, but she could hear a man moaning ahead. She dismounted, and ran forward, looking about in caution. The first two men she spotted were dead. The third was yet alive.

cb cb cb

"KYRIE *eleison*," Gianni mouthed, unable to tell if any sound left his mouth. But he screamed it in his head, trying to battle back against the pain. *Lord have mercy!*

The trees were swirling again, and high above, the white falcon, fighting off crows, seemed to suck him upward into the skies. "Wait for me, *Christe*," he prayed in a mutter, barely able to form the words. "Come for me. Don't leave me here, alone. Please, Lord Jesus. I've done my best to serve. Come for me, Lord on high!"

Dimly he wondered if Salvatore had survived the attack, if he could find him and . . .

It mattered not. Salvatore could not save him. No one could save him but God. Gianni could feel the poisonous arrow within him, a terrible sensation of collapse, as if it ate away at his vitals. This was no ordinary arrow. He struggled to breathe, to steel himself in order to take one more breath.

Vanquished. After all the battles, this was how he would die. He could feel the blood now, streaming from his body, oddly cool on the skin as a gentle breeze blew across him. Again his eyes went to that white falcon, circling, visible through the trees for a moment, then disappearing for long moments. A white bird against an impossibly blue sky . . .

"*Kyrie eleison. Christe eleison. Spiritus eleison. Kyrie . . . eleison . . .*" Again and again he silently prayed to the Father, Son, and Holy Spirit, waiting for the moment when he would finally be free of this world and in their realm forever.

God was nearing. The warmth surrounded him, entered him, made him feel light upon the rocks. His Savior! Coming for him at last! He could feel the smile spread across his face even as he tasted blood. . . . Glory! Glory to God in the highest!

"You will not die," a soft voice said, taking his big hand in long, thin fingers.

Irritated by this dim intrusion from what felt like someone behind him, beneath him, far away, he opened his eyes, almost surprised to see himself among a dancing, swirling forest and not flying with the falcon high above it. "Leave me . . . Leave me, woman."

"It is not your time," she said. She pushed him to his side, making him cry out in pain, sure that she had just sent him to heaven's gate, despite her words.

She gently moved his arm before him, exposing the arrow that he dimly knew had pierced his chain mail. Moving quickly, she placed a knee at his hip and someone grabbed his arm. Gianni cried out again as he felt the arrow tip rip through flesh as she pulled it out.

"*Christe eleison, Christe eleison,*" he panted. Why was his Savior not taking him now? How much more agony must he endure? Suddenly it felt as if God were taking a step back. "Wait!" he cried. "Wait for me, Lord!"

The woman pushed up his bloody chain mail, up toward his armpit, and placed a hand on his bare skin, never pausing. He gasped at the hot sting of her touch, wanted to strike her for inflicting any more pain upon him. But she stood there, unwavering, praying, and there were others with her, others who were praying . . . but the pain, it was too intense. Gianni passed out.

⚛ ⚛ ⚛

HE awoke with more clarity, feeling the woman splashing his side with cold water, washing away the blood like the mud from a child's fingers. But then she laid her hands upon the wounds at his waist and ankle again, still praying, and a warmth spread across his innards, as if the surgeon were stitching up a wound. It was as though he could feel his vitals sealing up again and the pain immediately edged away. So sudden was the change that Gianni struggled to grasp what was happening—

From a small vial, she poured oil across him, gently rubbing it across his side, down at his ankle, praying incessantly over him in a whisper.

"Who are you?" he managed to ask, slowly recognizing that

this truly was not his end. He trembled . . . not with illness now, but with confusion, fear. This woman had stolen him from heaven's gate! Who was she? A witch? Panting, he demanded she answer him. "Who . . . are . . . you?"

"It matters not." She continued her ministrations over him, touching his eyes, then his ears, then his lips as she repeated Jesus' name again and again. She was not a witch. He felt none of the cold fear he felt around the Sorcerer and his dark followers. He concentrated on her words. Christian prayer. He was in no spiritual danger from this one. But if not a witch, how—

Slowly, the forest ceased its madness and settled back into shape, gently swaying in a high breeze, but no longer swirling. The falcon landed on a branch above him. And the woman . . . he'd never seen such a beautiful creature. *Lord, who is this woman? If I am in danger, warn me now.* The edges of her cloak parted as she leaned over him again, head bent in prayer. Long, graceful neck, delicate collarbones, pleasing cleavage peeking above . . . a lady's brocade and beads, the finest.

"M'lady," he whispered.

She looked at him then, arched brows furrowed over dark brown eyes in which a man could find tales and wisdom . . . a stern angel of God. "You have work to do," she said, and his eyes went to her lips, formed in the shape of a perfect bow. "Cease looking at me like that."

"Yes, m'lady," he said, speaking normally now. He could breathe again, take a deep breath! He laughed at the sensation, filled his lungs and then laughed again. What sort of miracle had just occurred?

He was torn between the glory of an afterlife just barely touched, the promise, the glimpse that made his heart pound with hope, the desire to exist in that perfection and his relief at being alive. But in the midst of it was this angel, this servant . . . God's own hand, a wondrous creature. A healer. And beside her a priest and slave. What odd trio was this?

He rolled to his hands and knees and then slowly got to his feet, his legs still in armor, his sword still on the ground nearby. Gianni twisted to look at the wound at his side, verifying that this long, lithe woman before him had chased off death, that it was not some strange dream. Gingerly, he rolled his foot one way and then the other. The area was tender but not even bleeding! There was an ugly gash, but no blood . . . how could this be?

He whooped and raised his arms to the skies, grinning. "You saved me, mistress," he said loudly and joyfully. "You have done miraculous things—"

"Shush!" she said, stepping toward him with fear in her eyes, covering his mouth with her thin fingers. "It is not I, but the Lord God who chose to save you," she whispered. Her eyes were wide and her head went back and forth, scanning the forest. Instantly, he was on alert, taking her arm and sliding her behind him even as he withdrew his sword with the other hand.

"What is it?" he whispered over his shoulder. "Do they remain?"

The dry wind continued to brush past the trees above them, but there was nothing to be heard or seen that was out of the ordinary. Still, the hair at his neck prickled. He glanced up to the falcon, and the bird stared resolutely to the east, as if he spotted something. The crows were gone.

"Your assailants may return," she said. "You must return to your post, find more men, and pursue them. But you must not go alone."

"Nay. I am now your sworn servant," he said, turning toward her, eyes still canvassing the landscape. He saw her horse, halfway up the hill, her wagon on the road above. Her family crest—red peacock atop white background—on the side. A lady, she was, a noblewoman. "You have plucked me from the verge of death, fought back against the dark arts. You are a healer, and I am indebted to you."

"You owe me nothing. I must be away from here, soon. I must

not be seen. Traveling with a knight hardly makes me inconspicuous, along with my other companions."

"I will discard my armor, wear the clothes of a peasant. But I will be at your side."

"Nonsense. I was sent here to heal you. You were sent to fight the forces that seek to rule our world. I thank you for your generous offer but—"

Gianni sank to his knees before her. "M'lady. My name is Gianni de Capezzana. I have been trained under the finest and served with even finer." He took her hand in his and placed it over his heart. What could he promise her? "I only seek to serve. I must gain pardon from the cardinal to leave his service but then I shall give you my sword, my life. Do with them as you please."

Her dark eyes—the color of cliffs he had known above the Tyrrhenian Sea—searched his. He fought to keep his thoughts from her earthly beauty. He could have no expectations from her, must fight back his desire. He was a servant, a protector. *Lord, give me strength. Only to serve. Allow me to serve your servant. Thou hast brought us together!*

"You serve the Church," she said, pulling her hand from his. "You need not leave her service in favor of me. God healed you. Go back to your post."

"God healed me through you. I heard your prayers, know it as truth itself. You do not practice the dark arts."

"Go home, knight," she said, tilting her pert chin upward, lips clamped together.

"A healer." He paused. "God's healer. An art not sanctioned by the Church." His eyes went back to her family crest—the peacock. Where had he seen that before? He glanced over at the priest, back to Daria, and then quickly to the priest again. He took a step backward, eyes wide. "Who are you?"

The priest stepped in front of the lady, staring at the knight. "You know us. You *know* us!"

Gianni shook his head, then held it, feeling suddenly woozy. "I do. Somewhere. We have met."

"Nay," the woman said. "We have not. Go home."

"Wait," the priest said. "I think he is one of us."

"One of you?" Gianni said. "I do not know of what you speak, only that I belong with you. M'lady, you are in need of a protector. I am your man."

"Sir de Capezzana—"

"I am your man. God sent you to me. Now I will honor his gift by protecting you and yours."

"Surely you have promised allegiance to—"

"I must continue to pursue that one, he of the dark. Cardinal Boeri will understand that. But I am also your man."

She studied him for a long moment, as if she could stare into him, determine the value of his word. God in heaven, she was beautiful. But she was his sister, he reprimanded himself. His sister in Christ.

The priest interrupted then, breaking their gaze. "Sir de Capezzana, you have the gift of faith. Where God leads, you are clearly ready to travel. As the lady was sent to you, you have been sent to us. You are our man," he said, using Gianni's own words. He turned to face the lady so that Gianni could not see his face. "He is our man," he intoned. "The Lord has willed it."

The lady looked away in submission and the priest turned back to Gianni. "So be it. The Lord is ever before us. . . . Come then, knight. We must not tarry. Your other men, they will soon be here?"

"Yes."

"Then they will take care of your fallen comrades. We must go. It is not our time to face a Church garrison."

"But my other men, my cardinal—"

"As you said, we will send word to him once we reach safety," the priest said. He reached out and laid a hand on Gianni's shoulder. "These fallen men cannot be further hurt. The others will see to them. You said yourself that you were called to protect the lady. Come. Go where you have been called." He turned and the three made their way up the hill, seeming to care not whether he followed.

With a sorrowful glance back toward Aeneas's body and the others, Gianni rushed to catch up with the trio, just as Daria was reaching up to gesture for her falcon. As it landed upon her gloved hand, they looked like a portrait.

"May I ask thy name, m'lady?" he said.

She paused, skirts in one hand, falcon atop the other, regal lady from toe to fingertip. "I am Daria d'Angelo," she said.

Daria d'Angelo.

The Duchess.

CHAPTER EIGHT

THREE days later, Gianni wasn't able to articulate in his mind why he had sworn fealty to the lady and largely abandoned his oath to the Church. All he knew was that he had been dead, and God had saved him through her hand, and he was to guard her life. It was a confusing lot. . . . The cardinal would believe him dead, like the others he had left behind. But to wait for the other contingents to arrive, to try to explain about Daria and the mysterious healing . . . he was afraid that they would all end up in front of the Church's judges, defending themselves against charges of heresy and witchcraft.

He was certain that time would come. But with a knowledge as true as a sense of home, Gianni followed where his heart led. He followed where God led him. And his God had led him here. To her.

He looked back to the odd pair behind him. The older, odd-looking Dominican priest. The lady beside him, pure elegance, with a long, lean neck and chestnut hair that kept escaping her wimple and curling about her heart-shaped face. Her falcon remained high ahead, circling, circling. Occasionally he would swoop down and kill a rabbit. The priest had three carcasses bouncing against his horse's flanks. Daria met the knight's gaze unwaveringly, leaning forward to speak lowly to the mare as if sharing a secret about Gianni.

His eyes went back to the bird, high ahead, when the falcon screeched. It had been Bormeo that Gianni had seen as he lay dying, not some sentinel from God as he had thought. But when he had seen the lady . . . it was as if there were an angel before him. There had been angels on either side of her, he was sure of it. And together, they had delivered him.

He faced forward again and took stock, as if trying to emerge from a particularly absorbing dream. He fought the urge to lift his chain mail and run his hand over the wound at his side to confirm that it had been real, not some strange vision. He struggled to focus on this new commitment, and come to terms with his decision to leave the ranks of the Church without permission. But it was all he could do. She had saved his life. And deep within him, he was certain hers was in danger.

⚭ ⚭ ⚭

"You believe him to be one of us?" Daria asked Piero dryly. "Will we be turning up a new one of our gathering every day?"

So she had noticed it too. The passion within his eyes, the pull between them as if they all belonged together.

"I know not. God's ways are mysterious. I had thought we would at least get to Siena, and another of the Gifted would emerge in time. I never thought we would discover him so soon after departing."

Daria nodded, again bending forward to speak to her tiring mare. "You have become lazy, my dear horse, unused to long rides and eating too much while in the nuns' care." She looked again toward Piero, keeping her voice down. "And his gift?"

"I don't know. My assumption is faith. He's a knight of the Church—a position few take because they can make more money in mercenary work elsewhere. That indicates devotion, calling, faith."

He looked ahead to the knight, who was muttering to himself. "It could also be discernment. As a knight of the Church, his duty would call him to haul us before his superiors, allow them to decide if we were true believers or of evil."

"But he did not."

"Nay. He clearly decided who we were, as if he had been told of us. And he knew that we are in need of some protection. I would say that indicates some divine discernment. Or a mighty faith. The Holy One appeared to whisper in his ear and he obeyed."

"Could the Gifted who come to us . . . could they exhibit more than one gift?"

"Indeed. And yet as I read the letter, I would expect people with one primary, extraordinary gift, readily identifiable. As you are clearly a healer, I expect others to obviously present themselves. And as they do, it will become more and more difficult to move in secret until we know what God is calling us together to do. We have an interesting road ahead, m'lady."

"Indeed we do, Father." She looked up to Gianni, who had driven his heels into the horse's flesh and cantered up to the hilltop ahead. "And when do we tell him of what we know?"

"Soon. I wager that he will not allow us to keep our secret for long."

ɔ ɔ ɔ

GIANNI dipped his pen in the inkwell and fought to find the words of explanation he needed.

1 June 1339

Your Grace,

Please forgive my departure without a by-your-leave. As you will have discovered by now, I foolishly led my men into an ambush, and was nearly killed along with them. I was criti-

cally wounded and saved by a group of pilgrims and now travel with them northward. My hope is that in the coming weeks, I might pick up the trail of our Sorcerer and eventually bring him to justice. If I am successful, you shall be the first to hear of it, because I intend to bring him to your door.

I do not know how long this trail will last, Your Grace. Please accept this letter as my official resignation from your forces. I enclose remuneration for my horse, clothing, and arms. Please know I have reasons for this unorthodox departure. Someday, I hope to explain to you in person.

Gianni de Capezzana

He had wanted to sign his letter as he always had—*your faithful servant.* But what sort of faithful servant turned and walked away from his master?

The priest rounded their campfire and sat beside him. "You are fulfilling your calling as a knight of the Church in defending us. You were brought to us for a reason."

"What reason is that, Father?"

"There will be time enough to speak of such things. Just suffice it to say I am glad you are with us, Gianni. There are battles ahead of us, some requiring physical strength, others spiritual strength."

Gianni looked him over. "You seem to know more of me than I of you, Father."

"Yes," the man said dimly, looking down the hillside upon rows and rows of vines, bright green leaves sprouting, vines spreading. But no grapes yet. It was too early. "The wines of Toscana. Some of the finest anywhere."

"The best," Gianni agreed. "The lady lives within Siena's walls?"

"Yes. In a fine house. She also has a manor and vineyard outside the city."

"Defended?"

"I do not know."

"She has no male kin?"

"Her father was a wealthy merchant who passed away, along with the lady's mother, three years past."

"And the lady has no husband?"

"She was betrothed, handfasted. But the man broke their handfast and is set to wed another."

Gianni swallowed the questions that leapt to mind. It was improper to delve too deeply into such private matters. He had been spurned by a lady once. But they had not been handfasted. Such a turning caused much hurt.

"She came to the convent where I presided, in order to rest and allow her heart to heal."

"And in turn, became a healer?"

"I suspect she has always had the gift."

Gianni nodded, forced himself to ask the next question. "And there is no sorcery that you can detect. No witchcraft, Father? You are certain this is a divine gift from God? That we are protecting a true follower of the Christ?"

"Without a doubt. But you know as well as I that it will be difficult to convince the Church of such things. There is such upheaval right now—such political pull. At the moment, the men who seek to lead the world to the Gospel of Christ are more concerned with seizing and maintaining power. I fear that Daria's gift may be used for political gain. We must give it time, explore it further. For now, it is to remain a secret. Our plan is to get her home to Siena, and then see where God leads us. Change is on the horizon, Sir Gianni. Are you willing to go wherever God leads you?"

Gianni could see the questioning in the priest's eyes. "If it is God who leads me, without fail shall I go."

"Do you fear change, Gianni?"

"Father," Gianni said with a scoffing laugh, "in the last four days, I was nearly killed and brought back to life by a mysterious healer. I left my post of six years without notice to serve said healer. I swore my fealty to her because . . . because I could do no other. I would equate it to what you might have felt when God called you to be a priest. Do I seem like a man who does not welcome change when it is prudent?"

"Nay, sir," Piero said with a grin. "I would say that God has chosen you wisely."

⚓ ⚓ ⚓

THEY rode together for a time, and as they took the serpentine road through the wooded hills of Toscana, more and more fine country manors popped up; some were castles atop hills, some were walled fortresses, and others were simple, large homes with thatched roofs. Vineyards stretched for miles, and peasants worked fields of hay at the bottom of each, where the soil was best tilled for grains.

"You have more to tell me," Gianni said as they wove their way through a dark forest of beech and silver fir, their horses climbing hard as they neared the top of a valley road.

The priest dismounted and looked back to the wagon and Hasani and Daria, a short distance behind them. "Indeed I do. But we will wait, Gianni. We will wait for God's timing. In his timing, you will know all that we know."

Gianni accepted his word without further thought. The priest was protecting some measure of their story. Mayhap he was testing Gianni, making sure they could trust him. The black man clearly did not trust him yet, casting him long, studying glances as if examining the skin for a delicate thorn. Gianni did not blame them for their guarded inspection . . . a part of his mind was doing the same thing. But his heart, his heart was unaccountably tied to this group as if he had just discovered his own family on the road. An odd family, when one accounted for an old priest and freed slave, but a family. That was the best way Gianni could describe it.

"You are expecting trouble ahead. Is the lady in danger?"

"Possibly."

"Whom do you fear?"

"I am uncertain."

"On this count, you must not speak to me in riddles, Father. If there is a danger, please tell me of it so that I may protect her."

Father Piero sighed heavily. "Sir de Capezzana, not everything is laid out as clearly as our Roman roads. We must get her home and we shall take stock. I imagine that all will become clearer to us in the coming fortnight."

๛ ๛ ๛

DARIA smiled as they pulled through Siena's walls, so glad to be home. The city was bustling in preparation for St. John's Day, just three weeks hence. There were farmers driving herds of swine and others driving flocks of chickens to market. There were goatherders and fishmongers. Peasants hung their clothing on lines high above to dry and people argued on one corner, laughed together uproariously on another. As they left the marketplace and drew nearer to the Duomo, the great cathedral's striped marble towers sprouted up into the air, surpassing even her neighbors of wealth, each trying to outdo one another in stature as much as protection with their guard towers.

Her eyes briefly rested on the high tower that her heart tied to Marco, and she quickly looked away. It still burned, but it was no longer the ache, the dark wave that once threatened to overcome her. The terrible wounding her heart had suffered had apparently scabbed over. Given time, it might once again beat normally, even in Marco's presence.

Here in the city, it would be impossible to avoid him. There was family business to attend to, business that she could not make dear Vincenzo see to much longer. It was her responsibility. Not his. Her eyes ran in the direction of the del Buco mansion near the city walls, where Vincenzo's family tower climbed into the sky. She could not see it here, among the high, cramped brick homes and palaces and businesses that lined Siena's winding, cobblestone streets. But she knew it nearly as well as she did her own home.

The del Buco mansion was as uniform and elegant as Vincenzo. Her dear adopted uncle, where would she have been without him? Despite needing to care for his own young wife's needs and family business, he had seen to his best friend's child, Daria, watching over her and finally sending her away when her grief over Marco became life-threatening. She had lost so much weight, wishing on occasion to follow her parents into heaven. It had been Vincenzo who had had her trunks packed and his own knights escort her to the convent, the convent her mother had loved.

It was there that she had received a piece of her heart back, there that she discovered that she could live and survive, even without her beloved. And where she caught a glimpse of the future, a strange and wonderful and frightening future. Dear Vincenzo! He had known just what she needed. She could not wait to see him. In her wagon were gifts for him, fine cheeses from Roma. Spices from Morocco. Candles from England. They were not enough to repay him, but she hoped he would see her heartfelt thanks through them.

They made their way up the Via Banchi di Sotto, down Via Galgaria, turning again and again until they reached Via di Diacceto. Daria fought the urge to push her mare to a gallop across the cobblestones, eager now for home. When they pulled up outside the mansion, she forced herself to wait upon her horse until Hasani came and assisted her down. Gianni scanned the street, his hand resting on the hilt of his sword as if expecting an attack at any moment, and Daria stifled her frustration. *Cease such foolishness, knight! I am home! All will be well!*

Hasani knocked on the armored front door, and after a moment, Nico peered outward. "Mama! Mama! *Essi sono in casa! They're home!*" the boy called in excitement. Moments later, the gate's bar slid away and chains rolled up until the door could be opened. Four servants rushed out, hands aloft, shouting, "Welcome, welcome! Welcome, my lady! Welcome home!"

They were three siblings of a peasant family that her father had hired when she was but a babe—Aldo, Agata, and Beata Scioria. Only Agata had married and had children and now grandchildren of her own, one of which was the boy, Nico, who had first peered out at them. Every one of them worked in the d'Angelo household or woolen guild in some fashion.

"Agata," Daria exclaimed, allowing the old woman to kiss her on both cheeks and then her hands in delight. "Your Nico, he is growing as fast as a young sapling!"

"Indeed, my lady. And he eats as much as your horse!" The woman grabbed for Daria's horse's reins and led them all inward. "I am so happy you are home. It has been too long!"

"Just two months, dear one," Daria responded.

"Two months too long. This house needs her mistress."

"Indeed," Daria said. "You must catch me up on all that's happened here. But first, allow me to make introductions. Aldo, Agata, Beata, and Nico Scioria are the principal household servants in our villa. Father Piero is our new chaplain." She paused to allow the women to gasp and genuflect in praise, then raise thankful hands to the sky. For years they had lobbied for a new chaplain.

"*Grazie, Dio del cielo! Grazie, Madre benedetta!*"

"*Si, si,*" Daria said, smiling as she tried to becalm them. "And this is Sir Gianni de Capezzana, the new captain of our guard."

Again, the women twittered and whispered among themselves, again lifting praying hands of thanks to the rooftop, even as they circled Gianni in inspection like round hens circling a giant rooster. They nodded, as if approving of her decision, bowing toward Gianni in welcome. Aldo, their brother, reached out a hand and Gianni clasped it, smiling down at the little man.

"Yes, well, there is much to do!" Daria said. "Aldo, please see to the horses with Hasani. Nico, please run to the butcher and bring home ten of the finest capons. Also stop by the grocer and get some carrots and peas." She leaned down to the boy. "Please take the rabbits that Bormeo killed, skin them, and bring them to your *nonna*." She turned to the women. "Ladies, I am in dire need of a bath. Let us go and fetch water together and set it to heating."

She looked over to Father Piero and Gianni over her shoulder in merriment, unable to stifle her joy as the women carried her forward. "Hasani, please show Father Piero and Gianni around the estate and to their quarters!"

ꝋ ꝋ ꝋ

"I prefer to begin at the top and work our way down," Gianni said.

Hasani turned and led the way, with the priest and knight close behind. Gianni whistled in appreciation. The house was grand, with palacelike, wide stairs, leaded windows that let in daylight, and fine tapestries upon the walls. The family's affiliation with the woolen guild showed.

The house was constructed in a U shape and climbed for three stories—four, counting the towers. Gianni followed Hasani up the stairs to the roof level and Piero pattered behind them. There were two towers on the estate, but neither was as tall as some of the neighbors', making them more susceptible to archers. But having two was a clear tactical advantage, and Gianni nodded in respect to Daria's predecessors. Between them was at least a walled rooftop that could be defended. Gianni intended to explore it further, later, and figure out a way to better defend the top from archers on other, higher towers.

Hasani led them down to the third floor and waved toward the eastern wing and pretended to cradle a baby. That wing held empty rooms, presumably once for family. They moved into the central solarium, a parlor on the third floor. On one side were windows, open now to the Via di Diacceto below. On the other were more windows, open to the gardens below. Hasani gestured to the other wing and Gianni understood that was where Daria resided.

They descended to the next level. In the eastern wing were the servants' quarters and at the end, the knights' quarters. Hasani showed Gianni a wooden door in the corner, at chest height, that opened. Inside was a hook and bucket. Bathing water could be hauled up from the kitchen. To his right was a deep tub and drain beside it. Hardly private, but serviceable. And after six years of service with the knights of the Church, privacy was no longer an expectation anyway. Gianni looked across the wide hall, over sixteen empty bedstands—the straw ticks long removed—and felt lonely for his comrades, missing their jocularity and ribald voices, singing and wrestling.

"You'll soon fill this hall with fine men," Father Piero said, resting a hand on his shoulder for a moment.

"I lost five of the finest this past week," Gianni growled, pulling away, knowing it was not the priest's fault that they were dead. Only his. "How many men does the lady wish me to hire?"

"We have not spoken of it yet. Hasani, what would be safe to say?"

The tall man looked over to them and signaled two now, four more soon.

Gianni nodded. "I will set to work on that task on the morrow."

Hasani grunted again, showing him where he could put away his belongings in an old, curved chest. There was firewood laid in the fireplace, so dry and long laid that spiders had spun impressive webs. It had been many years since the d'Angelo household had felt the need for arms. Or since someone had protected it . . .

They walked out of the hall, past the servants' rooms, warm with use, and into the center—a common room. Beyond that was Hasani's room and then the hall ended abruptly. Hasani made it clear through gestures that it was the chapel ceiling. They came down more stairs to the main level and walked down the western wing and into the small chapel. Father Piero nodded in appreciation. "Such a nice little chapel, when so near to the Duomo. The lady's family must have been devout indeed."

Hasani bowed his head in quiet assent, then showed the priest the way to the back, through the sacristy, and out a narrow door to one end of the northwestern wing, where they discovered a small chaplain's room.

The three men paused, back out in the garden, gazing from the three-story wall along the Via di Fontebranda to the house that surrounded them on three sides. Gianni cleared his throat, hands on hips. "Hasani, how is this house defended under attack?"

Hasani gestured to either wing of the house at the corners, and with his hands, depicted two strong gates on either side that could be barred. Gianni grunted his approval. He had seen the iron gates within. The designer had relied on the ability to lock the central part of the estate up tight, becoming a virtual wall between the two towers and abandoning the outer wings and chapel. It was mediocre as far as city fortresses went, but it was somewhat respectable.

Father Piero grinned at Hasani and Gianni. "So, if under attack, the priest is sacrificed like a lamb led to the slaughter, eh?"

"Nonsense." Gianni laughed. "But you had better run like an altar boy if you hear the alarm, Father. We will lock you out behind the barricade if you don't get inside in time."

"Although I am old, I am yet quick on my feet when the need arises," Father Piero said with a grin.

Siena seemed like a bustling, peaceful city. But Gianni knew all city-states had times of peace that rapidly seeped into war. Daria was reckless to leave her home defenseless, in the hands of peasant servants, as dear to her heart as they were. No wonder Hasani had been anxious to return. She needed to protect what was hers. As an unmarried woman of means, she could quickly find herself overcome, with nothing. Had her absence already cost her critical ground?

CHAPTER NINE

THE d'Angelo household gathered in the dining hall on the main floor at half past seven, a late hour for supper, but delayed in order that the servants could prepare a feast and the travelers bathe. As Gianni hauled up water for his first bath in a week, using the ancient wheel and rope, it creaked and made quite a fuss. He had seen the rusty wheel and frayed rope atop the roof. It had been unused for more than the three years that master d'Angelo had laid dead.

How long had this house stood undefended? From his years within Cardinal Boeri's halls, Gianni well knew of Siena's shifting politics and the power of the Nine. How had the d'Angelo household not been overtaken? Divine providence? Daria's betrothal? Gianni shook his head in wonder. Whatever had preserved them, it was high time to do what they could to reinforce Daria's position.

A knock at the door echoed across the room and Gianni crossed creaking floorboards to open it. The servant boy, Nico, stood before him with a tower of linens nearly taller than he and a square of lye soap at the top.

He wavered when he spoke, and the entire pile began to slide from his arms.

"Whoa, whoa!" Gianni said with a laugh, taking the pile from him and setting it upon his straw tick.

"M'lady says to tell you we've sent for several new straw ticks. They shall be delivered on the morrow," the boy said. "Nonna sent these other things up from the cellar chests." He picked up one thing at a time and set them across the mattress. "A towel and cloth for your bath. The soap too. Two underlinens. The master's own old shirts and two overvestments with the house's coat of arms."

Gianni picked up "the master's" old ivory shirts and fingered the exquisite, soft weave. If they had ever been worn, he couldn't tell. "These are some of the finest linens I've ever seen made," he muttered. Appropriate for a house so central to the finest cloth guild south of Milano. He dropped the shirts and ran his hand across the light underlinens and then picked up the overvestments, long sheaths of an uncommon white and red, with the family crest on the front—a peacock. An odd choice for a family shield. And yet peacocks were majestic and could surprise you with their brilliant displays of tail feathers. . . .

"It is the family trade, cloth. The d'Angelos have been principals in the woolen guild here and the mistress's father once considered to be a part of the Nine. It is a shame he never came to power."

"So I've heard," Gianni said dryly. The knight studied the boy, perhaps ten. He had spent too much time in the company of hens, picking up a clucking tone, mimicking their phrases. Gianni could shape him, show him what it meant to be a man. He might prove a worthy squire . . . and yet his access to information in the kitchens was helpful. No one knew more about a house than the servants. "The mistress . . . her former betrothed. Is he a part of the Nine?"

"Nay. But there is one that is ailing and without heirs. We have not seen him at mass for five months or more. When he dies," the boy paused to genuflect, "may God bless his soul, it is rumored that master Marco will take his place at the table."

Gianni watched the boy's facial features. "You liked master Marco?"

Nico shrugged guiltily. "He taught me things. Played games with me." His expression hardened then. "But then he spurned my mistress. Can you imagine? Such a lovely lady? He was blessed by the saints above to have her! When I am grown, I will make him pay for the hardship he has caused her."

Gianni stifled a smile and placed a hand upon his shoulder. "I will begin your military training on the morrow, with your grandmother's permission. Then you will be prepared to challenge him when you are a man."

Nico's eyes widened. "Truly?"

"Yes, little man, if you see to your other duties and your parents approve, I will teach you to wield a shield and sword."

Nico clasped his hands together in a girlish gesture of excitement and Gianni rolled his eyes. There was much to do with this one.

"Nonna has one more bucket of water waiting on the pulley," he said, suddenly remembering the time. "Supper is late this evening to allow you and the others to bathe and change, and they are preparing a feast." He waggled his brows. "Such food!"

"How much time have I?" Gianni asked.

"Just enough to bathe, shave, and dress." The boy moved over to the tunnel and began hauling up another bucket while Gianni disrobed. As he pulled his shirt from over his head, Nico gasped. "Did you get that wound in battle?"

Gianni glanced at the boy and then down to his side, where the arrow had pierced him during the ambush. He ran his fingers over the wound, which appeared months—rather than days—old, then stared out the window. "*Si*. My last as a knight of the Church."

The boy came closer. "The saints preserved you, to survive such a wounding."

"Indeed." *The saints and your mistress . . .*

"I will leave you now, master Gianni."

"Thank you, Nico."

The boy shut the door behind him and Gianni grinned at the prospect of transforming the child into a man. He always enjoyed the process of training stable boys into squires and squires into knights. With no children of his own, he could take part in a portion of fatherhood without any of the lingering responsibility.

As he dumped the last of the water into the deep tub and eased into the steaming water, he thought again of Salvatore and Aeneas, men with children in villages about Roma who would never see them again. He frowned, lathering his hands and the cloth with the soap that smelled of milk, juniper, and eucalyptus, and then began washing himself from head to toe, as if he could scrub the memory off with the grime.

But then his hands rubbed past the wound at his ankle, where the first arrow had pierced him. He remembered the second arrow piercing his side at precisely the right—or dreadfully wrong—moment. Falling to the ground. The archers had been highly skilled, some of the best he'd ever encountered. He remembered Bormeo, circling high above him, and then Daria, an aura about her. . . .

What had happened to him? How could his path have taken so abrupt a turn? How had the lady healed him from his mortal wounds?

Fury at their evil assailants set his hands to shaking. Such treachery! And yet God had saved him, used the mistress to heal him, and perhaps through his serving her, protecting her, his path would more readily cross with the evil ones. Surely they did not live their lives riding from town to town! The Sorcerer was a man of means, elegant in manner. In protecting the lady, Gianni assumed that they would be invited to many feasts and gatherings of the wealthy. They would travel to other towns in seeing to d'Angelo business. He would be on the lookout, scanning for any man who might be the Sorcerer. He would root him out like a swine after a truffle, and one day run his blade through his black heart with satisfaction.

Gianni ducked under the water, washing suds from his brown hair and then rising, cleansed. *God is gracious. He has given me his own divine plan. Surely he is with me!*

✧ ✧ ✧

THE dining hall was set up in traditional fashion—with the lady's table on a dais at the front, set horizontally, then three vertically set tables before it, of which only the center one was set. Upon her invitation, Father Piero joined Hasani and Gianni at the lady's table. The servants sat below at the long, central table after bringing in steaming trenchers filled with roasted capons, vegetables, and bread.

The steward, Aldo, rose, with cup held high. "Welcome back to Siena, m'lady, master Hasani. Welcome, priest and knight. The manor feels like a home again with the four of you in it." He raised his chalice higher. "To your safe return."

"To our safe return," they all said. As was custom, they moved food onto smaller bread trenchers, which they shared between two. Each carried a small knife at their waist and used it in combination with forks, which were modern and quite new to the priest. He had heard of such things coming from France, but had never eaten with one. Following his lady's lead, he stabbed at the meat, cut through the tender flesh, and placed it in his mouth. Delicately seasoned, perfectly roasted, it was delicious. And the fork . . . the fork was quite useful.

He smiled in satisfaction, listening as the steward paused after several bites to begin his report to the lady. It sounded as if the household would soon move to the country for a time, to watch over St. John's Day feasting at the manor outside the city and to bring in and distribute the first of the summer hay. Other planting had to be be done. Cultivation with the vineyards had to be seen to.

The steward moved to another table to retrieve his notes upon a scroll. He was a servant with some learning, and Piero assumed that the d'Angelos had seen to his education themselves, since his sisters seemed to bear little of the same knowledge. It was common for fine families to "adopt" a certain family from surrounding lands, working together for generations. The decades served to build loyalty and peace while preventing intrigue and corruption.

"I distributed twelve ells of rough cotton cloth to the poor and sold the old wine from your cellars, m'lady," Aldo said, obviously pleased with himself. "Judging from the rain the Lord has blessed us with this spring," Aldo said, nodding toward the priest as if he had himself made the clouds gather, "we will have an extra portion of grapes from the vineyard. And the cotton crops are said to be the best in years."

"And the northern roof, Aldo?" the lady asked. "Did you see to its repair?"

"Indeed, m'lady. Just as soon as you were on your pilgrimage, we saw to it."

"Good."

"We have purchased marl to fertilize the fields in a fortnight, once the hay has been gathered, and Lord Vincenzo obtained seed for us."

"Excellent. And what of our mill?"

"The mill is already producing more cotton and finer silk than ever before, using that imported shipment we received three months past. The women talk of bringing to the guild more than three hundred ells of cloth by Michaelmas."

Piero took a bite. The man was a decent steward, from the sound of it, watching over everything from household to field to market.

"And the dyes? Were you able to obtain all we needed?"

Aldo's face fell a bit. "I have been less than successful in that endeavor, m'lady. Lord Vincenzo's man told me there is a new supply train expected in a new moon's time and we will be first at market in bidding."

The lady nodded. "We must have that soon, Aldo, if we are to make the most of those three hundred ells of cloth."

"Agreed, m'lady."

"Good enough, Aldo. Sit, eat. I am thankful for your work, and for all of you," she said, looking about the table. "You have kept my household in order."

Aldo paused for a moment, obviously wishing to say something else.

"What is it, dear man?"

"M'lady . . . mayhap we should speak in private."

"There are no secrets, here. Please . . ."

Aldo threw an uncomfortable glance toward his sisters, who quickly disappeared with the empty trenchers into the kitchen. "We have been visited upon two occasions by messengers from the Nine. They wish to speak of your assets at council. There are rumors. . . ."

"Rumors?"

Aldo cleared his throat, all business. "Rumors that our neighbor, Jacobi, has laid claim to the manor."

Daria wiped her mouth and rose, slowly, regally, a flush rising at her neck. "My father left the manor and the country estate to me. He saw to it that it was clearly in my name, and the courts blessed our documents."

Aldo nodded quickly. "Indeed. I have held them at bay with the copy you left to my care. But there is a call for you to appear before the Nine. Another has laid claim to a portion of your fields and the mill, producing an old note from your father."

"What claim could they possibly stake? My father was very careful!"

Aldo shifted, uneasily. "It is Lord Marco, m'lady."

"Marco! Any claim upon my property or my person ended when he broke our betrothal."

"As the baron has told him."

Daria settled back and Piero studied Hasani. He was fidgeting in his seat, notable only because the man was normally deadly still.

"If the baron has taken up my cause, then all will be well. And master Adimari, he . . . he will change his mind."

The steward remained where he was, staring at his feet. "Perhaps the lady should go calling upon the baron tomorrow."

Daria's eyes narrowed. "Why? Please, speak plainly."

The steward coughed and then met her gaze. "As you have no living relatives, m'lady, the baron has again laid claim to your wardship."

She shook her head. "It is all a mistake. Vincenzo would not . . . I will unravel this puzzle in the morning. The baron has been misunderstood. My betrothal, regardless of how it ended, left my father's estate in my hands and no other's. I am a woman grown. No one's ward but God's."

Aldo nodded, eager to please her, but all could clearly see that he did not concur with her assessment. Piero watched as Hasani rose, then slid out of the hall. A moment later, they could hear the front gate slam shut and a horse's hooves upon the cobblestones. Daria did not look up from her trencher.

⚭ ⚭ ⚭

HER large, round eyes at times reminded him of a small, world-wizened child. But her movements were those of a lady. The steward's news had clearly shaken her. Perhaps she had expected to resume her life here in Siena after her pilgrimage, imagining her life as a woman alone something she could control. But in this day and age, a woman alone was a property to be acquired, and only the smartest and most wily escaped. He had been right to be wary for her; forces were already moving against the house of d'Angelo.

Gianni wolfed down the last capon that Beata had served him, picking up a leg to nibble the meat from between knobs of bone. It was good to have a full stomach and he needed a full belly for the battles ahead. And there was the scent of battle upon the air already. If Daria went calling upon this baron on the morrow, he would attend her. In the wings, he might be able to better discern what was going on here in the old city, and how he might advise Daria in protecting what was hers.

Meeting the padre's eyes, he rose and followed him out of the hall after nodding at the mistress. Her eyes told him that her mind was already on the happenings here in Siena. The priest led him to the fire, away from the tables, which were suddenly silent.

"I am unfamiliar with the laws that pertain to such matters," Gianni said. "From what I gather, she was bequeathed most of her estate, over which this baron—"

"Baron Vincenzo del Buco," the priest supplied.

"Over which Baron del Buco has watched. He must have been a trusted friend in order to become the lady's warden."

"Indeed."

"So we can surmise that he arranged for the lady's betrothal to Adimari?"

"Perhaps. Or that could have been arranged before her father's death, when Daria was but a child."

"True. So our first order of business is to determine if the baron still has Daria's best interests at heart, or if he's seeking to further his claim upon her lands."

"I have heard of this baron, a burgher who bought his title a decade ago."

"As have I."

"Then you know what the servants told me? He is one of the Mercanzia, and counsel of the woolen guild. He and d'Angelo probably worked together for many years."

"I did not know that. Speak further with other household servants. Find out what they believe is really transpiring. I will go and see what the city's people can tell me. Any idea where the freed man went?"

"Perhaps to see what he can gather himself."

Gianni turned to leave, but the priest stopped him with a hand upon his arm. "Good knight, there is something I must tell you. . . ."

"What? Out with it."

The priest paused and then shook his head. "Nay. The time is not right."

Gianni studied the little man for a moment and then dismissed it. There were bigger things to discover than whatever he had to say. The priest could tell him of his secrets on the morrow. He turned away and strode down the hall again, approaching Daria and the servants. She was pulling a box out from a bag at her side and handing it to Beata.

The old woman stepped forward, tentative and servile in her motions. Nico was nearly as tall as she, stooped over as she was.

"Mistress?"

"Beata, I know that your eyes have dimmed in years past. That you have difficulty seeing anything close at hand. I miss your fine needlework. See if these can be of any assistance." Again, she raised the old box to the woman, and Gianni took a curious step forward.

With trembling hands, the old woman set down the box upon the table and opened the lid. Spectacles! Gianni had only seen two pair of the new contraptions—once in Venezia, the second in Roma. They were frightfully expensive, an extravagance of the wealthy. And the lady bestowed them upon a servant?

But one look at her face told Gianni that she was as thrilled to give as the old woman was to receive. Light emanated from her eyes and tender smile. "Please, Beata, try them on. Slip the wires across your face and hook them about your ears."

The old woman looked at Daria as if she had asked her to don a carnival costume, but obediently slipped the precious glasses from their case and did as her mistress bid. Her pursed lips opened in a soft gasp. She raised her hand to her face, looking upon the nails as if seeing them for the first time. She quickly bent to the table linen, examining the weave with reverent fingers.

"Well?" Daria asked, impatient. "Are they of assistance to you?"

"M'lady!" the old woman exclaimed. She turned and woefully took the glasses from her face, bowing her head in servile fashion. "It is not right. Losing one's eyesight is a part of the Lord's path for old people. This must be an instrument of the devil."

Daria rose, at once regal in her stance. "Not at all! Beata, this is a gift from the Lord! He has given man the way to correct eyes that no longer do what they were created to do. The angels are surely celebrating that you can once again count the hairs on Nico's head. Please, dear one, please. We will ask our chaplain to bless them, then wear them with confidence and enjoy the things you can once again see."

Beata paused for a moment, still contemplating her mistress's words, and then slowly, tentatively, reached out to take the glasses again. Her family immediately surrounded her, all asking at once to try them on. Beata was soon admonishing Nico for stumbling about the room, risking her precious gift. The family disappeared in a murmuring mass to the kitchen.

Gianni stepped forward, smiling down upon Daria. "So you can heal through other ways than prayer."

She gave him a small smile, obviously well pleased with her gift. "The Lord provides in many ways."

"It was an uncommon gift for a servant."

Her smile faded. "The Sciorias are the only family I have left. They have been loyal to mine for decades. There is nothing I would not do for them."

Gianni returned her look. If he was not careful, she would have his heart in a fortnight. What uncommon beliefs! What admirable and lovely qualities! To say nothing of . . . He turned away from her, trying to focus his thoughts. "M'lady, I ask your leave to go and see about hiring two or three mercenaries this night." He sensed her pause a moment behind him, contemplating his request. Obviously news of potential danger to the estate had opened her mind again to expanding her contingent of men at arms.

She stepped down from the dais, leading him away from the

servants and speaking in hushed undertones. "I would ask you, knight, to await Hasani's return and take him with you. He will know where the most reputable men in the city reside and where to find whom you seek."

"This city is familiar to me. I know where the reputable men gather."

Daria arched a brow. "You know our city?"

"I grew up in the hills of Toscana. My family tended to the Chianti vines for decades. My great-grandfather gathered enough land to send his sons to Roma for schooling."

"And others became knights?" she guessed.

"Indeed. My grandfather went on the fifth Crusade."

Daria winced. "An unfortunate end for those."

Gianni raised his chin. "But divine in its origin, and therefore blessed."

She strode to the far end of the great hall, toward the fireplace, and held up her hands to warm them. The summer eve held an uncommon chill. Gianni joined her there, and noted the fine lines of her cheekbones and jawline. What fool could have left such a magnificent woman? She was one of the famed beauties of Toscana . . . her title of Duchess more fable than true noble title. But she had the stance and beauty to rival queens, if he could only assist her in lifting her chin—there was a subtle air of defeat about her despite her efforts to hide it. Perhaps the residue of Adimari's departure.

"De Capezzana," she muttered, breaking his train of thought. "I should have recognized it."

"With three hundred thousand in Siena, ten thousand more between here and Firenze, it would be difficult to know all."

"Capezzana," she repeated. "I believe my father had dealings on occasion with those of your clan."

"Most of our family's business was conducted in Firenze, but they oft came to Siena as well."

"You are not in contact with your family?"

"I am the youngest of seven sons. My elder brothers, I do not see eye-to-eye with them. There was talk of my becoming a priest. My mother always wished me to serve the Church."

"So you fled?"

"It is no honor to follow a false calling. I am a servant of Christ, but nay, I am no priest."

She shot him a glance. "And yet you found yourself in the company of men and God."

Gianni allowed her a small smile. "Indeed. God makes us laugh at our own plans, does he not? At times he denies our own passions and dreams in favor of his own. But I find, dear lady, when I follow his lead, I am ultimately more satisfied." He dared to hold her glance a second longer than was proper.

Never dropping her own gaze, she stepped forward and turned, her skirts falling in a graceful line to one side. "And will you leave this house as quickly as you left your post as a knight of God?"

⚓ ⚓ ⚓

HER question clearly threw him. He faltered, working on a response, and a flush grew at his neck. This was a man unused to explaining his actions, and he obviously could not explain them yet to himself.

His dark eyes met hers. He was dreadfully handsome in a rugged sort of way, this knight. Different from Marco's lithe, masculine perfection. Marco was like the finest of Spanish horses, carefully groomed. This one was more raw energy, unkempt like a wild stallion just barely tamed. Mayhap two or three years her senior, and yet with uncommon experience about his eyes.

"M'lady, I will not so much as depart this manor without your leave," Gianni pledged to her with slow, measured intensity. "You may count on me as thy protector."

It was shameful to push a man so. What had gotten into her? She stared down at the floor, hearing her mama's voice in her head, admonishing her. She started from her reverie when he raised his hand, almost to lift her chin, caught himself before he touched her, and placed his hand over his heart instead. Slowly, he got down to one knee, into her line of vision. "M'lady, I have been called here as surely as I was called into service of the Church. I cannot explain turning from my post after you healed me, other than to say that God himself asked me to do so. I was willing to give the Church my life, and indeed, almost did. But then God gave me life again . . . through you."

The dear man was as confused as she. What was at hand? Again, her thoughts went to Father Piero's mysterious script. "And yet you did not accuse me of witchcraft."

"Nay. You are no witch."

"How can you be so sure, sir?" She dared to look back into his eyes. Even when he was on his knees, his head was just below her chin. He was one of the tallest, most powerful men she had ever met. A head taller than Marco. Broader than Vincenzo. She felt safer with him near. But she must press on, be sure of him now because later—

"Every day, my cardinal sent us out with his holy prayers covering us. For years I have been chasing infidels . . . those who seek the downfall of everything righteous and holy." He paused, looked to the stones beneath his knees, seeking words for thoughts that were bound to be as wild as hers, then returned to meet her gaze. "I was to die in that grove. I thought . . . I thought I glimpsed heaven itself. But then God, in his holy wisdom, decided to deliver me back to earth. To . . . you. Because of you, m'lady. For you. Through you. That is not witchcraft. That is God at work."

She needed to know one more thing if she were to trust him. "You believe that God can work through the lesser sex?"

"M'lady, God, in his grace, has used small children at times to do his good work. He has used slaves and even animals. Why would he not use a magnificent woman?" He bowed his head. "I am your sworn protector." He raised his chin again, this time with a slight grin. "And I will not leave you unless I die of a mortal wound that even you cannot heal." His smile faded and earnestness flooded his eyes. "I have offered to you my fealty. My life. Will you accept it?" He held out his hand, asking for hers.

He thought her magnificent. His eyes told her that. And worthy. She needed such strength and devotion. Another ally like Hasani, but different. Hasani was a protector too, but even as a freed man could not go everywhere this man could, generate the power he could. There was much at stake in the days to come. Her family estate. Her life. And moreover, her new calling, wherever it might lead.

She placed her hand in his and he slowly, tenderly kissed it, his lips covering the family ring and her knuckle, sending a shiver up her arm. She managed to cover her reaction and keep her composure, resisting the urge to yank her hand away. "I accept your sworn fealty, Sir Gianni." Daria leaned down and whispered in his ear, "I ask you to keep me alive until God sees fit to call me to his side."

Gianni looked away, averting his gaze for propriety's sake. But he was dreadfully still. "You fear for your life, m'lady?"

There was little left to hide. Soon he, too would fully know of the Gifted. If the Church did not put them to death at the stake, the dark adversary would attempt it in other ways. And there were those who wanted what was hers. . . . There would be battles ahead. Her thoughts flew to the grove where Gianni's own knights had been struck down, one after the other. "Yes. I do."

Gianni took her hand and placed it over his own heart, pulling her face uncomfortably close to his own, daring to look at her. It was highly unorthodox. "Daria d'Angelo, my lady. As long as I am alive, you shall come to no harm." She paused there a second, drawn by his intensity. A sound behind her made her rise quickly to a traditional stance.

"I accept thy pledge with gratitude, knight. I thank thee for thy sworn fealty and trust my life and my holdings and my people in thy hands. You may rise."

Gianni did as she bid. It was Hasani behind her; she could sense his presence. She turned.

"Did you learn of anything?"

Hasani gave her a sideways, halfway nod.

"Something," she said for him. "But not everything. See what you can learn as a relative newcomer to the city, Gianni. As you seek the first of our knights, listen to the words of peasant and nobleman alike. I need to hear everything you hear."

"Yes, m'lady." He moved off, toward the door, his thoughts on the horses in the stables and which he would choose.

"Gianni, I expect that you have gathered there is considerable opportunity for intrigue and treachery within this city and beyond," she said. Her words gave him pause and he turned to look upon her as she continued. "Choose your men wisely. It is of vital importance that they are as loyal to you as you are to me and the house of d'Angelo."

CHAPTER TEN

IT was late for visitors. Downstairs, he could hear a man open the large front door and greet whoever had come calling. Vincenzo wiped his mouth with the edge of the fine tablecloth, a linen out of the guild's finest, and rose. He was eating alone in the solarium, as was his custom of late. The dining hall depressed him, reminding him only of Tatiana's absence.

As he crossed the room, the door burst open and Marco Adimari rushed through. "You have heard?"

"Marco! Please, come and sit."

The younger man ran a hand through his dark and wavy hair. "You have not heard? She has returned."

"Daria? Of course. She sent word this afternoon. You did not expect her back? Siena is her home."

"Right." Marco paced before the cavernous fireplace. "Right. Yes, of course, I expected her to return. But . . . what do I say to her? How can I look her in the eye, Vincenzo?"

Vincenzo went to him and placed a hand on either shoulder. "Marco, Marco. Get a hold of yourself. Surely by now Daria has come to the same conclusion as you. Without heirs, neither of your houses can be sustained. There was no choice when no child came from your handfast. There was too much at stake." They were words well traveled, phrases repeated countless times. But Marco's heart continued to shake him from the path of wisdom. He loved Daria. Had always loved Daria. It simply was not meant to be.

"Her failure to conceive left you with no choice, man," Vincenzo said gently. "She knows that. Your own fathers would have concurred."

Marco lifted eyes of misery to his. "Why would God not bless our union? I loved her. I still love her, Uncle."

Vincenzo turned and walked away from him, trying to come up with a new way to convince him. "What of Lady Francesca?"

Marco gave a dismissive wave of his hand. "She is suitable. Already showing signs that she carries a child. Wishes to marry—"

"Marco, that is wonderful news! God has smiled at last upon you and the house of Adimari!" Vincenzo rose to clap the young man on the shoulder but Marco did not return his smile.

"It is good news. It is. But why can I not feel it as joy?"

"You will, in time. Francesca is a fine woman. Your union with her will prove very fruitful for the house of Adimari. Her dowry will bring you new lands, new houses, new power. And your sons will inhabit them. It is what your father wanted."

"My father wanted me to forge such a union with Daria. As did hers."

"We have been through this many times, Marco. Your father, and hers, assumed she would bear children. They spent many years speaking of their future joint grandchildren and the security it would bring to both estates."

"Mayhap . . . mayhap I did not give it enough time."

Vincenzo blew out a breath of frustration, walking away from him, repeating oft-repeated words. They had gone over this enough. When would Marco accept fate? The will of the divine? "Two years, Marco, two years. There was nothing to do but wed or break your handfast. You did the only thing you could. In two years, a fertile woman will bear fruit. Unless," he turned to eye the younger man, "unless she denies her husband . . ."

"She did not deny me. She was lovely and giving and everything I wanted in a wife, inviting me to her bed every day sanctioned by the Church."

Vincenzo forced the vision of Daria abed from his mind. "There you have it! The will of God, Marco. You have made a decision that you cannot overturn. You are handfasted to another. Another who assures you of future success, of increased lands and holdings. Of children. Do not look back."

"But Daria . . . my darling—"

Vincenzo grabbed his shoulders and shook him. "Marco Adimari! You behave as a lovesick boy. Be a *man*." He softened, forcing down the frustration that boiled to the surface. He reached up to try to stroke his cheek, but the man moved a step away, staring at him in silent anger. "Marco, Marco. We both care deeply for Daria. I will see to her welfare. You have my promise. I have petitioned to resume control of her estate as her warden until I can find a path that will bring her ultimate happiness."

Marco stared at him for another long moment and then he relented. "Of course. I know this. Forgive me for continuing to question your wisdom, Uncle. Forgive me for giving in to this madness." He began pacing again before the fire. "It is simply that . . . I cannot seem to get her out of my mind. I see her everywhere already . . . even when she was still in Roma. I bed Francesca wishing all the while she were Daria."

"Give it time, Marco. It has been but half a year since you two parted. Daria d'Angelo is not a woman easily forgotten."

"She was so hurt, so dreadfully hurt. And when she learns of my new handfast, so soon made after her departure, of Francesca's pregnancy . . ."

"She will understand. It might hurt again, bring her up short. But Daria comprehends all that is at stake. And ultimately, she will bless your union. In time, it will not hurt each time you see her. Nor will it hurt her to see you."

Marco sighed. "You speak of it as if you know how this goes. Did you once love another you could not have?"

Vincenzo gave him a small, sad smile. "Indeed. It is the nature of things, it seems. Rare is the man who loves one and is blessed to be loved in return. Rarer still is the man who loves his entire life."

Marco waved his head back and forth. "I am a fool. Forgive me, Uncle. Your own grief over your young wife yet burns within you and all I can think of is myself."

Vincenzo nodded, letting him absorb such a thought.

"You are in more dire need than I of an heir."

"Heirs will come, Marco," Vincenzo said with a sigh, placing a hand on his shoulder, guiding him toward the door. "For your house and my own. They will come." The words fell easily from his lips. Expected, reassuring words. This boy had always needed reassurance. Why was it that both Ermanno Adimari and Giulio d'Angelo had entrusted their children into his care? A childless man? Perhaps his younger age and vitality in dealing with the Nine had convinced them of his worth and reliability.

"You have heard that there are those that say I am claiming a portion of her fields and country manor?"

Vincenzo paused. "It is your right, Marco. You may not lay claim to all that would have been yours if your union had borne fruit and you had wed. But it is common to take a portion, your investment for two years—"

"No!" Marco stepped toward him. "I will not take yet a skein of wool from the house of d'Angelo. She owes me nothing, Uncle. She owes me nothing!"

Vincenzo sighed. "I understand your feelings, man. But it is common—"

"No, Uncle!" Marco ran a hand through his dark, curly hair. "She has given . . . she has given enough. The house of Adimari need not take what is not freely given. Please, see to it that such foolishness ends. Please."

Vincenzo looked at him for a long moment. "As you wish, Marco. I will speak of it with the Nine in the coming week."

"Good."

"They will see it as a sign of weakness. You lessen your opportunity to take the potential seat. The Nine expect ruthless adherence to laws and rights."

"So be it. If God ordains it, it shall be mine. If not . . ." He shrugged.

Vincenzo nodded. He was a fool. Daria understood the politics of the day. Marco should too. Vincenzo and even Daria needed him to take a seat with the Nine. It was all in their best interests. Long-term goals outweighing short-term pain. But he had pushed it as far as he could, this night.

Marco paused at the door. "And what of the house of Jacobi? I hear they are laying claim to her city villa, saying they hold some old note from her father."

"Bah! I will see to it. It is a minor attempt at her estate, one I shall easily put down. Cease worrying about Daria. She is my responsibility, not yours. Now go, go home to Francesca and invite me to the wedding before the new moon."

ふ ふ ふ

DARIA could not help herself. After reviewing the critical household and business affairs with Aldo, settling Bormeo into his falcon's keep, inspecting the gardens and new roof, peeking in on Beata—who was still busily inspecting minutiae she had not seen in a decade with repeated exclamations—she paced about her room for close to an hour and tried to settle into a night's rest before rising, pulling on an old gardening dress and a nondescript cape and covering her hair with the hood. She longed to walk the streets of her childhood, feeling the pull of the winding, cobblestone roads that led to the *campo*. At this hour, hardly anyone would be about.

As she slipped down the stairs and out into the garden, she sensed Hasani over her right shoulder. "I wish to go alone," she said, not meeting his gaze. He remained where he was, unmoving, until she took a step, and he with her. She fully turned. "I wish to go alone," she repeated.

A gargled form of "nay" came from his lips. He did not ask where she was going, or why, just silently insisted that he be with her.

Daria sighed. "Very well. But at least give me the illusion of solitude." She set out, feeling bad over her cross nature but she wanted, needed, hungered for a bit of breathing room, with no one but God to watch over her. Here in Siena, even with the potential of political danger, she felt safe and capable, courageous for the first time in two months. In years past, she had slipped from the villa to spy along the streets, observe, breathe in the city. Apparently that was no longer possible. At least not without Hasani.

She peeked around one corner and then hurried down the street, hugging the far building's wall. Hasani's footsteps behind her were nearly silent, and yet he was never more than five paces from her shadow. Daria had to admit that it was wise to have a guardian with her. No longer could she claim the invincibility of youth, the feeling that no one could ever wound her, take her life. And it was foolish for a woman to travel the streets alone at night. And yet . . .

Daria turned a second corner, listening to the sounds of the city—mamas yelling at errant boys at one corner, and cooing and singing to children at the next. Three men stumbled out of a tavern up and to the right, ceasing from their hilarity to stare in curiosity at the hooded woman across the way, until they caught sight of her dark guardian staring back at them as they passed, his hand on the hilt of a long, curved Arabian sword.

Her feet took her in the direction her heart longed to travel. In minutes she was on the corner across from the house of Adimari. A clattering along the bricks told her that two horses approached, and she sank backward, deeper into the shadows. Hasani echoed her movement. She cared not what he thought about her being here, staring into the windows of a man who had tossed her aside. All she knew is that she had to see it—test her heart and resolve to reside in a city where her lost lover still lived.

As soon as they rounded the corner, Daria knew it was Marco, riding atop his horse like the finest of the riders at tournament. The house of Adimari had twice claimed the tournament horse race prize, bringing pride into their neighborhood *contrada* for a year, until the next tournament threatened to capture the prize from them. Marco's older cousins had ridden in the race; one was even trampled to death. She supposed this might be the summer that Marco would ride.

She did not know the knight who traveled with him, but he was obviously a hired man, reminding her of Gianni in stature and movement. But her eyes only briefly flickered upon him. Instead, they covered Marco from head to toe, noting his fine clothing, lean forearm, dark olive skin. The barest of glimpses before he disappeared inside the villa, a man closing the heavy wooden gates behind him and sliding the iron lock shut with a high-pitched slide until finishing in a loud *ka-tunk* that echoed down the lonely street.

It was then that Daria realized she was holding her breath, found herself surprised she could exhale and take another breath and then another. The sight of Marco caused melancholy to spread through her chest, but no keening, breath-stealing cry escaped her lips as it had two months past. She was making progress. She would survive Marco's departure. Nay, at some point, she would thrive.

Resolutely, she headed down the street, her head ducked, her stride long and unladylike. She cared not.

All at once the steep street emptied into the wide, shell-shaped *campo*, like a river into a bay. She continued forward, to the very center, and once there, paused. Her father used to bring her to this very spot. He would crouch down and ask her to close her eyes. "Daria, close your eyes. Smell of this city. Feel her beneath your feet. Can you hear her heartbeat? Can you?"

Now, standing here, she could feel what he meant. There was a pulse to this ancient city, but at this hour, it was merely a gentle hum that one could feel all about. Dim sounds, flickering candlelight in windows, occasional shouts. But the city largely snored now, resting in preparation for another day.

A high, three-quarter moon edged up over the eastern wall of buildings, and to the right, Daria studied the silhouette of the top of Siena's monstrous church and tower, visible above the palaces of the Nine that lined the *campo*, up on the hill like a silent watchdog. To her immediate left was the sculpture of the she-wolf, the pagan icon of Siena. According to lore, the she-wolf had suckled Romulus and his brother Remus, father of Siena's founders. It was an ancient Ghibelline thumbing-of-nose at the papacy. While the city took pride in its faith, it took greater pride in independence.

Slowly, she circled, able to see in the moonlight the progress workmen had made on the red bricking of Il Campo—a burst of nine rays that were ostensibly to symbolize the folds of the Madonna's cloak, but more a nod to the Nine, the force that governed Siena. The façade of the Palazzo Pubblico was now finished, a fine town hall that served the Nine, with black and white shields symbolically covering the windows. Since Siena had defeated Firenze in 1260, the city never ceased to flaunt its power, even attaching captured flagpoles to the columns of the Duomo in a gaudy display of *braggadocio*.

Statues dotted Il Campo. Here, a white, naked Venus that seemed to starkly glow in the moonlight. Over there, Neptune. Daria moved forward, to the high point of the *campo*, the fountain. Water splashed in a delightful sound, another bold display in a notoriously dry city constantly thirsting for more. Streams and springs were jealously guarded outside the city, and many lives were lost each year in battling to keep the burgeoning city's wells from going dry. But here, here at the fountain, water ran freely from the aqueduct, splashing over the urn and down to a basin below. Her father had talked of funding a replacement, having a fine artist sculpt something worthy of the piazza, but it never came to fruition.

She bent to dip her hands and drink. Was that what she was doing this night? Rolling about in the dirt of her past when her Creator was pulling her upward, urging her forward? Ready to wash her clean? "Help me to rise, Father," she whispered skyward. "Help me to rise."

She glanced around the *campo* one more time and over to Hasani. "Come, friend," she said lowly. "See me home."

CHAPTER ELEVEN

GIANNI wandered the curving cobblestone streets, stopping in one tavern and then the next. He ordered ale or watered wine at each stop, pretending to drink, but ingesting little. He needed his wits about him, for there was much going on in this tight hilltop city. It felt good to be on his own, recollecting how one street led to another, even though he had not traveled these roads since he was a child delivering kegs of wine with his papa.

Memories of those years gave him pause, a pleasant, slow ache that filled his heart with longing. He would need to find time to visit the small valley that had been home to his people for centuries, and call upon the relatives that remained there, people he had not seen for nigh unto a decade. Home was home and he had a need to see the lush vines in summer swell, smell of the fermenting wines, taste of earthly tannins and fresh roasted bird upon a spit. In time, he told himself. In time. At present, he had a mission.

It was at the third tavern that he first heard townspeople speak of Daria.

"I hear tell the Duchess is back in the city," said a man to his companions at a table beside Gianni.

"D'Angelo? She dares to show her face back here?" blustered another.

"She has as much right here as that lout, Adimari," said the barmaid.

"It's what every highbrow lady needs," said the first. "To be brought down a couple o' notches, remember that they are but women."

"You are hardly Lord Adimari," the barmaid said, sending his companions into uproarious laughter.

"And you are hardly the Duchess!" the man returned, his face ruddy with barely concealed embarrassment. "Just look at how many kits this cat births," he said, reaching out to grab her and pull her to his lap. "One a year! Ach," he said, flinging her back to her feet. "You probably just made me a father again. You're as fertile as Persephone."

The barmaid tossed her hand and walked away from the raucous trio, moving on to serve others.

"If only the poor Duchess could've been so lucky within the womb as our Maura," said the second man.

"No, no. I think she was cold. She refused her man," said the third. "Crossed her legs tight each night."

"*Si*, that woman wants it all for herself. Had their betrothal worked, Adimari would've taken all she owned. The wench is a man in woman's clothing, ever since her papa passed on."

All three sloppily crossed themselves, as was common when speaking of the dead.

"I'll tell you what she wants. She wants to be of the Nine."

"Of the Nine? Of the Nine!"

"I will leave Siena and never look back should a woman ever take her seat at the table of the Nine!"

"I will move to Firenze and take up arms against Siena should such a travesty take place!"

His companions pounded the table together in agreement and tossed back glasses of wine, then hastily poured more. Gianni realized he was becoming more and more tense, ready to spring at these drunkards. He needed to remain calm, continue to gather information. It was then that he spied two knights on the far side of the room, quietly drinking and observing everyone in the tavern—including Gianni. Mercenaries, it appeared, not wearing the coat of arms of any house. Some of the free lances he sought?

Gianni turned away, staring at the barmaid as if she had his whole attention, trying not to show the knights that he was overly interested in the trio's conversation.

The drunkards were still talking, and that was when he realized one was of the house of Jacobi, Daria's neighbor who had threatened to try to claim her city estate. "My master has filed the papers. He says that he shall own the house of d'Angelo by winter's end. If need be, he says he'll make the Duchess his common-law wife. But he doesn't want her. She'd be a pretty ornament at his side, but if she's barren, she is of little use, especially if she refuses to warm her man's bed. Her house and holdings, on the other hand . . ."

Gianni rose and stared at the three, fingering the hilt of his sword.

Gradually, they felt the heat of his presence, and the first, of the house of Jacobi, rose to his feet. "You ha' something to say?"

"I am Gianni de Capezzana, and I have heard enough disparagement of Lady d'Angelo. Your master would not be fit to swim in her latrine, and you may not speak of her again."

"What is it to you, Gianni de Capezzana?" the first man blustered.

"I am captain of her guard."

"What guard? That house is an unguarded rattletrap. My boys and I could come and take it tonight!"

"Ettore, *fermate*—" his companion said in warning.

Ettore threw off his friend's hand, staring at Gianni, sizing him up.

Gianni moved his hand to his belt behind him and slowly pulled out a frightful dagger. He ran a careful finger down its blade. "*Per favore*, do come and try to take my lady's house this night. Then I will have reason to slice your throat just enough that your death will be slow and you can hear your own last, gurgling breaths."

Ettore ran his hand along the stubbly beard growth at one side of his face, thinking Gianni's words over. The tavern was suddenly so silent that Gianni could hear the scratching sound of it from three feet away. In his peripheral vision, he could see the two knights, standing, hands on sword hilts.

But his eyes remained on Ettore. His hands itched for a reason to beat the man, make him regret his callous, impolite words. But it was not what he was here to do. Defend Daria, yes. Attack, no. Not now. These men—the whole city—needed to know that Lady d'Angelo was no longer a woman alone. She was again a woman protected.

"My companions and I," said the man, cocking a half smile, shrugging his shoulders, "we were only having some fun. Three friends sharing some wine. We talk. We've been known to talk all night!" He lifted his hands in surrender, but there was murder in his eyes.

Gianni stifled a sigh. He had made an enemy, and the man lived next door. He nodded, slapped a silver piece on the wooden table, and then turned to walk out the door. Had he backed away, it would've shown fear. These men needed to know that he feared no one but God.

"Watch out, friend," shouted Ettore. "You might find a dagger like you carry in your back."

Gianni looked over his shoulder. "Such cowardice is what I would expect of men of Firenze, not of my neighbors here in Siena. Should I die with a dagger in my back," he said loudly to all in the crowded room, "you should know it was likely this man and he should be brought to the magistrate." He returned his gaze to Ettore. "Should you care to truly challenge me, I shall meet you wherever you wish. And your life will come to a swift end." Nodding curtly, he left.

He moved forward into the night, intent on getting back to Daria's home.

"Those were brave words, for a soldier walking the streets alone," called a voice behind him.

Gianni paused and smiled, turning slowly. "I had hoped you two would follow me."

"Better than those gents in there," said the second man. They moved closer to Gianni. One was short and blocky, dark haired, a head shorter than Gianni. The other was his height and sandy-haired, sturdy. The first reached out his hand. "I am Basilio Montinelli," he said. "And this is my friend, of Germany, Rune."

Gianni took his arm in the way of knights and nodded shortly. "A pleasure."

"It sounds like you are a captain in need of hiring an army."

"Indeed. Are you knights in search of a captain?"

The two eyed each other for a second. "More employment, than captain."

Gianni raised an eyebrow. "I see. *Arrivederci*, gentlemen." He turned on his heel and began walking home.

In seconds, the two flanked him. He looked from one to the other, then straight ahead, still walking. "I am seeking soldiers, but they must follow my direction without hesitation."

"What makes you capable of giving a man direction?"

Gianni pulled up short and lifted his chin. "Six years as captain of the knights de Vaticana de Roma."

The tall one, Rune, whistled lowly, while the shorter one, Basilio, crossed his arms. "And now?"

"I am on a new mission. No less holy."

"Protecting a beautiful, single woman of means is a holy calling now?"

"Yes. At times."

Basilio stared at him while Rune looked up and down the curving street, keeping an eye out for the men of the tavern or other dangers. "What are you offering?"

"I'm not. I don't need mercenaries. I need good men beside me, instantly responsive to my orders. I need soldiers." He turned to walk off again, and they fell into step with him.

"No need to get sulky," Basilio said. "I was simply being honest."

"As was I."

Rune spoke for the first time. "Our last employer . . . was less than respectable. We do not wish to work for such a man again. He made foolish choices for little gain. He looked upon us more as chattel than men. Many of our compatriots were lost for ill causes."

"I see. You have horses?"

"Each of us has a riding horse and pack horse."

"Armor?"

"Indeed."

"Specialties?"

"I am good with the broadsword," Basilio said. "And Rune is one of the best longbow men I've ever met."

Gianni's mind went to the forest where they'd been ambushed. Did he have a right to lead men again, after what had happened? He should've suspected something, should have waited for the rest of the troops before pursuing the Sorcerer, should've noted the archer's bows upon their backs. . . . "I take it you two have seen battle?"

"From the Rhine to Napoli. We two have traveled together for five years, working for two different men. We have been seeking employment for the last fortnight."

"Your last employer was?"

"Ilario Bicoli de Venezia."

"And why come to Siena?"

"I have always preferred Siena to Venezia or Firenze," Basilio said with a slight shrug of the shoulders.

Gianni paused again, looking from one to the other, trying to read their expressions, make a decision. "My charge is to protect Daria d'Angelo and her household. My mission may take us some distance and there is some potential that we may find resistance."

"Such as those men back there?"

"Mayhap. They are not who concern me."

"Who does?"

Gianni eyed him. "The Church."

Rune raised an eyebrow and Basilio chuckled. "Well, now. The Church, you say. That is an odd sort of potential enemy. Especially for a former knight of the Vatican."

Gianni stared back at him. "Indeed."

Basilio's smile grew. "I never was particularly religious. I'd like to work for a man such as you. I think I'll find it . . . amusing." He put out his arm in offering.

Gianni smiled back, taking his arm. "Welcome to the house of d'Angelo, Basilio, Rune," he said, taking the taller man's arm next. "I think you'll find me a worthy leader, and your mistress one they'll sing about across the ages."

"All a knight could ask for," Basilio said, spreading out his arms. "We shall go and collect our things and report to the house of d'Angelo after we break our fast on the morrow."

Gianni gave them a curt, farewell nod and then moved on through the city. He smiled, thinking about his two hired men. Not particularly religious. Something told him that service to Daria d'Angelo would soon change that.

꙯ ꙯ ꙯

DARIA knelt alone before the altar in the small family chapel the next morn, praying after their brief morning mass. It felt good to be in the chapel again, to see it alive. It was like opening an old gate. There were rusty hinges to get past, but once opened, oh, the garden one could see beyond it! Father Piero was reverent and peaceful and thorough in his duties; he would serve the household well. And even better—with an active household chapel, there was no need to attend the *contrada* church for mass until Sabbath. It would reduce her chances of running across Marco.

She was ready to see him, she thought. Not just from across a dark street, but in the light of day. She almost looked forward to the pain, knowing that in wrestling with it, she would eventually find healing.

It wasn't Marco that brought her to her knees this morning. There was a swelling in her heart that she could not name. Apprehension seemed to wash over her in waves, sending the hair on her neck upright over and over again. "What is it, Lord?" she whispered. "What is it you wish me to know? Give me wisdom and insight, Father. I need you here, with me. With all of us." She waited in the silence, yearning for a response, direction, anything, but nothing came. She genuflected and rose.

When she turned, she was startled to see Gianni, a respectful distance from her, standing with feet apart, hands behind him, head bowed. "No need to pretend to be praying, sir. You have need of me?"

"Yes, m'lady. Your newest knights have arrived, and I thought I might introduce you."

"Knights? You've found the time to hire two mercenaries already? You must have been out quite late."

"Not much later than my lady, I'd wager."

She shot him a quick look. How did he know she had gone out? Hasani would not have told him. One of the Sciorias . . . She would need to speak to them about keeping her confidences to themselves. If she wanted this knight to know her business, she would share it with him!

"How could you possibly have found any man of repute at such a late hour?"

He fell into step beside her, walking down the stone corridor to the main house from the chapel. "I cannot attest to their reputations. Only a gut feel that they are tried and true."

Daria paused and pulled herself to her full height, staring up into Gianni's eyes. The man kept his eyes respectfully forward, as if enduring a superior's inspection. "You did not verify their last employment? How can we trust them?"

"Oh, I will do some research, m'lady, rest assured. I will find out everything I can about these two, from birth onward, but right now we must fortify your household gates with any man I can find." He stared down at her then, his eyes full of confidence. "You have business to attend to, neighbors already poised to pounce if we do not show some strength. We begin here, today, to fight them back and hold a line. As we grow stronger, we'll go farther."

The man's use of *we* was not lost on her, and Daria let her eyes wander to the leaded window along the corridor. "Jacobi is an old dog with no teeth. I can easily put an end to his fruitless claim upon my father's house."

"Then do it. Go now to his door and seek an audience. And your first three knights will be directly behind you."

"Now?"

"No time like the present. Let us resolve this matter and gather strength for the larger ones ahead."

"I will face my neighbor, but I choose not to at this moment."

She moved again and Gianni was immediately beside her. "As you wish, m'lady." This time, he offered his arm, and after hesitating a moment, she laid her hand upon it. Her fingers brushed across smooth silk, a d'Angelo overcoat that she hadn't felt in years. She had to admit, it felt good to be under male escort again. And this Gianni seemed as wise as he was handsome.

ക ക ക

HER fingers were long and light upon his forearm, and Gianni fought the urge to smile. In all his travels with the cardinal, very few of the finest women he had met could measure up to Daria d'Angelo. She was a curious mixture of strength and fear and curiosity and bravado. In short, she was magnificent. The dogs in the pub had been speaking out of petty jealousy. Foolish words meant to try to make farmer and knight of equal caliber. But Daria was fine, a jewel that flashed different colors every time one glimpsed her in a different light. The Lord was good to bring him to such a lady.

"M'lady, if you have need of a nighttime walk again, please take me as your guard."

"Hasani was with me."

"I know. And he is a fine man. But even he could not fight off more than three men. There are enemies on the streets, mistress. I know it is your home, that you feel safe here. Perhaps you feel you are even surrounded by family. Undoubtedly, you are. But there is danger afoot. Please. Do not go out without a retinue of guards again."

"I will consider your request."

She didn't sound as if she would truly consider it, but all he could do was request prudence of her . . . and watch. If she didn't invite him, he would follow along uninvited. They walked through the huge inner barrier doors along the corridor. "I will need to hire a blacksmith. These doors and crossbeam need some fine Elban iron to fortify them. As do your rooftop towers."

Daria removed her hand from his arm and they stopped again. "This is a peaceful house, master Gianni."

"At the moment."

Clearly agitated, she circled him, her skirt dragging behind her. "There has not been a battle in our hall or outside it for decades."

"Nay."

"And yet you are insisting upon such expense and work to fortify it! Hired men. Armaments and horseflesh, I assume."

"In time."

"If my enemies do not already have designs upon my holdings, won't our rush to arm ourselves make us appear . . . vulnerable?"

Gianni stared into her wide brown eyes. "We are vulnerable. We are in danger."

"How do you know that?"

"Your steward's report last night made it clear enough. We fight off the enemy at your gates first, as we prepare for bigger and bigger enemies. There is word on the street . . . you are perceived as weak, already partially conquered.

"It is the nature of power, m'lady, to strike against other powers. I am assuming your father left his holdings safely in your hands, but he also planned on your betrothal to Adimari. Together, none would have dared face you. But now you are a woman alone, a woman spurned by a powerful family in this very city, and you are a woman with a very unusual gift—a power that will threaten many in the Church, when and if they come to know of it. We have no choice but to fortify our defenses. Strengthen your gates now, or prepare to surrender or flee."

He hated that his words made her wince, but they needed to make this clear between them. Here and now.

"You think you have discovered all my secrets?"

"There is no such thing as a woman without secrets, m'lady."

There. The tiniest of smiles. He realized that he, above all, might make her feel vulnerable. He was a relative stranger, and yet he now moved freely within her home, ate at her table, desired to make decisions for them all. As she had not grown up with men-at-arms in her home, it was bound to feel odd. Overwhelming. "Your secrets are safe with me, m'lady. I have pledged my service to protect you and yours. As you feel called to certain duties, please allow me to follow mine."

She studied him a moment, tapping one long finger against her full, pursed lips, an innocent gesture as she thought over his words. But he found it oddly stirring. He faced toward the main hall again. "Shall I introduce you to your new men, now, m'lady?"

Her hand again came to rest on his forearm. They moved forward together in silence. As they entered the main hall, Rune was just turning from the hearth, the burning embers having done their duty in warding off the morning chill, and he stood straighter when he saw the lady upon Gianni's arm.

Gianni bit back a grin, noting that Rune's sudden action had drawn Basilio's attention as well. It was good to have hired two men who had worked together for years—such men became a team, of sorts, and were oft stronger because of it.

"Gentlemen," Gianni said, "may I present to you our lady, Daria d'Angelo?"

Both men stood, side by side, and bowed, taking her hand as Gianni introduced each.

"This is Rune of Germany, m'lady. And this is Basilio Montinelli."

Daria nodded at each. "Thank you for coming, gentlemen. May I ask why you seek employment from the house of d'Angelo?"

"Because you are far more beautiful than our last employer?" Basilio quipped, but then swallowed his smile when he glimpsed Gianni's stern expression.

"We are soldiers, m'lady," Rune said. "We seek a fair wage and two decent meals a day. Your captain, here, seems like a worthy sort of leader."

"We would very much appreciate the opportunity to serve you," Basilio said.

Daria stared at one man and then the other. "We welcome you into our home, gentlemen. In addition to whatever rules master Gianni sets forth, please know that drunkenness, lewdness, sharing of house secrets to which you may be privy, or even common disrespect will be reason enough for immediate dismissal. I expect you to behave like gentlemen in a prince's castle. In return, I will pay you more than the common rate by sixpence a day, feed you *three* full meals a day, and give you a bed in the hall of knights and warm water that I insist you immerse yourselves in at least once a week. In addition, it is imperative that you attend daily morning mass with the rest of the household. Does all that sound amenable to you?"

"Indeed, m'lady," Rune said, for both of them.

"Good. If all is going well, in a fortnight, we shall have a swearing of fealty ceremony. We welcome you to our home. Thank you for serving us."

⚜ ⚜ ⚜

VINCENZO rode up to the house of d'Angelo, behind two of his own men. He took note of the fine horseflesh, packed with armor, on the four horses and donkeys tied to iron rungs outside. Knights? Giulio d'Angelo had never seen fit to arm his house and had been fortunate in never suffering an attack. As far as Vincenzo knew, the house had been unguarded for several decades. Considering the breadth of the d'Angelo business, he'd always thought it foolish, but Giulio had preferred to use charm rather than manpower to sway opinion.

His man knocked on the heavy wooden door at the front gate and Vincenzo stayed back, meticulously pulling off one leather riding glove and then the other.

Agata Scioria answered the door, and smiled when she saw Vincenzo's guard and then Vincenzo himself. "Master del Buco!" she cried, hands clasped and pulled to her breast. "Welcome, welcome! Come in, come in. I will announce your arrival to the mistress."

But Daria was there in front of him as soon as he entered, with more color to her cheeks and light in her eyes. When he had left her at the convent, she had been so heartsick, drawn, and terribly thin. Now she once again looked like herself, although there were new lines about her lovely, wide eyes, and an intensity to her jawline that had made her girlishness disappear, made her cheekbones more defined. "Ah, my Daria, more lovely each time I see you."

"Uncle! Oh, how I have missed you!" She rushed into his embrace and they kissed from cheek to cheek and back again in the manner of family. Her grin faltered a bit as she saw him take in the full room behind her.

"Come, Vincenzo, there are many you need to meet."

"I see, I see. You appear to have collected a man from each stop on your pilgrimage to Roma."

"Nay!" she said with a laugh. "That is hardly the way of it. Here, this is Father Piero, our new chaplain." The priest moved in a slight nod, his eyes never leaving Vincenzo's.

"May I present Baron Vincenzo del Buco," she said to the room, standing at his side. "And this is Gianni de Capezzana," she said. "He is the new captain of my guard."

"Your *guard*," Vincenzo said. His eyes searched for Hasani, who stood, as always, in the corner, like a silent sentinel.

"Yes. I knew you'd be pleased."

He had insisted for years that she consider hiring men, but while at the house of Adimari, she was protected by Marco's men, and before that, she was but a girl constantly escaping her father to ride among the hills. If she wanted to hire men, he would have seen to it that she was protected by the finest, most honorable—

Vincenzo focused on the man she was introducing him to and moved forward to embrace the knight's arm. As they looked each other in the eye, he leaned back to better study the man. "Have we met, Sir de Capezzana?"

"I do not believe we have," the knight said. But he looked at him as if he too recognized him from somewhere.

"Who was your last employer?" Vincenzo asked. He gave a half laugh then, to soften his tone. "If I may so inquire."

Gianni shot a look at Daria and then looked back to him. "The Church. I was a knight de Vaticana."

Vincenzo cocked a brow. "I see." His eyes swung to Daria. "My dear, when you go after knights, I see you only go after the best."

"I fear it was I who insisted the lady hire me."

"Ahh." There was more to the story, obviously. He would find out from Daria later. "And wasn't Father Piero in charge of the convent where my men left you two months past?" He gave the small priest a slight bow.

"Indeed. He has honored me by agreeing to serve as my chaplain." She turned to her right. "These two men, Uncle, are new to the house of d'Angelo as of this morning, Rune and Basilio."

Vincenzo nodded at the men and they nodded back. "My dear, I told you I would assist you in hiring guards when it came time. Is this because of Jacobi's foolishness? There truly is little to fear from him. I will see that it ends this day."

"No need, Uncle. I can handle Jacobi. And now that I have master Gianni," she said, smiling toward the knight, "he can see to the house's safety so you need not fret over me. Come, Uncle. There is much to tell you." She pulled him up the stairs toward the third-floor solarium, waving to Beata for some tea and leaving the men to talk among themselves.

༒ ༒ ༒

DARIA could sense that Vincenzo was tense and unhappy, but pretended not to see it. It was bound to be difficult for him to adjust to seeing "little Daria" home and so clearly taking charge of her own life. And she *was* taking charge of her own life. Or allowing God to lead her . . . or a little of both.

"Do you know these men, Daria?" Vincenzo asked, tucking her hand into the crook of his arm. "I am afraid for you, dear one. Suddenly a house of men, with no one to protect your honor?"

Daria stifled an acidic laugh. "The Sciorias are here, and will do passably well in protecting my honor. And who could be more trustworthy than a knight of the Church and a holy man? They strengthen my position as a woman alone."

They sat down in two chairs, to either side of a long, tall window that was open to the garden outside below them. The smell of the first summer roses in bloom wafted through on a slight breeze.

Beata soon arrived, a tray in hand. She set one cup in front of Daria, then another before Vincenzo, then poured from an imported English china pot Daria's father had given to her mother. Vincenzo studied the servant woman closely, but as was custom, she did not return his gaze. Slightly bowing once, she turned and left the room.

"Were those spectacles upon her face?"

Daria grinned at his bewildered expression. "Yes! Is it not marvelous? When I left, she could barely pour a cup of tea without her fingers on the lip of a cup. Now she can see the cup with excellent clarity."

"Daria, spectacles are quite costly. The remedy of princes, not servants."

"You know the Sciorias are as much family to me as you are. How could I pass them by, once I knew of them? In Roma, many more people have them."

"So they did not cost you twenty gold florins?"

"Nay." Daria stubbornly refused to say how much they had cost.

"As your guardian, I need to assist you in such decisions. Or you may soon find yourself bankrupt."

"Impossible. I have more than enough money. Those investments of Father's are still paying off handsomely, and we've enjoyed another good sale on the guild cloth. Not to mention my trade in parchment and ink. Speaking of the guild, have you had any fortune in obtaining the red and ochre dyes?"

"Red, done, ochre, I'm still seeking."

Daria breathed a sigh of relief. "Thank the heavens. I might go and see old master Carman about the ochre. He always seems to know someone who knows another who can obtain it."

"Good idea. He's more apt to give it to you than he will to me. He's still disgruntled over losing to me in cards last winter."

Daria laughed with him. She was so glad to see him! He was tall and lean, graying at the temples, but magnificent in stature. He deserved a seat with the Nine, but had deferred to Marco, preferring to increase his holdings through investments in various guilds, including their joint house venture in the cloth guild, rather than through city politics. Besides, he had already obtained his noble title. "Vincenzo, how does Tatiana fare these days?"

Tatiana was Vincenzo's third wife, a young woman barely older than Daria. They had been married for three years now, and like his second wife, who had died of a stomach ailment in her early years, this one too was ailing. And still Vincenzo awaited heirs of his own. After all Daria had been through with Marco, waiting month after month for her menses to stop and her belly to swell with child, she ached for their empty arms. Tatiana was lovely—one of the prettiest women of Siena, with golden-brown tresses that waved down her back and slanting green eyes. Or had been, anyway, before the illness robbed her of her vitality.

"She's a bit better, now, with summer's heat to warm her thin bones."

"So then, she's up and about again? That is good news." In the months before Daria left the city, she had taken to her bed and very rarely rose.

"For a time, each day. We went to Milano last month to obtain a remedy from a doctor there."

"And has it helped?"

Vincenzo waved his head back and forth, thinking. "Perhaps. I think your treatments were just as effective. Tatiana sends her love, my dear. Can you come and visit her soon?"

"I will on the morrow. I have missed her too. I obtained new herbs and a tonic in Roma that I would like to try with her. . . ." Daria longed to tell Vincenzo more, of this growing gift that seemed to be flowing from her, aching to heal every ailing person in her reach. While handfasted to Marco, she had continued her mother's habit of seeing to the ill of the city and distributing herbs and poultices and tonics to help heal them. It had always been a passion of her mother's, to reach out to the sick and in need.

Vincenzo was talking about Tatiana, of his desire to again take her north to Milano, perhaps even as far as Paris, in an effort to see her to wholeness. Daria bit her lip, repeating Father Piero's words in her mind that they must not share this secret gift until the proper time. But keeping it from Vincenzo, of all people . . . still, she decided to wait, nodding and listening to his plans.

"But enough of me and Tatiana," Vincenzo said, setting down his cup. "I have come to tell you that I have petitioned the Nine to take you on as my permanent ward—in essence, adopting you."

Daria attempted to smile. "That is so kind of you, Uncle. But there is really no need. I will hire my own attorney to make sure that I can maintain my father's position in the guild and see to other assets. Aldo is doing a fine job as steward. He shares everything with me that he once shared with my father. If there are things I do not understand, I will look to you for explanation."

Vincenzo set down his cup and leaned forward, then ran a hand through his wavy, graying hair. "My dear, you have helped me lead the guild only out of deference to your late father. The others on the board . . . unless I have some sort of legal bond with you, they are bound to chafe. A woman . . . it is simply not done."

"I intend to hold my seat for as long as possible. Working together, we shall show them what a woman can do."

"But—"

"I will send my attorney to see to the d'Angelo interests within the guild. I want my affairs in order before we move our household to the country estate to bring in first harvest. The summer feast days are just around the corner."

"None of this is necessary," Vincenzo said, waving about toward the open doorway that led to the great hall. "You needn't hire men; you may use my attorneys. You were once my ward, and

I your guardian. It is suitable for us to resume that relationship. I will see to your welfare, your holdings, and your estate."

Daria rose and walked up to him, looking up into his handsome face. "Dear Vincenzo. My father was so right in choosing you to see to my welfare. But I am a woman grown now. And while my handfasting did not end in the way that any of us could foresee, it does not mean my life is over. My time in Roma helped me to discover that." She reached up and cradled his cheek. "You helped me discover that. There is much, so much, before me."

Vincenzo closed his eyes and slightly leaned toward her touch. Daria drew back, surprised by his expression. At her movement, Vincenzo's confusing expression hardened, and Daria's hand went to her throat. The man was not, after all, her true uncle. Just a dear family friend. And his wife was ailing, probably unable to give him wifely comfort . . . was it lust in his eyes that she had glimpsed? It couldn't be. But then again, just because they had been dear to one another for decades did not make them immune to attraction.

"Baron del Buco, Vincenzo," she began, partially stretching out a hand toward him.

"Nay, nay." He stood and turned away from her. "Forgive me, Daria. It has been a long, hard winter and spring for both of us. It has left us . . . weak."

"We will not speak of it again."

"Nay." He took a deep breath, held it, and then blew out his cheeks. "Come, see to my wife on the morrow. And today I will lay to rest Jacobi's frivolous claim upon your house before I lay aside my petition for your guardianship. If you are certain that this course is wise."

"I believe that I can handle Jacobi—"

He raised a hand to shush her. "I can do this for you, dear one, and with half the effort. Allow me to assist."

Daria considered it for a moment and then nodded, once. "Thank you, Vincenzo."

"And afterward, you will come to me if you are in need of anything? To obtain advice? Protection?"

"Always, Uncle. I shall look to you."

Vincenzo studied her a moment before giving in at last. "Then it shall be so." He pulled on his gloves. "I will come and retrieve you on the morrow. If you are up to it, we must see to business at the guild."

"I will look for you," she said.

CHAPTER TWELVE

GIANNI watched Father Piero's eyes cover Baron del Buco as he said good-bye to Daria and departed. Gianni looked over to Basilio and Rune. "Go about town before you're tied too closely to the house of d'Angelo, and see what you can discover about our new acquaintance, Baron del Buco."

"The mistress seems fond enough of him," Basilio said, more in exploring his thoughts than challenge.

"And it is the mistress we're here to protect. To be her eyes where she may be blind."

Father Piero leaned toward them, arms crossed, hands disappearing into the arms of his robe. "He could simply be a ram—not a wolf in sheep's clothing."

Gianni looked to Hasani to cast his vote, but the man looked away. Perhaps the freed slave felt lost in the company of knights. After all, it had been his duty to protect the lady for years, and now there was a growing group before him, all with the same intention.

"You want me to look up a few of our old compatriots while we are about your business?" Basilio asked.

"Only the very best of your old compatriots. The ones you would entrust to protect your mother, sister, and own life's savings. Understood?"

"Understood."

"That said, I would like four or five more knights hired as soon as possible."

Rune whistled lowly. "That is quite a force for a villa in Siena. Especially for a house that has gone unguarded for some time. Why such need?"

Gianni stole a look at Father Piero. "We will get to that. In the meantime, trustworthy, admirable knights. And information on the baron."

Rune and Basilio departed, and in minutes they could hear the clattering of hoofbeats directly outside. They seemed like good men. Strong and independent at times, but willing. Gianni preferred such men to mindless soldiers. He needed men who could take direction, but also think upon their feet. He opened up a map of Siena that Nico had brought him, and began studying the various streets.

"Master Gianni," Father Piero said.

"Yes, Father," he said, still staring at the map.

"May I have a word with you outside in the garden?"

Gianni glanced up at the older man. "Certainly. In what regard?"

"We will talk of it . . . outside."

Gianni rose and followed the odd little priest to the garden. He took a seat and patiently waited for Piero to cease pacing. After a moment, he said, "It was no accident that we came upon you as you lay dying."

"I should say not. It was God himself, if I may be so bold, who orchestrated such a meeting."

"More than you can know."

Gianni opened his mouth, paused, and then shut it again. He stared into the priest's eyes, feeling an odd sense of recognition. "It is time. You will tell me of the secret you and Lady Daria carry."

Piero sat down beside him and related to Gianni the old story of the chapel outside Roma, of his teacher, and of the satchel—the same story he had shared with Daria.

"In all my life, I have not known a man I trusted more than my teacher."

Gianni nodded. "And? What did he say to you?"

✿ ✿ ✿

PIERO had looked to the teacher's eyes. The old man's face was aglow, warmly lit not only from the oil lamps, but also with excitement.

"You are about to be a part of an ancient secret, an ancient brotherhood of faithful. I was led to this same room in my days as a young student. It was then that my own teacher handed me this scroll and made me swear to keep it safe, passing it along to the next, only when I knew it was divinely ordained. He said that we are all heirs of the divine, and it was up to us, a special line of chosen priests, to help the world know it."

Piero forced himself to take a breath.

"Little did I know that you would enter my halls within my lifetime, that my successor would be *you!*"

Piero shook his head. "You confuse me, master."

"Nay. You know of what I speak. This resounds within you as knowledge as true as your God, an understanding as clear as your connection to the Savior through your holy vocation."

Piero licked his lips and remained silent. It was true. This felt like a mystery, frightening and overwhelming, and yet preordained, exactly how God had meant it to occur. That assurance gave him a measure of peace. "Go on, teacher. Tell me what you brought me here to tell me."

"For centuries this letter has been passed along through men like you and me. It was illuminated by a priest who professed to having been given the illustration as a vision. I know not from where this portion of the letter itself comes. It appears to be a letter of Paul, but not one of the canonized letters. I do not know if it was ever presented to the Council or if it was rejected. All I know," he paused to reach out and touch Piero's hand, "is that we are to protect it with our very lives."

Piero frowned at his intensity and opened the flap of the leather envelope. He carefully slid the pages out. They were ancient, indeed, hundreds of years old. The script was perfect in form, a monk's finest work. Piero's eyes followed the faded brown words in Latin. Pauline, to be sure, at least by inspiration if not from the hand of the great, inspired writer himself. And the illumination . . . primitive, but glorious in color. Here and there, even bits of gold leaf still clung to the sheet. Piero had never seen—

His head whipped upward, his eyes scanning the fresco, and then went back to the page. He pulled the lamp closer and bent nearer to the page, still scanning from letter to fresco. The woman had the same olive-brown eyes, the same long coil of hair at the nape of her neck. . . . It was uncanny, the resemblance.

The teacher laughed with delight and clapped his hands together once. "Yes, yes, you see it."

"It is the same artist."

"Nay." The teacher laid a hand on the wall. "The letter came from the east and our fresco here is clearly with us in the west."

"Then how, how is this possible, master? Coincidence?"

"Nay," the old man said, leaning forward and shaking his head slowly. His mouth was set in a whimsical smile, like a man in on a great joke. But his eyes sang of understanding and peace and glory. "We do not believe in coincidences. Please. There will be time for you to read the words later. Look at the last page."

Piero found himself fearful.

"Go on. It is your destiny, my son. Do not fear where the Lord himself takes you."

Piero tried to swallow, found his mouth dry. With trembling fingers, he slid the first page behind the next two then set all three

pages down upon the satchel again. He did not want to look. He
had to look.

In the margin of the next page was an image of a priest.

And like the fresco beside the teacher, it looked just like Piero.

ඊ ඊ ඊ

"It was you? A picture of you upon the page?" Gianni rose and
shook his head. "There is no explanation."

"Only God's, to which even I am not privy at the moment,"
said the priest.

"May I see it?"

"Of course."

"And Daria—she is the same woman on that chapel wall?
Wait! That chapel wall . . . was it in the ruins of the old outpost
west of Roma?"

Piero's eyes lit up with surprise. "Indeed."

"I have been to that outpost, camped there with my men."

Piero laughed softly. "You have seen the fresco?"

"Probably. But I confess I did not study it. It was . . . dare I say
I was drawn to it? It was five, six years past." He laughed in won-
derment. "It was the lady, with a peacock at her feet. . . . I could
not keep my eyes from her." He snapped his fingers. "That is why
you three were familiar to me! On the fresco, by the lady, was a
tall African and a priest in brown robes." Gianni stood abruptly,
consternation lowering his brows. "What is this? Of what do we
speak? Why are we together? Why now?"

"Sit down, man, sit down. I will tell you what I know. Unfor-
tunately, a great deal has yet to be discovered."

ඊ ඊ ඊ

Gianni's mind swirled as he followed Hasani and Daria down the
street that night, Rune and Basilio close behind. He didn't understand why she was out in her cloak, a heavy basket on her arm,
until they turned one corner and then another until they were in

the midst of some of Siena's most desolate and poor. There was a beggar at every corner, even at this late hour, perhaps because they had nowhere else to go.

He had seen Daria's expression change when Agata spoke to her sister Beata about an ailing young second cousin in the Contrada della Chiocciola. She had said he coughed so hard he vomited, over and over, and his mother feared for his life. It had not been lost to him that Agata shared the story loud enough that her mistress would be certain to hear. Perhaps it was their way, as it had apparently been with her mother, in tending to the sick.

Daria had glanced up at him, briefly seeking his permission, but when he shook his head, she looked away. He glanced upward to a star-filled, moonless sky. "You had to send me a headstrong one, Father?" he asked. "Couldn't my healer have been mild-mannered and unappealing? She would have been much easier to protect," he muttered, now more to himself than God.

"You say something, Captain?" Rune whispered.

"Nay," Gianni whispered back. His eyes were on Daria. She had stopped to speak to a blind beggar on the corner and offer him a piece of bread, but the man was crying, shuffling away from her in a crabwalk, as if in fear. The beggar cried out as Piero joined her. Hasani took her arm and urged her onward, and with one last offer to the mad blind man, who buried his head and wept, confusingly crying *no, no, no,* to their offer of assistance, Daria haltingly turned away. When Gianni passed him, he cried out again, as if he had been clubbed. Odd. It was no wonder the man was so thin—how could a blind beggar exist if he declined food given to him? Rushed away when anyone drew near?

His eyes went to Daria again. Could what Father Piero have told him possibly be true? His own miraculous healing made him more apt to believe it, but if what Father Piero thought might be in store truly came to be, his task in protecting Lady d'Angelo would become more and more difficult. And what of the illumina-

tions in the script? To say nothing of the ancient chapel . . . He
shifted uneasily.

Daria disappeared into a tall, decrepit, two-story building. Gianni sent Rune to a post on the far corner, and Basilio to the one
behind them. He himself stood outside the door. At the top of the
stairs, in flickering candlelight, he glimpsed Hasani. Uneasy sounds,
like the creaking of old hinges, fighting cats, and wailing babies,
were rife in this street. He paced back and forth, drawing his sword,
he was so ill at ease. But it was as much within him as without.

What was this madness? Ancient scripts with illuminations
that resembled Daria and Father Piero, with mention of others to
come. Spiritual gifts that, if they rivaled Daria's, would be difficult to disguise for long. He had had hopes of winning favor with
the Church for Daria, if her gift was carefully introduced and
blessed and condoned . . . but a whole group of people? Even his
own cardinal could not protect them from the wrath of the
Church. There would be a groundswell, mass hysteria once word
got out that such people existed. Crowds would throng to the
d'Angelo gates. His own former knights from Roma would arrive
to haul them in for questioning. . . .

Yet this was where he was supposed to be. Nowhere else. It
was as clear to him as if he weighed a rock in his hand and someone asked him if it was a feather. Here. Here. With Daria and
Piero. Somehow, they were inextricably linked. Destined for . . .
something.

How much to tell the guards? He sighed and eyed Basilio and
Rune. In time, they would learn more of the Gifted. If the priest was
right. Gianni glanced upward, hearing soothing women's voices,
Father Piero's deeper intonations, then prayer. Oh, Daria had a gift
all right. And nothing would be the same for Gianni ever again.

ↄ ↄ ↄ

DARIA awakened at two minutes past the midnight hour and
smiled over at the sleeping boy, then at Piero. They had packed his

chest with a thick herbal poultice of fennel, mullein, dill, and hore-hound, then prayed over him for hours. His mother reached over and squeezed her hand. "Thank you, Duchess. Thank you!"

Daria smiled back and shook her head. "I am not a duchess. But you are most welcome. I think your son will live to see man-hood. Be certain to come and fetch this poultice from my house to put it upon his chest once a week until he quits growing. His lungs cannot keep up with his growing body. And we must keep him from throwing up all his food." She turned toward the basket. "I've brought spelt, cheese, wine, and dried fruits. See to it that you give him enough watered wine, that he rests and sleeps most of this week. Get him to eat as much as you can. He'll be faring much better this time next week."

"Yes, m'lady."

A movement in the corner of the room caught her eye. "Be sure to keep it from the rats."

"Yes, m'lady."

"And here, I've brought this for you." She pulled an old dress, a tall candle, another loaf of bread, and a round of cheese from the basket. "You cannot care for your son if you are wasting away yourself."

Tears rolled down the woman's face, leaving twin tracks in the dirt. "You are so kind, Duchess. How can I repay you?"

Daria smiled. How often had she seen this with her mother? She had to admit, part of her had expected something more dra-matic when God whispered to her to come this night, a healing on par with Gianni's, but the Lord often worked in his own ways. "Simply help your son to grow to manhood and serve the Lord God in any way he calls."

"It shall be so," the woman said solemnly, wiping her run-ning nose on her greasy dress sleeve. She came around the bed and fell to her knees as Daria rose, grabbing her hand and kiss-ing it. "Thank you, Duchess, thank you."

"You are most welcome," Daria said, gently pulling her hand

away. "Will you accept this priest's blessing upon you and your son?" He would know how to guide her, tell her of the hope and healing that began within, convince them that the gifts they experienced were from God. With relief, Daria watched the woman obediently turn to Piero and receive his counsel.

"Come a week hence," Daria said, after he finished speaking.

"In a week. I will be there. Thank you, m'lady."

"One more thing," Piero said at the door. "Please . . . do not tell anyone we have been here."

A look of confusion passed over the woman's face, but she gave her assent. "As you wish, Father. Fare thee well, Duchess."

"I am not a duchess," Daria repeated in a whisper, as the boy stirred, but it was useless. The peasants had always called her mother Duchess, bestowing upon the lady a noble title for her countless noble deeds. Daria supposed she had inherited it. She hoped she could become half the woman her mother had been— so fine, so regal, so kind.

Hasani raised a lantern and took her arm as she made her way down creaking stairs, the whole stairwell waving beneath their weight. "Remind me to send a carpenter to repair this stair," she said.

Hasani grunted.

But even his omnipresent dour mood could not dim her joy. It was glorious, this gift! She suddenly felt like doing nothing but ministering to the sick. *Send me, Lord Jesus. Send me and give me a willing heart.* The last stair cracked under their weight and with a small cry, she jumped forward and out into the street. Even before Hasani brought his lantern up, she knew it was Gianni who stood before her, hands on sword hilt.

She expected anger, frustration, but one look at her and he was grinning. "You are glowing, m'lady. Resplendent." He offered his arm and she gratefully took it, weariness suddenly flooding her body. "Did it happen, then? Did you heal another?" he asked in a whisper.

"Mayhap," she said, eager to share it with someone who already knew her secret. "The boy now rests easily, but it is not quite what we experienced at the convent, nor with you. . . ." It was then she saw Basilio on the corner before them, alarm alive on his face, and looked back to see Rune rushing to join them. The men all seemed in a hurry to move her from this place and yet all she suddenly wished to do was sleep.

Hasani stepped forward with the lantern, Basilio matching his step. Rune stayed behind Gianni and Daria, alongside Piero. She could feel as well as see them canvassing each doorway, each alleyway as they passed, tensing in preparation of attack. What danger lurked? Were they truly in danger? She wanted to ask, but was afraid to utter a sound, suddenly wishing only to be home, safe.

As they got closer to the blind man's corner, his whimpering increased until he was fully wailing when they were directly in front of him. It took a moment for Daria to make out his words. "Away from us, Lion of Judah. Away from us, servants of Jesus of Nazareth! We want nothing of you!"

He began to scream, and Gianni pulled her close to him in a protective stance. "Hasani, blow out that lantern," he hissed. "Quiet, man. We mean you no harm!" he said to the beggar.

"Leave us! Leave us!" The man was on his knees now, beseeching them, and light appeared in the windows of the nearby buildings. The beggar clutched at his clothes as if they were burning him. His face was utter anguish, misery. "Leave us!" he screamed in a long, drawn-out cry.

Daria stared backward, stunned at his odd tone of terror, but Gianni pulled her forward.

"Someone's after the blind man!" shouted a neighbor.

"Someone's robbing him!" shouted another.

"Thieves! Thieves in the alley!"

Still another candle was lit.

"Run, m'lady," Gianni said lowly. *"Run."*

ↀ ↀ ↀ

THEY ran as the beggar screamed, screamed as if they had scorched him by their presence. Never had Piero heard such terror . . . this man's fear was tenfold any he had experienced. And in the face of such terror, it made his own heart pound as it had not in a decade.

Hasani and Gianni flanked Daria, and continually had to hold her upright when she stumbled. Basilio and Rune came beside Piero, who could not leave the screaming man before him. It was then that he knew—the man was possessed of evil spirits. And he knew them, recognized them. Already, the enemy had appeared!

Suddenly there were men behind them, torches held high, shouting. They were armed. What was this madness? They had done nothing wrong! Only sought to help! But it mattered not. All that mattered was the need to get Daria to the villa and the door barred behind them.

"Over here!" Basilio said, taking Piero's arm. "It is a shortcut." They rounded a corner and he quickly pulled them through a gate, shutting it behind them when Rune finally entered behind the others.

Their pursuers clattered past outside the gate and they all held their breath. Once they passed, Basilio whispered, "This way." He led them down a curving alleyway and down another. Gradually, they made their way to the middle-class Contrada de Pantera, and then the more wealthy neighborhoods. In minutes they were inside the d'Angelo gates, hands on knees, panting from their exertion.

Aldo was there, along with Agata. "Fellows, m'lady, what has happened?" the man asked in consternation.

"You must tell us, Father," Gianni panted, looking toward Piero. "We have just encountered the most odd of fellows."

Gianni glanced at Basilio and Rune. Their eyes betrayed the confusion they each felt. Basilio spoke first. "Is this the enemy you expected in beginning to arm yourself, Captain?"

Gianni shook his head. "I expected enemies. But not beggars in the street. Not the people taking up torch and sword."

Piero frowned and motioned to Agata to go and fetch water for the group. He went to Daria. "M'lady," he panted, hands on knees beside her, "you are well?"

"Shaken but well enough, Father. And you?"

"Fine. Simply winded. Come, let us retire by the fire." He led her forward and the men followed behind. Agata appeared with water and gave each of them a long draught from the ladle and pail.

"I think the man was beset by demons. He recognized us as of God when we first passed. The second time, so soon after the child's healing, made us more obvious somehow."

"Mayhap because we allow the Lord to use our gifts, the dark ones can more readily make us out."

Basilio and Rune overheard their conversation and yet held their tongues, simply staring from one to the other.

"He called us servants of Jesus," Gianni put in. "He appeared to see 'the Lion of Judah' among us. It reminded me of a man I once encountered, just once, as a knight of the Church. A bedeviled man, who wandered in the graveyard, dressed in rags, ranting, swearing, screaming. He clawed his flesh each day until he bled. And he became worse any time we drew near."

Father Piero was up, pacing. "He could see the Christ within you—and your power frightened him. Much like this man tonight."

"In Scripture," Daria said, "the first to note the presence of the Spirit in the disciples, those who recognized the Christ were—"

"Demons," Piero finished for her.

Basilio, face wan, hurriedly crossed himself. Rune remained, unmoving.

"It is too soon," Father Piero said. "We must not yet be discovered."

"Of what do you speak?" Basilio said, suddenly finding his

voice. "Rune and I must know what is transpiring here if we are to fully be of service."

Gianni said, "You have not yet taken an oath of fealty."

"We are already inextricably bound. Something has happened this night that I do not have words to cover. And yet I am to be here, with you. I know this in my gut." He looked to Rune and the tall, quiet man nodded his agreement. So he felt it too, this drawing together of their holy group. Piero was pleased. They were good men. Raw and bawdy at times, but trustworthy.

"Exactly what I felt," Gianni said. "Fall to your knees and swear your oath of fealty to the house of d'Angelo and we will share with you what is transpiring, or what we know of it, anyway."

Basilio and Rune did as he asked, kneeling before Daria, and Daria quickly led them through the oath. Both then kissed her hand and the family ring, then rose and bowed.

"So tell us," Basilio said, gesturing in invitation, sitting down as if to be regaled by a winter's night tale. "I take it our lady is more than your average healer."

"Indeed," Father Piero said. "But that is just the beginning of it. You men, and others you help us identify, may be called to protect us from unknown enemies, from robbers on the road to street mobs like you just encountered, to knights from other prestigious families in this city. You might even be called to protect us from the Church."

Rune and Basilio both looked to Gianni at that point, but his eyes were on the stone floor.

"Lady Daria healed Gianni from fatal wounds on the road from Roma," Piero said.

"Not yet a week past, now," Gianni said slowly.

"Dire wounds?" Rune asked.

"Deadly wounds."

"Not yet a week past," Basilio clarified.

"I speak the truth," Gianni confirmed. "I was called then and there to serve her, protect her," Gianni said, meeting their gaze. "I left my post, so strong was my calling."

"Your wounds were truly fatal?" Basilio asked, still trying to absorb their story.

"Indeed. I took a poisoned arrow at my side that certainly caused damage to my organs. Another at my ankle. The pain was excruciating and I glimpsed heaven itself before our lady—"

"God, not I," she interrupted.

"Before *God* healed me. Through our lady."

Basilio crossed himself again. "How?"

"Lady Daria came and prayed over me, and I could immediately sit, stand, even ride a horse. There was pain for some time, but there was a sensation as if my innards had instantly been knit back up, and scabbing formed upon my flesh within the hour. In all my years as a soldier, I have seen nothing like it."

This time, both Rune and Basilio crossed themselves.

"You can heal at any time, m'lady? Heal anyone you wish?" Basilio asked.

"Nay. I do not carry healings in my pocket. I can only heal as God wills. But more and more, I sense God's willing spirit to use me."

"There is more," Father Piero said. "I came into possession some time ago of a portion of an ancient script, something that appears to be uncanonized Scripture. Mayhap a lost letter of Saint Paul himself. There were illuminations in the margin. And the first two profiles in the margin bear an uncanny resemblance to me and Lady Daria."

"Holy, bloody Christ," Basilio muttered.

"Nay!" Daria and Father Piero cried together. "No blasphemy in this household, now or evermore!" Daria went on.

Basilio, turning a lighter shade of gray, said, "Forgive me! I forgot myself!"

Daria sighed. "The script, the words speak of a holy gathering. The author calls them—perhaps us—the Gifted. We are to be brought together, one with the gift of wisdom, another of healing, another of faith . . . visions, discernment, miraculous powers, prophecy."

"To do what?"

"We know not," Father Piero said. "In the letters to the Corinthians, Paul seems to outline the gifts to show us how we are all part of the Body—how the Spirit indwells—and how we are more closely tied to the Holy Lord than the Church wishes us to think. In this letter, it is more prophecy than admonishment, seeming to expand upon what Saint Paul speaks of in Corinthians when he outlines our battle against darkness: that we are but an arm or a leg that helps form the Body, but as a Body of strength, a Body that embodies the strongest of gifts—the most faithful of Christ-followers. Then amazing things will soon be upon us."

"Our letter speaks of tremendous battles, awesome victories for Christ through us," Daria said. "If we are, indeed, the Gifted who were prophesied coming together . . ."

"Yet it also speaks of dire circumstances, steep payment, sacrifice," Gianni added.

"Sacrifice is nearly always victory's closest companion," Piero said. "We are missing a portion of the letter. At this point, we must not get ahead of ourselves. It is reasonable to figure we must move forward, discovering what God would have us discover. That may include another portion of the letter; it may not. We only know that we have been called together for a divine service and can do nothing but follow where our Lord leads. I assume you feel the same. We must take on the task at hand, one day at a time, following as God illumines our path."

"And yet are we daft?" Basilo asked. "To take an illustration, a foreign letter, so to heart? One man's prophecy is another man's folly."

"I have seen more to make me believe that the prophecy is justified," Piero said. "My teacher gave me this letter, committing me to a lineage of many priests who have protected it. And he did so in an ancient chapel of some significance to us. A chapel Gianni and I have both seen."

Daria sat up a bit straighter as Gianni went on to tell them of the chapel.

Basilio's mouth dropped open. "And, once again, the pictures resemble you three, here?"

"To a great extent," Piero said. "The woman and the priest of the fresco greatly resemble what we see in the letter. And the knight, he is depicted on a Roman road that the priest and the woman are obviously bound to travel. I can only take it as the road upon which we encountered Sir de Capezzana."

"Coincidence?" Basilio at last managed.

"Nay," Piero said. "There is a symbol that ties all three figures together—a symbol that ties them to us, here."

"And that is?"

"A peacock. An ancient Christian symbol. And the one so prominent upon the d'Angelo family crest."

All were stunned into silence.

Father Piero nodded, resting chin in hand. "And so it has begun. What you experienced tonight on the streets, my friends, was the beginning of our spiritual battle. The stronger we become, and we do become stronger together, the more noticeable we will be to our enemies."

"I must tell you all," Gianni said, "that in Roma, my men and I pursued a Sorcerer, a man capable of great evil. We tracked him into the catacombs, where he and his followers had commited unspeakable acts. Days later, we nearly captured him, but he and two others ambushed us. They cut down every knight around me, did their best to kill me too. That was where Lady Daria healed me."

"So the enemy knows of her gift already?" Rune asked. "They will see us as twice the threat."

"They may have seen us going down, to attend him," Daria said. "The leader, the Sorcerer, looked up at us."

"And you, Lady Daria, and Gianni are the first of the Gifted to gather?" Basilio asked.

"Daria is undoubtedly our healer, and I have long been gifted with wisdom from God. Gianni has shown outright signs of tremendous faith. You two, or others within this house, may have gifts we have yet to unleash—it is enough to know that you have been brought to us because you have faith to believe in what we tell you. That gifting is no less in stature than anything else of which we speak. We must all continually give our gifting, our praise to God for this honor. Even with him beside us, we may indeed suffer. But without him, we will suffer even more dire consequences."

"You will seek the Church's sanction?"

"Mayhap. In time." Piero eyed Gianni.

"You do not think you can obtain it," Rune said lowly.

"Nay," Gianni said. "We can try, but it would be a hopeless cause. We will do best to try to work covertly for as long as possible, and when that becomes impossible, flee to gain more time to do as our Lord bids."

"To where?"

"Our Lord will show us our path when it comes time," Father Piero said.

"It is a most unsteady course," Basilio said with a grumble.

"Or the most steady of all," Father Piero said with a smile.

CHAPTER THIRTEEN

TATIANA had not been well enough this day to even rise from her bed. Her failing health, and inability to conceive a child, weighed heavily upon Vincenzo's shoulders. He disrobed and gingerly sank into the steaming hot spring, high above Siena. It felt good to get out and ride after such a long, eventful day. He needed space and time to think. He would stay here for a time after his business was done.

His men arrived, ushering Jacobi and several of his own men, to the mountaintop. "You dared to summon me, me here to you?" Jacobi said regally, a flush at his neck.

"Yes, I knew you would find it irritating," Vincenzo said in a dismissive manner. "Come, my old friend. You are literally on your high horse. Come and rest in the waters with me for a time and we shall talk."

The older, fat man dismounted and Vincenzo waved his guards away. "We must speak alone, Jacobi."

Jacobi assented and sent his own men a short distance apart. He disrobed and Vincenzo averted his eyes, not wishing to see the man's rolls of belly fat and pale flesh. It would be enough to have to sit and stare at his piggish face, round wide nose, and jowls.

"I assume you wish to speak of my claim upon the d'Angelo estate," Jacobi said, wincing as he eased into the waters. The flesh under his arms wagged like wings on a flightless bird.

"You assume correctly."

"I have a legitimate claim. Giulio promised me a portion of each fall harvest in exchange for an easement to keep his south-western tower where it has stood for decades—upon Jacobi soil. The surveyors have approved my claim. The house was not laid out correctly. It was built upon a portion of Jacobi land."

Vincenzo reached out and waved his fingers through the hot water, just his knuckles visible. He kept his eyes on them and his voice carefully neutral. "Why was there no documentation asso-ciated with such an agreement?"

"It was an agreement between gentlemen, neighbors."

"Dismantling the southern tower will make the house criti-cally vulnerable."

"Exactly why Giulio agreed to pay me for the easement."

"And yet you did not pursue your claim in the past three years."

Jacobi coughed, hearing the note of threat in Vincenzo's voice. "I thought it improper to bring it up while the daughter mourned, and then I expected to bring it up with Adimari, once they mar-ried, and now . . . now I find I cannot wait any longer."

Vincenzo sighed heavily. He tired of the lesser politics of the city, hated the close quarters that brought such squabbles to the surface over and over. With mansions and stores and cathedrals and banks built inches from their neighbors, land and newly drawn surveyor's marks were constantly of issue. It plagued the courts, often taking months to resolve, so neighbor often made agreement with neighbor to resolve such disputes.

"It is feasible that Giulio, whom we both knew as kind and overly trusting, agreed to your arrangement, Jacobi. But you bear no paperwork that supports your claim. Therefore, it is null and void. You must begin again if you wish to pursue your claim."

"And then I shall," Jacobi grumbled. "Tomorrow."

Vincenzo allowed the silence to settle between them before speaking. "If you pursue your claim, I shall bring my own surveyors out. They will be accompanied by my lawyers, who you know are the best of Siena or Firenze. They are well acquainted with the finest church officials and magistrates of either city. We will survey the land yet again. And we will not focus on just the line that you share with the house of d'Angelo, but also the line you share with the house of Monaco and also your back quadrant. Then we will set our eyes upon other Jacobi holdings in the city. We will dice up your land so that you will lose, lose much more than any improbable claim you have on the land beneath the d'Angelos' south tower."

At last, he let his eyes slowly lift from the water to the man across from him in the pool. Even in the dimming light of dusk, he could see the fear etched into the man's face around clenched mouth and eye.

"Do not pursue this claim. You shall pay a heavy price, Jacobi." He sighed and gave the man a half smile. "You are a friend. I do not wish you to spend any more time on such a frivolous pursuit. Accept this as worthy advice."

"What is she, to you? She is no longer your ward."

"Daria d'Angelo is like a niece to me."

Jacobi's eyes narrowed. "You are married, del Buco."

The silence grew long between them as Vincenzo seethed over his words. "The facts are this: You will not go to the Nine, you will not pursue this claim, and you will never more threaten Daria d'Angelo or her holdings. Is that understood?"

The man turned and lumbered out of the water, pulling on his tunic in an awkward manner where it clung to wet flesh. A guard appeared and handed him his overcoat, looking away in embarrassment.

"Jacobi, I cannot allow you to depart until you give me your word that this is over." With a gesture, his men were surrounding Jacobi's men, hands on the hilts of their swords.

The man shook his finger at Vincenzo. "There are others who are gaining in power and stature in this city. The sand is shifting. I will lay my claim to rest for a time, but you will deal with me again, del Buco." Vincenzo looked away from him, through the steam rising from the hot spring, out to the valley floor where shadows deepened into night.

"Nay," Vincenzo said, not looking back at the man. "You shall never disturb me in such a manner again."

After a long pause, Jacobi and his men mounted up and departed.

Vincenzo sighed heavily and concentrated on the dancing, swirling vapors against the darkening night sky. Jacobi spoke of several powerful merchants of Firenze, outsiders who already spun webs within Siena. Things were shifting in their city because of it and no one was more aware of it than Vincenzo. Still, he could hold his own. He could keep Jacobi in his pen with his smallest finger. Vincenzo sat back, following the steam's designs until he saw Daria's face and body before him, then splashed steaming sulfurous waters over his face as if to boil away the image.

Chapter Fourteen

GIANNI paced back and forth. The beggar's *contrada* this morning would be rife with rumors—of attack, of healing. The people would be looking for a lady, accompanied by guards. Only the idea that they would soon leave for the country manor assuaged his unease. He followed Daria out of the dining hall as she waited for Nico to bring her horse.

"I recommend you remain at home, m'lady."

"And I have told you that I must go with Lord del Buco to tend to guild business. I can hardly leave Siena again without it. Aldo will be with me," she said, eyeing her old steward.

"As will Rune and I," said Gianni.

"Your accompaniment will draw more attention," Daria said, leaning forward. "On this day, we must be most discreet, would you not agree?"

Gianni clenched his jaw and drew back, considering. "You are right, m'lady. We will follow at some distance. We will set Bormeo free and he will circle, following you. If you are in distress, if you wish for us to come to your aid, simply raise your arm and call Bormeo to you."

Daria smiled. "Most clever. I can abide by such a plan." Nico arrived and Gianni helped her mount as Rune brought two more horses for them. "Nico, go and let Bormeo out of his keep."

"Yes, m'lady."

"And you," she said, pointing at the knights, "do your best to keep to the shadows. I do not want Baron del Buco to interpret your accompaniment as a doubt in his ability to protect me."

"As you wish, m'lady," Gianni said with a slight bow.

♔ ♔ ♔

THE guild's factory was housed in five long, rectangular buildings, laid out side by side, just outside the city gates. Many merchants, importers, and exporters were a part of the guild; dyers, weavers, and even shepherds were part of the production aspect of the guild. Daria and Vincenzo, as elected co-consuls, led the council in decisions as to which cloth to weave, where and when to sell, and what and when to import.

In one long warehouse were their current imports just arrived from Milano and Napoli—silks from India, luxury cottons from Islam, with tapestry weaves and brocades, fine linens from France, and a poor man's German linen, nowhere near what their local industry produced, but much less expensive. From this warehouse, drivers loaded and distributed shipments across Siena, and to every town between Firenze and Roma.

In another warehouse was their own inventory—a medium-weight linen, favored for undergarments and gowns; a higher-quality linen that was sold at a premium; and lightweight cotton used for everything from veils to handkerchiefs to purse lining. There were also woolens of various weights and the fustian cloth— a blend of cotton warp and linen weft. And then there was their finest, softest cotton, the prize of Tuscan weavers and renowned throughout the trade routes. Finer, yet, than anything that even

Cremona or Piacenza were producing. As a child, Daria had loved to run her hands across that soft cloth every time she came to the guild warehouses. Her father would lean down and whisper, "No finer sheep live than those that graze the hills of Toscana."

Village women supplemented farm income by weaving and bringing their fine thread to the guild to sell. Taught generation to generation, Siena's woolen guild was still a generation ahead of others in terms of quality. But increasingly, others were pushing in on territory long familiar to the Sienese merchants and weavers.

In the third, fourth, and fifth buildings, women and men worked together to dye cloth and thread, to weave, and to wrap cloth onto large bolts, preparing them for export. In one end of the fifth building, two *segretari* kept track of the documents involved to maintain their business.

After Vincenzo and Daria had done their customary walk through the buildings—something that was usually done every other week—they stopped to speak with the secretaries and gain a report on the last quarter's exports and imports. Aldo hovered near, listening.

"As you know, we are looking at a magnificent crop this year and the word is that we will see increased imports from Sicily, Napoli, and northward," said one secretary. "There is even the potential of obtaining a portion of the business out of Cremona, if we can handle their need for exports."

"We have need of Lord Frangelico's connections in Venezia," said the other, summing up his ideas. "He has a business partner there who handles all oceanic imports. Six of his eight vessels now have cotton-screwing capability. If we could make use of those vessels, we could double the rate of export."

Vincenzo shot Daria a look and she shook her head in warning. She despised Lord Frangelico, as her father had before her. He was willing to bend any rule in a desire to reach his own goals, would cast his own kin aside if it led to money. She did not care if his ships could triple the amount others carried from the shore.

Vincenzo pulled her away from the secretaries to confer.

"Nay, Vincenzo, don't even think it," Daria said, hands on hips.

"Daria, we must. It is for the good of the entire guild if we can keep ahead of the world of trade. We must find wider, deeper export locations. If we do not, our neighbors to the north will do so without us. This plan would give us a portion of their profits as well as our own. Lord Frangelico's tie to the marine merchants would allow us better access to the nations of Africa, strengthen our tie with Cremona—"

"Nay. We are better served purchasing our own merchant marine fleet than entering into business arrangements with that one."

Vincenzo scoffed. "One does not purchase a ship on a whim, let alone more, unless he is a gambler. We are not merchant marines. We are running a business here, here in Toscana. Daria, we need to be wise. We need to work with men who have already built empires in other places if we are to build our own. There is one, Abramo Amidei, who may be of assistance to us. I wish to introduce you."

"Are you accusing me of being foolhardy?" Daria snapped. Vincenzo lifted his hands to ward off her fury and speak but she was not finished. "My father would have never made an agreement with Lord Frangelico, or outsiders like Amidei, never! Nor would you have, three years past!"

"Yes, but Daria, many things have transpired in this past three years."

"What things?" she said, throwing up a hand. "When did we decide to do business with people we cannot trust? And you speak of me as a gambler!"

He let her pace a moment. "If we could triple our exports we would become the richest merchants in Siena."

"Nay, Vincenzo. Think! Lord Frangelico will not enter this deal without an exacting price of his own." She shuddered. "We do not need to be beholden to that one."

"If we could triple our exports," Vincenzo went on, as if not hearing her, "even for a year, every person in our guild—people who look to us to make good decisions—would double their income. Can you imagine what that would do for our dyers? Our weavers? The villagers? Daria, think of the old women, alone in the hills, spinning until their fingers bleed. Think of them being able to set a few coins away, hire help to see to their chattel, their sheep, a chair to ease their weariness."

Daria sighed and looked at him. "You are not playing fairly."

Vincenzo crossed his arms. "You said you are a woman grown. This is a grown woman's decision. Choose wisely, dear one." He left her then, crossing over to the secretaries and asking for certain documents to look over.

It was then that Daria realized that all industry had come to a halt in the factory. Every eye was upon her.

"Come, Lord del Buco," she said, chin held high. "I think our inspection is done. Let us confer more on the way home." She turned and walked out of the long building, taking a deep breath as if she had been suffocating inside. Vincenzo was right behind her, Aldo a few paces back.

Daria was too furious to test words.

"I am sorry, dear one. I should not have surprised you so, with my views on the matter. I have been thinking about it for weeks during your sojourn to Roma. My timing was less than favorable."

Daria cast him a hopeful glance.

"And Tatiana . . . Tatiana is heavy on my mind. I am afraid that burden weighs upon me, makes me insufferable at times."

Daria studied him more closely. "She is growing more ill, Uncle? Why did you not tell me?"

"I had hoped Milano would give her ease. For a fortnight, it seemed it did. But two days past, she became worse."

Daria's mind went to the boy in the poor *contrada*, the one she had healed. Was Tatiana supposed to be next? Her heart fluttered in her chest. "I need to see her, Vincenzo. I shall send Aldo after my herbs, and let us go home to her."

Vincenzo nodded, unspeaking, and Daria's heart went to him. He was forgiven his indiscretions inside the *factoria*. Who would not be distracted with such strain upon his mind and heart? And she herself had been absent, less than a true partner in leading the guild. It was she who should be begging forgiveness . . . but she held her tongue, trying to discern why. Pride? Power? She knew not, only that she wished to say no more. They rode forward in silence, and at the crossing, Aldo headed home and Vincenzo and Daria turned toward the del Buco estate.

She looked up, spotting Bormeo flying high above her, circling, and smiled. Knowing that the bird, and her men, were near eased her throbbing head.

ↄ ↄ ↄ

DARIA'S heart pounded as they drew near to Vincenzo's magnificent home on the outer edge of the city, a huge estate conspicuously set apart, as if he had meant to tell one and all that he took from Siena what he needed and left the rest for the buzzards to fight over. Tatiana lay in the room high above, she knew, listening to birds upon the air and smelling the sweet loam of the earth that drifted over the city walls and into their own. At least, Daria hoped she did.

Vincenzo helped her dismount and with one more glance to her falcon, circling high above, she followed him into the estate. She knew Gianni and Rune hovered outside, undoubtedly frustrated by this change of plans. But they would need to know she trusted Vincenzo, that there was no need of protection if she was inside his walls. The sooner they learned that, the better off they would all be.

Vincenzo paused inside and came behind her to take her wrap, easing it from her shoulders in a slow move that sent a shiver down her spine. A man's touch upon her skin . . . One glance at his mournful face told her his mind was on his wife, not her. "I assume your lady is abed upstairs," she said, trying to keep relief from her tone.

"Yes. I will follow in a moment. Daria?"

She turned on the stair and looked backward. "Yes?"

"These last two months . . . they have been devastating for Tatiana. Do not be surprised by what you see."

She nodded sadly. "I understand." He looked so forlorn then, turning to stare out across the portico toward the heart of Siena, that she longed to rush down the stairs and into his arms. But there was something brewing between them that set her teeth on edge, something she was loath to name. Better to concentrate on his bride. Vincenzo needed his wife back at his side, again the pride of Siena with her long, wavy golden-brown hair and wide murky-green eyes. Few were as fair as Tatiana del Buco. A man like Vincenzo needed a companion that could match his stride, match his effect upon others. Tatiana was the perfect mate.

Daria lifted her skirts and climbed the steep, wide stairs upward, past the second and third levels and on to the fourth, thinking of the mousy bride who had preceded Tatiana and died early, and the one before her, who died in childbed. Tatiana was the one he had been sure would bring him heirs and happiness.

Daria paused outside her door, turning to bring her back to the cool stucco walls and breathing hard after her swift climb. "Please, Lord," she whispered. "Please heal this woman. For her. For Vincenzo. For me. I beseech you, Lord on High, help me heal this woman."

Finding her equilibrium, pausing for a moment more, she turned into the room and walked across the wide expanse to the other side, where Baroness del Buco lay atop her bed, attended by a maid.

She turned wide, smiling eyes in Daria's direction and reached out a hand in welcome. "Daria, Daria. There you are. How I have missed you!"

Daria drew near and took Tatiana's hand in both of her own.

"Sit, my friend. Tell me of Roma. And of your heart. Are you well?"

Daria did as she bid, sitting beside her on the large bed, covered with a feather mattress. "I fare much better than when I left,
thank you. I would not say that I am healed, but I am recovering.
And you?"

"Ahh," Tatiana said sadly. "How I wish I could say the same."
She paused to cough, a deep, fearsome bark resounding from her
thin chest and throat.

Daria shook her head. "You sound worse than when I left you.
Did you see the doctors in Milano?"

"Yes, yes. In Milano and then in Firenze. Vincenzo dragged me
everywhere. I saw more than twenty men. But none gave me treatments that gave me any ease. How I longed for your return!"

Daria leaned forward and touched her fevered brow. She did
not burn, but she was cold and clammy. "You should have sent for
me."

"Nay," Tatiana said. "I forbade Vincenzo to do so. You
needed your own time of healing."

"Oh, my dear friend. Always so selfless. May I become like you
one day!"

Tatiana raised a thin, pale hand to her face. "You are the most
selfless woman I know."

Daria scoffed. "Then you are in need of meeting more
women."

"Nay, Daria. In you I see such loveliness . . . such a desire to
serve, to care. Selflessness."

"And yet it is only myself about which I constantly think."

Tatiana shook her head, but Daria looked out the window, to
the Siena skyline. She searched her heart, waiting for God's urging
encouragement to heal this one, heal her now. She listened so hard
she was suddenly aware of the blood coursing through her ears.
But no gentle urging, no sudden knowledge that God was present
and about to act. She narrowed her eyes. Why? Why not this one?
Why not now? If there was ever a place and time that she longed
to change the course . . .

"Here is Aldo, with your apothecary," Vincenzo said, entering the room.

"Oh, good, good," Daria said, suddenly rising, trying to hide tears of frustration and fear that choked her. Vincenzo could not lose his third wife. Not Tatiana. It simply could not be.

ↈ ↈ ↈ

She tended to Tatiana and returned the next day, and the next, and by the time her household was packed to travel to the country manor, there were signs that the baroness was rallying and Daria had hopes that she would make a full recovery. She rose from her bed and even bid Daria good-bye from the front portico on that last day, but there was an uneasy fear in Daria's soul, a terror that all was not well, that illness lurked where she could not reach, where no one but God could reach. . . . And as much as she wished she could force the Spirit to work, she could not.

CHAPTER FIFTEEN

CARDINAL Boeri swept through the ancient catacombs to the papal crypt. Restoration work was progressing well. Now that it had been rediscovered, he intended to clean, protect, and make way for the faithful to come and pay homage to the old popes. It would do nicely to add another means of bringing in funds to the true Vaticana's coffers. This discovery aided him in strengthening the old city's position in drawing the papacy home.

But being here, in this place that the Sorcerer had so boldly defiled, made him vaguely ill at ease. On top of Gianni's sudden departure, the loss of his men—what was truly transpiring? Could this be part of the odd prophecy? The ancient letter?

His portion of the letter—what appeared to be a middle portion—told of a great battle ahead, between light and dark. The illuminist had drawn a dragon, with the peacock in its teeth. Only his trusted friend, the bishop, knew that he still held the pages in a secret chamber of his room, eager to study it, dissect it, so that he might better use it. Boeri had been vigilant, especially in the past decade, standing up for the Holy Church, and God had rewarded him richly. It had been he who discovered the ancient letter in the storeroom of the antiquities dealer in Constantinople. It had been he who had recognized the power of the prophecy, the importance within its uncanonized script. Not the Word of God, but of God, given to Boeri to do his good work.

The Church needed him. It was up to him to restore the papacy to Roma. And somehow, he would use both these prophesied "Gifted" and the Sorcerer to do so. If he captured the Sorcerer who had dared to defame the papal crypt, and then was able to directly channel the Gifted's efforts, his notoriety would spread. No one was better equipped to vanquish both forces than he and his men. In the college of cardinals, he was already a leader. Mastering this would put him in place for the papacy itself.

"It has begun," he whispered to the bishop as he looked about the crypt. "The Sorcerer's appearance, his growing power, will not go unanswered," he said.

The bishop's eyes widened. "The Gifted? You think they will rise?"

"Indeed, I do. And we alongside them."

ϕ ϕ ϕ

IT was a perfect summer's eve, there in the countryside with no moon, simply a sky full of stars and a blessed crispness to the air after the afternoon heat. Gianni praised God for the world around him, praised him for delivering him through Daria, bringing him into this odd gathering to do his good work. Gianni asked for protection for them all, for wisdom, for faith, to face what was ahead. And he asked for pardon from Cardinal Boeri, even though his old mentor did not yet know why Gianni had left his service.

Gianni had thought, long and hard, about sending his letter to him over the last weeks. He had destroyed several others, then rewrote them, searching for the right words, the right phrasing. He sought sanction; he sought blessing. In the end, he elected to send the first, the one he had written while still on the road to Siena.

Now, here in lands held by the house of d'Angelo, the timing seemed right.

The village nearby was small, merely a gathering of stores and supplies for those who toiled in Toscana's fields, but it was adequate. Come morn, either side would bustle with shopkeeper and shopper alike, the fishmonger, the grocer. Even now, in the dusty air of a midsummer eve, he could smell rotting fruit and spoiled meat juices. Here he would find his courier and send his message off to Roma.

Gianni met the man on the corner, as arranged. "Straight to Roma," he said firmly. "No pausing for wine nor water. You have what you need to make it there? A spare horse?"

"*Si*, sir. I will not fail you. Your letter will be delivered as promised."

"You are not to read it. It is sealed."

"No worries. I cannot read."

"No giving it to another."

"*Si, si*, just as we discussed."

The tavern door burst open then, and Rune and Basilio stumbled out, laughing and hitting their thighs. "Captain!" Basilio cried, obviously a bit chagrined to see him there.

"Go," Gianni whispered to the man, and the courier moved off as if he were a mare that had just been whipped.

"Who was that, Captain?" Rune asked.

"Never mind. You two have been drinking? You are on duty tonight."

"Just one glass of watered wine, Captain. Gettin' to know the villagers, keeping our ears to the ground, you know. We're on at midnight. We knew you and Hasani were about. . . ."

Screaming drew all three's attention to the village well. A woman, surrounded by what looked like a group of men carrying torches, cried out again in terror and then gave in to sobs, begging them to release her each time she caught her breath. They tossed her from one side of the circle to another, tearing her dress at the shoulder, then reaching out to tear her long skirts. Gianni, Basilio, and Rune looked toward one another and then ran. Most of the village and countryside slumbered at this hour. What was this?

They reached the group, just as the five men tossed the screaming woman down the well. Two seconds later, they heard a splash and the men cheered as one. "Consider that your baptism!" called one.

"What is this? What are you doing?" Gianni cried, shoving aside men to get to the edge. "Lady? M'lady? Are you all right?"

"She is nothing. A whore who claims to have found God," said one.

"We found her in the village church, praying!" said another.

"Well, is that not good? For a sinner to repent and ask forgiveness?"

"We need no whores in this village," spat out the first, waving his torch. "No blasphemers spoiling our holy places. Zola will agree to leave our village or drown this night."

"We have a relic in our church! She can't be in there!" cried another man.

"Bah!" Gianni cried. "I don't care if you have Saint Peter himself in there. You are unworthy of Christ's love if you do not show mercy to one such as this!" he said, waving downward. "Go! Be away from here! May God have mercy on your souls!"

Gianni, Rune, and Basilio faced the men down until three turned and walked away, one at a time. Two remained. All five men had a hand on the hilt of their sword or dagger.

Chanting from the well made them turn as one and peer downward. "Holy, holy, holy is the Lord God almighty. Heaven and earth is full of his glory. Holy, holy, holy is the Lord God almighty. Heaven and earth is full of his glory. . . ."

The sounds from the well bestilled them all, capturing them with their simplicity and might and pure, innocent tones of praise.

"Miss? Zola? Grab the rope! We shall pull you up!" Gianni looked with fury upon the villagers who still remained among them.

"Holy, holy, holy is the Lord God almighty!" Her sob was strangled then by a giggle, a mad cry of glee. "Holy! Holy! Holy!" It was then that her syllables ran together, garbled, and then emerged as an intelligible, ancient language, still in the same cadence, same tone of praise and joy. Her words became like song in their ears, and Gianni shared a long look of wonder with Rune and Basilio.

The village men backed away as one from the village well, eyes wide and fearful in the torchlight. "What'd we tell you? That's what she was doing in the church! Making devil sounds! We should've hanged her! Burned her! She's a witch! A witch!"

Gianni shook his head. "This is no witch," he said lowly. "I have met my share of witches. And this is no witch."

"What is it, then, Captain?" Rune asked in a low voice. "What language? I have not heard such words anywhere in my travels."

"We will burn her! She must die! A witch!" yelled the man, running down the small street. "Gather wood! Meet us in the village clearing! A witch! A witch among us!"

"We must get her to safety, quickly," Gianni said.

Gianni held one of the villagers' dropped torches over the well and Basilio immediately began hauling upward on the rope.

"What language does she speak?" Rune asked.

"That, my friends, is called the gift of tongues."

Basilio and Rune shared another look and put their backs into hauling the woman up. She emerged, dripping wet in her gown, feet in the bucket, clinging to the rope. A beauty, surely profitable in her trade as the town prostitute.

"Saints preserve us," Basilio said, reaching out his hand. "You are lovelier, Zola, than any woman I've seen."

She did not take his hand, just stared upward to the stars, fine sculpted cheekbones glistening in the soft, flickering light of a villager's forgotten torch, whispering in her strange words, smiling. They realized that it was tears that ran down her face now, not water from the well.

Voices in the distance gathered, a rumbling, threatening storm cloud. "Come, Zola. We will find you a safe place to praise God. But you must come now," Gianni said sternly, reaching out to her too. Basilio grunted with the effort of holding the woman aloft by himself as his companions reached for her.

"Holy, holy, holy is the Lord God almighty," Rune said, stretching out his long arm toward her.

For the first time she looked at one of them, at Rune, deep into his eyes, her gaze unwavering.

Gianni swallowed hard. Full lips. Jet-black hair. Deep olive skin. Voluptuous curves. As fine as Daria, but in a different way. Daria was delicate, refined, aristocratic. This one was earthy, sensuous, sinewy. He cast his eyes to the village road, anxious to get his mind back on the task at hand.

Basilio grunted and looked skyward. "Does the Lord not know that ugly women are much easier to hide and defend?"

He and Gianni shared a grin.

Gianni turned back to the woman. "Come, Zola. We will keep you safe. But we must get you out of here."

She ignored him, staring only at Rune. For the first time, Gianni noticed blood streaming from a gash along her ear and another at her jawline.

"Holy, holy, holy is the Lord God almighty," Rune said again softly, still reaching, looking only into her eyes.

"Holy, holy, holy is he," Zola whispered in response. She reached out and took his hand and he quickly swung her over the well wall and into his arms. He held her for a second, gathering her up. She passed out then, limp and hanging from him.

Rune carried her all the way to the manor.

When the servants had collected her and taken her into their quarters to care for her, Gianni looked hard at Rune, pacing outside her door. "We do not yet know her."

"She is one of us. One of the Gifted."

"Mayhap. We will know in time. But guard your heart, man.

At least until daybreak. We will ask the priest then, to help us discern the truth. The townspeople know her as a whore, not a Christian."

Rune took a step forward in defiance, caught himself and paused. "I tell you, she is no whore. Or she has left that behind her. You can clearly see it upon her face!"

"I know. Mayhap her adultery is a sin of the past. Mayhap she still is what she was. Be wary of the beautiful, of charm—that which draws you, Rune. The devil can confuse us with any of our weaknesses. We must be strong, man, careful on all fronts. There are battles waging here that we still have yet to identify."

Rune gave him a brief nod, then with head bowed, took a step backward. "By your leave, I shall spend the night in prayer."

Basilio guffawed. Clearly, this was not a typical request from Rune.

"I wish to seek the Lord's direction myself," Rune said.

Gianni paused. "Go, then. I shall take your watch."

⚜ ⚜ ⚜

FATHER Piero rose from his knees after morning prayer and slipped into his robes and then into his flat shoes. He would sweep the tiny chapel floor—nowhere near as large or beautiful as the one in Siena—before daybreak, so that Lady Daria and the people of this house would enter on clean stones. It was good to begin a man's day with an act of service for the Lord and his people.

Something niggled at him from last night's Scripture readings, something that he had turned over and over in his head all night. In Paul's writings to the Corinthians, he begged them to pay attention to what was right and good, to turn away from even religion that smacked of sin. His words were as appropriate today as they once had been—the Church often divided among those who sought power over faith. Even now the Eastern and Western Churches were divided, each claiming sanction from God. Avignon and Roma each fought to be the seat of the Holy Church! What madness! It was like the Corinthians, claiming superiority over others. Why could the world not remember that they were one, one Body, one Body designed to follow the Christ?

Piero had read until his candle flickered in the deep of night, drowning in a pool of melted wax. He had read and reread Paul's words in Latin and then other Scriptures in Revelation and translated them back to the original Greek, stewing over layers of meaning and message. There was something his Lord wanted him to learn, know this day. What was it? He was still poring over the verse in his Bible, moving toward the tiny chapel, reading in a whisper. He knelt and absently crossed himself as he reached the center of the windowless chapel, but then paused as he rose. There was a body stretched out, facedown, before the altar.

He padded forward. A woman, and she appeared to slumber beneath a blanket. Piero hunched over to get a better look at the woman and then crossed himself. The fallen one from the market! He crossed himself again and whispered, "Forgive me, Lord. Keep me from casting the first stone."

He rose, set down his Bible, and paced back and forth a moment, chin in hand, other hand on the cross he wore about his neck, waiting for her to rise. But she did not stir.

Daria arrived then, lighting candles along the wall of the chapel, and paused at the sight before Piero. She rushed forward. "What is this?"

"M'lady," Piero said. "It appears innocent . . ."

The young woman moaned and turned her head. That was when they saw the gash at her temple.

"What has happened?" Daria cried, moving from household mistress to healer in a moment's time. Rune arrived with a second blanket in his hand and rushed forward to them when he saw them with her. He knelt to help the woman rise, and placed the blanket about her shoulders. Daria looked at the knight with some accusation in her eyes.

He shook his head. "Not I, lady. Others, in town. We shall tell you the whole of it."

Zola looked from one to the other, furtively, like a trapped animal.

"They threw her down the well," Rune said.

"The well!" Piero cried.

"Yes," Rune said. "We saw it ourselves."

"Why? Why would they do such a thing?" Daria asked.

"I must go. . . ." Zola whispered, moving down the aisle.

"Wait!" Rune cried.

"I do not belong here," Zola said, tears welling in her eyes. She shook her head back and forth, miserable. "I am unworthy. My sins are too great."

"We are all sinners, my daughter," Piero said to the girl.

She met his gaze. "There are sinners, but then there are *sinners*, Father." She glanced at Daria, then back to the floor. "I am Zola, m'lady. A common whore."

Daria gasped. Her brow furrowed, and Piero could sense the pull between revulsion and mercy.

"A fallen one who appears to have the gift of speaking in tongues," Gianni said from behind them, newly arrived.

Zola was edging out again. "I will only bring shame to your house. I must go."

"Wait," Daria commanded. Zola stopped, pausing restlessly in the aisle.

"I found her in here last night," Rune put in, brushing a hand through his wavy blond hair. "Speaking again in that strange, heavenly language. If you could have seen the light upon her face, m'lady, you would know the truth of it. It brought me, *me*, to tears." He paced back and forth again and all were silent. "It was as if she could *see* the face of God himself. Watching her speak to the heavenlies was like glimpsing heaven. I threw myself upon the ground, begging for mercy. At some point, Zola slept and I could not bring myself to wake her."

Daria moved beside Piero, studying Zola, silently asking for explanation.

Zola nodded. "Something happened yesterday. To me. I was outside the village chapel, listening to the padre chant and pray through the window. I was tired, so tired, and it was as if the Spirit entered me, washed me. His language filled my mouth, spilled out of me. I could do nothing but enter that chamber and bow down before my God. I do not know what I said. I simply knew it was all I could do. That was where the villagers found me that night. I could not bear to leave the window—I remained in that place until the church was empty and I could enter. I understand the villagers' anger, your anger. But I am drawn to these holy places."

"I swear, m'lady," Rune said. "No unholy thing happened in this place."

"Nay," Zola said, shaking her head. "It cannot. I am . . . new. Changed. But I must go far from here. The townspeople, they shall never let my past die. I must begin anew where not a soul knows me. I wish you all a good morning. I will forever be grateful that your men saved me, Duchess." She turned and walked down the aisle then.

Rune looked from Piero to Daria and then down the aisle. "Don't you see?" he whispered. "She is one of us."

"Wait, Zola," Daria said again. "Wait just a moment." She motioned Piero away from the others, over to Gianni. "It is too much to comprehend, too fast. Another, such as this?"

Piero shrugged and smiled. "David was the least of eight brothers. Moses was God's mouthpiece . . ."

". . . and yet he could not speak without pause," she finished for him.

"Our Lord himself was born in a lowly manger, not the palace he deserved. Our Lord delights in using the most unlikely of servants. Why not this one?"

"Indeed."

"And yet our letter does not speak of one who speaks in tongues. Give it a fortnight. Tell her nothing of the Gifted. We shall pray and fast before we allow her into our inner ranks. For now, all she needs of us is to show her Christian love."

"Wise counsel," Gianni said.

"So be it," Daria said. She turned to the young woman. "Zola, you are a guest in this house as long as you care to stay. I ask that you abide with us for a fortnight, for reasons I cannot disclose as of yet. But you will be safe here, fed, clothed, and given a room of your own. Father Piero can give you spiritual counsel."

Zola's eyes narrowed. Confusion flooded her face. "I—"

"You are our guest, Zola. It matters not what you were. It only matters what you are now. I beg you to do as I request. I offer my hand in friendship and ask nothing of you but this. God led you to us. Let us watch together where he will lead us from here."

Zola paused a moment longer, then slowly, head bowed, walked down the short aisle and knelt at Daria's feet, taking her hand in hers and kissing it. "I am unworthy, m'lady. . . ."

"Nay," Daria said, smiling tenderly, helping the woman to rise to her feet. "You will soon see that only Christ makes each of us worthy, my friend. Now come, come and abide with us and we shall worship together."

Piero smiled and turned to dip his hand in the holy water, genuflected, knelt and prayed in silence, then rose and picked up his Bible. "The Lord on High has given us special Scriptures this morning." He nodded at Daria, and as was becoming their custom, she rose to translate as he read.

"*Et angelo Laodiciae ecclesiae scribe haec dicit Amen testis fidelis et verus qui est principium creaturae Dei. . . .*"

"To the angel of the church in Laodicea write: These are the words of the Amen, the faithful and true witness, the ruler of God's creation."

She paused for Father Piero to continue reading and then continued translating. "I know your deeds, that you are neither cold nor hot. I wish you were either one or the other! So, because you are lukewarm—neither hot nor cold—I am about to spit you out of my mouth. You say, 'I am rich; I have acquired wealth and do not need a thing.' But you do not realize that you are wretched, pitiful, poor, blind and naked. I counsel you to buy from me gold refined in the fire, so you can become rich; and white clothes to wear, so you can cover your shameful nakedness; and salve to put on your eyes, so you can see. Those whom I love I rebuke and discipline. So be earnest, and repent. Here I am! I stand at the door and knock. If anyone hears my voice and opens the door, I will come in and eat with him, and he with me."

"The Lord gave me this Scripture last night to contemplate and it is only in the light of day that I see it for what it is," said Piero. "Our Holy Church is the rich one, having acquired wealth, figuring they do not need a thing. But God sees her as wretched, pitiful, blind and naked. He is calling the Holy back to the Christ—to the only one who can clothe, give vision. He is rebuking her, rebuking us, preparing us all for change.

"*Ecce sto ad ostium et pulso si quis audierit vocem meam et aperuerit ianuam introibo ad illum et cenabo cum illo et ipse mecum. . . .*" Father Piero repeated from his Bible.

"Here I am! I stand at the door and knock. If anyone hears my voice and opens the door, I will come in and eat with him, and he with me," Daria said again.

"This is our verse, beloved," Piero said, staring at Zola, then looking to them all. "He is knocking. He is willing to come and abide with us, teach us, guide us. Any one of us who invites him in, be they priest or prostitute. Open the door," he said in a beseeching tone. "Open the door! Open the door!" A smile lit up his face. His voice dropped to a reverent whisper. "The Holy One draws near."

CHAPTER SIXTEEN

THE harvest came in and as the country manor bustled with preparation for the feast, Daria slipped out the gates, Bormeo on her arm. It had taken some doing, to escape unfettered. She had led Hasani to believe she was retiring to her quarters for a rest, and Gianni believed her to be in the kitchen, directing the staff in meal preparations. She did not wish to be deceitful. She only wished to be alone for a time.

Nico opened the back gate for her and she dug her heels into the mare's sides, nodding to the boy in an effort to seal their deal not to disclose her whereabouts unless she did not return before nightfall. She glanced over her shoulder and the boy was shutting the gate behind her, a worried expression on his face. No matter. She could dig him out of whatever difficulties he would face on her account.

Behind the manor lay a stream that led to a millhouse beside the manor's wall. The mare quickly forded it, the water not rising past her knees, and then they began to climb. *"Titt-titt,"* Daria whispered, unfettering Bormeo and watching him rise into the sky, immediately on the hunt. Warm afternoon light flooded the Tuscan landscape, giving everything a gold, softened tinge like something in a dream. For the first time in what seemed like weeks, Daria drew a deep breath.

It was all so much to absorb . . . Father Piero's assumption that they were the prophesied Gifted, gathering together under her own roof. Rune and Basilio locating another four men from the region who had agreed to join their ranks, bringing the total to seven men-at-arms, plus Hasani. Never had there been men-at-arms in the d'Angelo household, and she was beginning to fear that they were too many in number. And yet Father Piero did not disagree with Gianni's direction, so she acquiesced to their guidance.

Daria contemplated the Gifted—Piero with the gift of wisdom, Gianni with the gift of faith, herself with the gift of healing, and perhaps Zola with the gift of tongues. Piero had mused aloud that they needed an interpreter, that her gift of speaking in the tongues of angels did no one any good if there was not another present to decipher her words. Mayhap her gift was for Zola and God alone, Daria had returned. She was tired of dissecting everything in their path, everything about them. Daria longed for peace and solitude, for even a day as she had had at the priory in Roma.

God had been urging her outward, into the countryside. There was someone here, near the manor, that he intended to heal—someone beyond the beggar with pox that she had healed on the road to the manor—but she had not the strength to seek them out yet. Her thoughts went to Tatiana, and she wondered if she fared any better in Siena than when she had left. Daria shook her head—she needed her thoughts together, first, to renew her strength, take time with her Lord to hear from him. Then perhaps she would be ready to move out and do as he bid.

As she crested the hill, Bormeo swooped low, his high-pitched cry alerting her. But he was only playing, clearly happy to be free to fly and hunt. She watched as he circled high again, searching for prey. The tall silver fir, the dense oak, beech, and chestnut forests of the valleys grew more sparse as she climbed, while the sun sank closer to the western hills. Daria urged the horse still higher. At the crest of the next hill, she turned back and looked down into the valley. She could see small figures moving in and out of the manor gates, but no one seemed alarmed. The boy had kept his promise.

Then she moved on. She did not want the manor in her line of vision, only the trees and tall grasses, rolling hills and the beginnings of a sunset. Ten minutes later, she found her spot on the ridge, nestled perfectly between the towns of Briole and Gaiole in Chianti. A limestone cliff formed a hollow to her left. To her right was a dense grouping of juniper trees, the summer heat bringing their piquant, but warm and spicy smell to her nostrils.

Daria dismounted and reached to untie the blanket from the horse's flank, spreading it out on the lumpy grass next to a limestone boulder. She reached again for the parcel tied to the saddle, filled with her precious Bible and a flask of water. Then she let the mare free to chew on the rich hillside grasses. Bormeo swooped by again, marking her location as was his habit, and then climbed into the sky. Daria settled in, untying the large leather satchel and removing the precious Bible from its folds, thinking of Piero's letter. Her hand rubbed across the wide, smooth covering and her thoughts went to her parents, her grandfather, and her great-grandfather, all the d'Angelos who had read from this holy script. Holding this sacred book always gave Daria a sense of connection to her lost loved ones, a sense of peace as she opened it to read.

It was uncommon for anyone but priests to have a copy of the Holy Scriptures and even more so for a bourgeois family to own one. But when her great-grandfather began his trade in supplies on behalf of the monks of San Galgano and their scriptorium, and later learned Latin in order to read the Scriptures himself, the bishop had awarded him with a copy of the Holy Writ three years later.

Daria sat back against the rock, hugging the book that reached from chin to lap, and smiled. Could the Almighty have begun the work in the d'Angelo clan through that calling to the holy trade, a trade that had laid the foundation for this? For the Gifted?

❧ ❧ ❧

I⊤ was Basilio who noticed that Daria's horse was missing from the stable. He drew near to Gianni and Piero, who were talking in the courtyard. "Captain, is the Duchess on a ride this eve?"

Gianni frowned and rose. Servants moved in and out of the kitchen, but there was no sign of Daria. Rune emerged from the kitchen, carrying a bucket for . . . Zola, not Daria. Gianni glanced at Hasani, who stood guard on the upper portico roof outside Daria's quarters. It was then that understanding dawned; Daria had slipped away.

"She probably needed time to herself," Piero said, still sitting. "I do not think she will be in danger here."

"Mayhap. But she ought not be alone."

"There are times, dear man, that one can only commune with God in solitude."

"That is what this is about? She needs time to pray?"

"I myself walk the hills just after we break our fast, each and every day. Here at the manor there is too much commotion, too much going on to concentrate."

"She can pray in the chapel. She need not go outside the manor gates, especially with darkness drawing near."

"Do you not feel closer to your Creator outside the gates more than inside, Gianni? You are a man used to riding hard, riding far. There is something sacred about the natural world. Jesus himself used to draw away from the crowds, out into the countryside, to hilltops, to pray. Perhaps Daria felt a similar need."

"I would be more at ease if she had not healed that man of the pox as we neared the manor. Our secret will be ill kept if she insists on healing in so public a manner."

Piero shot him a wry grin. "I myself am thankful for that healing. There is no secret needed kept if we are all dead of the pox."

Gianni backed up in order to see more of the hills that rose behind the manor. His eyes scanned one valley and then the other. "There," he said, pointing. "Bormeo."

The priest grinned. "See? She is not alone."

Gianni rolled his eyes. "We will go to her," he said, waving Hasani down from his perch. "But we will keep our distance."

"The feast will be served late this eve, come nightfall. She knows the new men will be waiting for the ceremony, the harvesters more than ready to eat given the hour. Daria will return in time."

"Indeed," Gianni said, walking out. He intended to guarantee it would be so.

"Gianni," Piero called.

The knight turned to look over his shoulder.

"You must learn to trust me. Trust what I know to be true." Gianni looked hard at the priest. He was speaking of his gift, of wisdom, holy understanding. "I am still . . . still struggling to trust it myself, but I believe I would know if Daria were in immediate danger."

"I trust you, Father. And just as you were born with certain gifts, so was I. I must follow my heart."

Piero contemplated that a moment. "Go then. Keep an eye on your lady, but I ask you to do so at a distance. She has much to mull over and discuss with her Lord. What he has asked of her is . . . uncommon."

Gianni grinned. "I think that, my priest, is an understatement."

ॐ ॐ ॐ

SHE looked up from the long, even lines of Latin script and closed her eyes, feeling the welcome, cool tinge of eve on the hot afternoon breeze. "My Lord God, what is it that you need of me? What do you wish to do with the Gifted? Are we to seek the rest of the letter? Or was this all we needed to set our feet on this path you wish us to take? O Lord, lead us forward. Make us strong in our knowledge of you and in our faith. We long to serve you. . . ."

As she sat there, slowly inhaling the damp scent of loam on the wind, the Scriptures came back to her. "Thy word is a lamp unto my feet, and a light unto my path," she whispered. It had been a favorite of her mother's. Daria thought of traveling the streets at night in Siena, the high walls and buildings blocking any moonlight unless it was nearly directly above. When she carried a lamp, the light cast a mere three feet before her. It was light, but it was not the blazing sun. It was enough light to take the next few steps and no more.

Daria knew what they were to do, as they all apparently knew. They were to use their gifts, and as they did so, the Lord would show them where they were going, a few steps at a time. It was not theirs to know month to month what was to transpire, or even week by week, but more day by day. Mayhap moment by moment. Daria sighed. "Give me the faith, Father. Make up for me where I am weak. I want you to use my gift, but I am afraid, overwhelmed. . . ."

It came to her that she was not as overwhelmed as she thought she was. She knew that all was right about her for the moment. She felt whole and vital for the first time in months, an instrument in God's hands. "Use me, Lord God, use me." She moved to her knees and bowed deeply, stretching out her arms before her. "Forgive me my sins, Lord Jesus. Cleanse me of unholy thoughts, unholy actions. Make me a strong vessel. . . ."

She smiled again, accepting forgiveness, letting it wash over her as she prayed Zola would allow it to cleanse her too. After a moment, she sat back against the rock, praying for each of the people at the manor, from Nico to Piero to Gianni to Basilio—every one of them—as Piero had mentioned he too was praying. They ought to gather each evening for mass and prayer, she thought. If they were the Gifted, it was time they began to act like it—arming themselves within as Gianni concentrated on arming themselves outwardly. She would speak to Father Piero about it this evening, directly after the feast. In another week they would return to Siena. It was important that they get their internal affairs in order before it was too late.

Daria rose and scanned the horizon for Bormeo. She could hear his high-pitched screech in the distance, the sign he gave when he killed his prey. "Another rabbit for the feast table," she muttered, only half delighted. The bird screeched again. He was perhaps five minutes away, to the south. She made another soft sound to her mare, reaching out to her, but the horse already had head up, ears perked forward. Another horse approached.

Daria looked down the valley again, the hair on her neck standing on end. She realized she was holding her breath when Gianni and Hasani came into view, steadily riding up the path. Daria ducked behind the boulder, reaching up to smooth her hair and then shaking out her skirts, gathering her thoughts. She waited for them to round the corner, but they did not. Did they miss her? Were they heading elsewhere? She edged around the corner again, feeling like a girl spying upon her parents in the solarium, but they were heading out, toward Bormeo. To pick up the rabbit, she supposed.

She gathered her Bible and slid it into the leather envelope, but the cover caught and opened. It opened two pages in, on the presentation page that had the bishop's and her great-grandfather's names upon it. She smiled and turned the page, having not looked at those first pages in some time. On the next page was the peacock, the peacock of her family crest. For the first time, she saw Latin words nestled delicately among the feathers, almost undiscernible. She gasped. *Sapientiam. Wisdom*, she translated. *Healing. Faith. Visions. Discernment. Miracles. Prophecy.* She dropped the book and scrambled away, to the other edge of the clearing, just as Gianni and Hasani entered it.

"M'lady? Daria!" Gianni barked, alarmed by her face. He was off his horse and beside her in a moment. "What is it?" He turned and surveyed the landscape. "Whom do you fear?"

Hasani lifted the Bible from the blanket and looked over at her, obviously seeing the words there too. How often had they both pored over the book, reading from it as children, as adults? And yet never seeing the words? He handed it to Gianni and stared at her in wonder.

"What is this? A book? A *Bible*? You? You own a Bible?"

"Yes, with providing resources for the Galgano scriptorium, we were able to obtain one. And yet that—that is not what gives me pause. Look there, to the first pages, to the page with our family crest."

He stared at it blankly.

"You must let your eyes rest not upon the lines of the feathers, but on the spaces between. Do you see?" she asked.

And then he looked as if he wanted to drop it, yet couldn't tear his eyes away. He crossed himself and sank to his knees, still staring at the page. "How many? How many signs are we to be given?"

"I know not. I myself find them a mite frightful. I am convinced. Do you hear that, Lord? We are convinced!" she said loudly, to the sky. "Why is it that I feel that our lives are no longer our own?" she asked, reaching for the Bible. Gianni reluctantly let it go and came to his feet. She wrapped it and secured it again to the saddle. Then she mounted up and waited for Gianni and Hasani to follow.

"We did not mean to disturb you, m'lady," Gianni said, his eyes slowly focusing on her again.

"You did not disturb me. I was preparing to leave."

Hasani grunted his disapproval and Daria felt a twinge of guilt run through her shoulder blades. She glanced back at him. "Forgive me, friend, for slipping away. I needed . . . merely an hour to myself." Hasani didn't meet her gaze. He would punish her, silently, for a day and tomorrow all would be well. That had always been their way.

"I do not warrant an apology?" Gianni asked.

She slid her eyes over to him, saw the grin in his eyes. "You are a hired man, not a friend."

"Ahh. So the woman for whom I *work* cannot be trusted?"

"I did not lie to you. I was in the kitchen for a time. It is not my responsibility to let you know every step I plan to take."

"If my chief goal is to see to your health and welfare, Lady Daria, then I do rely upon you to tell me."

"That is a problem, Captain. I am used to making decisions for myself. Freedom."

"You are altogether a different woman, m'lady," he said, shaking his head. "In all my travels, I have not met many who are as headstrong and independent as you."

"So I've heard. Yet there are not many women in my position. Without father. Without spouse. But with means."

"Nay. There are not. And yet I was thinking not of your familial status but more of you as a woman. On the outside, you are . . ." He cleared his throat nervously. "What I mean to say is that you have the heart of a lioness. You appear to fear nothing." His left cheek dimpled. "Other than signs and wonders from God."

"A lioness still fears, even if she appears not to." She could feel his eyes upon her, feel the weight of his unspoken words. On the outside, she was what? She refused to meet his gaze again. Let him look. Let him wonder. He might be the captain of the d'Angelo guard—a needed contingent to protect her holdings and their strange group—but she had not settled into the idea that she herself needed constant guarding. And his obvious interest in her as a woman . . . well, that was a path that ought not to be taken. Daria had tried her hand at love and come up short. God clearly had another path in mind for her. And Daria had just determined through her time in prayer to take that path, and none other.

She would not sway. She would not waver. She was God's servant, on a path as holy as a nun's or priest's.

CHAPTER SEVENTEEN

AGATA and Beata Scioria hurried Daria along to her quarters for a deep, warm bath. They could hear the clattering of hoofbeats outside the courtyard gates, cries of welcome, as the new men arrived at the manor. Makeshift tables and benches had been erected in the courtyard, and the Sciorias had decorated all ten with wild mustard greens and purple flowering sage. In the center of each were enormous stacks of pomegranates, oranges, Daria's favorite pears from the Cistercian abbey, and almonds. Heavenly smells of roasting pig on a spit, stuffed partridge, lamb, and spiced squash wafted through the air.

Passing the kitchen, Daria glimpsed simmering haggis and freshly baked custards and tarts and rolls. Through a window she saw a village cook at an open fire, carefully stirring a sauce in an enormous pot—a Scioria family recipe of verjuice, wine, ginger, and salt. In an hour the courtyard would be full of the villagers who had toiled in their fields, ready to celebrate a strong first harvest in the sheds and the midsummer eve feast.

Daria shed her clothing, sank into the juniper berry-scented water, and quickly scrubbed her body and hair. Agata remained behind to assist her in dressing while Beata returned to the kitchen. Daria rose, drying her body, and Agata came to her, a fine new gown in hand. "It is lovely, m'lady. I am glad you saved it until now."

"As am I," Daria said. "It will be perfect this night."

She took the delicate creamy undergown from Agata, letting the fabric settle over her arms and torso and legs. Then she reached for the darker silk overgown, slitted deeply at the sides to allow for maximum ventilation, and pulled it over her body. It settled just under the knobs of her shoulders, exposing a bit of the gown beneath. The fabric was a rich moiré pattern, with alternating stitches that gave it an uncommon depth. The Sienese seamstress had done an excellent job—the entire front panel flowed smoothly to below her waist and below that, to just above her feet.

Agata moved to run a bone comb through her tangle of curls, making Daria wince. But soon she had Daria's hair combed out, a silver fillet settled around the crown, and her hair bunched into a crispinette made of finely woven cream-colored silk. She moved away from Daria as she rose. "Ah, m'lady, you look worthy of court."

"Thank you, Agata." She smiled and went to a looking glass in the corner, where she could see her dim outline. It had been more than six months since she had donned a new gown—since before she and Marco parted ways. But her mother had always said a feast day warranted a fine new gown.

"Come, m'lady."

The musicians were already playing—Aldo had hired three from the village to play lute, mandola, and viola. It had been too long since music had graced the d'Angelo household. She hoped one or two of the knights had both instrument and a keen ear for music—that would make their part in the household all the more welcome come eventide.

Hasani met her at the main entrance and she took his arm. The people milled about and raucous laughter overtook the music at times. Flags with the family herald of red peacock on a brilliant white background hung in the still night air. Torches blazed. Later there would be a bonfire. Daria's heart quickened at the thought of so many people about . . . the last festival she had taken part in had been Twelfth Night, and had not ended happily. By the end of the festival, she had left Marco's household. She looked up to Hasani and he smiled gently down at her in encouragement, as if reading her mind.

He squeezed her hand upon his arm, then led her outward and the crowd hushed and gathered as if welcoming a noblewoman.

Gianni drew near and bowed deeply. "M'lady . . ." He looked at her for a long moment, smiling appreciatively, clearly wanting to say more, but resisting. "May I present to you the villagers and the new men of your guard?"

"Indeed," Daria said. She moved from Hasani to Gianni's arm and accompanied him down the line of villagers who gathered to greet her. She remembered many by name, and was introduced to others by Aldo. Two-thirds of the way down the line, an old villager held on to her hand. "M'lady, I beg of you to pay our cottage a visit on the morrow. I remember your mother, and her way with the medicines and herbs. She once saved my own mother from a harrowing illness of the lungs. Would you do me the honor of coming to visit my wife? I would trade the season's wages if you would agree to do so."

Gianni moved in between them as if to break the old man's hold, but Daria moved in closer to him. *This is the one. Go, as he asks.* Daria's heart pounded as God's urging flowed through her mind. Never had he been more clear. "Will she be all right if we tarry through the feast? The games? Or ought we go this moment?"

"Ach, no, I cannot take the lady away from the festival. Please, if you will but come visit us on the morrow, I'm sure it will be well."

"We will be visiting your wife soon, good man. There will be no fee, no wages traded." She looked into his eyes and smiled. "Be calm, friend. Your wife will soon breathe easily. I promise. And be sure to take a basket of the feastings home with you to share with her."

"Thank you, Duchess, thank you."

She moved on to greet the rest of the harvesters and then arrived at a group of men at the end of the line, to whom she would be introduced by Basilio. They had been gathered from the far reaches of the region, some from as far away as Roma. The first was Lucan, one of the strongest, tallest men she had ever encountered, a head taller than Rune and Gianni, even, and yet he moved like a gentle giant. She immediately took to his shy smile.

The second, Ciro, was a broad, strong man—as powerfully built as Gianni—the only one from the village, who eyed her with too much familiarity and little honor. She bristled as Ciro bent to kiss her hand, holding it several moments too long. And when he straightened, he glanced over to Zola, lust clearly lacing his eyes. Daria pulled her hand away and glanced back at the woman, who kept her eyes on the ground, then pulled Basilio and Gianni a step away. "Dismiss him. He is unacceptable."

"Ciro is a fine swordsman, the best in the village, m'lady," Basilio said.

"I care not. He is unseemly."

Gianni nodded. "Done. As soon as you greet the rest of the men, we shall escort him out."

She was grateful for Gianni's immediate deference to her opinion. Perhaps he had glimpsed what she had seen.

The third and fourth men were brothers, Ugo and Vito, obviously eager to please. One wore a lute across his back and a sword at his side. The other had a flautist's case across his chest. They laughed with the freedom of children but the depth of men as one cracked a joke.

Daria shoved her apprehension over Ciro away and was quickly laughing with them. "My musicians!" Daria exclaimed, clapping her hands together lightly. "I had so hoped that some of our newest household members would bring music into the house as well."

The men nodded as one. "It is our pleasure to serve with our instruments, be it by sword or with music," said the elder brother, Ugo.

"I think you shall find," said the younger, "that we are adept with either, m'lady. We are pleased to serve you."

Daria smiled at both. How happy her parents would have been to find musicians again in their home! Not since she was a little girl had melodies flowed through the halls at any other time than the feast days.

"Gentlemen, we will have the fealty ceremony in a week's time," Gianni announced. "As per Lady Daria's rules, there will be no swearing, no raucous behavior—other than during tonight's feast," he said loudly with a grin, bringing laughter from the crowd, "and you will behave as if you are the lady's brother himself. Your actions reflect upon the house of d'Angelo and any infractions will be punishable by immediate dismissal. Understood?"

"Understood," said the group as one.

"Father Piero," Daria called.

"Yes, m'lady?"

"Please say a blessing over this heavenly smelling food so that we can begin eating!"

"Hear, hear!" cried a farmer in the center of the crowd, his fist held high.

"As you wish, m'lady!"

Just as the priest finished, the people gave a cheer and moved toward the tables. Between each setting was a bread trencher, ready to be piled high with roasted meats and bird, and covered with the thin verjuice sauce. Daria's mouth watered and she realized she had not eaten since breaking her fast that morning.

Gianni was in the corner with Rune, Basilio, and Ciro. Daria could hear Ciro's voice getting louder, his hands moving wildly as if to emphasize his words. Suddenly the disgruntled knight spun around and strode over to Daria, Rune and Basilio right behind him. They each took an arm as he leaned toward Daria, the veins at his temples popping in rage. "How dare you, *Duchess*. How dare you! I deserve this position! I deserve it! I have done nothing to warrant dismissal!"

Hasani moved in front of her from the left and Gianni caught up and moved in front of her at the right. "Stand down," Gianni said lowly. There was a dagger in his hand. "Depart now and you leave with life and limb. If you continue this attack, I cannot promise you that."

Daria laid a hand on Gianni's shoulder and after a moment, he moved slightly aside. "I am sorry you were called here in hopes of taking the position. We are clearly ill suited. I bid thee well. Go in peace."

"I hear I am not the only man to whom you are ill suited," Ciro sneered. "Perhaps that is why you surround yourself with men. You must hire them since you cannot win their hearts. And you must hire the town whore to entertain them to keep them here!"

"Enough!" Gianni shouted.

"You appear warm and beautiful, but within you are a cold-hearted—"

"Be gone!" Gianni shouted. As one, Rune, Basilio, Hasani, and Gianni moved the struggling and venomous man outside the gates, shutting the door in the face of his threats. Daria, shaking, motioned to the musicians to help disguise the noise and the villagers began speaking in hushed undertones, guiltily looking away from her.

Zola moved to her side. "You chose well, m'lady. That one is cruel and evil hearted. Pay him no further mind."

"Thank you, Zola," Daria said, looking after the woman who shrank back into the shadows instead of joining her neighbors at the tables. Had she herself suffered at the man's hands? Daria did her best to hide a shiver. She was glad the man would be locked outside her gates instead of sleeping this night inside the manor walls.

"The others seem like solid sorts," Father Piero said, moving beside her to escort her to the head of the table. "Concentrate on them instead of the riffraff."

"We will know in time," Daria said.

"Indeed. The making of a man becomes clear in the face of danger, as the ancients said."

Daria glanced up at him. "So you too expect danger."

The priest sighed as he lumbered down to sit beside her. "Danger. Glory. Peace. Peril. We are on an uncommon path."

"I prayed this day for strength to remain on that path. For courage to be used as the Savior sees fit."

"As I prayed for you and the rest of us. Keep praying as such and he will see us through," Piero said, patting her hand. He leaned closer. "I take it you are to heal the old man's wife this night?"

Daria grinned. "God will heal the woman if he sees fit. I believe he has asked me to go and serve."

"Well said, daughter. Always God, not us. If we begin to claim our gifts as power, use them for any other purpose other than to honor the Lord, I am afraid that our Lord will not honor our gifts."

Basilio and Rune joined them at the table, along with Gianni. "We beg your pardon, m'lady," Basilio said. "He seemed the perfect gentleman in town. We did not expect what we saw here tonight."

"Never thee mind," Daria said. "I am just glad he was a weed we could quickly pull from our garden before it took root."

☙ ☙ ☙

HIGH on the hill above Daria's manor, the spurned knight cantered up to join the men astride horses, hidden in a copse of trees. One was his master; the other he had not met. Both were as finely dressed as princes on the hunt. From this vantage point, they could clearly see the people moving in and out of the gates.

"Half the town moves in and out of her gates freely," growled the first man, "and yet you are tossed out like a drunkard from the tavern."

"I did nothing. She seemed to see through me."

"I should have sent another. You are like pond scum, just beneath the water's surface. Anyone can see through you."

The knight shifted in his saddle and clenched his teeth together. His master's words pierced, but he deserved them. Ciro had failed him. After a moment, he found his voice. "What shall we do? How may I serve you now?"

The man did not look at him, merely stared downward at Daria's gates. "Did you learn anything while inside? How is she armed? Why is she bringing in men-at-arms?"

"Nothing was said. The two who brought me in shared little, only that she was to soon return to the city and perhaps beyond. That I had to be without farm or dependent clan because our road was uncertain."

The second man grunted and tapped his pursed lips. "Curious. The lady's road should be most certain. Summer in this valley. Bring in the harvest. Return to Siena to do her business and winter. What is uncertain about that? The weather?"

Ciro shrugged his shoulders. He sensed neither was truly asking him the question anyway. "Forgive me, master, for failing you. I beg you for another opportunity to prove my worth."

Hard, dark, piercing eyes studied him for an uncomfortable moment. "In truth, there is another already inside. I will make use of you outside, with me."

Ciro's eyes widened. Another! Already inside! Shame washed through him over his failure. If another had succeeded, so should have he!

"But we shall not be seen together. We must meet under cover of darkness. Now that you are known to Daria and her men, you must not be seen as associated with me. Understood?"

Ciro nodded. "How shall I obtain my orders from you?"

"I will call you to me when I have need of you. In the meantime, find out what you can in the village. Where they are going, what they are up to."

"Done."

"Nothing else was said? What were their immediate plans?"

"The villagers said that they would wait until second harvest and then return to Siena, as you expected."

"Good, good. When they leave, you shall trail them and we will meet in the hills above Siena."

Ciro hesitated, shifting under the weight of silence, wondering if he had been dismissed for the night. "There was one other thing . . ."

Again, the hard, dark, piercing gaze upon him. Ciro was angry at himself for even bringing it up.

"Yes? What is it?"

"The lady. She promised to go and attend an old man's wife this night."

"This night? But there is a feast to attend."

"She promised. If not tonight, then very soon. There is talk in the village . . . of the lady being a healer."

The second man let out a dismissive sound. "An herbalist. As her mother was before her."

Something within Ciro resisted. "Nay. The villagers . . . they speak of her as a *healer*. For the past year a beggar has hovered at the edge of our village, never able to draw near because he has the pox. He was on the road to the manor the day the lady and her troop came to the valley. The Duchess and her priest dropped from their horses, surrounded the man, and prayed over him for nigh over an hour."

"And then?"

"The story goes that they dropped him off at a farmhouse,

with two florins for new clothing, a place to stay, and assistance in finding work. They asked the farmer not to tell of their identity, but word spreads quickly through such a small village."

"The man was healed?"

"Healed. Not a mark on him."

The master shifted in his saddle. "It is very curious." He sighed and stared thoughtfully down at the manor.

"You say she is to go out this night and attend a peasant?"

"This night or on the morrow. A farmer's wife, at the north end of the valley."

"All right, then. We shall follow them. You, watch the farmer's house. What you see, their formation and pattern in guarding the lady, what transpires. I want every detail. Report to my aide what you learn. He will await your return here, two days hence."

Ciro bit back a smile. An opportunity to serve! To recover his stature with the master! "As you wish."

cb cb cb

THE two men watched Ciro make his way down the hillside, to the west this time in order to avoid being seen by knights or villagers in the manor below.

"They grow in strength as well as number," said the leader.

"You think they are the ones. The Gifted?"

"Potentially. Their coming was foretold. There is a strength within them. . . . If they are our enemies, they must be quickly turned or vanquished. Our master demands it. They are drawn into the simple faith right now, and if we can bring them into the ultimate knowledge, they will be powerful allies. We will find ways to draw each of them in, appeal to them. They are unique creations; each will have a unique weakness. The letter is bound to be useful in this. They will be curious . . . and as eager as we to know what the rest of the letter contains. We must beat them to it. We can then use it as a tool to bring them along. . . ."

"And if they do not wish to join us?"

The master set his lips in a straight line and left the apprentice's question hanging in the air. "Every step they take. Anything they gain, anything they lose. Their strengths. Their weaknesses. Accomplishments, failures, I want to know it all. Discover all you can, man, and report to me. We shall meet again in Siena."

"As you wish, master."

         ക ക ക

AFTER the feast, after the wine ran out and the bonfire turned to glowing embers, after their wish boats with candles upon them were sent down the creek, the villagers departed for their cottages about the valley.

Daria asked Agata to gather her basket of herbs and tonics and Beata went with her to change out of her glorious gown and into a plain work shift. The cotton was old, but age had made it soft, and it felt welcome against Daria's skin. She donned a cape that tied at the neck, happy to have a hood to disguise her hair under the bright full moon.

"Tell me you do not intend to go out this night," Gianni said when she rounded the corner. Her hand flew to her throat. He pushed off from the wall and grimaced, obviously dismayed to have frightened her.

Daria brushed past him and walked back into the courtyard. "Very well. 'I do not intend to go out this night.' " She took the basket from Agata and settled the hood over her head. The boy, Nico, emerged from the stable with her mare tiredly trailing behind him.

"M'lady . . ." She turned back to him, his handsome face warm in the flickering lamplight. He brushed a hand through his hair. "It is late, very late. The man's wife is likely sleeping by now."

"Or ailing. Ofttimes, night is the worst time for those who labor with illness. The farmer departed early because he was so concerned."

"That knight, the one you dismissed, he made some ugly threats."

Daria took a step forward. "Are you telling me that you have hired five men-at-arms and I cannot go where I wish, when I wish?"

"I simply ask that you not take unnecessary risks."

"This is necessary, Captain. Assemble the knights I need to take suitable precaution but not attract undue attention. Despite our best efforts, the villagers speak freely of me healing the beggar of pox. If the farmer's wife is healed, word of it must not spread— or at least be tied to me. Your men will need to watch over me, but from some distance."

"No. That is not acceptable."

"That is most unfortunate. It appears, then, that God has asked me to do something *unacceptable*."

Gianni swallowed hard. "The Lord himself has asked you to go? Does he speak to you?"

"Prepared me, urged me when I met the man, nudged me from within. I suspect you know of what I speak. I am to go, and go this night." She ignored his move to help her mount and swung her leg across the mare, but then paused. "Hasani cannot go with me. He is too identifiable. Father Piero ate too much and is suffering from indigestion in his quarters. If you change into some peasant garb, you may go with me."

Gianni grinned. "Give me but a moment," he said, raising one finger. He leaned over to the boy. "Saddle my horse quickly, will you, Nico? If I'm not ready to ride in a minute or two the mistress is liable to leave without me."

"Right away, Captain!" said the boy, scurrying off.

ॐ ॐ ॐ

THEY rode the path under a wide, glittering moon, side by side. A knight rode a distance before them, another behind them, and still another rode opposite Gianni, on Daria's other side. But they were good, moving in and out of the trees, off the main road—Daria could barely make them out and she was looking for them. "Our own angels, on watch," she said. "I am more afraid for the manor than for myself."

"Hasani is on watch, as are Lucan and Rune. They will remain at their posts until we return."

It seemed like a faulty plan to Daria, and she shifted under the weight of such attention. Surely their stores of grapes and cloth at the manor were more desirable than she! "His threats were idle," she said.

"Mayhap. But there was a spirit about him that left me . . . disquieted. I intend to learn more about him before we leave for Siena. If my lady had stayed at home as instructed, I would have tracked him this night."

Daria smiled. "I have never been the obedient sort."

"I noticed that."

They rode in silence for a time before Gianni spoke again. "Has Father Piero allowed you to study the letter further?"

"Most of it. I am still trying to link thought with experience with knowledge. It is like knitting together threads that keep unraveling back to the beginning. How could it be that our likenesses are on the first three pages? What is in the portion that is missing? What clues are we missing that are before our very eyes, like that of the peacock in my very own Bible?"

"Aye. The same questions ramble through my own head. How could it be that God would choose to heal through you? How could he have brought you and Piero together at the convent? You and I together on the road?" He let out a deep breath. "God is at work in a mighty fashion."

"It appears as such. But what are we to accomplish? Or what if this is all some grand illusion? Coincidence?"

"Nay. This is not mere coincidence. God is afoot."

Daria sighed. "I confess I agree with you, but it does not bestill my mind. I feel a strong urge to keep my healing a secret, and will obey that call, but I can't help but think that it might help us in some way. Would it not aid us to gain a following? People who would support us, protect us?"

"It could, in time. But if news of your gift spreads, we would not be able to travel without a throng of people following us. We have some foundations yet to build. We must solidify as a group if we are to work together and that takes time. Heal as God urges you to and await his illumination of our next step."

"Wise counsel. I have read enough of the letter to know that two more are bound to soon join us.

"The Bible clearly lists them too, in the same order. Wisdom, healing, faith . . . There are seven, a perfect number."

"What are the next two?"

"Visions. Discernment between evil and good."

Gianni laughed under his breath. "Mayhap they will tell us what is next and ease my mind in protecting you from those who would wish evil upon your life. They can tell me when I can take my rest in my bed on a night such as this or send you out with a full retinue of guards."

"Only God alone can do that, Gianni," she said with a smile.

"I know, I know. But a weary man can dream, can he not?"

The light was burning in the small cottage beside the dark forest and Daria glanced at Gianni, glad they had come and not waited for morning.

ᚼ ᚼ ᚼ

A soft whistle from the edge of the woods and from each direction let them know that all was well, and that his guards were on the watch. Gianni looked to Daria, wondering if she had heard the whistles, but her focus was entirely on the cottage before them. Her eyes were wide and staring, her brow furrowed, and her lips moved in constant, silent prayer.

"Give her strength, Lord Jesus," Gianni offered, quickly dismounting, this time a step ahead of Daria. He helped her to dismount, lifting her from the saddle and settling her on the ground. She was light in his arms and he fought the urge to hold her small waist between his palms for a moment longer. Again, she paid him no heed, simply turned to untie her basket of remedies from the mare's saddle, strode to the door, and knocked.

"I will wait here. Call if you have need of me," he whispered.

"I have need of you now, knight. Come in with me." Gianni paused, instantly on alert, uneasy. Daria never asked for assistance.

"Who's there?" a man called. They could hear the labored breathing of the woman even outside. She sounded as if she were under water. Surely she was about to die!

"Daria d'Angelo," she said lowly, her lips nearly touching the wooden door.

"Duchess!" the old man cried, opening the door wide. "I cannot believe you are here. I thought you would wait until sunup before paying us a visit."

Daria smiled. "I could not wait until sunup, nor could your wife. Have faith, good man. This night you shall see a new decade ahead with your woman, not a life of solitude." She glanced back at Gianni, the question in her eyes. *Why do you not follow?*

It seemed foolish to Gianni to leave the door unguarded, and yet his men surrounded them, kept watch over them. If his lady needed him inside on the Lord's business, surely the Lord would keep watch over the cottage himself!

The beggar on the road had been healed quickly, his angry red rash disappearing as they watched in wonder. He sensed this one would take longer. The woman tried to smile at them, but was quickly drawn back into a panic over her labored breathing. She sounded as if she were at the water's edge, sucking in a bit of water with each breath. Gurgling as she inhaled, coughing violently with nearly each exhalation. Daria lifted one of the woman's hands up to the candlelight and then brought the candle to her face. Her nailbeds and lips were blue. Gianni crossed himself and joined Daria at her side, already praying as she set out her medicinals. Surely this old woman would be meeting Saint Peter this night!

He opened his eyes after praying to glance at Daria and find her staring back at him. Wide, golden-brown eyes studied him accusingly. "He called me here, Gianni," she said, her eyebrows lowering. "Believe or get out of this cottage."

"Forgive me my unbelief, m'lady," he whispered, shaking his head. "I will do my best to believe."

"Nay, not your best. Believe in the God who saved you and he shall do the rest. Think back, back to that forest and your mortal wound. Consider what he did for you there, and for the beggar on the road, and *believe* in the God on high." She turned from him then, asking the old man to bring clean cloths and to put water on the hearth grate to boil, filling the room with steam, and another kettle filled with sage and fennel tea. Watching her move, minister to the woman, was like watching an elegant dance performed by one well versed in her steps. But Gianni knew that much of this was new to his lady—mayhap watching her mother before her had made her steps assured. . . .

Daria pulled box and bag from her basket, one after the other, and then a small stone and pestle. She pulled out a small bundle of yew branches from her bag and asked Gianni to set them atop the fire. In minutes a pleasant, sweet odor filled the room as the yew spat and smoked its juices upon the fire. She ground together a vast amount of four herbs, creating a thick paste that nearly spilled from the stone. She rose, and put her ear to one side of the woman's chest and then the other.

She glanced at him, silently asking him to avert his eyes, and Gianni rose to put his back to the old woman as Daria untied the old woman's shift and uncovered her chest. He could hear Daria crooning to her, speaking in soft, dulcet tones that soothed and encouraged.

The old man passed him with the boiling water and cloth and after Daria stirred a bit into the herbal mixture, she began patting it across the woman's chest, praying now, a constant petition to come and be present, to wash the woman's lungs clean, to allow air to flow without impediment, for healing to come.

She bound the poultice to the woman's chest with a long, cotton strip, wound around and around her with the old man's help. On and on she prayed, for the illness to be gone, for the light of Jesus Christ to reign, for darkness to be banished. As the old woman was lowered back against the cushion, slightly elevated rather than flat now, she sounded worse, not better.

At Daria's touch to his elbow, Gianni turned and went to his knees, echoing Daria's petitions, shoving aside the dark thought that raced through his mind that the woman would die, not heal. He concentrated on Daria's words, imagined himself kneeling before God himself, beseeching his Lord to come and do his good work again, here, right now.

"Death, you have no place here," Daria prayed. "This woman has been claimed by the Lord of life and promised more days upon this earth. Be gone, evil one. Be gone, illness. In the name of Jesus Christ, only life and healing are welcome here. Come, Lord Jesus. Come, Holy Ghost. Come and heal this woman. Ease her breath, ease her life. Bring her your gift of peace, Father. . . ."

As she prayed, the sounds from the woman's mouth became less like slow suffocation and more like labored breathing.

"Thanks be to God," the old man whispered slowly in wonder. He squeezed his wife's shoulder but she appeared to be sleeping.

"Our Lord's work is not yet done," Daria whispered. "Quickly, the green bottle in my bag." The old man retrieved it and Daria gave the woman several small sips of the hart's-tongue tonic from a spoon.

They continued to pray over her and the woman's breathing continued to ease within an hour. She drew deep, clear breaths through her nostrils and allowed easy, soft breaths out from her mouth.

Gianni laughed, tears running down his cheeks in wonder. "Do you hear that? Do you hear *that*?"

Daria opened her eyes and grinned back at him, then reached

to touch the old man's arm. He opened tired eyes to gaze upon his wife and then smiled at Daria with a mouth devoid of but three teeth. "You have done it! She is well—I have not heard her breathe as such in years. You have done it, m'lady!"

"Nay," she motioned with her hands, trying to shush his exuberant shout. "Our Lord has done it. He has answered your faithful prayer, good man. Not us. Our Lord."

"But you—"

"Nay," she said, rising. "Be very clear about this, dear man. God, not us. God through us, but not us."

The old man shuffled over to her, still on his knees. "How may I repay you? How can I repay such a debt? You have restored to me my wife, my helpmeet."

Daria smiled, shifting uncomfortably under his gaze. She bent to help him to his feet, urging Gianni to do the same. Together, they brought the old farmer to his feet, holding him for a moment to make sure he would not fall. They had spent a good hour on their knees. "You may pay me with continued good service. You have watched over my fields for a generation, and before that, over my father's fields. It is my honor to serve you and my Lord this night in ushering healing into this house."

"I will sing of your praises to everyone I meet—"

"Nay," Gianni and Daria said together.

"Please, dear neighbor, you may praise me as your lady but not as a healer. It is imperative that you keep this news to yourself. You may tell of my visit and poultice, but do not speak of the Lord working through us."

Confusion ran through the old man's shining eyes. "But why? It is a miracle, is it not? It will bring encouragement to the people, to know that God is working in such a manner. To know we toil in the fields of such a faithful, blessed servant . . ."

"They are good questions. Honest questions. All we know is that we are to attempt to keep this gift a secret until the proper time. There may well be a day we will call upon you to defend us, friend. For now, please abide with your wife in peace and prosperity and thank God daily for the gifts he has bestowed."

"So be it, m'lady. So be it."

❧ ❧ ❧

CIRO watched the cottage, aware that one of the lady's knights was a mere twenty paces away. The man had to be drowsy at this late hour, the feast's heavy sweetmeats and large tankards of ale probably having their effect. Ciro crept a bit closer, wishing to get a better view of the cottage, and hopefully a glimpse through the window.

Just then, the old man shouted out, not in fear, but joy. Ciro's eyes narrowed. The guard to his left rose and paced back and forth, having heard the shout too. It seemed to arouse his senses and he paused, staring in Ciro's direction for several long seconds. Ugo, the musician. True knights were never musicians.

Ciro remained completely still and in a few minutes, the guard walked in the other direction, resuming a twenty-pace guard stance that he had earlier abandoned. Ciro swore under his breath. The ten paces he took came very near to where he hid. If he had to take down the man, it would alert Gianni and the lady that there was danger about. His master would be extremely displeased. And yet if Ugo discovered him . . .

Gianni appeared at the window and peered out, as if he could sense his presence too. They appeared to be preparing to go. What had transpired? The knight moved aside, and suddenly, Ciro had a plain view of the old woman, resting on her bed. The old man was beside her, grinning like a dog having just finished a butcher's finest bone. So it had been done. The woman had healed another. How did she do it?

And why was his master so interested in a healer?

❧ ❧ ❧

GIANNI paced before the window, noting the moon that crested and began to sink on the opposite horizon. Were they to be here all night? Were the men asleep at their posts? It was impossible to tell. All Gianni could tell was that he felt warm and becalmed by the door of this cottage and jittery and ill at ease as he looked outward. What was out there awaiting them?

"Come, m'lady," he said lowly. "We must hasten home. The hour is late."

"Indeed," she said, turning weary eyes upon him. The healings seemed to take something physical from her, as if all her lifeblood seeped into the one that ailed. She bent to gather the last of her things in the basket and he hurried over to take it from her, then went to tie it to her mare's saddle outside. She paused to give instructions to the old farmer, setting out carefully allotted piles of herbs on the table and telling the farmer to continue to administer the poultices through the week, each night, and to feed his wife a hearty horehound soup, as much as she could eat.

Gianni slipped outside and studied the silhouette of rolling, wooded hills in the bright moonlight. He whistled, and from the west, the north, and the south, corresponding whistles sliced the air. Gianni looked sharply to the east, made a hollow with his fist, and whistled again.

No answer.

In minutes, two knights came on horseback, kicking their horses to a speed that was dangerous, even on a moonlit night. Something was indeed amiss. Gianni grabbed Daria's mare's reins and his own horse's too, holding them taut as the horses pranced and shifted, sensing with excitement the guards' approach.

Daria emerged and Gianni rushed her to her mare. "What? What is it?"

"One of the men failed to report." Basilio and Vito appeared beside them.

"When did Ugo last check in?" Gianni asked Basilio sharply.

"Not more than an hour ago."

"All right. You two take thy lady home. I want her surrounded, understood? Do not leave her side."

"Yes, sir," Basilio said, leading the others.

"Get her inside the manor gates, then close the gates and lock them. Take her inside, to the inner chamber, and bar those doors too. Bring in basic provisions and armament. No more."

Gianni lifted Daria up into the saddle and she slumped forward.

"Captain?" asked Basilio uncertainly, looking at Daria.

"She has healed another. The healings seem to exhaust her. You may need to ride with her to keep her from falling."

"No, no . . ." Daria said weakly, but the men shared a look that told Gianni they would do what was necessary to keep her safe.

"Sir, it is my brother who is missing," Vito said. "May I have permission to remain and see to his welfare alongside you?"

"Nay. I need you with Basilio. I promise, I will see to your brother." Gianni studied the man, saw his hesitation, and nodded in appreciation when he submitted to his captain's orders. A well-trained knight, was he.

Gianni dared to glance at Daria. She had made herself sit up straighter, fighting for some sense of decorum. She was a warrior within! Still, she was but a woman, and she was an aristocrat, not country-hardened. It was good that she had allowed him to protect her.

"Do not emerge from the inner chamber until I myself knock at the door."

"Yes, sir," Basilio said.

"Sir de Capezzana," Daria said to Gianni, "are you certain that we are not overreacting? Mayhap your guard merely slumbers through this peaceful night."

"For his sake, I hope he does not. If he slumbers through his first duty as a knight of the house of d'Angelo, it will be his last." He whacked Daria's horse then on the flank, and she took off beside Basilio's horse.

Vito held back, studying the dark hills. "Ugo does not sleep

while on duty. He did not drink more than one tankard of ale at
the feast."

"Understood. I will see to him, Vito. Trust me."

With a nod and one last glance at the woods, Vito rammed his
heels into his horse's sides and galloped off to flank his lady.

Gianni mounted and paused, listening for anything he could
hear. There, a horse, carrying a rider. Gianni held his position but
unsheathed his sword. The horse was moving very slowly, not like
a mount carrying an attacker. "Who goes there?"

Ugo emerged from the forest's shadows and into the stark
moonlight, hunched over his horse, barely holding to the saddle.

"Ugo!" Gianni shouted, rushing over to him.

The young man's face was covered in blood, a huge gash at the
temple still oozing. "It was a spy. I discovered him in the brush,
watching the cottage. We scuffled and he must have struck
me. . . ."

"With a rock," said Gianni, squinting in the near dark. "Or
broadsword." They looked all about them then, deadly still,
searching for any hint of the enemy still about. Was it the knight
who had been dismissed? And if so, what did he hope to achieve
in spying upon them? Gianni glanced back at the cottage. From
this angle, he could plainly see inside the window; he watched as
the farmer attended to his wife.

"Ugo, could you see us, inside the cottage from your vantage
point?"

"Yes, sir," the man said, trying not to moan through his words.

"Could you hear us?"

"Only at times. I heard the old man shout out. I—I take it the
Duchess healed his wife, eh?"

"Indeed." Again, Gianni studied the shadows about them.
There was no longer any sense of danger. Ciro, or whoever had as-
saulted Ugo, was long gone, perhaps spooked by the other knights.
But had he seen what Ugo had? Had he noticed that the lady appeared to have healed the woman?

"How is that possible?" Ugo asked. "The villagers said that woman would die any day. Now she appears to be ready to go milk the cows on the morrow." Gianni looked back toward the cottage window. The woman was sitting up, speaking to her husband.

"A miracle, isn't it?" Gianni whispered, a smile pulling at the corners of his mouth. But then he remembered the danger at hand. If Ciro or another had seen Daria heal, then the secret might not long be kept. . . . He didn't understand their call to keep the Gifted a secret, only knew it to be a truth sent to them all from God. "Quickly," he said to the man. "We must get to the lady and make sure all is well, and tend to your wound. There is much to tell you in time about our company, much yet to be discovered."

CHAPTER EIGHTEEN

HE found her the next morning in the shed beside the stables, hanging bunches of herbs from the rafters to dry. She glanced at him and continued with her work, using her long, thin fingers to tie another bunch of greenery together and then fashion a loop. Gianni glanced upward. Across each rafter were hundreds of hooks.

"I take it you do this each summer?"

"Each and every."

"About last night—"

"You nearly frightened old Aldo to death," she said. "When you came to the door, he thought fifty men would chase in after you."

Gianni grimaced. The old servant had looked a shade more gray than usual, a battle-axe in his hands as they allowed them through the door. "Your servants are not prepared. The household is changed. They must know how to protect themselves and those they love. Every person counts. Even little Nico."

She paused and stared at him. "It was one man, Sir de Capezzana. We were not attacked by highwaymen or robbers."

"Nay. But I would much prefer highwaymen to what we encountered last night."

"It was probably just Ciro, disgruntled over his dismissal. He sought retribution. Your man chased him off. He will not dare to bother us again."

"Mayhap." How could he put into words what he felt, surmised? There was a shifting about him, sudden flashes of cold that sent chills running down his spine. He had not felt that since he had come close to the Sorcerer and lost him.

"I tended to Ugo's wound again this morning," she said, reaching up with a bunch of purple foxglove. Gianni averted his eyes when her body was silhouetted against the bright morning sunshine, streaming through the window.

"And?"

"Definitely a sword. He was backhanded, luckily for him," Daria said.

"Did you heal the man?"

"I tended to his wounds," she corrected. "God will do the rest in time. He has a terrible headache. I gave him some tea and tonic and ordered him to rest for the day. There is not always a call for God's intervention, but rather a call to use what he has provided us on earth."

Gianni picked up some dried herbs from the table where she worked, crushed them between his fingers and then smelled of the deep licorice scent. Anise. "How is it my lady knows the difference between sword wounds?"

"I cared for several while at the house of Marco Adimari. He employed six men-at-arms and they skirmished daily to stay in fighting form. Sometimes they inflicted damage they did not intend to their comrades."

Gianni scrambled for something to say. He had unwittingly ventured into very personal territory. "So you believe Ugo was intentionally spared?"

Daria met his gaze. "Anyone who can backhand a knight with the flat of his sword can as easily slice him open. Ugo was lucky."

Gianni grunted and turned. "Or blessed."

"That too," Daria said. Happily, he could hear the smile in her voice again. "If I were Ciro, I would not want the rest of you after me. Perhaps it was as he said—Ugo discovered him in the brush and he inflicted only enough damage to escape unseen."

She stood on her tiptoes to reach a higher hook with a bunch of rosemary. "Did you fare well this morn? In trying to find Ciro?"

"Nay," Gianni said. "He is not to be found. The villagers say he left."

"When?"

"Yesterday, after we dismissed him. They said they saw him on the road toward Siena, heading out. That he was off to seek other employment."

"So it was *not* Ciro?" Her smile faltered. Apparently, she favored known enemies to the unknown. So did Gianni.

"Impossible to know. He could have doubled back."

She reached up with a bunch of lavender to an even higher hook, but was just shy of it. Gianni rounded the table, took the bunch from her, and hooked it on the rafter. He looked down at her and saw the concern in her eyes, resisted the urge to reach out and touch her, comfort her. "That road would have led him directly past the farmer's cottage. It was idle curiosity that kept him around."

"And yet now he knows our secret. He might tell others of it."

When he did not respond, she looked up from tying her next bunch of lavender. "You are disturbed by the thought."

"Something odd is afoot. I have not felt such stirrings since I trailed the Sorcerer into that grove of trees. . . ."

"The grove where your men were killed?"

"The grove where I was very nearly killed." Simply remembering that day made his side ache. But there was little other than the faint scar to remind him in fact. He had been healed. By this woman. For the thousandth time, his mind raced ahead, trying to put various clues together, trying to understand what lay before them.

"I think it is time for us to meet, to review the priest's letter, to pray and to fast. We must decide how much we tell of our secrets to our new men, come to agreement about what we do, where we go. . . ." He shook his head in confusion. "I am overcome by this sense of apprehension. That we have not simply encountered a ribald knight but rather an enemy to our cause."

"An enemy? This soon?" Daria asked, fingering the herbs and then raising those wide, brown eyes to meet his.

"An enemy. We cannot wait any longer. We must ask our new men to swear fealty to you. But before they do, everyone in this household must know the truth of our calling. Everyone must decide if they are willing to face what comes, whether friend or foe."

⚭ ⚭ ⚭

THE entire household rose the next morning and, as agreed, began a two-day fast, sipping of water but taking no food. Only Ugo was allowed a hearty, healing soup, and had to heat it himself, alone by the hearth. The others spent a great deal of time either in chapel or riding among the hills, seeking solitude or time with their Lord. Daria had promised to remain within the confines of the manor's gates.

Father Piero gathered them together daily to chant the Liturgy of the Hours, once at daybreak for Lauds and in the evening for Vespers. He usually chanted through Compline as well, looking forward to the day ahead, and a few of the household would join him. But everyone attended morning Lauds and many came to hear the afternoon Vespers. Nico entered the chapel as each service began, swinging the censer wide, casting great arcs of scent-rich smoke this way and that. Daria inhaled deeply, seeking the peace and direction they all sought. By the end of the first night, they knew they had to bring the men in on what they all knew. Either they were together in this, or they would soon become splintered. Together, they could be strong, but still, Daria was ill at ease over telling the others.

After Vespers that night, they gathered around the large table in the great hall. A fire crackled in the large hearth, spreading warmth as well as deep shadows into the room, but still Daria fought back a shiver. Everything was about to change.

"Let us begin with prayer," Father Piero said, sitting down at the head of the table, opposite Daria. All bowed their heads. "Lord God on high, we ask for your blessing over this, your faithful gathering. You have brought this group of people together and we offer ourselves to you to do as you bid. Give us your direction, Lord. Give us your protection. In Christ's holy name, amen."

"Amen," rumbled all about him. Two of the men shifted awkwardly and glanced at one another. Clearly, they were unused to such prayers or happenings in other households. Daria had rarely seen anything like it herself. She smiled.

Father Piero pulled the leather envelope from his robes. He paused and looked solemnly about the circle of faces, now numbering thirteen, counting everyone from maid to knight. "We thought it time to bring you into the circle of knowledge. Each one of you, servant or knight, lady or lad, is important to us. You have each been brought to us for a reason. Together, we are stronger. We need each of you to be in constant prayer, seeking the Lord's righteous ways, seeking to do as he bids."

Ugo shifted and laughed. "Have we taken the wrong path? Have we ended up in a monastery and not in the house of our lady?"

Others laughed and even Daria smiled, but they soon sobered as Father Piero awaited their entire focus. "You are in the house of a fine lady, indeed. But moreover, you are in the house of the Gifted."

"The Gifted?" Vito asked, looking toward Gianni.

Gianni nodded back toward Father Piero. "He shall explain. Be patient."

"When I was but a young man . . ." he began. He unrolled the envelope and slid out the pages, slowly explaining how his mentor had passed to him the sacred secret of the letter, showed him the fresco in the ancient ruins. He concentrated on all who had not heard it before. Beata leaned over his shoulder to get a better look at the portrait that appeared to be the priest, straightened her spectacles, and gasped at the next one that so closely resembled Daria. All were silent, staring with round eyes as Father Piero held up the pages.

Gianni picked up the story. "On the old Roman road from Roma to Firenze, we tracked an evil Sorcerer, a man who had led many in evil rituals."

"Did you catch him?" asked Basilio.

"Nay. He and his followers ambushed us. They killed all five of my men, some of the finest knights I have ever known."

The women gasped and Daria sighed. It pained her to remember the sight of all those fine men, in the prime of life, never to breathe or love or sing again on this earth. And then she remembered Gianni, on the brink of death. . . .

"You were that knight on the road," Basilio said. "The one pictured in the fresco!"

"Our lady here came to me, Bormeo flying high overhead," Gianni said, pacing now before the fire. "I was at death's door, my eyesight dimming, and she brought me back."

"Brought you back?" Lucan asked.

"Healed me in miraculous fashion. I had wounds here and here," he said, raising an arm, gesturing toward his ankle. "The arrows were like none I had seen. The archers were uncommonly adept at their dark art. Had our lady not been present, I would have died alongside my men."

"You used your herbs," Vito said to Daria, clearly hoping there would be some earthly explanation.

She shook her head. "Holy oil. And prayer."

"And Gianni was not the first she healed," Father Piero said, rising. "There was a nun at the convent."

"And the boy in Siena," said Basilio.

"As well as that beggar on the road here . . ." said Rune, understanding and fear washing over his face.

"And two nights past, the old farmer's woman," said Lucan slowly.

Vito crossed himself and rose, pacing in a dark corner. "A

healer. Not just a herbalist. But a true healer. There will be some who claim she is a witch! Beggin' your pardon, m'lady."

"We are aware of that," Gianni said, glancing her way. "It is part of the reason we need to keep this gifting a secret for a time."

"But I am just the beginning," Daria said, leaning forward. "Father Piero has the gift of wisdom; we must all listen to him when he speaks. Gianni has the gift of great faith—we can rely on his faith to bolster our own." She lifted her eyes to meet his.

"There is more," Piero said. "Lady Daria discovered this, two days past," he said, gesturing for her to hand him her Bible. He held it up for all of them to see. "This Bible was given to Daria's great-grandfather, nearly sixty years past. While reading it, she saw something she hadn't seen in all her years of studying it. Here, on the front pages." He opened the book for all to see. "It is the peacock, the herald of this household, the symbol of the d'Angelos' *contrada* in Siena. It is also an ancient Christian emblem that symbolized resurrection. Saint Augustine believed a peacock's flesh had antiseptic qualities—that even buried, it did not corrupt. The peacock's feathers are shed each summer, but return even more luminous and beautiful than before.

"At the feet of each of the three figures in the fresco, there was a peacock. Here, in the border of the illumination on the letter itself, you see the distinctive eye and colors of a peacock feather, repeated, over and over. And if you look back here, to this Bible, you can see words among the feathers."

The group crowded around, all trying to see. "They are in the white space, not written out. But can you see them? *Sapientiam.* Wisdom," he pointed. "*Sanem.* Healing. They're all here—faith, visions, discernment, miraculous powers, prophecy. Again, in the same order as the other maps we have been given. It is a listing of our Gifted, already present here, and those who are yet to come."

Beata crossed herself, over and over, ashen faced. Her sister did the same. Aldo paced in the aisle. The knights frowned or smiled with looks of awe or consternation.

Zola began to chant in praise, falling to her knees with her arms upraised, whispering as tears streamed down her face. Gradually, her words became intelligible, but her face alight in peace and joy told them what they needed to know.

"Our Zola is obviously gifted with tongues, speaking a heavenly language that flows about us, strengthens us," Father Piero said. "Do not let it frighten you. Absorb it, sense it in your ears as you would sense a musical note. Perhaps others will exhibit this gift in time. Perhaps one or two of you will soon be able to interpret her words. But I am counting on the fact that you all exhibit signs of great faith, of service. Those are two of the most important gifts of all."

The men who stood gradually sat down in their chairs. "Why? Why would God bring us together?"

Father Piero's eyes roamed over the ancient script and he shook his head. "It is not entirely clear. We have here only the first portion of the letter and it reads partially as prophecy, partially as a letter. It tells only of the Gifted gathering, in part to usher in change. Just as it begins to tell how they will usher in change, beyond telling of Christ's great love, it cuts off. The rest is missing."

"Missing!" Basilio said with a scoff. *"Perfecto."*

"It is potentially a letter penned by Saint Paul himself, but we do not know. It is unlike any other of Paul's letters, similar in verbiage but dissimilar in style, content. Perhaps it is why the Church fathers never embraced it, never included it in the Holy Canon."

"So it is not endorsed by the Holy Roman Church?" Vito asked.

"Nay. I am not certain it has even been examined."

Ugo rose and paced, running a hand through his thin black hair. "Could this not easily be an instrument of the devil? Could we not as easily be succumbing to his dark plan as we are to bringing in God's holy light?"

"A worthy question," Father Piero said. "But nay. I have lived with this document for decades, prayed over it, dissected the words, the phrases. There is nothing that is incompatible with the rest of the Holy Scriptures. It emphasizes following Jesus, above all others. But it also encourages us to live as living sacrifices to the Christ, each and every day."

"I am not a sacrifice," growled Basilio, bringing a fist to his chest. "I am a knight."

"Indeed," Father Piero said. "The question remains, would you sacrifice yourself if Christ himself asked you to do so?"

Basilio laughed again, eyes wide, mouth aghast. Then abruptly, he shut it. "If the Lord asked me to do so, I suppose I would."

"And would you lay your life down for your friends, your lady?"

Basilio looked about the table and nodded, slowly. "I would."

Father Piero stared down at the letter and then again to the knight. "There may come such a time. I want to be very clear here. There is a battle before us. Perhaps many."

Rune sat back, hands behind his head. "Against whom?"

"Flesh. And spirit."

"And what is a knight to do against spirit?" Rune returned.

"Pray," Father Piero said lowly. "Pray and pray and pray some more."

"And yet it is the words that bespeak of power—clearly power within the Gifted but moreover in all Christian people that will unnerve our brothers in the Church, mayhap awaken our dark enemy to fight us before we are strong."

"We are but thirteen, counting the boy," Rune said. "How can we take on such enemies?"

"That is why we must put off a confrontation as long as possible," the priest said. "We must learn to draw more fully upon God's own strength, more and more each day. We will have what we need, in the Lord's time. If God is for us, who can be against us?"

"If God is for us, who can be against us?" Gianni repeated, pausing over each word. He looked about the room, looking into the eyes of each one present. He held out his fist before him. "If God is for us . . ." he led loudly.

"Who can be against us?" they said together. And all laid their hands atop his.

CHAPTER NINETEEN

DARIA awakened the next morn to the clattering of horses' hooves in the courtyard, the gruff sounds of male greeting. Four, five horses, by the sound of it. She pulled back her thin blanket and left her bed to go to the window, edging open the shutter. When she saw Vincenzo, her heart pounded with joy and she was rustling through her chest for a gown even before Beata appeared in the doorway.

"Ah, mistress, it is Lord del Buco!" Beata said, pushing the spectacles back up to the bridge of her nose. "He said he came to check on you." She lifted the gown from Daria's fingers and waited for Daria to raise her hands. "I think it is his wife, in truth, who brought him here. One of his men told Vito that she is ailing again."

Daria's smile faded. Tatiana? She shook her head and waited, hoping for that quickening within her that told her she was to heal her too. But it was her stomach that tightened in dread, not her heart.

"Mayhap you are to heal her next, m'lady?" Beata asked, her hopeful eyes magnified by the spectacles.

Daria gave her a rueful look. "I . . . I do not know. In any case, we can go and tend to the dear girl, do our best to ease her symptoms."

"Begging your pardon, m'lady," Beata said hesitantly. "But you cannot heal anyone you wish?"

"Nay. I'm afraid it is only those that God leads me to heal. I feel not the . . . *inclination* and direction toward Tatiana that I have felt toward the others."

Beata pursed her lips and moved behind her. "A pity, that. Poor Lord Vincenzo may have to bury yet another bride."

Daria closed her eyes at the maid's words, feeling the truth of them slice her heart in agony for her beloved uncle. And poor Tatiana with a lung ailment like the one that plagued the farmer's wife.

Thinking of the farmer's wife gave Daria hope. Perhaps she could use the same poultice . . . perhaps God had simply waited until this hour to save Tatiana, so that both she and Vincenzo would know his holy power.

As Beata finished brushing her hair, Father Piero appeared in the doorway, Hasani just beyond him. The priest stared at her, sorrow washing over his features. "You must not speak of it, m'lady. All of us must keep still. It is . . . it is not the right time. I know Lord Vincenzo is close to your heart, but it is imperative that you remain committed to God's call first and foremost."

Daria brushed past him in irritation. What was this? Challenging her commitment to God's call? Asking her not to tell her guardian, practically her only family in the world, nothing of what she had discovered? Vincenzo had fallen away from routine mass attendance when his second wife died in his arms. Perhaps her news would restore his faith! And if she could successfully heal Tatiana . . .

Hasani stubbornly blocked her way. He agreed? How could they know? Father Piero reached out and caught her hand, pulling her around gently, forcing her to look into his eyes. He shook his head. "I cannot tell you why, daughter, only that we both have a very clear word not to say too much. Keep your discussion to the business at hand. Go to the lady if you must. But do not speak of the Gifted."

Daria pulled her hand away, frustrated. Vincenzo had always kept her confidences, clearly loved her as surely as her own father had loved her. What kind of gift had to be kept as secret from even her most trusted confidant? And yet she sensed the wisdom at the base of Father Piero's words. They rankled, but she understood them too, as truth.

She swallowed hard. Abiding by them would be another matter. . . . Vincenzo had always been skilled in wrestling the truth from her. They had shared the most intimate of confidences when she broke her handfast with Marco. Over the last year, he had become more like an older brother than an uncle. If only he truly were blood kin!

"May we pray before you go to him?" Father Piero asked.

"I confess that I do not feel like praying," she said. There was a visceral pull to the courtyard for her. Vincenzo . . .

"Be that as it may, stand there and let Hasani and me pray over you."

She bowed her head in mock obedience, going through the priest's ministrations in order to be free of him, confessing her guilt in her heart even as she did so. The priest prayed for protection and wisdom and strength from within as they faced the men in the courtyard and soon, anyone else.

He was a good man, a wise man, to be sure. But was this not going too far? Daria lifted a hand to her temple, feeling the tightening of a headache beginning there. "Amen," she repeated after the priest, avoiding his eyes, even more so Hasani's.

"Tread carefully, Daria," he said solemnly. "How and when we move into the world, decisions we make could cost us our very lives."

Daria could not help herself from letting out a derisive sound.

"Does everything have to hold such monumental weight, Father? Could this not simply be an old friend, coming to call upon me out of love and concern?"

Father Piero held her gaze for a moment. "Of course. It could be that. Or it could be used by others for evil. Tread carefully," he repeated. He squeezed her hand and then strode away from her. She met Hasani's disapproving look. "What? Must you stare at me like that? Go, go to a post outside. I do not wish you with me when I greet Lord Vincenzo."

Daria felt cruel as she left her friend behind, but she could not help herself. Suddenly all the men about her irritated her like a thick layer of road dust upon the skin. Was there not a one of them that could simply abide in her household and not prowl about like a cock about his hens? She shook her head. Mayhap this arrangement would not work. Mayhap God intended the Gifted to take another form, rather than all this power in weapon and brawn. Were they not to be a spiritual force? The letter said nothing of physical force.

Seeing Vincenzo at the end of the portico, staring out through the manor gates and down into the valley, warm morning light washing across it in glory, swept away her ill feelings. He turned and opened his arms in greeting, gazing at her with affection. She grinned broadly and rushed to take the tall man's hands, kissing one cheek and then the other, then backing up to smile at him in pleasure and greeting.

"Saints above, Daria, you are more beautiful every time I see you," he said.

"You flatter me, Uncle."

"No, no. You are truly one of the most beautiful from Firenze to Napoli. I swear it. It is no wonder they call you the Duchess."

She brushed past him and stood on the other side of the portico post, looking out to the valley. "It is this place, the joy of midsummer. The first harvest is in and I am somehow . . . edified. Restored."

"Oh, darling girl, I cannot tell you what joy it is to hear such words from you." Gently, he urged her to face him and he looked down at her with those warm eyes, eyes that held power and passion and the sorrow she longed to ease. She closed her eyes and gave in to his touch as he caressed her cheek lovingly. Vincenzo took her hand, then, and tucked it into the crook of his arm, leading her on a walk down the stone portico, away from the curious eyes of everyone who worked in the courtyard.

"You have acquired more men."

"I have," she said. "We return to Siena soon and as you know, some of my neighbors have been less than hospitable of late."

"I resolved the matter with Jacobi myself, several weeks past."

"You did." The news, although expected, still chafed. She was used to Vincenzo looking after her, but it also made her irritable. Did he think she could not yet look after herself? Was there not one man in her life who could see her as capable?

"Indeed." Vincenzo laughed softly, still thinking of Jacobi. "He did not take my warning kindly, but he took it nonetheless. I am most confident that he will give you no more trouble."

"And what of Marco, his claim upon a portion of my estate?"

"He has withdrawn the petition. It was in his political interests to pursue it, Daria; you understand that. But he could not bear to inflict any more pain upon you." He paused and held her gaze steadily. "You must know before your return to Siena that he has married—"

"Married?"

Vincenzo gave a sorrowful shake of his head. "They were handfasted but a month before she conceived. They married a week past."

Daria stared out toward the valley for a long moment, then cleared her throat. There was little more to say about Marco Adimari. It hurt, this turn. But her time with Marco was clearly past. She must think of the present, the future. "Vincenzo, there are others that I must prepare to battle, others who will wish to prey upon a woman alone. You have your own interests, our guild, to protect. You stand to lose much if you stand beside me."

"I swore to your father that I would look after you."

"And well you have," she said gently, turning toward him. "I cannot thank you enough for sending me to the convent when I was so . . . less than myself. But I am now a woman grown, a woman who has loved and lost and survived, a woman with assets, and a woman trained to think for herself."

Vincenzo laughed in delight and crossed his arms. "It is one of our most difficult obstacles in finding you a suitable spouse. My old friend mayhap has injured you by educating you so."

Daria put her hands on her hips. "I think not! Any reasonable male would see it as an asset, not a hindrance. Marco himself loved that we could read together, dialogue, debate. . . . If I may be so bold, m'lord, you yourself have loved that about me."

Vincenzo kept smiling, watching her as she spoke. "I've often thought that we would make a good coupling ourselves, had you come of age or broken your handfast when I too was available. Think of it. You could have been a true baroness instead of the fabled Duchess."

Daria could feel her eyebrow shoot upward. "I can hear the talk in the streets now. 'There goes the barren baroness.' No," she said, shaking her head with a smile. "That would not do at all. My failure to conceive would not bode well for the house of del Buco. You are in as dire need of an heir as are the houses of Adimari and d'Angelo."

"Do not tell me you haven't thought—"

"M'lord, it is hardly a suitable conversation, this. You are married." She shook her head. "It only proves how troubled your heart is, to speak of such things. Tell me, tell me of your heart, of Tatiana." And yet his words echoed through her mind. He thought of her as a potential bride. Thought of her as a woman now, not a niece.

Vincenzo took several steps forward, away from her, and

stared once more to the valley. "Forgive me, Daria." He clenched his fists in anger, pulled at his shirt in a self-loathing manner before bringing one hand to his neck, massaging. "You are quite right. I am not myself." He stared out to the valley and then glanced back at her. "Tatiana is most unwell. I came here to beseech you to come home to Siena now. The foolish doctors from Firenze and Siena—even Milano—have done nought but bring her closer to death's door. I know you and your medicines could bring her some relief, at least. . . ."

Tears edged the corners of his eyes. He was plainly exhausted. How many nights had he stayed by Tatiana's side, hoping and praying? Daria's heart went out to him, knowing what it meant to have a partner rent from your side. It was a physical wound as much as an affair of the heart, and Vincenzo was saying the slow good-bye to his bride just as she had been forced to say to Marco. How well she knew this exquisite pain! Surely it was the reason he forgot himself, spoke to her in such a forthright, unseemly manner.

"We will leave at once, my friend."

Vincenzo's grateful eyes searched hers, tears lacing his dark lashes. He took her hands again and nodded, gratefully. "You bring me hope, Daria. Thank you."

They stared at each other and there was a force between them that startled Daria. "I will pack thee a basket and you must rush home to tend to your wife. I will follow within days, and return here, if necessary. But we will go and see to dear Tatiana. Rest in that knowledge, Uncle. I will be there shortly."

Vincenzo stared at her in misery. He was confused, lost in his pain, casting about for comfort, hope. Surely he did not desire Daria! She was barren!

Without children, all three of their lines would be soon lost, and the fortunes that their fathers and grandfathers before them had struggled to attain would be scattered. For Daria, that was a matter for God to decide. Not having heirs freed her to do what she was about to do—to go where he called her, to do what he bid.

As she walked away from Vincenzo that day, for the first time, she saw her barren state as a blessing rather than a curse.

She glanced over her shoulder at the man, once more looking out upon the valley, lost in thought. Could his unmet desire for heirs mean that God intended to use him too? If he did not intend to spare Tatiana, did that mean God wished him to remain single, unencumbered? Daria shivered. She glanced up at the manor, seeing Father Piero, watching, and bristled. She had kept their secrets. She knew that she was overstepping her bounds in trying to ascertain God's own thoughts, a job only for holy men and women, not a merchant from Siena.

But if God deigned that Vincenzo join their mission, who were they to say no?

CHAPTER TWENTY

GIANNI knew not what troubled Daria, but he could feel her confusion as they drew near the del Buco estate, back in Siena. When the guard opened the broad wooden fortified gates to allow them access, Daria hung back as he and Father Piero entered, staring ahead at the horses tied to the iron rungs on the wall of the stables. Two horses were there, each bearing the mark of the house of Adimari.

Marco Adimari.

Gianni awaited his lady to come alongside them, not looking back, affording her a moment of privacy. It was most unfortunate that the hour she had chosen to come and attend to Tatiana del Buco was the hour that Marco and his wife had chosen to call upon the del Bucos. Father Piero dismounted and looked from Daria to the other horses and then downward, muttering a prayer. A man led his horse into a stable and then came to collect Gianni's.

Gianni moved to Daria and helped her dismount. "Come m'lady. Surely the encounter will be brief."

"It is all right. I can do all things through Christ who strengthens me," she said with a smile. She had been reading Scripture to them all each morning after mass. The household had taken to attending morning and evening services each day, leaving Father Piero to attend the other hours by himself. After breaking their fast, Father Piero read a chapter of Scripture aloud in Latin, and Daria translated it into their native tongue as he did so. For the first time, the Word of God entered the ears and surrounded the heart as none of them had ever experienced. They dared not speak of their household practice. Indeed, uttering the Holy Scriptures in anything but the Church-ordained language of Latin was enough to bring the wrath of the Church down upon their heads. And yet, once it had begun, they could do no other. Hunger to discover other holy words, holy understanding, drew them forward.

Gianni surveyed their surroundings. The del Buco estate was one of the finest he had ever visited. Two men stood on the high porch of the fine house, hands on the hilt of their swords, returning his gaze with bored expressions. One set a foot upon the wall above them, his eyes never leaving Gianni until Daria came into view. Then both men followed her with vivid interest. Gianni moved into their line of vision on purpose, staring upward in silent challenge. *You will leave this one be. You will give her the respect she deserves.*

Father Piero made their introduction at the front door, greeted by a maid who bowed and bid them entry. Another guard introduced himself and led them up sweeping stairs, past the grand salon on the second floor, opening out onto the portico and terrace where the other guards stood, up another floor to the third. This salon was enclosed, with high, narrow windows and but two small, narrow decks, overlooking Siena. The house was four stories tall, even though it was not surrounded by immediate neighbors like the d'Angelo estate in the center of the city. According to custom and security, Gianni assumed the sleeping chambers were on an upper floor.

At the far end, Marco Adimari turned from the light at the window to gaze through the streaming shadows in their direction.

A nondescript woman lounged on a padded bench beside him, moaning over her queasy stomach, the curse of pregnancy. She seemed unaware of the tension in the room, chattering on. But her husband's eyes were on Daria.

Gianni expected Daria to pause, but his lady moved forward in fluid motion, pausing a proper distance before Adimari and curtseying demurely, setting her mouth in a tender, but formal smile. "Lord Adimari," she said.

Marco moved with a start, as if coming out of a dream, pausing two paces from her and bowing in similar fashion. "Lady d'Angelo," he greeted her.

He stared at her as if he wanted to memorize her features, but she was turning toward his bride, who moved from the bench. Gianni wanted to whistle in appreciation. Whatever his lady was feeling within, she showed little without.

Stumbling over his own words, Marco said, "May I . . . May I present my wife, Lady Francesca Adimari?"

The woman stepped forward and took Daria's hands in her own. "Oh, Lady d'Angelo," she said, blushing at the neck. "What a joy it is to meet you. I am, well what I mean to say . . . it is a joy," she finished lamely. Gianni admired her warmth if not her lithe manner with words or decorum.

"Quite," said Daria, smiling toward her. "And may I present my new chaplain and the captain of my guard? Father Piero, Sir de Capezzana, I am pleased to introduce you to Lord and Lady Adimari."

Both bowed toward Gianni and the priest.

"You have come to visit Tatiana?" Lady Adimari said, trying to fill in the sudden, suffocating silence.

"Indeed. Lord del Buco asked me to return to see to his wife. I have brought fresh herbs and medicines from the countryside."

"We have been waiting here ourselves for nigh unto an hour," the woman said. "Mayhap Baroness del Buco will see none of us this day."

Marco looked at Daria with an embarrassed smile. "Francesca," he said to his wife, "I believe Baron del Buco requested that Lady d'Angelo return to the city and attend the baroness as fast as she could."

His wife was very young, but at least she was well meaning. Gianni hoped Daria could see that the girl in no way compared to herself and take some measure of peace in her stature.

The guard again appeared in the doorway, alongside a maid. "You may go up to see her, Lady d'Angelo," he said.

Daria turned back to the Adimaris, focusing on the young bride. Moving quickly, she reached out and gently squeezed her arm. "It was a pleasure to meet you. In time . . . in time I hope that we might be friends." She glanced at Marco and then back at the girl. "And if you need attendance during your time of confinement, I might be of some assistance; at the very least I can give you something to still your heaving stomach. If it is too awkward to see me, rest assured that I will keep you and yours in prayer."

The girl smiled shyly, blushing as her pregnancy was noted in such an obvious way. "You are as kind as Marco told me you were, Lady Daria," she said lowly, bowing in deference.

"And it is obvious that Marco has found a lovely . . . bride. I wish the Lord's richest blessings upon you both."

"And upon you, m'lady," Marco said. He did not glance toward Gianni or Father Piero, only covered Daria with his hungry look. Their parting had obviously been as painful for him as it had been for Daria. Gianni turned and walked alongside his lady, admiring her again for her strength. It was uncommon for an arranged marriage to be so impassioned. For the blessed, love flourished at times, but most often couples dared pray only for affection and nothing more. And to have to part after sharing such love . . .

Gianni looked back at Marco and the man met his glance with eyes full of confusion. Even though he had taken a bride, it appeared that Adimari was behind Daria along the path to inner healing. His love for Daria might assist them, later on their journey. Or could it endanger them?

"That took courage, my dear," Father Piero whispered, offering Daria an arm while holding his robes with the other. They climbed another curving stone staircase to the top floor and Gianni's skin prickled in apprehension. What was next? Why did he have such a reaction to Vincenzo? He had first noticed it when the man had visited the country manor. Was it competition? It was a vain hope, indeed, that a lady such as Daria d'Angelo would ever look upon him as anything more than the captain of her guard. But if she were to do so, Vincenzo was a more likely competitor than Marco. Marco's hands were again tied, and this time more thoroughly because of his bond to his impregnated wife. But Vincenzo . . . unless God acted quickly, Tatiana was unlikely to survive another fortnight. And Vincenzo was closer to Daria's heart than any other that he had seen. The only thing that would keep the two apart would be Daria's inability to bear children. So if that was the driving force behind del Buco's life, and that unavoidably kept him from Daria as surely as it had driven her from Adimari, then why the apprehension? He shoved his unsettled feelings aside and greeted Vincenzo with a deferential nod as Daria kissed him and Father Piero was led by the maid to meet Tatiana.

Gianni took position as guard at the door, staring straight ahead. There was a small salon on this top floor, by the staircase, but it was dark. Judging from the light streaming through doorways along the edge, the windows had been reserved for the sleeping quarters. As his eyes adjusted, he noted fine paintings that adorned the walls, making them appear as if they were draped with high-caliber weavings, hung from painted pegs at the ceiling. The paintings were throughout the house—wherever there was not a true weaving—something he had not seen in but the finest of estates. Only princes could afford true weavings hanging on all walls. Lesser nobility simulated their taste in style.

Gianni preferred the comforting ochre of aging plaster, himself. Warm woods. Rich carvings. The paintings felt false to him. He stared harder into the darkness, listening to Daria's soothing voice as she spoke to Tatiana and the woman coughed so hard she fainted.

"She has broken ribs, coughing this hard. . . ." Daria's voice carried easily over the wooden floors and Gianni winced at the thought of it. "The doctors?"

"All they can tell me is that she is riddled with the cancer. They are amazed . . . we are all amazed that my bride still . . ." His voice cracked and Gianni frowned.

"It is all right, Vincenzo," she said tenderly.

"Please, I have need of warm water." A maid appeared and scurried past him, down the stairs to the kitchen.

"They bled her, Daria. While I was with you in the country, they took her to the hospital. Set leeches all across her beautiful skin . . ."

"I can see that," she said softly. "Bleeding can drain the body of the dark humors, but Tatiana . . ." She sighed and stroked Tatiana's forehead. "Vincenzo, will you do me the kindness of allowing me time alone with your wife and my priest?"

There was a pause and then Vincenzo appeared at the doorway, striding out of the room but then leaning against the wall as if in pain, closing his eyes. Was he ill himself? Or merely grieving? Gianni forced himself to stay still, say nothing, keeping his eyes upon Daria through the doorway.

Vincenzo came toward him and passed by, never looking his way. But he paused just past his shoulder. "Never give your heart to a woman, Sir de Capezzana. They steal it from your very chest." He descended down the stairs then, but his words hung in the air as a question for Gianni.

Did the man speak of his wife? Or of Daria?

cb cb cb

DARIA and Father Piero stayed with Tatiana for hours. Vincenzo came for as long as he could bear, then left, then returned again.

For every notch they wrestled back, pulling Tatiana toward life, they seemed to slip three notches. They had prayed for hours, administered poultice and steaming vapors, but Daria felt helpless against this attack. It was as if they were taking proper action, but it was meaningless.

"God is not in this room," Daria said, looking wearily in Father Piero's direction. "What are we not doing? Where are we failing?"

"There is not a room that God cannot enter. But there are rooms where he must enter uninvited. He only does this at times. Most often, he wishes to be welcomed, sought."

Daria stared at him, trying to decipher what he was saying. Surely they had invited the Savior in, again and again. What was keeping the ultimate Healer away? "Sometimes, I think our efforts are useless, despite what I have seen. At times he simply wishes to take his beloved home," she whispered, bending to wring out a wet cloth and sponge off Tatiana's sweating face. The woman was cold, but drenched in perspiration. Her hair, once the glory of Siena as a crown of golden-brown waves, was plastered against her head and neck.

"Do not lose hope, Daria. We must hope and pray. But at times, God says no to our prayers in order to give us the best of yeses—a welcoming home to heaven."

That made Daria cry for a bit and her shoulders shook as she covered her face in her hands. After a moment, Daria asked for more water and soap laced with lavender. Lovingly, she washed Tatiana's hair, lathering the long strands and rinsing them in buckets of warm water. The young woman awakened then, her breath coming in a high whistle as she inhaled and a low whine as she exhaled. She smiled at Daria, squeezing her hand, thanking her wordlessly for understanding.

"Fear not, dear one," Daria said through tears. This bond of death, hovering outside Tatiana's door, was powerful. "You will soon be free, I promise. I promise. You shall be either healed and at your husband's side or in heaven itself. *Fear not,*" she said, kissing her forehead in empathy. Her tears dropped to Tatiana's skin and glittered in the candlelight. The woman's furrowed brow eased into peace as she once again slept. The tonic was helping her, at least, with rest.

Vincenzo came in, then, and spying his wife's lovely hair, drying in shining waves about her on the pillow, had to turn and walk back out, his face in his hands.

ॐ ॐ ॐ

DARIA looked to the empty, dark doorway. "Do you think that God punishes us, Father?" she whispered dully. "That he sends us tragedy so that he might prove that he is God? That even the Gifted's hands are tied until he frees them?"

The priest mulled over her words. "God need not prove anything. He is God. There is nothing beside him, so it is difficult to compare his ways to anything we know. And yet the Word says we were made in his image. So think of it this way. A father would never push his child down, and yet can use a scraped knee as a lesson to be more careful in the future. I see him not punishing us with tragedy, but using tragedy for his gain, our gain. Tragedy is as much a part of this life as breathing, Daria. You know this, have experienced it firsthand. If we allow it, he can use our sorrows to winnow away the dead branches."

"So that we might be fruit-bearing vines." She stared into the darkness, her hand falling to her belly, remembering that God had promised her a child. That promise seemed distant, otherworldly, impossible. "Winnowing away. Such as my parting from Marco. As much as it eviscerated me, it brought me to you . . . to realization of my gifting, to our gathering."

"Right."

"Could he not use this moment to bring life to Vincenzo's vines? I am a healer, am I not? Why has he not chosen to heal, here?"

"The Lord's ways are a mystery, indeed, Daria. We may be of the Gifted, but it does not mean we can discern all his ways. We might awaken tomorrow to find that he has used you, after all, to heal this woman. Or we may find that she has gone on before us, and he will use grief to get to Vincenzo's heart again. We must remain confident that our God can use all things, *all things*, for good."

"All things," she whispered. "It is an attitude of hope."

"It is an attitude of survival."

රු රු රු

FOOLS. Vincenzo dug his nails into his palms in an effort not to give in to the sobs. God was robbing him, again. He had robbed him of his first wife and son, on the eve that they were to greet his first heir. God had robbed him of his second wife, afflicting her with a stomach ailment that even Daria's mother could not ease. She had screamed, screamed at such a high, deafening pitch that when he closed his eyes, Vincenzo could still hear it.

Countless nights, he had stood outside her door, sweating, panting, pacing, fighting against the urge to enter her room and place her pillow atop mouth and nose . . . he had dreamed of slicing open her neck and letting her bleed to death. Surely it was a kindness compared to such that she suffered! But each time, Daria's mother had been there, praying, standing watch, hoping against hope that God would intervene.

But he had not. And now, Tatiana.

Tatiana. They had been the talk of Siena. He, powerful. She, his beauty, his light. It had been promised to him—deep within, as if from God—that she would be the one to bring him longevity, a part in history with a bloodline that lived on. They would have strong, handsome sons. Beautiful, coveted daughters. And a business that would gain in fame as well as wealth and power. Once he saw her, he had placed his heart in her hands, knew that she was his future.

And now she lay dying.

Vincenzo cried angry tears, sinking to the floor even as Daria and the priest once again commenced their hopeless prayer.

His beautiful, laughing, singing Tatiana.

His joy. His prize.

Slipping away from him . . .

Vincenzo rose then, stumbling down the stairs and outside the manor, past the guards and maids, out into the deep shadows that drew him, welcomed him. . . . The cool air becalmed his hot nerves. He made his way to the city gates and outward, walking the well-worn paths of shepherds and villagers bringing their wares to the city. Remembering the day he had brought Tatiana home, remembering, remembering.

ଙ ଙ ଙ

SHE was leaving. Her breath came in labored measures, with frightful pauses that had them holding their breath with her. She was frightfully pale, even in the warm candlelight. "Vincenzo," Daria called.

When no one answered, she called, louder, "Vincenzo . . ."

She looked at Father Piero, hands cradling one of Tatiana's, praying. She closed her eyes and listened to the words in Latin. Last rites.

"Vincenzo!"

Desperate sobs leaving her, she rose and stumbled out of the room on wooden legs, finding herself surprised at the empty salon. Where was Vincenzo? Gianni?

"Vincenzo! Gianni!" she called down the stairs, through choking sobs. She had failed. The woman would die. She had failed her dearest friend, this woman's husband. How could the Lord have let her fail him?

She moved down the stairs, swallowing past the knot in her throat. "Lord, Lord, bring an end to this awful night. Welcome Tatiana into your arms, but let Vincenzo—"

She gave in to sobs then. Her friend, her dearest friend's beloved, was about to die! She stumbled onward, tears blinding her, taking several steps at a time, nearly falling, until Gianni was there, catching her in his arms. "Daria? What is it, m'lady?"

Daria had no room for decorum. She leaned into his arms, absorbing his strength like a fainting maid. She fought to cease her tears, but was overwhelmed by the sobs that gnawed at her aching throat. "Please . . . Tatiana . . . she is . . . she will die at any moment. I must . . . we must find Vincenzo."

Gianni leaned back from her, looking at her helplessly in the flickering candlelight. "He left, m'lady. An hour past. Stumbled outside. I know not where he went."

"Ask his guards. Find him, Gianni," she said, forcing herself to step away, clinging to his hand. "Find him. Please. We haven't much time."

He turned from her then, rushing outside, calling to the guards outside.

Daria turned, and with stiff steps, forced herself back to Tatiana's deathbed. What was to come was out of her hands. With each footfall she prayed that God would grant her last request this night. That Vincenzo would arrive back in time to kiss his wife's lips before they were cold in death.

ↂ ↂ ↂ

"Hurry, man, we must find your master," Gianni said, rushing down the stone steps in the moonlight.

The guard roused from his position and stood. "The lady?"

"We have but moments before she passes from this earth."

"He left, with one guard trailing him. I think they were heading for the city gates."

"Let us go then. We must not tarry."

The man joined him, and they hurried down the rest of the stairs, down into the courtyard, where their horses still remained, tied to the iron rungs. "Do not pause to saddle a horse. Take Lady

Daria's," Gianni said. "She wants nothing more than Lord Vincenzo to return before it is too late."

The guard did as he bid without question. Another opened the
gates and they galloped out, the horses making an eerie, hollow
sound upon the bricks as they departed.

It was good that the del Buco guard was before him. He took
one turn and then another that Gianni was not familiar with, obvious shortcuts his master would take to the city gates. They rode
hard and fast, not encountering another soul at this hour, even galloping through the marketplace where normally crowds gathered
around fruit vendors and fishmongers. At the city gate, a guard
challenged them, but after a curt word, lazily opened the gates,
muttering under his breath.

Gianni paused just outside. "You shall not shut the gates. We
will be back momentarily with Lord del Buco."

"I cannot do as you ask! It is my sworn duty to keep the city
gates shut."

"Be that as it may, know that the time it takes you to open them
again will be the same time I will take to exact payment in a beating. Choose well."

The thin man raised his hands in surrender. Even in the thin
moonlight, Gianni could see the whites of his wide eyes. It gave
him a moment's reprieve of humor.

But as they galloped forward, through the winding streets of
the poor man's village and down through a graveyard, to where
the rocky hills gave way to nothing until one reached Firenze, his
grin quickly faded. He was seeking a man, a man who would be
forced back to his wife's deathbed, only to say good-bye.

Memories from his years as a knight of the Church cascaded
through his mind. Son ripped from a mother's arms . . . wife from
husband . . . father from daughter. Each time he had dealt the condemned their sentence with an underlying sense of righteousness,
not always understanding, but bowing to the Church's greater understanding. But there was none of that sense here. No, as they

reached Lord del Buco and his guard faltered, he felt cold inside, weary, as he approached the man. "Come, m'lord. Daria sends for you. There is no time to tarry."

Vincenzo looked outward. "I cannot. I must not."

Gianni paused, unable to find words to coerce him.

"Have you ever buried a loved one, Sir de Capezzana?" The man stared at him with tired eyes.

"Comrades. A grandmother."

"But nary a wife?"

"Nay." Gianni looked to his feet, kicking at the rocks. "Baron del Buco, we really must go. . . ."

"You have never heard a woman cry out as if she had been flayed open? Not felt her life slip from beneath your fingertips?" His tone was becoming hard, angry.

Gianni took a step to the left, spreading his legs in a subtle defensive position. "Nay, m'lord." He crossed himself. "May I never suffer as you do now. As you apparently have before."

Vincenzo turned to the valley and gave a guttural cry, fists clenched, dropping to his knees. It was as if he were wrestling the devil himself. Upon the ground, he bent and sobbed.

Gianni gave him a moment, waiting until the wracking sobs seeped into weeping. Then Vincenzo's guard stepped forward and grasped his master's shoulder. "Come, m'lord, take my horse. I will return to the estate by foot. If you do not bid thy bride farewell, you most surely will regret it."

Vincenzo hung his head, then wearily rose to his feet, tears still streaming down his face. He had loved her, then. Or they were the tears of anger, of the fiercely vanquished? Gianni was uncertain.

He only knew that the man defeatedly climbed atop Daria's horse and followed Gianni through the city gates—cracked and immediately open as they approached—and back to the del Buco estate.

Gianni gazed up to the fourth floor in fear as they approached, concerned that all would be dark by now, the candles extinguished as was custom with last breaths. But still, candlelight flickered from the three open windows, dancing in the evening's summer breeze. She yet lived. His heart jumped, hoping that Daria had once again healed. That this man did not go to say good-bye to the condemned, but to greet the pardoned.

And yet, as another guard led Vincenzo up the stairs, urging him forward when he paused, Gianni could feel the chill of death in the air as they rose. He would have left them there, alone to say their parting words, had not Daria reached for his hand. He helped her to her feet and she clung to his arm.

She cried as Vincenzo lowered himself to Tatiana's bedside, and Gianni wiped his nose, feeling tears edge his throat for the first time. Surely if Daria cared so, so should he. Father Piero receded into a dim corner, praying in Latin in a quiet chant, and periodically forming the sign of the cross toward the lady's deathbed like a dark angel of death.

"Enough!" Vincenzo cried, thrusting a savage hand in Piero's direction. "No more, priest! The die has been cast. Your words will not alter the hands of fate. Please . . ." His tone faded from anger to utter sorrow in a breath. "Please."

Father Piero fell silent.

Vincenzo took Tatiana's hand and she opened her eyes partially, and looked toward him. Tears streamed down his face. "Fare thee well, Tatiana. I have loved you." She gave him a tender smile, took a half breath, the barest of whistles now, her back arching as if reaching for the rest of it, and then slowly, slowly, she released and lay still. Her lips remained parted and Vincenzo leaned forward, tears dripping to them and sliding inside, like nectar into a hummingbird's beak. Quietly, reverently, he kissed her still lips and then sank to the ground, his back to the bed that held his dead bride.

Gianni stood transfixed, putting an arm around Daria when she leaned into his chest, shuddering as she cried harder still. Father Piero moved from the corner and crossed Tatiana's arms and closed her eyes, making the sign of the cross and praying again.

"Leave us," Vincenzo growled, still facing away. "Leave us. Please. Be gone from this house. I need . . . please." He bent to cradle his head in his hands, elbows on knees.

"Vincenzo—" Daria began.

He raised one hand. "Please. You have done all you could. Leave me and come to me in three days."

Daria nodded, a movement that Vincenzo could not see. But he appeared not to care. Gianni led her from the room, Father Piero trailing behind.

Chapter Twenty-one

Daria donned her mother's white mourning clothes as if her own kin had passed. For two days, she did not speak, barely ate. Father Piero watched from afar, vaguely troubled. It was not good that she be so tied to any man. There were unaccounted tasks ahead, roads they must travel. Would Vincenzo hold her back?

With Daria remaining, in large measure, in her quarters, Hasani had disappeared as well. Gianni had thrown himself into completing the renovations to the city estate, bringing in workmen who specialized in brickwork, woodwork, and ironwork. The household teemed with activity this morning, the knights' and workmen's jostling and laughter echoing oddly among the silent halls. A pall was cast upon their evening gatherings in the dining hall by the lady's conspicuous absence.

When Daria missed Lauds and then Prime—a service she rarely missed—then Terce and Sext, Father Piero went in search of her. He passed Hasani's quarters on the second floor, heading for the third, and noticed the tall African stooped over his work. Judging by the inkwells at the top of his desk and fine parchment to his side, he was drawing something. Was he a copyist or illuminist? Father Piero smiled and shook his head. Most unusual. He would have to ask the man to show him his work at some point; perhaps he could make inroads with the silent man.

Father Piero reached the third floor, the floor that housed Daria's rooms, the solarium, and the empty wing of family rooms. He topped the last step and coughed loudly, then rang a small bell.

"Who passes?" she called.

"Father Piero," he responded. "I am concerned for you."

She appeared then in the dim hallway, hovering just inside the doorframe to her suite. "No need to be concerned, Father. I am well. Only . . . wrestling with sorrow."

"Indeed," he said with a nod. "Might you meet me, here in the solarium? I thought we could share a cup of tea," he paused to lift the pot at his side in gesture, "and some Scripture that might bring you succor."

He held his breath, waiting for her to respond, and after a moment she said, "Very well. I shall meet you there."

Piero hid a small smile of victory and moved into the salon, a very comfortable sitting room, vaguely feminine in décor. He set down the metal teapot, far from the delicate pages of the Bible— and went to the shuttered windows, opening them to the evening air. There were seven windows, as tall as Nico, as wide as a man's spread hand, coming to an arched point at the top in gothic style. They were easily defensible, too narrow for a man to gain access, wide enough to shoot an arrow through. And they provided some light, long beams cast across the stone floor to the other side of the salon. He stared outside, considering his words to the lady, praying.

He heard her footsteps and turned, smiling gently. "Daughter. Thank you for seeing me." He felt awkward, like an ill-trained suitor. He had spent years in the company of women who hung upon his very word, but never had he needed to console. That task was always left to the abbess. When she sat back in a chair, hand to mouth, gazing out through the windows, he poured tea himself, usually a woman's duty, noblewoman or not.

"You will return to Lord del Buco on the morrow?"

"I had intended to do so. But I cannot imagine having the courage."

Piero sat back, absorbing her words. "Ofttimes, God asks more of us than we expect to give. But it is in those times that we learn how great a God we truly serve."

She sighed and rose, walking with slow strides to the nearest window. She was truly lovely, worthy of a Sienese portrait in oil. But even the finest of artists would not be able to capture her beauty, her vitality, even when subdued. She brimmed with life, perhaps a vestige of her gifting. And yet she felt utterly alone, removed. He had to reach her.

"Daria, we are on a path together that we cannot turn from."

"I am aware of it."

"This path might call us to leave loved ones, your beloved home. I know not where the Lord wishes us to go."

"He wants me to heal Old Woman Parmo, the one who sells cloth in the market."

Piero sat up straighter. "He told you this?"

A humorless sound left her lips. "On the very night that Tatiana died. As we came home, through the market, at her stall, he was very clear. She is to be the next one."

Silence moved between them.

"And you are wondering why an old woman? Why not Baroness del Buco?"

"Indeed." She let out an exasperated sigh. "Why a woman old in my mother's own day, a woman who has buried most of her own children, and not Vincenzo's love?" She waved her hands wildly, pacing. "Why not one of the kindest and loveliest of women? Why not preserve Vincenzo's hope for an heir? Why kill love?"

She continued to pace, obviously working on forming her thoughts into words. Piero waited silently.

"I do not understand, Father. I do not understand this God we are called to serve. Where is the justice? Where is the logic?"

Piero raised a steaming cup to his lips and then sat back. "You are not yourself. You are overcome with grief."

"Nay! This is not grief! This is fury!"

Piero took another sip. "Please. Come. Sit. Let us drink tea, and pray and discuss this in calm fashion."

"Calm fashion? Calm fashion!" She laughed again, this time with bitter tears that rolled down her face. She wiped them away angrily. "Explain it to me, and I shall be becalmed."

Piero rose and went to the opposite window, on the far side of the room, sensing she needed distance. "I cannot."

"Cannot? Or will not?"

"Nay. There is little to say. I do not know why God takes action at times and remains conspicuously absent in others."

"But you are a priest. You have dedicated your life to studying the Word . . . God himself."

"It is true. But the mysteries of God cannot be defined. Only so much is known to us; we see but through a glass darkly—"

"It is not enough. How can he call us to such a radical path, ask such things of us as have *already* been asked, and not bring us into a deeper understanding, a deeper knowledge?"

It was Piero's turn to laugh lightly. "Do you not already understand, know him better than before, Daria?"

She did not answer, but he could feel her assent. "My daughter, we *will* know him, more and more each day if we earnestly seek him, honestly accept how he acts or how he fails to act. It is the heart of discipleship. Painful at times, glorious at others. Seeking him in all things. Difficult at times, indeed. But well worth it. Have faith, daughter. Have faith."

Daria swung her head back and forth as if struggling with his words. She closed her eyes and tipped up her chin, then lowered it to look at the priest. "I believe I am in need of confession."

"Confess, then," he said, holding her gaze steadily in his.

"Right here? Right now?"

"Right here, right now. Tonight, alone, in your suite. In the garden come morningtide."

"With you."

"Nay. Aye. However you are so moved. You do not need me to speak to your Lord. You've said yourself that he already speaks in your ear."

Daria blanched, her lips parting in dismay. "Do you think me mad?"

"Nay!" Piero jumped up. "It is glorious!"

But she was not looking at him. "Father, what you say is blasphemy. The Holy Church condones only confession before a priest, proclaiming we are in need of the holy brothers to make our case to the Christ."

It was Piero's turn to pace. "Have you read any Scripture that supports such doctrine? Does not Paul speak of it in his epistle to the Romans? Does not Acts clearly say that all one must do is believe in Christ? 'Believe in the Lord Jesus, and you will be saved?' We are in need of leadership in the Church, yes, to make sure we do not stray. But it is not necessary for salvation. Your pontiff is not your bridge to God, Daria; Jesus is your bridge to God."

"It is heresy, what you speak," Daria whispered.

Piero nodded and smiled. "*Si.* Heresy. Heresy. Or . . . is it? Have we been led astray? Has the Church become so enraptured with itself that it has forgotten to be enraptured by the Savior himself?"

Daria shook her head, backing away. "You speak of yet another reason to bring the Church's wrath down upon this house."

"Mayhap. I begin to see that there are many reasons that they will one day arrive at our door."

Daria paced on the opposite side of the room, then moved to the chair and sank down into it. She poured a cup of tea and sat back, lost in thought. At last, she spoke. "There truly is no Scripture that supports the idea of confession through priestly help?"

"Support, yes. Other Scriptures could certainly be interpreted that way. It was an honest practice once, I am certain. An effort to protect the people. The ignorant might be dissuaded from truth, persuaded by lies, without priestly direction. . . .

"I met a brother outside the Duomo last night, a man I hadn't seen since we were boys in seminary. Lady Daria, he whispered of corruption in the Church, terrible decisions, misguided choices." Piero shook his head back and forth in sorrow, his mind back on the priest's tormented face. "Here in Siena, as well as in Roma, Avignon. We are holy men, but we are but men, as fallible as any other.

"Most people cannot read—a decided disadvantage in finding God's true way. But, Daria," he paused to lean over the back of the chair, "you can read Latin, Greek. You have the education, mental capacity of three ordinary priests, combined. You read the Scriptures with me and decide for yourself. Look for reasons to support our current direction. Look for what I have seen. Ask God to show you truth. See what God illuminates for you. I do not claim to know God's mind. But I believe that he has shared with me . . . truth."

Daria raised a hand to her forehead, brushing aside rich, brown coils from in front of her brow. "You ask too much."

"Nay. You are perfectly suited for this task, daughter. Together, we will decipher what God wishes us to know. Perhaps bring Gianni into it. And then together, we will decide who we tell. It is part of our task as the Gifted. . . ."

"To know the Word, the Word that is Life itself. To know the Word and tell others of it," she quoted from the first page of the letter.

Piero shot her a smile. "You remember the second sentence, after having seen it but twice?"

She met his gaze. "Perhaps if it is leading my chaplain to challenge the basic tenets of the Holy Church, it is time that I study every one."

ზ ზ ზ

CARDINAL Boeri looked up from his desk as two knights escorted a bedraggled man inside the chambers. "What is this?" he demanded.

"Your Grace, this man maintains that he brings a missive from Sir Gianni de Capezzana," one said.

"It is!" said the small man. "It is from him! It has his mark upon it!"

The cardinal rose. In the corner, the bishop did too. He strode toward the trio. "How did you come by this letter?" he demanded.

"The knight gave it to me. Said if I brought back your mark, he'd give me more pay for my trouble. Said to give the letter to no one but you."

"Where is he? This knight?"

"I met him in the country outside Siena."

"Siena. How long ago?"

"A fortnight, mayhap a little longer," he said with a shrug of one shoulder.

The cardinal chided the man. "Siena is but three days' travel from here. Why did you tarry?"

"I had other business to attend to," he said defensively.

"Mm-hmm. In every tavern between the cities most likely," he said, wrinkling his nose in disgust. The cardinal took the letter from the man and turned it over. The de Capezzana seal. He waved a hand over his shoulder. "Take him out. Give him the seal he requests, and then show him to the gates."

The bishop hovered near the cardinal as he tore it open and read. "He's alive. Still on the trail of the Sorcerer." He smiled at the bishop. "If the Sorcerer is on the brink of doing battle with the prophesied ones, mayhap Gianni will discover both." He clapped the bishop on the shoulder. "My brother, God is at work, here, looking to our best interests. I am certain that de Capezzana's loyalties may lead us to both. And with the Gifted and the Sorcerer both in hand, we shall use it to strengthen our position in bringing the papacy home."

CHAPTER TWENTY-TWO

VINCENZO was not in the house when Daria arrived. The stable boy had told her the baron had gone out for a ride that morning and not yet returned. Daria welcomed no debate when she told her guards, Ugo and Vito, to remain behind. She nodded to Hasani, whom she trusted to be discreet.

Shifting uneasily, obviously torn between their captain's order and their lady's request, one stayed in the courtyard and the other followed them into the house, but remained behind on the first floor. The maids led her up the stairs, maintaining a silence that Vincenzo had demanded since the dawn he had awakened a widower. With leaden feet, Daria climbed up the stairs behind them. With Vincenzo having no female relative in Siena, Daria assumed the duty of making the baroness's corpse ready for burial.

The summer heat had made its way through the shuttered windows and on the upper floors, it was stifling. Combined with the odors of a decaying body, Daria had to reach out for a doorjamb and steady herself before entering. She did as the maids before her and covered her face with a handkerchief, concentrating on breathing through her mouth, and moved forward.

Vincenzo refused the customary ceremony of public viewing while Tatiana's body lay in their home, awaiting transfer to the Duomo. Daria saw that he had, however, allowed the maids to dress the baroness in her finest white gown during the first few hours of death. The gown was trimmed in gold, a gown she had worn during their sacrament of marriage, and the sight of it brought fresh tears to Daria's eyes. How happy her friend had been on that day!

She was glad she had washed Tatiana's hair while she still lived. Reverently, she went to Tatiana's jewelry box and opened it. On top was a gold hairpiece—three strands that crossed the head at the crown and held a crispinette at the neck. Daria thought for a moment and then decided against the crispinette. Tatiana's hair was too beautiful. It would be better down in these final hours, regardless of what the old women might deem unseemly when they moved her body to the Duomo for vigil. Vincenzo always found pride over his bride's hair; mayhap this small gesture would bring him some tiny measure of joy.

Daria wished Father Piero were with her. But the last rites had been said. All that remained was to carry Tatiana's body to the Duomo, then see Vincenzo through the vigils, the Office of the Dead, and burial. The bishop himself would oversee the ceremony, and Tatiana's body would be taken to a coveted part of the cemetery for burial.

She brushed Tatiana's hair until it fell in smooth waves, then placed the gold crown atop her head. She took a tiny bit of French rouge and dabbed a bit on her cold, blue lips, and a bit more on her cheeks, making her appear more lifelike, less ghostly. Daria had thought that this tending would make her teary again, but she felt empty, numb, as if she had no heart, no more tears to cry even if she wanted to.

"Why would you do such a thing?" Vincenzo said suddenly, from just behind her.

Daria looked up in surprise, feeling unaccountably guilty. It was custom. . . .

"Why?" He took her arm and lifted her roughly to her feet and then a step away from Tatiana.

"Uncle, I was simply—"

"I did not ask for this!" he thundered.

"No," Daria stammered. "No. Please forgive me. I, I assumed—"

"You assumed I would want my dead bride to appear lively?"

"Vincenzo, I only meant—"

"What? To rend my heart even further?"

Daria's hand went to her mouth and she shook her head in horror. "Nay. Never." The tears came then, the tears she thought were all dried and gone, just as Vincenzo leaned one arm against a wall, sobbing. Dimly, Daria noticed Hasani, hovering in the hall outside the room. But her eyes were drawn to Vincenzo, rocking back and forth.

She came behind him, wrapping her arms around him from behind, crying with him, and after a minute he turned, taking her into his arms as he wept. A quarter of an hour later, their sobbing ceased, but still he held onto her. Daria prayed, prayed for his entire household, for peace, for healing. That was when an odd thought entered her mind and heart.

Leave the dead to tend the dead. You are to bring life to those who seek life.

She longed to shake it from her mind, but it remained, echoing through her head like a shout in the hallowed halls of the Duomo.

Leave the dead to tend the dead. Her eyes raced around the room, looking for someone else who might be speaking, but only Hasani hovered in the doorway. She gently pulled away from Vincenzo, but still, he held onto her hand.

"Daria, forgive me . . ."

Leave the dead to tend the dead.

". . . I . . . I do not know myself. I know you only meant to help, dear one."

You are to bring life to those who seek life.

"Vincenzo," she said. "I will return at dusk to accompany you to the Duomo."

He nodded and slowly let go of her hand. She swallowed hard. "You . . . you will be all right? Do you wish me to remain with you in vigil?"

Leave the dead to tend the dead.

"Nay."

You are to bring life to those who seek life.

She wished she could bring her hands to her ears, stop the voice. "Father Piero? May I send him to tend to you? Perhaps a man—"

"Nay." He turned lifeless eyes to her. "Go in peace, Daria. Thank you for seeing to Tatiana. Come back to me at dusk. It is . . . enough."

She turned and left him then, no parting word seeming right in her mouth. What did one say to a man who was in such deep despair? Who could only see the morrow's burial ceremony before him?

You are to bring life to those who seek life.

"Do you hear that?" she whispered to Hasani as they went down the steps. She paused to look at him, but he just shook his head and sent her a questioning glance.

Was it God? Speaking to her heart like an angel to a shepherd? Like the burning bush to Moses? Had she failed him by not understanding? She paused on the steps halfway down, wondering if God had urged her to speak to Vincenzo, share with him some Word from Scripture that would bring him peace, assuage his wounds, give him hope. But even now, no Word came to her that seemed enough to send her back upstairs. She wished Father Piero were here!

Hasani touched her arm.

"No, no, it isn't anything. Give it no more thought. Let us get home."

She hurried down the rest of the stairs, past Vito and out into the courtyard. Ugo, surrounded by several of Vincenzo's men and involved in animated banter, jumped to his feet when he saw them.

She glanced at the brothers. "Come, gentlemen. I have need of your music after we take our noon meal. Are you willing?"

"Certainly," Ugo said, while uncertainty laced his eyes. "You wish to continue mourning? I have—"

"Nay," she said, turning to touch his arm. "Nothing that speaks to me of death." She shivered, in spite of herself. "I am longing for joy, light. Not feasting music, mind you. But something with breath to it."

Ugo smiled and nodded at Vito and then at her. "And you shall have it, m'lady. It will be welcome to mine own ears as well."

ↀ ↀ ↀ

THE lady and her guards hurried from the del Buco estate, unaware that Ciro trailed behind them. Halfway home, Lady Daria dispatched the tall, black man on an unknown errand but kept the two other guards near her. At the same time, she raised her arm and the great white falcon rose into the air and circled high above, like a silent sentinel. As they entered the market, they moved to single file, one guard in front and one in back.

Ciro easily trailed them, blending into the crowded street, bending to look at grape or silver among the vendors any time one of them glanced his way. His mission was to know more of this woman, what her connection to the baron was.

He was beginning to think this pursuit was unworthy of his time. In the past week, the lady seemed content to tend to normal business, and of late, her friend, the baron. She certainly had not healed his woman. Mayhap she simply had an eye to assume the dying baroness's position. But he had to agree with the master that it was odd, the preparations the man, de Capezzana, continued to make at the estate, fortifying gate and tower as if expecting impending battle.

Vito glanced back his way suddenly, actually turning in his saddle to gaze about, as if sensing his presence. But Ciro remained calm, moving ahead to yet another vendor, and leading his horse as if he had seen nothing odd. It sent a chill of power down his neck to dare the knight so, to move closer rather than away. If Vito saw his face, he would recognize him, shout out. Ciro's fingers rolled over the hilt of his dagger when he took another three steps, coming closer, smiling as the blood rushed through his veins.

But when Ciro dared to turn again, Vito was peering forward once again, watching as his lady paused over the old woman who sold French linens and their own country's cotton and woolens.

Ciro moved closer, still edging forward until he stood directly across from the lady. He feigned interest in a butcher's newly plucked hens, hanging from their feet at the edge of the vendor's tent, pretended to examine them while he listened to the conversation behind him.

He smiled. The lady was but two feet away now. Apparently, the two brothers were better musicians than guards. Could they not see him right beside their lady? He considered turning and pulling her from her steed, bringing a knife to her throat before her guards even unsheathed their swords. The master would be pleased with his ability to get so close, his capability, his calm demeanor. He was learning much from the master.

"M'lady?" the first guard asked, looking backward to her. "Is there something that I may fetch for you?"

"Nay," Lady Daria said, nudging her mare with her heels. Even as the horse moved forward, her eyes lingered on the old woman, puttering about her stall like a donkey on three legs seeking fresh hay, crippled by the rheumatism.

Why such interest in the old cloth merchantess? Ciro studied her a moment and then watched the Duchess depart. He could have taken her if he had so wished. In one swift move, he could have had her off the mare and pulled her through the crowd. . . . Yes, the master would be pleased. He was maturing as his master taught him, learning to obey his master's will over his own desire. Nothing gave him more pleasure than the combination of a woman's flesh and danger. Daria's ankles showed above her slippers, and he imagined the length of her leg . . . the fabled barren Duchess. Mayhap she only needed the right man in her bed.

He felt the old woman's eyes upon him and casually turned to meet her stare. Her eyes were unwavering. His smile faded into clenched teeth. He didn't like the way she looked at him, looked through him. He fought the urge to slice her neck open like the chickens down the row, take a bolt of her finest linen and make it appear a robbery. Who would miss such an old woman? Surely she would die at any moment anyway.

He took a step toward her and the old woman's eyes narrowed.

Just then, a boisterous French nobleman arrived, parting the crowd, greeting the old woman with a shout and wave as he dismounted. He waved several black attendants forward, each carrying several bolts of cloth atop their heads.

Now was not the time. The old woman would live another day. Perhaps it was for the best. There was something about her that tied her to the Duchess. And if Ciro could find out what it was before he killed her, the master would take even greater pleasure in his actions.

Ꮿ Ꮿ Ꮿ

DISQUIETED, Gianni paced before the gates of the d'Angelo estate as the woodworkers and blacksmiths departed for the day. Daria had expected to return an hour past. Why did she tarry? Had they come across some mishap? Did Baron del Buco keep them there?

The priest emerged through the massive wooden doors and stood there, hands clasped. "What is it, Sir Gianni?"

"I do not know," Gianni said, still pacing back and forth, his hand going to his sword hilt again and again. "I should not have let the lady go without me."

"You had business here. And she did not wish you present. You were fortunate to get her agreement on the other three. Had you insisted upon going, she would have tried to slip out, entirely alone."

Gianni eyed the priest. He already had gleaned her ways as clearly as Gianni had himself. It relieved him that the priest had come to the same conclusions. "Still . . . there is something odd in the air. Like the night Ciro attacked Ugo."

"They are present," the priest said softly.

"Who? Who are present?"

The priest sighed. "Our enemies. Those of the dark." He tossed Gianni a halfhearted smile and cocked one brow. "Not that we are ever apart from them for long, but I too feel their presence. They are watching."

Gianni stopped his pacing then and looked about like a scout suddenly discovering he was being watched himself. "They are here? Nearby?"

"Here. Nearby. Far away. They are everywhere." He shrugged. "We reside in enemy-occupied territory. But it is as God wishes. We must pray for his divine protection and time to seek his desires for us."

Gianni took a step forward. "And the lady? She is in harm's way?"

"Mayhap."

Gianni let out a guttural cry of frustration, tossing his hands in the air. "How can you be so calm?"

Father Piero lowered his voice and slid his eyes left and right, making sure they were still alone. "The blessed Father did not wait hundreds of years to bring us together simply to watch us die. We may suffer, yes, but we shall live. We must live to fulfill the prophecy. . . ."

"Which prophecy?" Gianni said.

Father Piero raised his hand. "We know not the entire prophecy, since we only hold a portion of the letter. But it is time that together we read the rest of the fragment we do have. Find a way to understand and commit to what we know, and not obsess on that we do not. Mayhap the lady will feel up to it this day."

Gianni tapped at the priest's chest. "Whether or not the lady is prepared, you shall read it to me," he said, jabbing at his own chest now. "I must know what there is to know. If battle is soon upon us, and neither wood nor metal will make a difference, then you must prepare us in ways that will."

CHAPTER TWENTY-THREE

"AGAIN, what you propose is heresy," Daria said, staring at her priest across the table. Beata and Agata departed, arms laden with leftover food from the noon meal. But the others all remained, huddled about the main table at the front of the room, on the dais.

" 'Repent and be baptized every one of you, in the name of Jesus Christ for the forgiveness of your sins, and you will receive the gifts of the Holy Spirit.' That is the entirety of the text. From Acts, no mention of priests. Another from the same book: 'Then Peter said, "Can anyone keep these people from being baptized with water? They have received the Holy Spirit just as we have.' " You know these verses as well as I, Daria. If we are holy, if our hearts are committed solely to following the risen Christ, holy work is accomplished. You must embrace this fact if we are to move forward together, daughter. The Church cannot remain between us."

Daria straightened, staring down her priest. It had come out in conversation as they supped that Ugo and Vito did not believe themselves baptized. As the group prepared to read the letter fragment, Ugo had spoken up, expressing his concern.

"I cannot believe that I must defend the Church to her priest."

"I cannot believe I must defend the ability of all to access Christ without the Church, to you."

"We could wait for the bishop as the Church advises," Vito suggested. "Go to him after the del Buco funeral."

"He is a good man, Bishop Benedicto," Daria said. "I see no reason why he would object to these men being baptized. We simply must wait for the next Eastertide—"

"There is no time," Father Piero said, still looking into Daria's eyes. "It can take months. He would force them to attend mass, meet with him, until he deemed them worthy."

"Bishop Benedicto is a good man," Daria repeated. "I cannot imagine they need wait past Easter. And the reasons to make one wait for the sacrament are good."

Father Piero took a deep breath and stood. He repeated the words slowly, clearly enunciating each one. "There is no time. What we sense, what I venture to say we all sense to some extent, is the enemy approaching. They know we are here."

"Is that what I keep feeling?" Vito asked.

"Who? Who knows?" asked Rune.

"Are you saying the Church is our enemy?" asked Basilio.

The priest ignored them, concentrating on Daria and Gianni. "The battle is soon upon us. We must begin earnest preparations this day. We need every soldier and every soldier with spiritual armament." He opened up his Bible to the thin, yellowing pages. "Yet there is something we must discuss that is of even greater concern than the impending battle, my friends. Our mission, I believe, is as much about sharing the love of Christ—our free access to him—as it is in sharing our gifts."

"To share . . . love?" Basilio asked, in a high-pitched, strangled tone that made Piero smile.

"If we're squired away here, how can we accomplish anything?" asked Ugo, his hand on the still strings of his lute.

"A good question, that. I think our captain has been wise in fortifying this house, in case we must stave off an enemy who attacks with weapons."

Basilio and Rune scoffed. "How else might an enemy attack?"

"Consider that," Father Piero said, raising a hand to quiet them. He did not return their smile. "How else *would* an enemy attack a fortified house?"

"Tunnel underground," said Vito.

"Infiltrate through a spy," said Zola quietly. The men looked at her for a long moment. Then they all chimed in.

"Fire. Burn us out."

"Cut us off from supplies, drive us out with hunger."

"Or thirst. Water would open our gates before food."

"No water, no way to fight fire."

"But if they set us afire, they endanger the entire city. All of Siena could be aflame."

"All right, all right," Father Piero said, raising his hands to quiet them. "You understand—there are many ways we may be attacked by others *physically*." He turned page after page of hand-lettered script in his Bible, then turned to Daria. "Will you translate?" he asked softly.

"Mayhap we've taken this too far, Father," Daria said. "Reading the Holy Writ in our common language—"

"Scripture cannot be heretical," Piero said in irritation. "Christ spoke in the language of his people." He sighed. "Let us discern this day what is of God and what is not. Do so for yourself. Let it be a testing ground for the Gifted. They will not burn you at the stake if you come to the conclusion that I was the lone heretic in your midst and simply led you astray for a time."

Daria nodded slowly. "I will translate."

The priest began reading, pausing to allow Daria to translate as he went. "From Ephesians: *'De cetero fratres confortamini in Domino et in potentia virtutis eius. . . .'*"

" 'Finally, be strong in the Lord and in his mighty power. Put on the full armor of God so that you can take your stand against the devil's schemes.' "

" ' . . . *quia non est nobis conluctatio adversus carnem et sanguinem sed adversus principes. . . .*"

" 'For our struggle is not against flesh and blood, but against the rulers, against the authorities, against the powers of this dark world and against the spiritual forces of evil in the heavenly realms.' "

The knights looked at Daria and the priest with consternation. Only Gianni seemed unsurprised.

"You are wondering what it means to take on the full armor of God," said Piero.

They all nodded.

"God is gracious in his Word. It is right here. . . ."

Daria continued in her translation, echoing the priest. As she spoke the holy words, warmth covered her skin and surrounded the group at large. She watched as their eyes grew round in wonder and then became soft, as the Spirit pierced every one of their hearts.

" '*Propterea accipite armaturam Dei ut possitis resistere in die malo et omnibus perfectis stare. . . .*' "

" 'Therefore put on the full armor of God, so that when the day of evil comes, you may be able to stand your ground, and after you have done everything, to stand. Stand firm then, with the belt of truth buckled around your waist, with the breastplate of righteousness in place, and with your feet fitted with the readiness that comes from the gospel of peace. In addition to all this, take up the shield of faith, with which you can extinguish all the flaming arrows of the evil one. Take the helmet of salvation and the sword of the Spirit, which is the word of God. And pray in the Spirit on all occasions with all kinds of prayers and requests. With this in mind, be alert and always keep on praying for all the saints.' "

Father Piero stopped reading and looked up. A hush fell over them all, broken only by Zola's odd, nonsensical tongue of praise. She rocked in a corner by herself, arms upraised, tears running down her cheeks.

"I have never heard such words of Holy Scripture before. Is it all like that?" Ugo asked reverently.

"If God is for us . . ." led Vito.

"Who can be against us?" they said as one.

"That is exactly what it says here, my friends," Father Piero said, lifting his Bible.

"And you . . . you and Zola and Lady Daria and our captain, here," said Rune to the priest, "your gifts . . . they are of the Spirit?"

"Indeed," Piero said. "And yet what you'll find it says in the letter," he paused to tap the goatskin-covered pouch that held the sacred manuscript, "is that no gift matches God's greatest gift, and that is to love. That there is nothing more powerful than God's own love, living in each of us. It speaks of the gifts among us, but moreover, it speaks very thoroughly of loving our neighbors as ourselves, echoing what we know from the Christ."

"To love?" Vito asked, eyebrows lowering to a frown.

"To love." He turned to Corinthians and translated himself this time. " 'If I speak in the tongues of men and of angels, but have not love, I am only a resounding gong or a clanging cymbal. If I have the gift of prophecy and can fathom all mysteries and all knowledge, and if I have a faith that can move mountains, but have not love, I am nothing.' "

He looked about the room, solemnly. "Do you not see? It matters little who exhibits extraordinary gifts among us . . . the greatest gift we can share with others is *love*."

"It is hardly love I gain when I attend mass," said Basilio.

Father Piero nodded. "But it is what *we* are here to do. The Gifted. Each of us. In sharing our other gift—be it healing or miraculous powers or faith—we will gain more and more opportunities to share the true Gospel and the greatest of gifts. We will draw them by our gifting, but the greatest thing we will teach them will be to love as Christ first loved them, to seek God with all their mind, heart, and soul. That is something every one of us must convey, first and foremost, in *everything* we do and say."

The group was silent.

"Might we go back and read the Scripture about heavenly armor again?" quipped Vito.

They all laughed, even Piero. "I promise you, my son, that this will eventually make perfect sense. Think of it as knightly honor. Knightly devotion. As you have sworn to uphold Lady Daria, here, protect her, see to her welfare, watch over her property, so must you swear to uphold Christ's Gospel. To learn to know it so well that you shall breathe the Word, speak the Word, live the Word. Working together, we can accomplish mighty tasks. We will begin with your baptisms. I am satisfied that you are ready. We will invite the Spirit to cover you as one of his own."

He cast a questioning eye in Daria's direction, but she did not hesitate. Regardless of what she knew was customary, she understood that Father Piero was right. "Christ have mercy," she whispered, as she followed the group out of the dining hall and toward the chapel. Outside, a summer storm had come in, covering the city with pewter clouds that held on to their load of rain like a jealous mother. She paused and closed her eyes and let the bracing breeze wash over her. "Heaven help us."

&c &c &c

"The heavens are astir," said the master, gazing out of the cave mouth. "It is the perfect night for our ceremony!"

Three women scurried by them, whispering, and both men followed them with their eyes. "Every time we meet, more gather," said the man. Still others, cloaked in dark robes, passed by them. Young and old, landed gentry and commoner. Here they came. But his master's eyes scanned for one key individual. . . .

Not seeing him, the master raised his hand and nodded once,

indicating ongoing patience. "It is good. The enemy gathers force this day. We have who we need. It is understandable that he has not come. We will pray for power and strength, so that we might be what he needs when he does turn to us for assistance."

"You think he will come."

"I do." The master laughed. "They will all come, in time."

"And what of the Duchess's gathering? Does her group not . . . give you pause?"

"Nay, nay," said the master, turning to lead him deeper within the cave, walking past one dripping ivory candle after another along the wall. "It is only logical that as we gain power the enemy will do his best to keep his faithful at bay. He is a jealous god but we know how to pursue his people. Soon they will be ours. Man hungers for change. We are the change that offers them power. Glory. Strength. Choices."

The Sorcerer paused and turned to his apprentice. "You have been faithful. I will honor you."

"Nay, master. It is unnecessary—"

The master lifted his hand to cease his talk. "Nay. Tell me. Tell me her name and she shall be yours."

The apprentice smiled and thought of glimpses of noses and chins and lips. . . . "I know not her name."

"Pay it no heed. Simply point her out. She will be but the first. . . . We shall baptize you in the ways of the dark, and evermore, you shall hunger for more of what you taste. And in turn, greater and greater will your power be."

He turned and swept into the cave, his followers immediately coming to silence as he drew near them. Nodding to the drummer, the master began to speak. "Our god gives us what we need to live—water for the sheep and vine, water in our wells. He is the god of the earth, the god that birthed us into being. . . ."

The people about him began to sway in ecstasy, his words cascading over their ears like wine in a drunkard's mouth. The drummer beat his drum, picking up the tempo a half step.

A massive black cat prowled the stone altar, as if watching all that was happening.

"We are all kings and queens in this place. There is none greater amongst us, no one higher than another! We are washed in the river and made one. . . . 'Sin' is the creation of disreputable priests. We are inherently good. All we must do is to go back to the garden, eat of the fruit . . . and then we will know *power!*" He raised his fists in the air and the people shouted out around him.

"There are others who proclaim a god who would bow down to the earth and become one of us," the master said. "We proclaim a god who takes us and makes us gods ourselves!" The drumbeat picked up in tempo again. Bodies writhed, robes fell.

"We are the communion of new saints."

"We believe!" they chanted. "We believe!"

"Together, we hold the power of the gods. Together, we gain in strength. We belong to one another!" shouted the master. The beat of the drum was at a frantic tempo now, and woman fell upon man, man upon woman in a frenzy of lip and bare leg. Some women reached for other women. Some men reached for other men.

The cool of the cave washed over the apprentice, even as his skin grew hot as if in fever and with trembling hands he covered his woman with his touch. . . . "I believe," he whispered. "I believe. . . ."

⚓ ⚓ ⚓

FATHER Piero went to the altar for his oil of catechumens, genuflected and then picked up the vial, turning back to the young men. Daria, despite her best intentions, was fascinated with the rite, normally reserved for the privacy of the baptistery, and finally gave in to watching all of it. The priest had not asked them to avert their eyes, seemed instead to invite them to more fully take part. Piero gestured for the brothers to kneel before the altar. The brothers now handed their shirts to their comrades behind them and bowed their heads in prayer.

The priest paused at the basin of water, a makeshift font, praying in Latin, asking God to make the time to come for no mere physical washing—but instead for a supreme action of the Holy Spirit. Rather than turning to the cross as was custom, the priest turned to the people assembled and bowed his head, arms raised, and prayed, "Father in heaven, at the baptism of Jesus in the River Jordan you proclaimed him your beloved Son and anointed him with the Holy Spirit. Make all who are baptized into Christ faithful in their calling to be your children and inheritors with him of everlasting life; through your Son, Jesus Christ our Lord, who lives and reigns with you and the Holy Spirit, one God, now and forever."

"Amen," they said together.

He gestured for the men to rise and poured oil into his palm. He made the sign of the cross in the air and then anointed each man's heart, shoulders, and head with a small cross, saying, "You shall meet the powers of darkness in the waters, but our God lays claim to your heart, your strength, and your mind. He is stronger than the dark one. Trust the Holy One will save you, both now and forever *and you shall be saved.*"

Daria noticed the uncommon stillness of both men, the lack of witty words upon their tongues. They knew the gravity of this ceremony, and in their knowing, Daria knew it was rightly done. Here. In her house. Never had such a thing been done, since the early ages of the faith.

Father Piero led the brothers to the font, his eyes full of wonder. "In holy baptism our gracious Father liberates us from sin and death by joining us to the death and resurrection of our Lord. We are born fallen; but in the waters of baptism we are *reborn children of God* and inheritors of eternal life. By water and the Holy Spirit we are made members of the Church which *is* the body of Christ. As we live with him and with his people, we grow in faith, love, and obedience to the will of God."

He waited until Vito and Ugo raised their eyes to meet his.

"Do you desire to be baptized?"

"We do," they said together.

Daria sat back, stunned to see tears welling in the knights' eyes. Never had she seen a man cry, other than her father weeping over her dead mother or Vincenzo over Tatiana—or Gianni when he witnessed the healing. But as she looked about the chapel, she noticed all felt the power of this moment, the majesty, the intensity in the room. It was overwhelming. And a lump grew in her own throat as her attention again turned to Vito, Ugo, and Piero.

"Vito, I ask you to profess your faith in Christ Jesus, reject sin, and confess the faith of the Church, the faith in which we baptize. Do you renounce all the forces of evil, the devil, and all his empty promises?"

"I do."

"Do you believe in God the Father?"

"I believe in God, the Father almighty, creator of heaven and earth."

"Do you believe in Jesus Christ, the Son of God?"

Vito paused, searching for the more complex response Father Piero had taught him. "In your own words, man," Piero said, placing a hand on his shoulder. "Make it your own, my son." He gave him a moment to think. "I ask again, do you believe in Jesus Christ?"

Vito nodded solemnly. "I do. I believe in Jesus, God's Son, my Lord, conceived by the power of the Holy Spirit and born of a virgin. He suffered, oh how he suffered. He was crucified. Died. And was buried." He paused and swallowed hard, as if seeing Christ suffer before him.

"He died for *you*, Vito," Piero said softly.

Vito nodded. "For me, yes. He even descended into hell. For me." Now tears freely flowed down his face. "But on the third day, on that beautiful third day, *he rose again*." Daria could see the victorious knight within him when he said those words, and smiled. "He ascended into heaven, and is seated at the right hand of the Father. And yet he will come again to judge us all, living or dead."

Piero smiled at him with approval. "Vito, do you believe in God the Holy Spirit?"

"I believe in the Holy Spirit, the holy Church, the communion of saints, the forgiveness of sins—even mine—and that I will be resurrected after death and know life everlasting."

"Now *that*," Piero said, tears streaming down his cheeks as well as he clasped the younger man's neck and looked into his eyes, "that is the knowledge of the *holy*. That is *love*." He turned to the font and dipped his hand in, covering Vito's forehead with the sweet, clear water with each phrase to come. "Sir Vito, I baptize thee in the name of the Father . . . and of the Son . . . and of the Holy Spirit. Amen."

The priest looked down upon Vito like a proud papa, and then turned to Ugo and went through the same steps with him, with swelling impact for all assembled. The Spirit washed over them all as Ugo completed his testimony of faith and a strong scent entered the room on the breeze. It smelled of orange and of cloves.

Rain pounded down then, drowning out Father Piero's words as it ran down the roof tiles and pooled on the ground. It was as if they were all being baptized in that moment. . . .

"Holy, holy, holy is the Lord," whispered Daria. She looked around for Zola, thinking she might be in her customary corner, praying in her holy language, but she was not present. In fact, she did not remember her in their company since they left the dining hall.

Mayhap she felt unwelcome, unworthy. Father Piero would continue to soothe her with the Gospel of love, and Daria would pray healing upon her. And soon, she would know the forgiveness and peace already known to all present in the chapel and beyond.

"The Lord be with you," Father Piero said, drawing her attention forward again.

"And also with you," they said together.

He bowed his head to pray again. "God, the Father of our Lord Jesus Christ, we give you thanks for freeing your sons from the power of sin and for raising them up to a new life through this holy sacrament. Pour your Holy Spirit upon Vito and Ugo: the spirit of wisdom and understanding, the spirit of counsel and might, the spirit of knowledge and the fear of the Lord, the spirit of joy in your presence."

"Amen."

He turned to Ugo, first, pausing with awe-inspired wonder. "Ugo, child of God, you have been sealed by the Holy Spirit and marked with the cross of Christ forever." As he said the words, he marked the first man with the sign of the cross upon his forehead.

Father Piero turned to Vito and smiled. "Vito, child of God, you have been sealed by the Holy Spirit and marked with the cross of Christ forever." As with Ugo, he marked the second man with the cross over his brow.

"Let your light so shine before others that they may see your good works and glorify your Father in heaven. Amen."

They all opened their eyes and smiled upon their new brothers.

"Come. Come closer," said Piero. "Let us pray over these two."

They did as he bid, surrounding the brothers and laying hands upon their shoulders in a crowded circle. Father Piero led them in one last prayer. "Through baptism God has made these men new brothers of the priesthood we all share in Christ Jesus, that we may proclaim the praise of God and bear his creative and redeeming Word to all the world. . . ."

⚓ ⚓ ⚓

"CEASE!" the master cried. He cocked his head as if listening. Gradually, the group becalmed, but reluctantly. "Do you not sense what is happening? Do you not feel the attack?"

Everyone was now deadly still, looking to him.

His bride reached up to whisper in his ear, but he tossed her aside and strode to the cave mouth. "Nay!" he screamed. "Nay! Not this day! You may not have them!"

He stared outward, where the clouds were clearing after dumping their loads of rain at last. At last he turned and spoke to them. "The enemy has gained strength, but all is not lost. This is but one battle among many. This is war." He cast his eyes back, about the group. "Bring others. We need each and every one. Tell them of the power that is here, the strength that will preserve their livestock and purse. Tell them that they will be greeted as dukes and duchesses. Tell them that the time of change is upon us, and they must join the winning forces." He lapsed into Latin, chanting unintelligibly as he bowed to the ground.

His bride turned to the valley and let the rain-fresh wind blow across her cheeks, wishing she were different, that her life had been cast in another direction.

She sighed. It was simply not to be. There was nothing she could do.

This was where she belonged. To him. To the Sorcerer.

And she would do her part to deliver the Gifted into his hands.

Chapter Twenty-four

At midnight, Daria walked with Vincenzo behind the men carrying Tatiana's corpse on a bier and covered in a gossamer-thin linen into the huge Duomo. They set her upon a dais near the choir, and monks sang a low, mournful song, the official beginning of wake night. Daria stood with Vincenzo for hours, until he turned her gently toward the door. "Go, Daria. Go and rest for a few hours. Tomorrow will be long and I'll need you with me again."

She nodded and laid her head on his shoulder for a moment before departing. He clung to her hand even as she walked away, although he faced Tatiana the whole time.

The next morning, the Duomo was packed. Every person who had ever been touched by Vincenzo or wished to be touched by him was present and accounted for. The crowd, mostly of the upper middle class and some of the nobility, wore the customary white. *This is what heaven might look like,* Daria thought. Pristine. Whole. One.

She liked the majesty of the great church, the towering dome, the giant pillars striped with white and black marble, the magnificent white marble pulpit that rose atop the backs of lions and columns. She liked to pray before the high altar, studying di Buoninsegna's famous Maestà. Her mother used to tell stories of the parade of people and dignitaries who ushered the masterpiece into the Duomo. Daria's friend Ambrogio, an artist himself, had once dressed her as a man and sneaked her into the lumbering church, to within a breath's space of the altarpiece. He wanted her to see di Buoninsegna's poetry up close, the twenty-six panels that adorned the back of the altarpiece, representing the Passion of the Christ. Even now, staring at the mournful Madonna in blue and Christ Child in royal purple and gold, it was those scenes she thought upon.

Daria loved this church, so much a part of her history, her life. She even liked the monastic dirge that twenty monks sang together, perfectly annunciating the dreadful pall of death. The acoustics were perfect, sending Scripture in Latin out of the bishop's mouth and out over the crowd. Even those standing at the back would hear every word.

Tatiana's body was in a coffin at the front, the lid now closed and covered with green vines that symbolized eternal life. A part of Daria wondered why they did not celebrate in some measure— Tatiana was free of her illness, unencumbered, at rest. Or dancing! Dancing, in heaven.

Daria stole a glance to her right—Piero stood beside her—and then to her left. Zola was a stunning beauty, dressed in a glorious white gown that Daria had worn as a younger girl. Beata had let it out here and there and it fit her to perfection. They had finished the ensemble with a new crispinette, and suddenly a woman who was once the town whore looked like the purest of ladies. Rune followed her around all day like a cat seeking a mistress with a bowl of milk, when Gianni allowed it.

Daria stole another glance. Only Zola's eyes and the cut of her mouth told Daria that she was ill at ease. Was it the service of death? Or was it her previous occupation, her old life? Certainly the priests would have a fit if they knew. . . .

Or did she feel smothered, stifled, unable to use her gift in this place? Daria felt it too. As glorious as this church was, it held none of the power and warmth of the Spirit that they had all discovered in their chapel yesterday during the baptisms. It was not the Duomo itself, Daria decided. It was the people within, this service of the dead that made her feel as if she were in a crypt as surely as Tatiana's body would soon be. Daria resisted the urge to shout out, to wake her sleeping people. Her eyes widened. It was the same holy urging when she felt called to heal another—the same passionate desire to reach out and minister to them, address their ailment.

Daria clamped her mouth shut. But the more she tried to focus on Bishop Benedicto's words, the more she seemed to see the bored, deadened look in the congregants' eyes. Did they not see what this service was all about? Tatiana was free, released into the Savior's arms, ready to enter heaven as soon as the Christ reached for her. To be that close to him! To know heaven! It would be joy, peace, satisfaction, healing at its fullest. And it was Christ's love that had given them the drawbridge.

The love of Christ. Her eyes passed over Bishop Benedicto. He knew of this love, Daria was sure of it. But high up on his pulpit of marble, reading in Latin—the majority of his people could not understand a word he said! They could not know the full power of the Gospel, understand the impact of the Messiah's life on their own. To them it was a mysterious mix of faith and magic, the realm of holy men alone. Most felt as interlopers in their own Church!

She shifted her weight, longing to sit or run—anything but stand a moment longer—eager for the service to come to a close. Vincenzo had remained on the opposite side of the congregation from her and never glanced back at her—something he had done since she was a child.

Daria supposed it was childish, missing that action today of all days. But she still could not avoid it. She longed to reach out to

Vincenzo, to tell him of love, to share with him all that she had learned. But the timing was not right.

Vincenzo had always held the Church at arm's length. He dined with the bishop, sent extravagant presents to the priests who worked within the Duomo's walls. He had purchased gifts of parchment and ink from Daria to give to their scriptorium. He had given a portion of their joint proceeds from each year's sales of cotton and linen to the bishop as tithe. Daria shifted her weight and considered it for the first time. She had always seen it as devotion. But was it more politics than piety?

She remembered long, heated debates between her father and Vincenzo in the garden . . . over the nature of God, the role of the Church. Vincenzo had attended mass regularly until his second wife had passed away. Tatiana had encouraged him to attend with her, and he had done so, now and again. Daria tapped her toe on the marble floor, trying to concentrate on not making a sound rather than crying again. She would not cry for Tatiana again. She would not. Tatiana was free!

Zola tugged at her arm, and Daria looked up with heated cheeks to see that the mass had come to a close, that people moved forward as one to kiss their fingers and then touch the coffin in a parting gesture, to shake Vincenzo's hand or kiss both his cheeks, depending on how well they knew him. Lord Frangelico and another tall man, dressed in the finest of coats, neared her uncle and he greeted them with solemn dignity. Daria grimaced as he kissed Frangelico from cheek to cheek, hating the idea of being so near him. Who was the other noble with him? Could it be the fabled Abramo Amidei of whom so many on the streets spoke? He moved with ease, chatting with Frangelico as if at an afternoon garden party, but his expression remained appropriately solemn. His dark eyes flicked across the crowd, seeming to rest on every person, then moving on. He radiated power.

When his eyes came to rest upon Daria, and she did not look away, she thought she saw the smallest of smiles. When Daria dared to glance his direction again, he was deep in conversation with Lord Frangelico as they exited the church.

Daria and Zola, along with her knights and Father Piero, entered the line and made their way forward. Within ten minutes, they reached the front. Although Daria had seen Vincenzo that morning, she still reached up to kiss him on both cheeks. "It will soon be over, Uncle."

He held her hands for a moment. "It matters not. Nothing ma—"

She looked up to see him pause over Zola and hid a smile. "Baron del Buco, may I present my companion, Zola Apressi?"

"I am so sorry for your loss, Baron," Zola said.

Vincenzo bowed deeply, holding Zola's hand, and then nodded once, moving on to the next lady to avoid the twittering of old women.

Daria spotted Marco and his bride, Francesca, coming up behind them. Marco neared Vincenzo, his hand on his wife's shoulder. But his eyes were on Daria. She turned away, linking her arm through Zola's. "Come, my friend. We will go to Baron del Buco's home and eat delightful dishes and stand on his porch and toast to Tatiana's memory. The hardest part is over."

Zola smiled and matched her step. The knights were immediately behind them. Basilio and Rune moved in front of them, casting back smiles to the ladies. Father Piero and Gianni were on either side, and at their backs, the others trailed them. Daria sighed. "You expect battle here, in the Duomo's shadow?"

"Always at the ready, m'lady." Gianni smiled.

"That was the hardest part?" Zola whispered.

Daria sighed. "For me. Certainly watching her die was much worse," she said, crossing herself. "But this feast afterward . . . it all seems like a waste. Tatiana surely cares not! It seems only to drag out Vincenzo's pain. There is something cruel about it all. We go off to a death feast at his home while he watches his wife put in the ground. Odd, isn't it?"

"Odd," Zola said with a somber nod.

Daria shook her head. She was in a foul, contemptuous mood. She would need to avoid Marco at the house or no one would be able to tolerate her. She glanced at Gianni on her right, resplendent in her father's finest linens and overcoat, bearing the d'Angelo coat of arms. Perhaps she could spend time talking with him on the portico, make Marco jealous. . . .

"We must keep our thoughts on the purest plain," Father Piero whispered.

Daria whirled, her cheeks heating. Could he read her thoughts?

He smiled, as surprised as she was. "No, I do not know what you were thinking, daughter. But I can see some of your thoughts upon your face!" His smile disappeared. "I only say it because I sense something. . . ."

"Wicked," Gianni finished for him.

"Wicked?" Daria asked.

Both men nodded.

A chill ran down her spine.

"The Spirit is preparing us. We all must be wary," Father Piero said to the group.

"Shall we go back to the estate?" Gianni asked him.

"No," Daria said, resting her hand upon his arm as she looked toward the marketplace. "I am to go and heal Old Woman Parmo."

"Now?" Basilio asked.

"Now."

"But it is not yet dark," Rune said.

"Someone will discover us," Vito said.

"Baron del Buco is expecting you, m'lady," said Zola.

"It is very poor timing." Daria gave a little shrug to her shoulders, feeling helpless.

"Do we question our God?" Piero said. "Or when he says leap, do we leap?"

"We leap," Daria said.

"But Baron del Buco," Gianni said. He ran an agitated hand through his hair. "He is important to us. His contacts are numerous. There will be many at his house tonight."

Daria frowned at him. "I do not understand."

"The baron—what will he think if you are not in attendance?"

"Mayhap it is time I tell him the truth." She turned away, speaking mostly to herself, trying to reason it out. "Mayhap it will bring him more fully to the side of the righteous. He hovers over unknown chasms . . . as though—"

She turned but they were all shaking their heads, clearly in disagreement with her line of thinking, still desiring secrecy for their mission—a mission that was as yet unclear to any of them. "All right. All right," she said. She folded her arms in front of her.

"Zola. Vito. Ugo, Rune, Lucan, you five will go to the baron's home and proceed to enter into the gathering," Piero said. "If the baron sees you all, he will assume Daria is present, that he has not come across her yet. We will pray that the Lord does his good work in quick order."

"And we will go with Lady Daria?" asked Gianni.

"Yes," Daria said. "My most trusted spiritual and physical guardians." Her thoughts went to Hasani, back at the estate. Slaves, freed or not, were not welcome in the Duomo. But she was glad he was there. If something wicked was already upon them, the Sciorias would need help in securing the house and defending themselves.

They all shared one last look and then moved forward, splitting into two groups at the crossroads between the marketplace and the del Buco estate five blocks away.

⚜ ⚜ ⚜

OLD Woman Parmo was just locking up her last chests when they arrived. A young man, perhaps her grandson, loaded them onto a wagon, preparing to head home, while she reached a hand to a painful lower back, struggling to stand upright after bending.

Daria, Gianni, and Piero came to a stop in front of her.

She looked around, deep wrinkles forming around her eyes as she smiled at Daria. "I am packed up for the day. Perhaps I may tend to your needs, Duchess, on the morrow?"

The old woman purchased from Daria's guild each autumn. Daria's presence—and the late hour—obviously confused her. Daria looked down the street. "May we speak in private, my friend?"

Old Woman Parmo squinted her eyes at Daria and her companions, cast a welcoming look to her grandson, and led them to the back of the stall.

"My friend, I have some wonderful news."

"Eh? What is that?"

"God has sent us here. We believe he means for us to heal you of your cripplement."

"What? No, no. It is nothing, nothing but gout, the rheumatism. Part of the penance of the aged, you know."

Daria took a half step forward. "I have seen you. For years I have seen you, struggling to get along when your fine young grandson is not here to help you. Please. Will you not give us a chance?"

"What you speak of . . . it is not possible."

"I assure you, friend, it is possible," said Gianni. "I have seen the duchess at work. She healed me two months past. I suffered grievous wounds. She saved me, I swear it. She can heal you too."

The old woman looked from Daria to the priest. "There is no foul play here, Father?"

"Nay." Piero leaned closer. "We strive to do only what our Lord urges us to do. Only what he approves."

The old woman's lips parted in wonder and then she shrugged. "I have reason to believe you."

"What is that?" Daria asked.

"An old family treasure—something I've always wondered over. Yet as soon as I saw you today, Duchess, I knew the time had come."

Gianni looked over his shoulder, watching as two men moved slowly by, studying the odd ensemble. "We must not tarry here," he whispered.

"Come," the old woman said. "My house is close by."

"We really must not waste a moment," Daria said. "I am absent from someplace I should be. I had thought to take you to my estate where it is safe."

"Come," the old woman repeated. Gianni, Daria, and Piero shared a look of concern and surprise, but then followed the woman and her grandson down one alleyway and then another. The five of them hurried along, casting glances to the shadows that now clung to each doorway and alley. But no one appeared. The streets were quiet as dusk bled into the edge of night.

"Come, come," she said yet again, at the door of an old building in a neighborhood full of warehouses and merchants. They followed her inside. The first floor was largely a great room and storehouse for the del Parmo trade—linens. Daria recognized that three-quarters of the piles had come directly from Siena's woolen guild. Being surrounded by her own cloth gave her an odd sense of peace. She smiled at Piero, thinking she would point them out to him, but his face was intent. What was it? He hurried to a table to grab a beeswax candle from the boy, then rushed to where the old woman stood, beside an ancient tapestry that hung from the far wall.

Gianni walked in front of her, apprehension running across his shoulders. She could tell when he was wary now—he held his chin up, braced his shoulders as if readying himself for impact. She felt the same way within—wanting to see, and yet uneasy about what they were about to discover.

"Come closer, daughter," Piero said, encouraging Daria forward.

"It has been in this city for generations beyond my grandmother," the woman said.

"We recognized your family crest," said the boy, pointing to a small female figure in the corner, bearing the d'Angelo coat of arms.

"We thought it was there because of your family's involvement with the guild," the old woman said. "And the woman tending the other—I always thought of your dear mama, tending the ill, God rest her soul." She genuflected and then held up the corner of the tapestry. There was a tall woman kneeling, with head bowed as if praying, a woman with long, curly hair, her coat bearing a red peacock on a white background. Daria would've dismissed it as the old woman had—her family had been involved with the woolen trade for centuries—but then her eye caught sight of the other woman upon the ground beside her. The woman in the d'Angelo coat faced the holy family, looked as if she were praying like all the others about her, but she had one hand upon the old woman's leg. Daria gasped and drew back, looking over the entire piece. "What is this? Is there more? Have you seen other things?"

"Nay. I do not believe so," the old woman said. "It is an old altarpiece, once used to grace the Duomo's altar in the days before the Maestà. But not for some time. The priests were about to discard it, but I paid for it, thinking I would put it above my own chapel altar."

"It is beautiful," Daria said with a smile. "Your own divine message that I would come to heal you."

"Indeed. But, Duchess, there is something else you must see," the old woman said. Her face clouded over with concern, and with weary movements she pulled down the tapestry and slowly turned it over. Daria thought that she meant to show her the artistry of the back—often the backside could be more beautiful than the front, given the talent of the weaver.

It was a magnificent piece. Daria bent to admire the craftsmanship, shaking her head in wonder. The Maestà was a wonder, to be sure, but the priests had been ready to discard this, this?

"Daria," Piero said lowly.

She glanced up at him and then backed up to see the tapestry as he saw it.

From several paces back one could see a peacock, clearly outlined in white at the corner. Daria's hand went to her mouth. Because it was then that she saw the second figure—a towering giant dragon above the peacock, about to strike.

CHAPTER TWENTY-FIVE

"In all my travels with Lady Daria, in all my visits to her home, I wonder why I have not had the pleasure of meeting you," Vincenzo said, reaching for Zola's hand and holding it between his in a friendly, fatherly way. "How long have you been a guest within her home?"

They all stood in the grand salon of the baron's home, which was lined with candelabra. Servants circulated with trays of feast food. Countless nobles and merchants, the *grandi* of the city, rotated about the room, and their combined hushed conversations still made it difficult to hear.

"Lady Zola is new to Siena, Baron del Buco," Rune said. He was a head taller than Vincenzo and there was a sudden desire to protect Zola within him. He knew not why, only that it was there.

"Oh?" Vincenzo said. "New to the city, you say? From where do you hail, lady?"

"You simply must get to Roma more often, Vincenzo," cut in another nobleman, this one as tall as Rune. The knight eyed him, a bitter taste lining his mouth for no apparent reason.

"Lord Amidei," Vincenzo said with a nod. "May I present to

you Lady Zola and Sir Rune, of the house of d'Angelo?" The new-comer had dark, wavy hair, and a long, patrician nose. He appeared more French than Italian. On his arm was a striking woman with sable hair. She faded into the crowd behind him, however, as the no-bleman entered into the conversation.

Rune's eyes went to Basilio. But his friend was watching, with vivid interest, as the woman walked away.

"Lady Zola," the nobleman said, bowing lowly.

"Lord Amidei," she said in a deep curtsey.

Rune eyed the newcomer more thoroughly. She knew him. From where? And he referred to her as a lady, a noblewoman? Could he be from her past? Did he not know what had happened to her in that small Toscana town?

Amidei glanced apologetically at Rune and tucked Zola's hand in the crook of his arm. "Come, my dear. You must tell me of your adventures. You do not mind, Sir Rune? Baron? I assume you must see to your other guests."

"Nay, nay," Vincenzo said, waving them off, turning to a cou-ple beside them, acknowledging their condolences. . . .

Rune looked back to Zola, intending to follow her, but discov-ered she had already disappeared among the throng of guests with Lord Amidei.

⚜ ⚜ ⚜

"What is that?" Daria whispered, casting a frightened glance to Piero. His eyebrows were lowered in consternation, but he did not look afraid. "What does this mean?"

He took her arm and pulled her a few steps away. "A warning, mayhap. We are of the light, Daria. The dark always seeks to eclipse the light."

"The evil ones. God is telling us that evil draws near. We are in danger. In danger, Father!" She backed up as she spoke, bump-ing into Gianni. He put his hands upon her shoulders, facing the small priest with her.

Piero shook his head. "Do not give in to this fear, Daria. They count on you fearing them. Scripture tells us repeatedly, fear not! Take courage! This is a warning, a reminder that we must be vigilant, to watch out for the dragon who may hover. But our God is stronger. You must never release that ideal. Our God is stronger. If God is for us . . ."

Daria swallowed hard.

Piero took her hands. "Daria, there will be many times when we feel such terror. You must leave it all, to find that place within you where you are willing to leave it all at the foot of the cross. To care not whether you live or die, only that you are serving the Master. Can you find that within you?"

Daria closed her eyes, aware that Piero prayed for her, that Gianni did the same behind her. Gradually, she realized that Old Woman Parmo and her grandson had joined them, all bowing their heads in prayer. As they did, she could feel her heart lifting, recognized lightness, as if chains had been stripped from her torso. She took a deep breath and smiled. "Thank you, m'Lord, Jesus," she whispered. She lifted her chin. "He brought us here so that you might be healed. Let us be on with it. You said you had a chapel here?"

The old woman led them out of the warehouse and into the chapel. Once there, Gianni lit the incense lamp and Father Piero began praying at the front, consecrating the hall for God's sacred work. In hushed tones, Daria told the woman and her grandson what to expect, that they must join them all in the most fervent of prayers.

"The greatest thing you must do is to submit to hope," she said, staring into the old woman's watery eyes. "I know it is difficult to believe, but you must. God intends for you to experience his miraculous hand, this day." She raised a hand to the dark window. "Put your fear at bay, as I just had to. Trust in all that you know to be good in the Savior. He has sent us to you. It will not go awry. Believe," she added with a smile, raising excited eyebrows.

Her muscles tensed in anticipation. She could feel the Spirit enter the sanctuary and surround them like a veiling that touched and blew by the skin. At her neck, across her forearms, over her head . . . She knelt and entered into prayer with Piero, reveling in the Presence. The others followed.

When it felt right and the prayers had ceased, Daria rose and nodded to the grandson to unfold a blanket upon the floor, near the front and center of the chapel altar. Daria went to Old Woman Parmo's side, and her grandson took the other. "You must lie down upon it," whispered Daria.

The woman cried out in pain as Gianni and her grandson lowered her on the blanket, as gently as they could. Daria had had no idea she suffered so, so good was she at hiding it in her movements at the market. She knelt beside the old woman on one side, and Father Piero knelt on the other. The old woman's grandson stood nearby, and Father Piero asked him to echo every prayer out of their mouths.

Daria placed one hand on the woman's forehead and bent low. "May I touch you? I must see what God is about to do."

The woman nodded, an edge of fear still in her eyes.

Gently, Daria felt down the length of each arm, feeling the heat of pain radiating mostly from wrist and finger. Then she did the same with her legs, pausing at the hip and knee. Quietly, she helped the old woman turn to one side. The lower back, near the tailbone, was where the most heat emanated.

The old woman whimpered and Daria helped her roll again onto her back.

She smiled into her eyes. "And now it begins. You shall see. You are most blessed, my friend. You have been chosen to be healed. Believe. Believe. You must believe. Close your eyes and feel the Savior's presence. He is here. Feel him washing over you, preparing your body to change, to be renewed. . . ."

"I will be young again?" the woman asked.

Daria smiled. "Nay. Nay, we cannot do that. But God shall

ease your pain. You will live your last days without this plague upon you. . . ."

೮ ೮ ೮

VINCENZO looked about the room, feeling as if he were in a fog. Where was Daria? Her people were here; she must be on the other side of the room or outside on the portico where there was a bit of air to be had. He needed her here, beside him. Needed her to make appropriate conversation with these people, to help him make appearances. Tatiana had been good at this. . . .

He examined faces as he looked about the room. Only five of the Nine were present. What sort of slap to his face was that meant to be? The five present were men he assumed would be in attendance, men with whom he had good political ties, those who owed him as much as he owed them. But there were two he had assumed would make an appearance, two with whom in the past year he had solidified ties, deepened their relationship—Lord Frangelico and Lord del Loren. Both had made an appearance at the Duomo, but hadn't bothered to come for the feast. Favors had been exchanged. If those two did not feel beholden to attend his wife's death feast, then how could he know they felt tied to him at all?

It was vital to the guild, to his future, to Daria's and Marco's future as well, that they maintain and deepen their stronghold among the city's noblemen and then move beyond them. The Nine could maintain stature and hold public position—Vincenzo had never wished for that—but he wanted to own a piece of every one of them. He was close to attaining his goals, their goals. Where was Daria? What could be keeping her?

Abramo Amidei's presence niggled at him. He was an outsider from Firenze, a man with whom Vincenzo had done a little business, but who threatened his own political pull by what he could offer his city's people with increased trade. Did he wish to circumvent Vincenzo, bring trade directly to the guilds of Siena to and from Firenze? For decades, Siena had refused most business with their archrival, Firenze, but market demand was answered by market supply. If there was a coin to be made, what businessman could turn it away? Had Abramo circumvented Vincenzo's efforts with the two missing *grandi*, those of the Nine he expected present this night? And what of the other two—those with whom he had never made inroads?

Vincenzo had been absorbed with Tatiana's decline of late. It had cost him, in more ways than one. The only time he had left the city in the past three months was to go and fetch Daria home, hoping against hope that God would heal his wife—or to take Tatiana to see doctors in Firenze and Milano.

God had turned his face from Vincenzo. He had always been rather distant. But this last week had been like a shove backward, a visible divine affront, losing Tatiana.

His head was splitting open with a pounding headache. He had difficulty breathing, felt as if he were drowning in this sea of supposed mourners.

Mourners! No one cared for his Tatiana the way he had! No one knew that he had lost not only a wife three days past, but also a child, small but present in his mother's womb. . . .

こ こ こ

DARIA closed her eyes and felt the Spirit continue to wash over them. The air hummed with his holy presence. It was as if she could feel every hair on her scalp, rising in attention to their Creator, as if she could feel every one atop the old woman's head as well! She smiled, praying and praying along with Father Piero, dimly hearing Gianni and the Parmo boy repeat their phrases, their petitions.

It was time. Daria, still closing her eyes, took the woman's right arm in her hands and prayed, prayed fervently for God to heal every joint. Slowly, steadily, she caressed the woman's arm, gently but firmly pulling it straight.

The old woman cried out.

Daria opened her eyes and smiled when she saw the look of wonder as she rolled her right hand around, feeling the freedom in her right wrist. The skin was still mottled with age spots and wrinkled, but it was inside, inside that all had been made new!

Again they prayed, prayed over each finger as Daria held them in her hand and then carefully pulled each straight.

As each one clicked back into place, the woman sobbed anew, looking through wondrous tears at her right wrist and fingers, waving them about in an exotic, hypnotic dance of movement.

Daria moved to her left side and Father Piero moved to the right. They repeated the same prayers, watched in glory as the old woman's left arm and wrist and fingers gained the same flexibility as the right.

They moved on to pray over her knees, then turned her to the side again. Old Woman Parmo cried out as before, cutting off her sobs of joy with that of pain. This was the most difficult, the greatest obstacle.

"Believe," Daria said, leaning close to her ear. "Your God has asked us to heal you, completely, of this terrible rheumatism. You will be free. Look at your hands, pray to God for total freedom, and believe that your back will once again be free of pain."

∞ ∞ ∞

RUNE emerged on the second floor of the estate, on a balcony above the portico where countless people meandered. He nodded to the guard, attempting to put him at ease. "I needed some air," he said, looking down below them to the crowd. "Care to join me?" He waved a round bottle of red wine at chest height, and the guard took a hesitant step forward, looking side to side.

Rune took a seat on the ledge, hoisting a foot to the rail to appear totally relaxed and therefore put the guard more at ease. But he could feel the guard keep him within his gaze as Rune's own eyes washed over the people below. There was Vincenzo, in a corner, trying his best to be civil to the well-wishers but clearly feeling miserable, glancing about on occasion as if he were looking for someone. Mayhap Lady Daria? She needed to make haste. Her absence was conspicuous.

He spotted Basilio, weaving his way back indoors, apparently giving up on finding Zola out on the portico. Good. He could look inside while Rune remained here, searching for a glimpse of the beauty or Abramo Amidei.

Feeling the guard's glance, Rune took another casual swig from the rounded bottle, let the wine sit on his tongue a moment before sliding down his throat in the manner of all true Sienese enjoying their wine.

There. Amidei was leading Zola up the staircase from down below—they had apparently been in the garden—and toward Vincenzo. Amidei was smiling, greeting other men, bowing gracefully to the women, introducing Zola as if she were his wife. It was highly inappropriate, unseemly. Did the man not know he was doing damage to her character? One did not draw a lady down into a dark garden alone! Perhaps it was done differently in Firenze, but here in Siena, the women would gossip and the men would look upon her with baser desires. . . .

Rune came to his feet and did not tarry down the staircase, ignoring the guard's words behind him. If he hurried, he could intercept Zola and encourage her home before any more damage was done.

It was not jealousy that pushed him forward.

It was fear.

ॐ ॐ ॐ

OLD Woman Parmo and her grandson saw the trio back to the marketplace.

The old woman reached yet again for Daria, her movements of a woman twenty years her junior. "How may I repay you, Duchess? How may I repay you?"

"Not I," Daria said, smiling upward. "Your Lord and your

God. It is he who has healed you. I am but his emissary." She paused and glanced to the dark but empty street. "But I ask you not to speak of this to another. It is imperative that this gift be kept a secret."

The old woman cackled. "How can I keep this a secret?" she said, waving down the length of her body. "Shall I remain hunched over, pretend pain?"

"Nay," Daria said, finding it impossible not to meet her joy with joy. "You shall enjoy your new lease on health and vitality while you have it, this side of heaven. But when people ask . . . tell them that it is a miracle. That your God was so gracious, so loving, that he healed you this night. It is the truth. Just leave my household out of your tale."

The old woman nodded vaguely, clearly not understanding. "As you wish, m'lady." She turned to her grandson and took a bundle from his arms. "I wish you to have this, m'lady. It is the tapestry. It belongs to you and no other."

"Oh, I could not."

"Please keep it for us," Piero said, leaning forward to pat her head. "May the Lord bless and keep you both. And us. We would be thankful to know you will pray for us and ours."

"Daily, Father," the woman pledged.

"Farewell," Daria said. She turned and mounted, as did Gianni and Piero. They had to get back to the del Buco estate! Hours had passed. . . .

A shadow caught Gianni's eye and he wheeled his horse toward a narrow alley. "A man! Halt!" He tried to follow, realized, too late, it was too narrow, and backed up, dismounted, and ran forward. In minutes, he returned, running a hand through his hair and sighing. He slid his sword back into its sheath at his side. "It is all right, m'lady."

"But there was someone there."

"But he is gone now." He turned and mounted up again.

"A spy?" she whispered.

"Mayhap." He eyed Old Woman Parmo and her grandson and then leaned toward Piero and Daria. "Despite our best intentions, the secrets of this house may not be long kept."

"We must get you to the del Buco estate," Piero said. "Lord del Buco is surely looking for you by now and wondering over your absence."

"Indeed," she said, gathering her skirts, steeling her resolve. She wished for nothing more than a retreat to her suite, to discard her gown and sink into her bed. But there was work yet to be done. "God give me strength," she whispered.

CHAPTER TWENTY-SIX

"MAY the gods give you a more prosperous year than this one, friend," Abramo Amidei said, coming closer as the crowds thinned. Vincenzo noted that Zola was still on his arm. Where had he seen her before? It troubled him, his inability to place her before first catching sight of her on Daria's country estate, then in the Duomo.

"It is the unending hope, is it not?" Vincenzo said, eyeing him. "That the new year will bring new opportunities, greater wealth, be it mind, body, or spirit?"

"Indeed. We should speak of it sometime," Abramo offered. "I know of ways that would improve your lot."

Vincenzo's eyes narrowed. Was the man speaking of business? Politics? Then why was he staring down at the lovely Zola?

"My mind is hardly on business at the moment."

"Nor is mine," Abramo said, raising his eyebrows.

Vincenzo shook his head. It was hardly appropriate to bring up matters of the heart at this, his wife's death feast. . . .

Abramo took his arm and pulled him to the edge of the portico, leaving Zola behind. "You seek me out, Baron. I will be in the city for another several weeks before I must depart to see to my other interests. When the clouds lift, when you are ready for more . . . When you wish to obtain the power that has eluded you, just out of your reach, come to call on me." He smiled at Vincenzo. "You well know what I have accomplished in Firenze. You are like me. We understand that true power does not reside in the roosters that parade about," he paused to gesture to two of the Nine on the other side of the room, even smiling at one, "but rather in those who toss them their seed. Working with me, we can gain wealth, power, greater than you have already accomplished. Together we could control eventually both Firenze and Siena."

Vincenzo stared outward, to the dark gardens below his home. Power, wealth mattered little if he could not keep a bride alive. And if there were no heirs to inherit the fortune, why bother at all?

"There is much to live for, despite how it may seem now," whispered Abramo lowly, sipping from his goblet and staring out to the crowd that remained. "You can attain more than you ever dreamed."

"More than I ever dreamed? I have dreamed of a great deal, Lord Amidei."

Abramo smiled and slid his eyes to meet Vincenzo's. "Ask for one thing, and I shall give it to you."

Vincenzo scoffed. "Has Lord Amidei departed? It appears that a god is standing at my portico rail."

Abramo threw his head back and laughed. "One thing," he said again, as if in challenge. "After that, you shall need to give something in return for each favor you ask."

"A business partnership? Is that what you propose?"

"We shall name it whatever you wish."

Vincenzo shifted uneasily. He was used to holding the power, controlling others. This man was one of the few who could send him reeling. He licked his lips, preparing an answer, when he felt Abramo straighten beside him. Vincenzo did the same, standing and turning back to the crowd. It was Daria, coming through at last, making her way to him from across the grand expanse.

"Ahh, the duchess," Abramo whispered. "So intriguing. Who is that with her?"

"The captain of her guard, Sir Gianni de Capezzana."

"Her lover?" he asked under his breath.

"Nay. The lady—"

"Oh, she is your lover?" he interrupted.

"Lord Amidei!"

Abramo laughed, raising his hands. "So provincial, you Sienese! What would be the harm of it? She is barren, is she not?"

"Mayhap," Vincenzo said lamely. He suddenly wished that Daria were back and safely handfasted to Marco Adimari, that it were she instead of Francesca that carried the child, that men like Abramo Adimari would no longer give her more than momentary notice.

"There are other ways to obtain heirs," Abramo said lowly in his ear. "Is it the enticing Duchess that I will first help you obtain?"

Vincenzo scoffed. If he wanted Daria, he would have her. What audacity, to think that he needed his assistance in obtaining a bride! Especially one as dear to his heart and life as Daria!

"M'lady, you are as beautiful as legend has it," Abramo said brazenly as Daria walked up to them, a tender smile upon her face as she looked to Vincenzo. Haltingly, she allowed the man to take her hand and kiss it as he bowed. As soon as she could, she withdrew her hand from him.

Gianni moved in closer to her, standing directly over her shoulder so that he was directly in Abramo's line of vision, his lips clamped in a solemn line.

Vincenzo hid a smile of approval. Daria had chosen this one well.

"Ahh, Sir Gianni de Capezzana," Abramo said, bowing lowly. His knowledge of the knight's name obviously threw him. "Have we met?"

"Nay," Vincenzo said. "I gave him your name. May I introduce you to Lord Abramo Amidei de Firenze?"

Gianni countered Abramo's deep bow. "The only Amideis I have met hailed from Roma."

"The black sheep of the family, I'm afraid," Abramo said with a winsome grin. "There are others in Venezia. But only our finest are in Firenze." He turned to Vincenzo. "I must depart now, Baron. Again, please accept my deepest condolences. Leo del Loren has been kind enough to give me use of his smaller city home while I am in Siena. Feel free to come and call upon me there should you feel up to the task."

At the mention of one of the Nine's names, a man that Vincenzo expected to attend this night, he turned away from Daria to face Lord Amidei again.

"Ahh, yes. We shall speak of him, then," Abramo said with one cocked eyebrow and another smile. He turned and gestured to a companion, a beautiful woman whom Vincenzo had not seen before, and she took his arm. The duo cascaded down the garden stairs in a flow of cape and gown, the finest of fabrics, and Vincenzo could not keep his eyes from them. Abramo did not look back. True power, he held. Would it be wise to see what the man could truly offer him? Offer them all?

"Uncle?" Daria asked softly from behind. "Forgive me for not standing by your side this evening."

He turned, remembering his frustration. "Yes. What kept you?"

"I was . . . detained. There were so many people here to see this night, so many who knew my parents. . . ."

The girl had never been a decent liar.

"Ahh." He scanned Gianni's face, but the man gave away nothing. Vincenzo took a sip of wine and felt it flow down his throat with a warm burn. If Daria could not be counted upon, mayhap it was time that he put every card into play.

He would see Lord Abramo in three days' time. He would let

the man wonder, show him he was not overly anxious, but then he would see what he had to offer. With luck, he could control Abramo more than he would attempt to control Vincenzo.

∂ ∂ ∂

"I have disappointed him," Daria said sorrowfully to Gianni and Father Piero after Vincenzo bid her household good night. Daria's knights, Father Piero, and Zola accompanied her down the stairs to their horses.

"He is distracted, for good cause," Gianni tried.

"Nay. I failed him," Daria said. She bit her lip and tensed as Gianni took her waist in his large hands and lifted her to the saddle.

"What was your choice?" he asked, looking up at her and passing her the reins.

"I know not. It was clearly the moment for the old woman. For us to see one more sign that we travel the right path. That the stakes are high. God could not have been more clear."

"Then you cannot question it," Father Piero said.

They wove through the streets, two by two.

"Lord Vincenzo's sorrow runs very deep," Gianni tried. "Your presence might have made this evening easier, but never palatable."

"Indeed." She appreciated his attempt to calm her.

"What do you make of Lord Amidei?" he asked, leaning forward, so that Zola could not hear them from three horses behind.

"He seemed . . . charming."

"That is it? Charming?"

"No. Well, yes. Charming. Wily. Powerful. Disturbing. Soothing. All at once."

Gianni nodded.

"Why? Do you know him? Of him?"

"Nay. I intend to soon."

Chapter Twenty-seven

By morningtide, word of Old Woman Parmo's healing had filtered through the entire city and within hours, the streets outside were clogged with people, carrying wounded or ill, crying out for attention, running toward the marketplace.

"Miracle worker!"

"Healer! In the market!"

"The old woman! She walks like a young virgin, healed, I tell you. . . ."

"Get your boy and bring him to the market—"

Gianni eyed them through his tall, narrow windows and then made haste through the solarium and over into Daria's suite. He met up with Father Piero as the man rushed up the stairs. "Are you aware—"

"Well aware," Gianni cut in. Hasani stood guard at Daria's door, his hand moving to his curved sword as they approached.

"Stand down, it is us," Gianni said, emerging from the shadows. The man grudgingly stepped aside and Gianni knocked upon Daria's door. "M'lady. Please, may we have a word?" She had not come down for mass or to break her fast. Was she ill?

Beata came to the door, and sliding her spectacles higher atop her nose, gestured inward into the dark room. Slits of lights peeked around the closed shutters, and the people's collective cry came to them.

"I must go to them," Daria said. She stood with her arm against the shutter, as if pulling back from a force outside.

"No, m'lady," Gianni said, shaking his head. "There is no way to protect you, out there. There is no control. . . ."

She dropped her arm and straightened. He saw now that tears streamed down her face. "I must go to them. How can I ignore their cries?"

"You feel the Spirit moving you to do so? Then why not? Why not go to them?" Father Piero asked quietly. Gianni threw him a look of exasperation. He supported her mad plan?

But her attention was solely on the priest. "I am afraid again. This time I am afraid that God will not work, that they will think I am a fraud, masquerading as healer."

"It is not what they think that is important, daughter. It is what God thinks. And how can you question the Almighty, after what you witnessed last night?"

"Nay! Nay! She may not depart this house!" Gianni cried.

"We could bring them in, then. One at a time," she said.

"Nay! If they discover that it is you, they would inundate this house. There would be a riot, no control. They would crush us."

"There has to be a way, Gianni," she said, coming closer to him. "He is calling me, asking me to go to them. It is much stronger than when I was called to the old woman . . . it steals my very breath."

"It could be the Lord afoot, Gianni," Father Piero said. "Mayhap it is with this event that others will hear of Daria and be drawn by her gifting. Mayhap we will gain the prophesied others—our missing discerner, prophet, or those who see visions or hold miraculous powers. We are incomplete. We must follow our given path."

Gianni let out a humorless laugh. "If word reaches our other Gifted, then it most assuredly will reach the Church. As well as others," he said, thinking of men in the shadows, spies that followed their every move but could not be intercepted. Who were they? What did they want? He ran a hand through his hair. His task was impossible! If she wanted to wade into that crowd, what good was his presence at all?

"God will protect us," Father Piero said.

"I will go in disguise. I will wear heavy veiling," Daria said.

"They will be in awe, they will not rip it from her head," Beata added.

"If I do not go, they are liable to hurt the old woman, tear from her the truth." He could hear the decision in her voice already. She was going. Now it fell to him to protect her.

"How will it work?" Gianni asked helplessly as Beata bent to pull veiling from a chest at the corner of the room. "Healing can take hours upon hours. Days. You cannot expect to heal as the disciples healed. And you've said yourself that God chooses to heal only here and there. What will transpire if healing does not occur? What if the crowd turns against you?"

Beata wound gray veiling around Daria's head and face, leaving only her wide, olive eyes exposed. "All I know is I am to go, Gianni. God gave me this word at Tatiana's mass. I suggest you change clothes. Out of the family crest and into a disguise of your own. I depart in ten minutes' time. With or without you."

"With me," he said, pointing a finger toward her. "You shall wait for me and my men and you shall give us thirty minutes."

"Twenty."

"Twenty-five!" He threw up his hands. "You are impossible. And you, Father, you may as well administer last rites to us all right now."

⚓ ⚓ ⚓

IT was Basilio who thought of nearing the market across the rooftops. The streets were fast becoming clogged with throngs of people, only one in twenty carrying along someone in need of healing, the others there to glimpse a vision of "the healing angel."

As they made their way toward the market, sometimes stealing across porticos and balconies, other times through windows and down alleyways . . . they heard shouts of visions of the Holy Virgin, of the apostles, just at the next corner, of Moses and Abraham, descending from the clouds. . . .

"Pray, dear priest," Daria whispered to him as they walked across another rooftop, two stories above the crowd, getting closer. "Pray for me—for wisdom and clarity and protection."

They jumped to the last rooftop, one that served as the edge of the market street, the farthest from the d'Angelo home.

"My prayers have been unceasing since this morning," Father Piero said. "You know what to do. He has not abandoned you." He reached out and took her shaking hands. "I must leave you, now. I do not want anyone to see us together, but we are near, dear one. All around you. We are near. God is near."

Daria looked into his eyes. He seemed like an entirely different man, out of his priestly robes and in the garb of a house servant. She glanced around and watched her knights drop to the ground on either side of the house, blending into the crowd. The plan was that if things went awry, they would fight their way to Daria's central point, cutting off any attempt to take her away, then pull her to safety above and back home, the way they had come. She turned. Gianni was pulling a cape hood over his head and nodded once to her.

Daria strode to the corner of the flat roof and stood there until someone noticed her.

"There! Look up there!"

"There she is! She has arrived!"

"It is the holy Mother!"

"An angel!"

Women screamed. Men shouted. The crowd moved as if it lived as one body, pushing en masse toward her.

"Wait!" Daria cried. "Be quiet!" She held up her hands and in minutes, the crowd hushed, as if holding its breath. "I come to you with a message of peace and hope. A message of love. Jesus the Christ loves each and every one of you. He longs to abide within you."

"My daughter, m'lady, she needs your touch!" cried out a forlorn, desperate mother holding a babe.

"My mother, Angel! She needs you!"

"Wait!" Daria shouted again. "I will leave if you refuse to listen!"

The crowd immediately hushed again.

"I have a gift, a gift of healing for many of you today. God has told me this."

A cheer went up and Daria waited for it to subside. "But I must share with you a Word from Scripture before I do. My gift, while remarkable, is nothing compared to what each of you holds within your heart. God himself has planted your gifting within each of you—the power to hope, the power to have faith, the power to love."

She gazed down at their sea of faces, bathed in wonder, and her heart skipped a beat. They were so hungry, so thirsty for the good Word. . . .

" '*Si linguis hominum loquar et angelorum caritatem autem non habeam factus sum velut aes sonans aut cymbalum tinniens. . . .*' These are holy words, the Word of the Lord. Let me tell you what it means. 'Though I speak in the tongues of men and of angels, and have not love, I am only a resounding gong or clanging cymbal. If I have the gift of prophecy and can fathom all mysteries and all knowledge, and if I have a faith that can move mountains, but have not love, I am nothing. . . .' "

A murmur moved through the crowd. "She dares to utter the Word in our language!"

"Who is she?"

"The Bible clearly teaches us to love," Daria shouted. "Jesus clearly teaches it. To love is our greatest gift. To love your neighbor as yourself, to accept that the Christ loved you enough to die for you, such love will bring the greatest healing of all! Embrace this teaching! Turn to one another, and tell thy neighbor, 'Thou art loved.'"

They stared up at her, unmoving, silent. "Do you not believe it? Thy Savior proved it to each of us," she said, beating her breast, "when he died upon the cross! I bear the truth of it, this day! I shout it to the heavens!" Words filled her mouth, words that were not her own. Daria felt her mouth moving, but it was the Spirit, the Holy Spirit that flowed through her. She fell to her knees and the crowd gasped.

It was love. The purest of loves that flowed through her.

All that was right and good in life was present at this moment. Daria wept. It mattered not that her mother and father were dead. It mattered not that Marco had turned from her. Her heart was whole again, bursting with this love inside her. God had healed *her*. And now she had to share it.

"I will come to you, my people," she said, tears rolling down her face beneath the veil. "God has sent us to you. And I am here to tell you that God loves each of you. Please . . . feel those words enter your heart as they have mine and let them do their healing work. You are loved," she said slowly, pausing over each word. "You are loved. You are loved! You are loved! You are loved!"

The crowd began to echo her words in a chant. "You are loved! You are loved!"

Daria laughed, and light and awesome joy surrounded her. She raised her hand and closed her eyes, praying the Scriptures, asking God to infiltrate each and every heart with the sword of truth. " '*Caritas patiens est benigna est caritas non aemulatur non agit perperam non inflatur. . . .*' Hear now, Saint Paul's word for each of you! 'Love is patient, love is kind. It does not envy, it does not boast, it is not proud. It is not rude, it is not self-seeking, it is not easily angered, it keeps no record of wrongs. Love does not delight in evil but rejoices with the truth. It always protects, always trusts, always hopes, always perseveres. *Love never fails.*"

"Love never fails!" echoed Piero from below her and to her left. In hooded cape, his face was mostly hidden from view. But Daria could see his smile!

"Love never fails!" shouted another.

"Never fails! Never fails! Never fails!" chanted the crowd.

Again, she waited for them to calm. "I tell you the truth. I have this gift now, but I do not know how long God will grant it. I will move between you now, if you will but part into two equal halves along the road. I ask you to pray for the healing you need now, and as I pass and afterward, thanking God, not I, for the gift. It is your risen Savior, Jesus Christ, that heals you, if he chooses to heal this day. It is he who shows us the way to love, the way to everything good," she said, making the sign of the cross before her. "Glory be to God!" she said, her voice strangled by tears. "Glory be to God!"

"Glory be to God!" shouted Father Piero.

"To God! To God!" shouted the crowd.

A ladder emerged from the storefront beneath her, and Daria turned to climb down it. Gianni was beside it, holding it when she touched ground, and she took his arm with a trembling hand. Basilio joined them from the right, and the crowd surged, pushing again, but obediently kept a path open to her.

From either side, hands reached out to her, but eerily, they did not shout. As Daria moved between them, slightly ahead of Basilio and behind Gianni, touching each and every hand, she continued to weep. "Your Savior loves you," she kept saying. "Your risen Savior longs to heal you," she said, over and over. "Your Savior wishes to know you. Believe and be saved. Believe and be healed. Believe and know that he is God!"

She paused on occasion to lay a hand upon a fevered brow, the mouth of a babe who had not cried since birth, the eyes of an old man who had not seen in decades, a youth's jaw riddled with infection. She touched hundreds upon hundreds of fingertips, praying that Jesus would enter each heart, each mind, each soul and bring them ultimate peace and healing through his love. And should God grant them amazing favor, to heal some of their physical ailments as well.

⁂ ⁂ ⁂

FOLLOWING behind her, Piero heard the cry of the babe mute since birth, the shout of the old blind man seeing his grandchild beside him, the young boy opening and closing a mouth once fused shut. He saw for himself the strapping young man who rose from his pallet, his fever now broken. The hairs stood up on his neck in awe at what was transpiring, nothing like he had ever seen before. But it was not danger he sensed, but the presence of the Holy. Here in this street, greater than any time he had felt the Spirit draw near, be it in cathedral or chapel or home, *God was here.*

His mind spun with the possibilities. Was this what they were called together to do? To minister to the weak? The sick? The aged? To spread this Gospel of love? His mind went back to the Church, of all the time spent in writing letters, coordinating new rules, new laws for the people. Their desire was holy—to keep the people in line, to teach them the right ways of men when so many strayed. But they had forgotten this, this truest of lessons, this greatest of stories, to tell the people that *they were loved.* As they were. Now and evermore. Loved.

After two hours of praying, Daria reached the end of the line and began to make her way back, still reaching out to touch her people. She wavered on her feet, obviously exhausted. "Captain," Basilio whispered, suddenly at Gianni's side. "The guards from the Duomo. And the bishop. They are present."

Piero turned. "In the name of Jesus Christ, I command thee to cease your evil doings!" shouted Bishop Benedicto in fine robes from three hundred feet away. He hurried forward, a contingent of armed guards hurrying before and behind him.

"It is in his name we move and breathe," Piero said. "You cannot keep us from this truest of callings! My friends," he said to the crowd. "Do not hurt your dear bishop nor his men. But the time is not yet right for us to talk. Please . . . close in and block their way. Send them back to the Duomo until God himself asks us to meet."

Obediently, the crowd moved inward, closing the men off from Daria and her people, like the Red Sea after the great crossing. She turned and prayed over a few more people, then paused over a baby, spasming in a convulsion.

Gianni looked back to the Duomo guards, trying to fight their way forward. Precious minutes passed as she prayed, seeming to have forgotten the danger behind them. "M'lady," he said, bowing low to touch her shoulder as she continued to pray over the child, while his mother wept and watched.

Piero glanced back at the guards. Despite the people's best efforts, they were making headway. He did not want anyone injured on their behalf. The crowd was already in a frenzy, moaning, screaming, shouting all about them. "Mayhap it is not this one's time, Daria. We must make haste. . . ." His words faded into a smile as Daria leaned back.

The infant suddenly stilled and began to coo, smiling in perfect peace up at Daria and his mother. The young mother swayed back and forth, sobbing in joy and wonder. "Bless you, bless you, m'lady."

Daria stood and rocked back and forth on her feet. Her eyes were rolling back in her head and she slumped into a faint.

Gianni scooped her up into his arms. "She is all right," he said to the gasping crowd, still eyeing the guards behind them. "She is simply exhausted and must return to her home. Please, do not follow us. Let us depart in peace and guard our backs. Your lady only asks that you remember what she has told you this day—to love one another as the God of love loves each of you."

CHAPTER TWENTY-EIGHT

VINCENZO made his way to the de Loren estate, just two blocks away from Daria's home. The streets were still agog with rumors of the healer. The story was that the same woman had healed Old Woman Parmo—even though the old woman denied it—the night of Tatiana's funeral feast. Vincenzo's eyes flicked down the winding street in the direction of the d'Angelo home, remembering Daria's odd, late entrance that eve, her attempt to hide her absence.

He turned in the opposite direction, thinking of the story of how the healer's men asked the crowd to cut off the Duomo guards and the bishop, how one had picked up the healer and carried her away. There were rumors that she died that day, giving the last of her life for those around her and for her Gospel of love. Vincenzo let out an exasperated breath from between his lips. The city was rife with simpletons. They were anxious to embrace any new messiah!

At the de Loren estate, Vincenzo pulled his horse to a stop and waited while his guards rapped upon the giant door. This was Lord

Leo de Loren's second estate in the city, a smaller abode that was just about as big as Vincenzo's sprawling home. The Nine lived in the nine largest homes, with the highest towers in the city bordering the *campo*.

The gate swung open and Vincenzo rode into the courtyard, dismounting as Lord Abramo neared him. "Welcome, welcome, my friend."

Vincenzo followed Abramo into the house, into the ground-floor salon, which had tall, leaded Venetian glass windows that opened to verdant gardens outside. He nodded in appreciation as Abramo noted one fine feature after another in the home. "I think my sojourn will someday turn into full citizenship, I enjoy it here so," Abramo said, gesturing toward a chair for Vincenzo as he sank into another. "I just brokered a deal to purchase this estate from de Loren."

"You do not miss Firenze?"

"Nay," Abramo said, with a dismissive glance to the window. "I always prefer to embrace what is before me, be it in Roma or Firenze or Siena. There is much here to be done, much before us."

Vincenzo shifted in his seat. So they had arrived at the point of this visit already. Abramo was swift. Vincenzo sat back in his chair and steepled his fingers, staring at Abramo. "Lord Leo offended me, by not attending my wife's funeral feast as promised."

Abramo nodded, as if he understood. "It is difficult. To run a city such as this and tend to all the important people. As I understand it, he was called away on another matter."

"And I suppose Lord Damien was called away on that same business?"

Abramo nodded, furrowing his brow. "Yes, yes, I believe he was."

Vincenzo studied the tall man, thinking of Tatiana and her family in Firenze. When she had known Abramo, he was traveling, unmarried, building his father's business. Vincenzo remembered her talking about him with an edge of wonder to her voice. He always remembered talk of men who might become a competitor.

"Are you married, Lord Abramo?"

"Me? Nay. Women are like business to me. Always a new one to be had."

Vincenzo watched Abramo as he pretended to laugh with him. Clearly this man was used to power, infiltrating his city as easily as he had infiltrated Firenze. Firenze was larger; perhaps he had set his sights on the smaller, noble city of Siena as a secondary base of operations.

Vincenzo needed him as much as Abramo needed Vincenzo. He spoke the truth when he said that together they would both be stronger. The man seemed to shake excess power from his shirtsleeves. He would most assuredly rise in stature and strength. And Vincenzo wanted to go with him. Set aside his need for a new bride, an heir for a time, concentrate on business, build an even greater empire. Something he could control. He looked at Abramo across his steepled fingers, keeping his tone carefully neutral. "I obviously need both Lord Leo and Lord Damien if I am to control the Nine. With them in tow, I could increase the guild's exports and imports threefold."

Abramo nodded, considering it as if it were a new idea to him. Vincenzo knew it was not. In fact, he was certain that it was Abramo who had moved casually between Vincenzo and these two, knowing it would gain him leverage. He had probably seen to it that they would be absent the night of Tatiana's death feast, in order to best maneuver Vincenzo into his hands.

"And if I bring Lord Leo and Lord Damien to your side, if you gain subtle control in this city, Baron del Buco, what do I obtain?"

"I do not know. What is it you want?"

It was Abramo's turn to steeple his fingers. The warm laugh lines around his eyes faded. Vincenzo fought off the urge to shift in his seat and remained as deadly still as the man before him.

Then the smile lines reappeared and Abramo shrugged with a laugh. "I confess, I do not know. We can discuss that later. But my friend, I like you. I have a good feeling about you, of how we might work together. I offer you not only Lord Leo and Lord Damien, but Lord Frangelico as well."

Lord Damien! Vincenzo's attempts in making inroads with him had seemed futile, and Daria had reacted so strongly against Frangelico that he knew she would never come to his aid in establishing the vital link. Frangelico had been at the Church to maintain public appearances, but Vincenzo doubted that he had ever considered attending the death feast in order to honor the del Buco name. Abramo must have gotten to him through ties in Firenze, in Venezia. If he had Lord Frangelico, then ultimate power within Siena lay within reach of him.

Or them. His mouth was dry, as if he were a thirsting man panting while he waited for a drip of water. It was better, he reminded himself, to have a portion, if not all.

Abramo rose. "Yes. Yes, I see it all now, my friend. This will be the start of a grand partnership. Together, we can obtain greater wealth, greater power than anything you have known!"

Vincenzo smiled and rose, reaching to shake the man's large hand and kiss his cheeks to solidify the deal. They walked to the courtyard, Abramo's hand on his shoulder, speaking in his ear how they would move in the coming week to maintain the control that Vincenzo had already gained, and make three bold strokes to commit Lord Leo, Lord Damien, and finally Lord Frangelico to every one of their desires—be they whim or winsome endeavor.

Vincenzo found himself liking how Abramo talked, moved, reached out and brought people together as they strolled through the garden, through the kitchen, through the women's salon, where three of the prettiest of women reclined.

It had been many years since he had met a man he admired. Many years since he had had a mentor. It unsettled him in a way, sparked new life and interest in others. And after saying such a long, dismal good-bye to Tatiana, any interest in life was welcome indeed.

He was mounting up to leave, when Abramo asked him a casual question. "What do you make of this mad story of the marketplace healer?"

Vincenzo's eyebrow shot upward. "I spoke to the bishop. It happened. They discovered her, the people, claiming miraculous healing. The crowd turned against them, kept the Duomo guards from her, but did as she asked—turned them away unharmed. They spoke of love. They say she was translating Scripture into the language of the people."

Abramo's hand rested on Vincenzo's horse's neck. The horse shifted uneasily. She had always been high-strung. "Most curious. See what you can find out, Vincenzo. We need the identity of our mysterious healer. Knowledge," he said, tapping his temple, "is power."

ტ ტ ტ

THE city swelled with people from all around Toscana as news of the healings spread. Vito and Ugo brought back stories from the pub that hundreds had been healed even though her men could quantify only fifteen to twenty from that day. It mattered not; the city was agog and seeking the mysterious healer. Daria and her household remained at home, daring not to venture out again until the attention dried up.

It was only when news arrived that another healer was in the countryside, in the hills above Siena, that the Gifted rose to attention.

"Is it another? Another of us?" Daria asked the priest.

"Mayhap."

"Mayhap?"

"It could be an interloper, an agent of the enemy. The dark one does not like it when the Lord of Light makes such strides as we made in that marketplace."

"But it could be one of us, one of the Gifted."

"Mayhap. Or it could be a witch or sorcerer, pretending to be a harbinger of healing."

Gianni sat upright. "What leads you to that conclusion?"

"The Church is not our greatest concern; those of the dark will gather to counter our every move and they are prolific, legion. It is logical that after our marketplace spectacle, they will attempt to seize the attention."

"I could make an appearance again," Daria said.

"We are not actors," Father Piero said.

"I did not mean it in that way—"

"I am certain you did not. But we must be very careful. Every move must be examined, thought out, prayed over. Gianni feels that enemies already study our movements. Daria, you must tend to your days as usual—for appearances as well as for the sake of your business. You are gathering protection because you are attempting to hold on to everything your father built; your peers will see your weaknesses as a female and pass it off as nothing more than plumage."

"Understood," Gianni said. "Let me send two of my men to attend this healer's service. Discover what they can."

Father Piero paced back and forth for a moment, considering. "Not you, Gianni, nor me or Lady Daria. It must be two others. The dark might recognize our presence and expose us. It could prove dangerous." He eyed the knights and Zola, hovering in the corner like a mouse trying to blend in.

"Rune, Vito, and Zola. You are the three that shall attend. Rune most often travels with Basilio, Vito with Ugo. Mixing it up might make them less obvious."

Zola shook her head. "Not I, Father. I am not strong enough."

Father Piero gave her a queer look and then smiled. "Nay. You are as you should be, woman. Please, go with the others. And come back to us with news."

"M'lady," Agata said, pausing in the doorway. "You have a visitor."

Daria frowned in irritation. "Who?"

"Master Ambrogio Rossellino," she said with a small smile.

Daria squealed with joy and flew from the padded bench, out toward the front entry, Agata and Gianni just behind her. "Ambrogio!" she cried, rushing into the young man's arms. He was still so much the same—standing eye to eye with her, curly hair cropped close to the skull, the newest fashions, shining green eyes, dark, bushy brows. They kissed from side to side and back again.

"Daria," the man said. "My dear friend. It has been too long!"

"Indeed! Come, come! Let us walk in the garden!" She ignored Gianni, just over her shoulder, ignored Ambrogio's curious glance into the hall filled with men. It had been two years since she had seen him, what with his work in Firenze and her own exile as she broke with Marco. Their fathers had been dear friends, as had Marco's father and her own, and there was a time that Marco, Ambrogio, and Daria had ridden high into the hills of Siena every summer eve. It was upon that tender, innocent age she wished to dwell for a time, not the intrigue and fear that rambled through her house and eaves like a pigeon seeking a roost.

She took his arm and they wandered into the garden as she suggested. Ambrogio complimented her, made her laugh. But soon, he could not ignore Gianni any longer. "So, who is the hulking knight that seems intent on remembering every stitch in my vest?"

"Gianni de Capezzana," she said lowly, whispering. "Captain of my guard."

"Captain? Of your guard?" he asked with furrowing brow. "Since when did the house of d'Angelo need guards?"

"Since . . ." She paused to absently finger a rose, trying to find light words for so heavy a subject.

"Oh, Daria, forgive me. That was careless of me. Of course. Without your father, without Marco . . . It is a wise course."

She nodded, eager to be past the subject. "So, you have returned to Siena. For good?"

"I hope so. I have a new assignment at the Palazzo Pubblico. My paintings make the priests cross-eyed with concern, but the nobles continue to pay for them, so what can they say?" he said with a sly shrug. A child prodigy who had picked up on the unique, three-dimensional structure of the painters of Firenze, Ambrogio was known far and wide for his unique perspective; now as he gained maturity, his paintings were creating a stir from Roma to Venezia, even though the priests did grumble about his Christ figures that did not maintain the typical sovereign detachment.

As long as Daria had known him, Ambrogio had been fascinated with the bond between Holy Mother and Child, as well as Christ's humanity, with man's fascination over him. In his paintings, the Christ was frequently a squirming, restless babe, or a suckling child staring out at the painting's viewer with intense curiosity. In one he was so distracted and frightened by the attention of the viewer that he appeared to have crushed his pet goldfinch.

"So who is your latest victim?" she asked conspiratorially.

Ambrogio smiled and wiggled his brows. "The chapel in the Monte Siepi abbey."

"You were working upon that when I last saw you, two years past!"

Ambrogio nodded. "It was massive in scope." He gesticulated wildly, dramatically, stepping away from her, swooping his left arm in an arc, then his right, telling her of the frescoes, of walls depicting Galgano's vision, portraying a procession of saints and angels on the side walls covering, covering, covering one panel after another, sweeping along the visitors inside the chapel, toward the Madonna enthroned as queen of heaven. "By using the entire chapel space, it is as if we are inside Galgano's head. Do you see? Do you *see?*"

Daria clapped her hands, grinned, and nodded. "It is a marvelous concept. I cannot wait to lay eyes upon it."

He sobered. "You cannot go. They have destroyed it."

"Destroyed it?"

"Yes. The fools! On the front panel, my Madonna was cowering in utter terror beneath the angel, not wishing to hear the annunciation. I would not care for an angel to appear before me with such news, would you?"

"Nay," Daria said with a fearful grin.

"I had the Maestà above her, enthroned, crown, scepter, all that. I had both. Both the girl-child, Mary, discovering she was to bear the Baby of all babies, and the Holy Mother, queen of heaven. But it was not enough!"

"Not enough?"

"Nay. They had some foolish interloper come and paint over my front panel. Can you imagine? They painted over it!"

"Impossible! With what?"

"An entirely boring, meek Madonna and mother with Christ child on her lap. Ooo. Fascinating. Where have we seen that before? Umm, mayhap in every other church from Venezia *a* Roma?"

Daria hid a smile behind her hand. Ambrogio was always impassioned, and very nearly always on the other side of some great force. "How do you do it, Ambrogio?" she asked, sinking to a garden bench. "How do you put so much of yourself into your work and then walk away? After two years? How do you accept the destruction of your work, the dismantling of a masterpiece?"

"Bah," he said, blowing out his breath and sinking to the bench beside her. "Ever forward, dear friend. One cannot look back, only forward. I immerse myself in what might be rather than obsess on what might have been."

They talked for hours, until their backsides grew sore, sitting on the stone bench, and they were forced to move. There was no lover's interest from Ambrogio, more a brotherly love. Oh, how she had missed him! Missed his easy camaraderie. It had been like that with Marco, once, but with something more. . . .

"What is that sad smile?" he asked, pulling her to her feet.

"Nothing. I have missed you."

"Well, I am back," he said, swinging her around. "Wait," he said, pausing suddenly. He pulled her back toward a sliver of evening light, lifted her chin, and made her stand there a moment.

"I really must paint you m'lady. You were stunning as a girl, but now, as a woman—m'lady, you are . . ." His eyes narrowed. "If only you did not have such a large, hairy mole upon your nose." He *tsk*ed under his breath. "Most unfortunate."

"Brogi," she said, smiling and shaking her head. He always loved to tease her.

"Nay. You are beautiful, Daria. More fair than any real duchess."

She moved away from him, embarrassed, wishing only to escape his intense gaze. "You have always overemphasized truth, Ambrogio."

He held onto her hand so when she took another half step, she was forced to stop and look back in his direction. He smiled then. "Nay. And yes. I am apt to overdramatize things. But art, subjects. That has always been my heart. You know that, better than anyone. Believe me when I tell you this. You *are* magnificent, Daria."

"I am suitable. Pleasing to the eye at times—"

Ambrogio feigned heart failure, gasping and sinking backward to the bench. "Such lies! My heart cannot take such lies!"

Daria crossed her arms and waited for his drama to be over. "Will you take the stage next?"

"I tried that, once. Let us just say that it works better for me to work alone." He stayed there, on the bench, arms on knees, looking up at her. "Were you so wounded, dear one, that you can no longer accept the simple truth of your own blessed countenance? Did Marco so injure you? Shall I go and cut out his eyes as punishment, so that he will be forced to think of nothing but your visage every time he looks into the ever-night?"

Daria laughed under her breath. "Nay, nay. That would not suit at all. He is married now. A father-to-be at last." She turned her back to him and took a few steps. "Our parting was almost as painful for Marco as it was for me. Love . . . love sometimes is simply not meant to be."

"Nay. Nay!" he said, rising and walking to her, turning her

around to face him. "I can hear in your voice that even you do not believe your own words! Love is always meant to be. Always, always, always. It is our sin, our folly, our feeble eyes that lead us astray. But love . . . love is *love*. Beyond us. Otherworldly. Godly. We capture a bit of the heavenly and hold it close and then it escapes us. We are so foolish, letting it depart! That is when tragedy occurs. You have suffered a tragedy, dear girl, with Marco. A tragedy. And it is not just that after your parents, after all you went through, you had to suffer this. But know this: Love . . . love is always meant to be. It may escape us, but it hovers nearby, waiting to be recaptured, held close."

She looked into his earnest eyes, hearing the echo of her own words in the marketplace, feeling them minister to her heart again, realizing he would not let this moment go until she accepted his impassioned words. "I thank you for thy kind words, Brogi. Know that healing has already occurred, deep within me." She considered telling him all of it, beginning in Roma, but Hasani caught her eye. "God has healed me, Ambrogio. It is only when I talk about the past, think of what might have been, that this huge, melancholic hole gapes open in my chest like an old wound with a light suture. Now, please. Help close it again. Speak to me of other subjects. Any other subject than that that leads me to Marco. What are you to work on next?"

He stared at her solemnly for a moment, letting her question hang in the air. Then, "I am at work on a piece for the Nine. Something that has not one Madonna or Child in it, I hope."

She laughed. "That is marvelous, Ambrogio." She took his arm again and they walked back to the front gate. "You must come and call, at least once a week. You have done my heart good, being here. Please say you will."

"I will look forward to it, m'lady," the man said, sweeping into a low bow. "I will return, one week hence."

"Good." He turned to leave and she reached out to him with one more word. "Brogi?"

"*Sì?*"

"Why did you not come? To the baroness's death feast. I assumed you would be there, since you were but a half day's ride away."

Ambrogio's bright green eyes clouded and he tried a half smile. "The baron and I . . . We had a parting of ways. I have not been welcome in his home for some time."

Daria shook her head with a start. Vincenzo? He had become this angry with Ambrogio? Or vice versa? She could not imagine what would have led to that! "There is obviously more to that story. You will tell me the whole of it, when you return next week."

"If you insist. Fare thee well, dear one. It is so grand to see you." They kissed, cheek to cheek, and Basilio rolled the chain to open the gate. Ambrogio looked over at him, and Rune in the corner, and Hasani over her shoulder. He wiggled his eyebrows again at Daria. "A princess in her castle, surrounded by her knights. It is at last as it always should have been."

"Good night, Brogi."

He swept out of the gate then, and into the dark night. And for the first time in a long time, Daria found herself smiling for little reason at all.

CHAPTER TWENTY-NINE

FATHER Piero had prepared them well, and all had prayed over them, prayed for their protection as they moved out into the streets of Siena toward the hills, but still he could not rest. There was something off about Zola, something deeper where she would not allow access. By all appearances, she seemed healed, renewed, but there was still something dark that lingered in the depths. Why could he not get to it? What was it?

"They will be well, priest," Gianni called from the corner. "Cease your mutterings."

"I cannot. There is something that keeps me from rest."

Gianni peered over at him. "Be more specific."

"It is Zola," Piero said, hating that it sounded like a confession. But it was, in a sense. They all considered him to be the wise man of the group, the one who guided in spiritual matters, but this one was a conundrum indeed.

Gianni sat up straighter. "You do not trust her."

"No. Yes." He shook his head. "There is something disquieting about the woman."

"You are a priest!" Gianni scoffed. "You do not succumb to the ways of man around a maid. . . ."

Piero shot him a doleful look. "It is not that."

Gianni shrugged. "She has been through much. Perhaps her darker years resonate within her. It takes many years of light, at times, to counteract a year of shadow."

"Indeed. Indeed." Piero tried to take in the knight's words, absorb them as clarification, encouragement. But there was something that niggled at him. . . .

♂ ♂ ♂

THE trio drew near the outskirts of the crowd, now eighty strong, but the Sorcerer could easily pick them out. The way they moved, observed, a half step away. *They might as well be wearing white crosses.* It was just as well. Zola was with them. Perhaps between them, they could turn the two knights who walked with her, even while the moon still hung in the sky. *Prepare for battle, knights!*

He smiled from beneath his hood, reveling in the glory of it. Two days prior, twenty had been present. Yesterday, fifty. Today, eighty! The Gifted would have no opportunity to escalate their power again while he was within reach. He offered the people a consistent story to tell—one that eclipsed the mysterious, disappearing healer of the marketplace. He offered the people a taste of glory! A taste of wonder!

The sun had set two hours prior and on the horizon, a waxing moon glowed in the night sky. *Lughnasadh.* A true holiday for the people!

Slowly, reverently, the Sorcerer raised his arms and held them there in the air until all quieted and drew near. He closed his eyes and listened to them all, breathing, coughing, sniffling. Directly before him was a paralytic, a paralytic from the marketplace who had not been near enough the healer to taste change. Tonight, tonight, the man would discover change.

"Air!" the Sorcerer shouted, digging a stick into the soft, fine

Tuscan-red dirt in front of him. "Fire!" he shouted again, drawing a line.

In tandem with his shout, a huge pyre was set aflame, the fuel-covered dry tinder alight in a sinuous, dancing flame.

"Water!" he yelled, and a plebe took a gourd filled with water and sprinkled it across the crowd as the Sorcerer drew in the sand yet another line.

"Earth!" he growled, drawing the fourth line and then dropping the stick to stretch his arms out, turning, as if absorbing power from the depths. "Earth! Earth!"

Slowly, carefully, he bent to retrieve the stick and said lowly, "Spirit." He turned and walked away from the pentagram, taking five steps up the hill, listening as the crowd whispered back a report to those behind them of his last word.

"Tell me, my friends. What do all of these elements have in common?"

The crowd hushed and then someone dared to answer.

"It is us!" dared a man. "They are things all around us."

"Indeed," said the Sorcerer. "All around us. Us. Us." He paced back and forth, observing each face, each expression of fear and interest and bewilderment and confusion and intrigue. . . . "Us. You. You, and you. Every man, woman, and child here. Around you.

"All our lives, we have been taught by the holy men in churches that it was all about another. But I am here to tell you that it is all about us. We hold the reins in our hands as to what happens here and now, what happens in the hereafter, if we will but reach out and lay claim to it!

"We are children of this mighty earth! The Holy Scriptures tell us of it, right there in the beginning. In Genesis, what did God create first?"

"Earth!"

"And when he turned to us, from whence did Adam come? Of what matter did he fashion the first man?"

"Earth!"

"And when our bodies give out, when the worms come and eat our flesh and bones, to where does this body go?"

"Earth!"

"Yes. Yes. Now you begin to see what others have kept from you. We are one with this land. One with this place. Birthed from it, returning to it." He drew a circle in the air. "And we have been kept from her powers." He let that thought settle among them a moment, feeling like he watched water draining away down a thirsty hole. "Her powers may be yours if you simply reach for them. Be you noble or slave. Man or woman. Human or animal. Tree or blade of grass. There is no greater than another. All are equal here, in this place.

"And if the earth gives us life, takes us in death, it is also here to give us rest when we ail. From it we can absorb what we are missing, and absorb other elements from water, fire, air, and spirit. When you set to work, to learn the craft—to learn what others have strived to keep from you in an effort to maintain power—you will master everything around you. There is no great secret, here, friends. There is only knowledge.

"The priests try to keep knowledge from you. They do not trust knowledge in your hands. But I give it to you freely today. Close your eyes, breathe in the scent of the earth. . . ."

The Sorcerer moved to an older woman nearby. "Sister," he said, bending down and reaching a hand to touch her shoulder. "You ail."

"Why . . . why, yes."

"Why do you suffer?"

"Well . . . because it is my lot."

"It is your lot to suffer? Nay! Tell me how you are suffering."

"It is my back. My back gives me terrible trouble."

"No longer," said the master, shaking his head slowly. "No longer!" he shouted. The crowd was silent before him. "I need your help, my people. I need you to work with me if we are to call the forces here today that will heal this woman. . . ."

ᚯ ᚯ ᚯ

"CHARLATAN," Rune said.

"He is after their money," said Vito. "He wants something from them. Men like this never move without an—"

"Hush," Zola said, leaning toward them. "You must be quiet."

Rune glanced across Vito to her, wondering at the intensity of her tone. Fear. Why, fear? He looked beyond her to others in the crowd, most wearing hoods. Why such secrecy among the followers? Did they know they erred in their presence in this place? He covered a shiver down his back by turning in the other direction. In Germania, there were gatherings like this in the Black Forest. Rumors of healers and magic, white and dark. . . .

"This woman desires healing!" shouted the leader. "She wishes for a back that is free from pain! Shall she have it?"

Yes, yes, yes, shouted the crowd. *Yes, yes, yes.*

The leader began to chant and pray in Latin, quietly enough that it was difficult to make out his words. He circled the old woman, who was on her knees, rocking, wailing.

Every time the leader passed by the bonfire, the flames seemed to spark and swell, larger and larger although no fuel was added to it. He nodded to two men and they lifted a large bucket of water and slowly poured it over the old woman's head. The leader continued to chant, waving his hands above the woman, now drenched and shivering before him.

"Say it with me!" the leader shouted.

The crowd, with rapt attention, immediately repeated his words.

"What is it?" Vito asked. "I do not know Latin. What does he have them saying?"

"Thou will find new life from Mother Earth," Rune translated, another shiver running down his back. "Thou will find your thirst quenched from the Water, thou will find your bones warmed from the Fire, thou will find the Spirit to heal you—"

The master looked up then, out in their direction as if he had heard them. They were just beyond the light cast by the bonfire, deep in shadow. But it was as if he could see them clearly.

The man returned his attention to the woman.

"Did that just happen?" Vito whispered.

"Hush," Zola said.

"No, I mean . . . did he see us? Look to us?"

"Hush," Zola insisted.

"He cannot hear us, not above this din—"

"Earth! Sky! Water! Fire! Spirit!" the leader screamed, his arms outstretched. He reached forward and lifted the old woman to a standing position and moved behind her. "Earth, sky, water, fire, spirit . . ." he chanted. He took her arms at the shoulder and put what looked like a knee to her back. "Woman, embrace thy healing!"

The bonfire exploded then, as if a boulder had been cast into its very center and engulfed in flame, becoming twice as big as before. The crowd fell back, gasping.

But when they turned their attention forward, the woman had her hands to her face and was weeping, weeping with joy. "My pain! My pain is gone!" she shouted out to the crowd, arms outstretched.

Rune looked at Vito, who shared a confused expression. "It appears real," Vito said, giving his head a little shake.

But when Rune looked to Zola, she was smiling, tears drifting down her face, clapping with the rest of the crowd.

"Zola!" he whispered, but she ignored him, her eyes only upon the Sorcerer. She stared blankly forward, as if she saw but did not truly see. "Zola!"

"It does not end here!" the leader shouted. "Who else? Who else seeks healing this night?"

Five people filed upward and lined up in front of him. With a nod, he sent two men behind the five and began chanting over all five of them, bending to hear each one's complaint. He walked back and forth, back and forth, chanting the same Latin words as before, and the crowd enthusiastically chanted along with him.

He returned to the man at the far right and took his face between his hands. "Man of the Earth, take in you what you need to be healed. Take in you the heat of Fire! Take in you the cleansing of Water! Take in you the life of Air! Take in you the vitality of the Earth. Take in you the Spirit now!"

The man seeking healing fell back with the leader's last word and the fire again grew as if dry fuel had been thrown atop it. The crowd gasped again. Sparks flew up into the dark night sky as if inhaled by a giant. The leader's men caught the falling man and gently laid him down upon the ground.

"Now!" shouted the leader, pushing the second backward as if a force leapt from his hand.

"Now!" shouted the leader, pushing the third, then the fourth, then the fifth.

Slowly, the first man sat up, holding his ear. "It's gone! The pain! I've been healed!" he shouted. The second followed suit, rising to a sitting position and shaking his head in wonder. The other three did the same.

"What you see here, tonight, my friends," said the leader, pacing back and forth, "is nothing that you cannot accomplish yourself. This is the power of God within our hands!"

"Blasphemy," growled Rune, stepping forward.

Vito reached out and grabbed his arm. "Speak not," he hissed. "Remember Father Piero's words. But listen to this man, Rune! Listen to him! Are his words not words that our own might speak?"

"Yes," said Zola, her eyes dreamy with wonder. "I've considered the same thing."

"It is not at all the same thing—" Rune began.

"This is what God wanted for us, when he created us!" called the man. "Why else, how else can you explain the wonders you have seen this night? Come back to me again, my friends, while we still have time together. Come tomorrow, here, and my people will lead you to our secret meeting place. I will teach you, show you the wonders of this natural world. . . ."

"I cannot abide by it," Rune said, shaking his head. "We must speak up. All these fools shall be led astray."

"Nay," Zola said, turning to him. "Come. You have seen enough. We will return to the house of d'Angelo and tell our people what we have seen this night." She tugged at his arm. "Come. Come away, Sir Rune. We will return on the morrow if you wish to hear more."

She turned and walked down the hill and Vito followed her, casting an eye of wonder back up the hill where the healer had been. Rune frowned. Could these people not see what they had just encountered? Could they not see it?

CHAPTER THIRTY

DARIA awoke three nights later in a cold sweat. She could still see the girl child, shaking, reaching out to her. She hadn't much time. The child was alone and dying. And she was important to God. And to the Gifted?

Daria pulled back the covers and stepped into slippers, then hurried into an old gown that was meant for gardening and little other. She wound her hair up into a knot and then the veiling around that. One week she had waited to venture out again, the urge to move and do as God bid welling up inside her like a flood building against a dam. No longer. She could wait no longer.

She hurried to the door and pulled it open, rushing through, but then paused with a gasp. Her hand flew to her chest as a man stepped out of the shadows.

"Hasani," she whispered, trying to still her pounding heart. Then she looked at him more closely. He was fully dressed. And holding an unlit lantern and sword. "How did you know?" she whispered.

The tall African lifted one shoulder and then turned to go.

Daria followed, through the hallway, down the stairs, and to the front gate. A guard, Ugo, roused from his doze and walked toward them. "M'lady? Where are you going?"

"Out," she said, staring at the doorway as Hasani opened it.

"Out? At this hour?"

"I have been called."

Ugo paused a moment. "Let me go and retrieve the captain."

"Nay," she said, placing a hand upon his arm. "I am not alone. I have Hasani. We will be less conspicuous alone. It is for my safety that I must travel thus."

Hasani raised his hood and covered his head.

"Right," Ugo said, crossing his arms. "No one will notice a hooded giant and a woman in veils moving about the streets at this hour."

Daria smiled, in spite of herself. "No one will be about at this hour. There is a girl, Ugo . . . we must get to her now." She moved ahead, now irritated that she had paused at all.

"I will go with you."

"Nay. You must stay at your post."

"Then I must go and report to the captain, m'lady."

"I am not a child," she said over the shoulder. "Do what you must, Sir Ugo. But know that I am and will always be the mistress of this house. And that the only one—the only one I capitulate to—is God himself. It is he who sends me on this mission tonight."

"Blessed be your task, m'lady," he said, with a slight bow.

"Now close the gates so that I know the house is secure."

"As you wish, m'lady."

When the gates were cranked to a secure close, Daria looked up at the guard in the tower—she could not make out who it was—and gave him a little wave. Then she looked left and then right, pausing. She had no idea where she was supposed to go. She closed her eyes and prayed for direction, for God to lead her to the child. Hasani tapped her on the shoulder and hooked his thumb right. He set off down the street.

Did he know where they were going? Was that possible? It felt right, somehow, as one felt when reaching the last road leading toward home. She hurried to match his pace, taking one and a half strides for every one of his.

⚭ ⚭ ⚭

GIANNI was on his feet out of bed, hand on the hilt of his dagger, before Ugo reached his side, panting.

"What? What is it?"

Vito rushed in, then, behind, from the tower.

"What? Are we in danger?"

"The lady, Captain. She and Hasani . . . they've left the house. She said she was called."

"They set off in the direction of the Duomo," Vito said.

"The Duomo? Is she mad? A contingent from Roma has just arrived. They've certainly been told of the marketplace, told of the dark healer in the hills. Does she seek to get herself thrown into prison?"

Both men shook their heads helplessly.

The other knights were awake now too, all except for Basilio, who snored away in the far bed. *Nothing can wake that man except morning.* "Rune, you go to the tower. Release Bormeo from his keep. He will find Lady Daria and circle above her. Vito, you come with me. Ugo, to the front gates."

The men strapped on belts that held swords and slipped on dark capes. Within minutes, Ugo was opening the heavy gates for them and the two exited. Gianni gazed upward, past deeply shadowed windows. Up top, Bormeo's cage was opened and with a screech, the falcon took flight. He circled several times, passing through the orb of the moon, then moved toward the great church, the Duomo.

⚭ ⚭ ⚭

DARIA and Hasani entered the narrow, empty Piazza del Duomo that swarmed with people during the heat of day. Only drunkards and the most pitiful of Siena remained out at this hour, snoring away in doorways. Others slept along the rim of the fountain. The few who awakened as they passed by them seemed afraid, slinking away to the opposite side of a statue or rising and scuttling away, casting fearful glances over their shoulder.

Daria and Hasani walked forward as if pulled, ignoring the onlookers, their eyes only on a man on the wide, shallow cathedral steps, holding a girl in his lap. Daria's heart raced. Gianni would consider her foolhardy, risking the Piazza del Duomo. *Here, Lord? Here is where you have asked us to come? Protect us, Holy One. Protect us, Lord Jesus!*

They were fifteen paces away before Daria pulled up short. It was Bishop Benedicto. The bishop himself who held the child.

But Hasani was already fading backward, concerned the old bishop would know them, together, immediately.

The bishop lifted his head, and streaks of tears ran down his face, glittering in the moonlight. He peered at her for a long moment and then wiped his cheeks. The girl gasped and then whimpered.

The bishop looked down at the child and then back to her. "You are the healer? The healer of the marketplace?" he asked. Two guards appeared at the top of the cathedral steps above him. Hearing his words, one immediately whirled and turned inside.

"Your Grace, may I have a word with you?" Daria asked, as calmly as she could. Her eyes remained on the elderly priest; she fought to keep them from the menacing guard. She had heard Gianni say that a force from Roma had made its first appearance, alerted by the stories told of Siena's healers.

The bishop peered over at her again. He raised a hand when the guard began to descend the stairs, hearing his clanking metal and rubbing leather, and seeing Daria begin to back away. "Nay. Stay where you are!" he shouted over his shoulder.

"May I approach, Your Grace?" she said, gesturing toward the girl.

"You may," he said.

She drew near and knelt before them. The girl child was delicate, about seven years of age. "What is her name?" she asked gently.

"Tessa. She is a beggar of the piazza. For years, I have given her bread each day. She is a good child, with a good heart. But these are troubling days. . . . I could never find a home for her where she would stay. . . . This morning, she was missing. I could not sleep, knew I had to find her if I was to have any rest." He glanced at Daria. "I found her an hour ago, like this, barely coherent. Shaking. I was afraid to move her. I fear she is dying."

Daria reached out and touched the child's wrist. Her pulse was weak and slow. "Yes. It appears she is."

She allowed him to ask the question she knew would come.

"Why are you out at this hour, woman?"

"Because God awakened me as well." She smiled softly from beneath her veils. A movement in the sky caught her attention. A bird? "Your Grace, I assume you know by now that the healings that occurred in the marketplace were real."

The aged bishop kept his eyes on the child, struggling to breathe. "So they claim."

"Your Grace, this gift is from God. I did not ask for it. But he asks me to use it for his good."

"God does not need us to do his mighty work."

"Indeed," she said, thinking. "But at times he gives us mighty work to do. See for yourself all that men of the Church have done on his behalf! As for me, all I can tell you is that I can feel his heart, his urging. . . . He has asked me to do this tonight, to heal your young friend. He wants her to be saved."

The bishop scowled at her. "I have prayed over this child for nigh unto an hour."

"You have laid good groundwork, then. Again, this is not about me. And if I may, this is not about you. This is about God and Tessa. Will you permit me to heal her?"

The bishop scoffed. "Such audacity! A contingent has just ridden in. . . ."

"Yes. I am aware of them. Surely you can see that I am not foolish—that this is an acknowledged risk. And yet when God calls, a devout follower goes. No one knows this better than a priest, yes?"

He gave her a reluctant nod.

"Please. Let me do as our Lord bids. If you decide I am an interloper, that this gift is not of divine origin, then I will willingly submit to your guards." She glanced up and saw that six more had joined the first. They wore the same cape that Gianni had once worn, with the tau cross. "Consider it your own trial of my gifting. Even if I were unwilling, it would be difficult for me to escape."

He stared at her, considering. "You are daring."

"Please, Your Grace. There is little time. Examine me firsthand and see if you are not convinced that the Lord is at work."

Still, he paused. She could feel the child fading. Her neck prickled as if angels were drawing near. . . . "I invite you to call down prayers of protection, for the evil one to be driven out, for life to come back to this child. Surely if I were of the dark I would not invite this! I would not ask for God to do one of his greatest works tonight, through us! May he permit us to be involved," she said, with a subservient tuck of the head.

She remained with head bowed while several long, silent seconds passed by.

Tessa groaned, deeply, as if her innards were tearing apart.

"Lord God on High, we invite you into our midst here. . . ." the old bishop began with a tremulous voice, in Latin. As he went on, his voice became stronger. And Daria could feel the Holy Spirit enveloping them, warming them, warding off the chill of night.

๙ ๙ ๙

GIANNI was well into the piazza before he realized it. He tapped Vito on the arm, pointed ahead of them, and moved in close. "We are not alone."

Vito nodded, not looking anywhere but forward, awaiting direction.

High above, Bormeo circled but remained silent.

Near the great cathedral, Daria hovered near the figure on the steps, talking to a man in robes, on the steps. Where was Hasani? Above Daria, high on the steps, were six men, men he could identify by silhouette of form alone. Gianni's breath caught in his throat and he set his mouth in a grim line, studying the entire potential battlefield. On the far side of the piazza, two shadows moved, making their way toward Daria. And still, there was at least one behind them. Who were these others? Too many shadows made it impossible to know.

They had to get closer to Daria! If the two on the far side of the piazza got to them first, they would be too late to attempt protection. Where was Hasani? His eyes narrowed as two guards stepped forward at the top of the stairs with lit torches, joining two others, casting down long streaks of light toward his lady.

The man at the bottom raised a hand, and the guards stopped their descent.

Who held enough power to stop the guards? Gianni frowned. This did not bode well. Did Daria not realize she was tangling with decisions that could cost her her life?

ಚಿ ಚಿ ಚಿ

THE sixth man entered the piazza stealthily, taking quick note of the torches at the front of the Duomo, the six guards, and what looked like two people—a man and child?—at the bottom. Two people stood before them. He scanned the rest of the L-shaped piazza. There, on the far side, two men hovered in the shadows. And nearer him, two others. His own men.

Was this healer mad, going to the holy church herself? Did she wish to be burned at the stake? He grinned. He loved such audacity. Would that he himself had such courage! He wanted this one with him, to turn her to his own cause. Together, they would draw

them all . . . he needed only to make sure of her identity, have time
to persuade her.

He moved forward, confident that the knights across the piazza were concentrating on his own men and had not yet detected
his presence. Besides, he had learned many ways to deceive the eye.
If necessary, he could disappear in a moment.

He paused and sniffed the air. Orange blossoms? And clove.
Something else, indefinable. Just the faintest . . . and then it was
gone. Perhaps it was simply the orange groves, their blossoms fading and falling to the ground. And yet it was so stunningly strong
for a moment. . . .

ᛣ ᛣ ᛣ

DARIA knelt before the old bishop and gently laid a hand on the
child's forehead. Fever. She looked down her body, noting again
the wrist bones and knees that protruded. She was terribly thin,
and therefore it would be more difficult to ward off whatever
ailed her.

She nodded to the bishop. "Please, your Grace. Continue your
prayers so that you know that our God smiles over what happens
here. He will not allow anything to touch this child if you are praying—unless he wishes it."

The bishop eyed her and then nodded, praying now in Latin,
ancient verses of Scripture. *"Non rogo ut tollas eos de mundo sed
ut serves eos ex malo. . . ."* Daria listened to the man pray, absorbing his words as strength within. *My prayer is not that you take
them out of the world but that you protect them from the evil
one. . . .*

"Father God, Lord God," Daria began. "You have called us
here, to this child. We ask that you bring her healing this night, this
hour. We ask that you surround her with your holy Presence and
enter her body, ceasing this terrible fever. We ask that you drive
away the illness that plagues her tender young frame." In Daria's
mind, she could see the fever like a black cloud clinging to the girl's

chest and head, like a giant spider. "Please Lord, you've called us and we have answered you. Enter this child, Great Physician. Enter her and cast out this illness, Lord Jesus. Make her well—"

The child gasped and sat up suddenly, a hand going to her shallow chest. She panted, eyes wide.

The bishop and Daria waited.

And then the child smiled, smiled so broadly that Daria and the bishop had to join her. In a moment, she burst out laughing, pure joy, and her companions laughed with her. Even the guards chuckled, staring on in wonder from high above them. It was as if the Holy Spirit had been inside her, working, working, working, and was now bursting outward, infecting them all.

"I am well," she cried out to the bishop. "I am well!"

All of a sudden, her face fell and her big eyes scanned the piazza. She paused over two men behind Daria and then whipped her face to the other side. Two others.

Hasani drew his sword, emerging from the shadows by a statue.

At the top of the stairs, the guards drew theirs.

Tessa rose, on shaking legs, fury sliding into her tender facial features. She pointed across the piazza, to the two men still in shadow. "There!" And then to another, near a statue. "There!" she screamed in terror. "There, there! He is coming! Watch out!"

CHAPTER THIRTY-ONE

GIANNI paused in confusion. He thought he should go to Daria, but the girl's screams turned his heart in the direction of the piazza spies. "God be with us," he muttered. And then he took off running toward the men in shadow, sword drawn.

From the corner of his eye, he saw the guards descending the stairs, two pausing by Daria and the man and child, two others heading in the same direction—to intercept the men on the far side. Two remained at the top of the stairs, guarding the church.

The two spies turned and ran. It was no use. They were too far ahead.

"There!" the girl screamed, her voice echoing about the stones of the piazza. "He is still there!" she cried.

Gianni turned slowly and a man emerged from a dark doorway and then around a tall statue. He leaned casually against her curving form, from the side. Was he sliding on gloves? He was in robes, a hood over his head. Why was he so familiar?

All at once, he knew.

The catacombs.

The Sorcerer.

ᚼ ᚼ ᚼ

"I must go," Daria said to the bishop. "We are in danger here."

The bishop turned wide eyes from the scene across the piazza to Daria. He clearly had not heard, could not hear over the girl's repeated cries.

"God be with you," Daria said. Then she turned to flee.

"Wait!" the girl said, turning to them with a sob. "I am to go with you."

Daria turned and shook her head in confusion. "Nay. We have no place for a child. The bishop will look after you."

"Please. He told me . . . I am . . . Contessa. Do you not know me?"

Daria still shook her head in confusion. There was no time for debate!

Hasani took her shoulder and turned her to face him. He opened wide eyes as if she were missing something obvious. No! It could not be! This child . . . was one of the Gifted?

Daria swallowed hard. She was dear to the bishop. Would he let her go?

"Bishop, I ask your permission to take this child and give her a home."

The old priest threw out a protective hand and drew the girl to him. "Nay. I do not know you—"

"Nay!" the girl screamed. "Do not let him escape!"

Their eyes turned back across the piazza.

ᚼ ᚼ ᚼ

Aɴɴ, the knight of the church. He had not been able to place him before, at the baron's home. But here, now, in this light that was so similar to the catacombs, he remembered. A worthy adversary.

One he thought was gone and buried. "You are a hard man to kill," he said, careful to keep his face hidden, deep within his hood.

"You certainly tried," Gianni said. He took a step forward, echoing the Sorcerer's move.

The two guards from the church paused, five paces away from them. "Captain!" said one, recognizing Gianni.

The Sorcerer and the first knight circled one another, the others standing a few paces away. "Ahh, yes," said the Sorcerer. "Your captain. This man led his men to me like lambs to the slaughter. We were able to pick them off, one by one."

Fury rumbled beneath the surface of Gianni's calm façade. The Sorcerer could see it. It was good, anger. Anger fed his people. . . . "You were foolish, following us into the grove. You ought to have known better."

The man sucked in his breath quickly but held his tongue.

"I particularly enjoyed taking down the man you were trying to save." He paused, shaking his head. "But it is most puzzling. I was certain I left all of you dead or near death behind me. I could feel your life force fading away."

"You did. But my God is bigger than anything you can conjure up."

The Sorcerer laughed, nodding in sudden understanding, glancing across the piazza. "The healer. Of course. She was there."

Gianni raised his sword, seething now. "God is with us. I will deliver you to the authorities."

"And what of you? Surely the Holy Church has not sanctioned your healer's endeavors? She remains hidden in her veils. Is that because you fear your own? That must be quite the quandary for you, a knight of the Church—"

"Enough," Gianni cried, lunging with his sword. "You shall burn on the stake for your crimes. This is where it ends."

"Nay," he said with a chuckle, delighting in the game. "This is but the beginning."

❧ ❧ ❧

THE Sorcerer swirled then, suddenly, a tornado wave of robe, then a bright, blinding light made them squint, fighting to see, even as a loud explosion reverberated through their ears. After a moment, Vito and two Duomo guards ran to where he had stood. But there was nothing, nothing but a curving, flat pad of robe where he had been.

"It is a trick!" Gianni cried.

The Vaticana guards stood, with mouths agape. Their eyes filled with fear and they backed away. "What sort of black magic is this?" said one.

"It is just that! Magic! Tricks. Call upon your Lord God and he shall protect you! Ye must rally, men, not cower in fear! *Quoniam mihi adhesit et liberabo eum exaltabo eum quoniem cognovit nomen meum. . . .*" he said, raising his hands as the cardinal had in Roma. "Because he loves me, says the Lord, I will rescue him; I will protect him, for he acknowledges my name."

The bishop gasped, clearly chagrined at Gianni's translation of Scripture into the common tongue. Gianni ignored him. "Fear not, this evil! We must give chase!" But the men continued to back away.

Across the piazza, people were emerging from the city's hospital, holding lanterns and candles aloft, wondering what could be transpiring at this hour.

"Captain," Vito said. "Hasani has set out after the Sorcerer. We must concentrate on the lady."

❧ ❧ ❧

"PLEASE, Your Grace," Tessa said, looking up to the old bishop, her hand in his. "No one else will give me a home. God has answered your prayer. I am to go with this kind woman. I have been waiting for a lady such as she."

The bishop looked from the girl to Daria. "What is your name?"

"Forgive me, Your Grace, I cannot disclose that. Not yet." Gianni came up beside her, sheathing his sword so that the guards would not become further agitated.

"You must. You cannot take the child without telling me where you are taking her."

"I am one of the faithful in your fair city," she said. "I promise to send her to mass here every Sunday. You shall see for yourself how she flourishes. You have my promise that she will be in good care."

Six more guards appeared on the Duomo steps.

Gianni knelt on one knee. "Please, Your Grace. As a former knight of the Church itself, I testify that the child will be in good hands. These men," he said, waving upward, "will tell you that my word is good. Search your heart and see if you do not feel God's peace over the decision."

The old man cast doleful eyes from one to the other and then closed them in a moment of prayer.

Give him wisdom, Lord Jesus, Daria prayed silently, casting a fearful glance around the piazza. *Keep us, O Lord, from the hands of the wicked; protect me from men of violence who plan to trip my feet. . . .*

The bishop opened his eyes and with one last look at Tessa gestured forward. "But do as the lady has promised, Tessa. Come back each Sunday at mass so that I might know you are well."

"I promise, Your Grace!" she said, stepping over to Daria and taking her hand.

Guards rushed down the stairs and surrounded the bishop, one on either side. He held up one hand to bring them to a halt, his eyes on the trio before him. "I have prayed for you, Contessa. I have prayed that a fine lady would take you in and make you her daughter. I confess, it was not like this. . . . This is not what I imagined."

Tessa smiled and looked up at Daria. "No? This is just like it was in my dreams."

CHAPTER THIRTY-TWO

DARIA had put the child to bed in her own bed, ignoring the filth, unwilling to awaken the Sciorias to draw a bath in the middle of the night. She had laid beside her for hours, until the pink dawn light sneaked through the edge of closed shutters, observing long, sable lashes and hollow cheeks, delicate bones. Daria smiled. She might be barren, but God had fulfilled his promise to give her a child.

She reached out a hand to caress the girl's cheek, but as soon as she touched her, Tessa sat up straight and flew out of the bed. She stood, feet akimbo, panting in fear. Daria raised herself on one arm. "I . . . forgive me. I only meant to caress your cheek."

The child looked down at the ground. Embarrassed? "Forgive me, m'lady. I have spent many nights in the streets. I do not sleep soundly. I did not wish to offend you."

"Nay," Daria said. "It is I who was unthinking. You do not offend, child. It is understandable, your guard. We will get to know each other slowly. I am thankful . . . thankful that God has brought us together."

The child relaxed, but still stood apart from her.

Daria considered her for a moment. "Contessa, tell me what you need to tell me. You said . . . you said last night that you had been waiting for me."

"Yes," she said. She took a few steps and sat down on the edge of the bed, out of Daria's reach. But it was a gesture of trust. "I had dreamed about you. Even in your veils, in the dark, I knew you were the one."

"Your dreams . . . do you often dream?"

"Yes," the child said, frowning. "Sometimes even in the middle of the day."

"I see. And what sort of things do you dream about? Other than those you had of me?"

"People, mostly. Good people. And bad." She fiddled with a hole in her gown.

"The bad people, Tessa . . . had you dreamed of the men in the piazza last night?"

"Nay. I mean yes. I mean it is not that I truly have dreaming dreams. It is more like knowing things, given to me like dreams. Last night, the bad men meant us harm. They wanted to pull me away from you, just after I had found you." She looked at Daria then, big tears welling in her eyes.

"I see."

"Sometimes I sense things that are about to happen. Sometimes I can change what happens. But sometimes I want it to happen as I have seen, so I simply watch."

"Give me an example."

"Like Roberto—he's a child of the Piazza il Campo too—there was a man who was going to take his satchel. Roberto had just earned a whole silver coin, a whole silver coin, working for the baker on the corner, and had it in his satchel. It was under his head as he slept. I saw a man enter the piazza, and I knew he was there to do Roberto harm, mayhap to steal his farthing."

"What did you do?"

"I screamed and it scared him away. Roberto shared his farthing with me, then. We ate for an entire week because of it."

"And you had seen it, in your dreams, before then."

"Nay. It was more that I knew why he was there when he started across the piazza, even while I was asleep."

"And last night?"

"I knew I was becoming more ill. I had to get to the bishop . . . and when you came, as ill as I was, I knew that all would be well. There is such light about you, m'lady. . . ."

"What about the men? The men across the piazza."

Tessa shivered and shook her head. "When they entered the piazza, when they drew nearer us, I could feel them. . . . I know not how to explain it better than that. I simply feel a person nearby and know if they are a good person or a bad person."

"You have the gift of discernment. You are our discerner."

Tessa cocked her head, looking confused. "I do not know what those words mean."

"You shall, child."

"Your man, Hasani. He knows things—I think he knew the bad men would be there."

Daria darted a look to the child. "Hasani? How could he have known?" Daria rose and walked to the shutters, opening them, letting the sunlight wash over her. Hasani had greeted her at the door last night. Several times in the last few months, he had surprised her, like that, as if he knew what she needed before she told him. She had considered it the fruits of their childhood bond . . . but was there something more?

"Those men in the piazza. Not your knights, but the others. Who were they, m'lady?"

"I do not know," Daria said.

"They did not wish us well."

"Nay, they did not." She reached out and pulled the child to a standing position, holding both of her hands. "Tessa, I believe you have been called to us, to this house because you are one of the

Gifted. God is doing something beyond our dreams, beyond our capacity to imagine. And our call is to simply follow. I did not think a child would be one of us. You will be asked to be more brave than any other child I know in the days that come. But we will be beside you. Are you willing?"

Contessa studied her with wide, saucerlike eyes, old wisdom within their depths. She nodded.

"I take it from what the bishop said that you have no family?"

The girl shook her head, offered no explanation.

"You will not be alone, Tessa. If you allow it, we will be your family. You will always have a home in this house, with me."

"I shall like that very much."

"Good. Then let us see to a morning bath and new clothes. A young lady of the house of d'Angelo cannot be seen in rags!" She smiled, but Tessa's mouth dropped open.

"You . . . you are the Duchess?"

Daria smiled. "I hold no formal title."

"But you are . . . you are Lady Daria d'Angelo?"

"Indeed." She bowed lowly as if meeting a fine lady herself. Then she took Tessa's chin in her hand and grinned down at her. "And you shall be the next."

CHAPTER THIRTY-THREE

As agreed with the new captain of the Church guard, Gianni returned to the Duomo the following morning at daybreak. He was greeted with smiles and tentative arm braces, then led into the inner chambers of an adjacent building. It was not until this morning that Gianni had learned that Cardinal Boeri himself had ridden in from Roma. Bishop Benedicto and Bishop di Mino stood before the cardinal as he entered, turned and parted to flank him when they heard the men enter the hall.

Cardinal Boeri rose and smiled, stepping down from his chair upon the steps to go to Gianni.

Gianni sank to his knees. "Your Grace, I am thankful to see you again."

The cardinal laid a hand on his shoulder. "As I am to see you. Rise and report, sir."

Gianni did as he bid. It was so good to see his old friend! Relief flooded through him like reinforcements arriving on a beleaguered field. "I will tell you what I can, Your Grace."

"Good. Come, come and sit." He gestured for a chair to be

brought for Gianni, to be set before the dais. The bishops sat on either side.

Gianni longed for a private moment with the cardinal, the chance to open up to the man, test his thinking, verify with his trusted confidant that his bewildering experiences were of God. . . . In the company of the two bishops, he felt strangled, caught between his oath to protect Daria and his desire to serve his old master.

"Our Sorcerer again escaped you," the cardinal began.

"Indeed. My lady's man gave chase, but he eluded him among the alleys."

"Who is this lady that you serve?"

"Forgive me, Your Grace, but I cannot answer that."

"It is only a matter of time until her identity is uncovered," Bishop Benedicto said beside him.

"Every man in this room knows why I must protect it as long as I can."

Silence settled about them.

"And the Sorcerer. Was it me that he sought? Or your lady?" asked the bishop.

"I know not," Gianni said. "Cardinal Boeri, I am here to tell you that the lady I serve is on a holy path, one I have never encountered before. She is gifted—in uncommon ways."

"As I have heard," the man returned, dryly. "Is she alone?"

"Forgive me, again, I cannot tell you such details. I have sworn to protect her."

The cardinal rose, fury edging his jawline. "You swore to protect the Holy Church."

Gianni nodded, eyes to the floor. "In a way, I see that I am serving both."

"A man of divided loyalties is a man destined to fail."

"They are not divided, Your Grace. Please, may we speak in private?"

"Nay. You have edged into dangerous territory, knight. It is safer for the men of the Church to stand together, to test our knowledge together. If you are truly with us, you will not be fearful of the same examination." He stepped down and paced to the window. After a moment, he said over his shoulder, "The only reason I have not yet sent my men to track you and yours down, bring you to Roma for interrogation, is because your lady has apparently caught the eye of the Sorcerer. He wants her, for some reason. And I want him, first."

He traipsed back to Gianni's side and laid a hand upon his shoulder. "I trust you, Gianni. I know your heart. And our bishop here, well, Benedicto agrees that there is something holy about your lady. She was appropriately subservient to the Church, to the Christ. He could detect no malice about her."

"Indeed. That is what I mean when I say that I feel that I am still serving the Holy Church, as well as this lady."

"She is obviously a noblewoman with some wealth. Our men saw that you had at least two others with you this past night. So she employs three, mayhap more men. There are no more than a couple hundred men of the city who employ that many. We will learn of her identity quickly. Tell us, and we will aid you in your oath to protect her."

"Nay, Your Grace. I cannot. It is not yet time."

"Time? Time for what?"

Gianni rubbed his hand over his face as if he wished to wring clear thoughts from his head. "I know not. Only that I am to do what I have been doing. The Lord has not shown me what we are doing, where we are going, other than to minister through our gifts."

"You speak of gifts. What does that mean?" the cardinal asked, leaning forward.

"Bishop Benedicto witnessed her gift of healing. There are many who need healing," he hedged, suddenly wary.

"Healing is an act of God," the cardinal said.

"Indeed," Gianni said.

Silence flooded his ears as the cardinal studied him, fingers steepled. "Because of my love for you, Gianni, and Bishop Benedicto's testimony of last night's healing being tainted by no evil, and because I want you to catch our Sorcerer, I will grant you more time." He leaned forward again. "But you must send me reports, on a weekly basis. Tell me what you can, where you are. I think you will remember why you've trusted me, all these years. And you can persuade your lady to trust me as well. Then you both shall fall under my arm of protection." He sighed and rose. "These are difficult times, sir. You know it as well as I. Should you and your lady fall into the wrong hands of the Church, it may mean your very lives will be forfeit."

"I understand."

"I must return to Roma immediately. But if you catch this Sorcerer, or need my counsel, you must come to me with haste. You may be this lady's protector, but you were the Church's sworn servant first. I will allow you to serve both, for a time. After that, we shall see."

"Thank you, thank you, Your Grace," Gianni said. This was exactly as he had hoped. Pardon, sanction. Ability to come back to the cardinal for help.

ᚦ ᚦ ᚦ

Bishop di Mino hovered beside the cardinal as Gianni and Bishop Benedicto exited the hall.

"You are wondering why I did not force the issue," the cardinal said.

"Nay. I am still stunned that our own man appears to be among the Gifted."

The cardinal raised one brow and nodded. It was remarkable news. "God is good. He clearly means for us to do just as I had hoped—to ensnare the Gifted, corral them, study them, as well as the Sorcerer. This is just what the Church of Roma needs. If Gianni is able to do as I bid, we could accomplish all the Lord has desired.

We will use it to testify to Roma's strength. It will become the reason the papacy must be returned to where it belongs. Signs! Wonders! Miracles! Avignon has nothing but political puppets to maintain the papacy. We have God's very hand at work. The people will demand it."

"But Your Grace . . . the letter. The illumination. The dragon, taking down the peacock. Shall we not warn de Capezzana?"

"Nay," the cardinal said, staring out the window again. "If these are truly the Gifted ones, they will know it themselves."

∽ ∽ ∽

BEATA and Agata delighted in the opportunity to hover over a girl child again, taking Tessa under their wings and flitting about the kitchen as if they had just discovered a pile of gold florins.

Water was set upon the hearth grate to heat. Bread was brought out and buttered, a thick slice handed to the dumbfounded girl. Hard-boiled eggs were cracked and peeled, salted, and placed on a trencher for her. An orange was sliced and put upon the trencher next. Tessa sat with wide eyes, gobbling the food as if she might never eat again.

"There will be time enough to work on table manners," Piero said, reading Daria's expression. The girl had to settle into the idea that there was food, and would be food the next day and the next. When she relaxed with that knowledge, her frantic eating would ease into normalcy.

Nico stood in the corner, leaning against the wall, arms crossed. He was a little older than Contessa, and was most likely torn between disliking another child in the house—he was clearly accustomed to being doted on—and getting excited over a potential playmate.

"Nico," Daria said, waving him forward. "Come."

Obediently, the child crossed the floor and stood beside Tessa.

"Nico Scioria, this is Contessa, or Tessa is what she prefers. She has come to live with us. Tessa, this is Nico."

The two nodded at each other warily.

"Nico, after Tessa finishes breaking her fast, I would like you to show her around the entire house and gardens. I want her to know every room, know her new home." She bent down and whispered, "You can show her the secret passageways too."

She could see by his expression that he was warming to the idea of playing the one in the know, teaching this new arrival the intricacies of the estate. "Nico, Tessa is important to us."

Gianni came into the kitchen then. He had been out this morning. Piero knew not where. He clapped Nico on the back. "Your first lady. See to it that she comes to no harm. The weaker sex are in need of our protection." His eyes flashed at Daria, but she ignored his taunt.

Nico nodded sagely. It obviously appealed to him, this sense of guardianship. Gianni had been working with him, teaching him the ways of sword and shield, had commented he would make a fine squire. Daria knew his grandparents would never bless his departure to serve with fighting men. But his interaction with the knights of her home might give him enough experience to become a knight himself, when he came of age. She could sponsor him, if need be.

"Tessa, you must stay hidden on these grounds, for a time. There are things afoot—what you experienced last night was just a bit of what might happen. Do you understand?"

The girl nodded and continued to stuff food into her mouth.

"Have you never eaten before, girl?" Nico asked with consternation as Tessa dropped a portion of her bread to the floor. His eyes widened as she bent to retrieve it and hurriedly stuck it too in her mouth.

"Not for four days," she mumbled after him, swallowing half of what was in her mouth. Yes, Daria would have her hands full, teaching this one table manners. She would have to keep her from sitting with Basilio and Rune in the dining hall—they were hardly fine examples of genteel society. Vito and Ugo were little better. . . .

"M'lady," Aldo Scioria, her steward, said, as he entered the kitchen. "I have need of speaking with you. There are several guild issues at the factory that we must address and a report from the manor I wish you to read."

"Very well," Daria said. "I know I have been preoccupied of late. I appreciate your patience, Aldo."

"Of course, m'lady," he said. "Baron del Buco also sent word that he would like to meet us at the factory this afternoon. Midafternoon, he said."

"Then let us go. And I will reserve an hour for you to inform me of the business at hand before we leave."

"Good. Thank you, m'lady."

Piero studied Daria, but was distracted by a delectable smell emanating from the fry pan tended by Beata. She was frying thick slices of ham to go with the porridge. When she turned away for a moment, Piero snitched a slice from the pan, tossing it back and forth in his hands in an effort to rapidly cool it.

Beata turned and saw his mischief, and immediately began yelling and shaking her hands in the air. "What has this household turned into?" she cried to the heavens. Then she brought down her long, wooden spatula in a *whack* across Piero's shoulders. "Out! Out! Consider that your morning meal! You may not steal from this kitchen! Does not the Bible mention stealing as something we ought not do?"

Daria laughed as she followed Piero out the door into the courtyard garden. He split the ham in two and offered her half.

"No, thank you. Someone has to have a sense of decorum in this house. I will not be a party to your sin."

Piero shrugged and popped the rest of the ham into his mouth. He kept step with her as she walked into the courtyard garden, pausing to finger various roses. "My mother loved this color, especially," she said, touching a crimson rose that was almost blue, it was so dark.

They continued walking.

"You healed the child last night, m'lady."

"Yes. Contessa knew me, knew she belonged with us. Her healing had begun before I even arrived."

"Why did you go without me? Without Gianni?"

Daria sighed and looked at him. "I thought we would be less conspicuous if we traveled alone. I did not expect . . . others. The dark ones. I did not expect her to be in the arms of the bishop himself. They released Bormeo," she said.

"Yes. Gianni knew he would find you."

"He has still not returned."

"He will, will he not?"

Daria gave in after a moment of challenge. "Yes. He will eat his fill from the hills and then come home. If another doesn't capture him."

"I think he is rather like his mistress. Neither of you will be caught unless you wish it."

Was there another comment beneath the first? Daria scanned his face, but he had turned away, walking again. "It was foolhardy," she admitted. "Forgive me."

He turned and faced her. "Lady Daria, no matter when the Father calls you, no matter how late the hour, no matter how silly the idea sounds, I wish to be with you. So does Gianni. Will you allow us to fulfill that call?"

She paused a moment, considering. "Yes."

"Good. Now tell me about the girl."

"You may as well tell me also," said Gianni, joining them. "She is one of us? One of the Gifted?"

"You may judge for yourselves. But I believe she has the gift of discernment."

Father Piero nodded. "Odd. I expected the one with visions to next arise. Discernment is out of order of the listing, but mayhap none of the rest will fall in such a line. Discernment is highly useful to us, especially at this juncture." He eyed her more closely. "And she appeals to you? You think she will be trustworthy?"

"I do not know. She has spent years in the *campo* as a beggar. Surely that does not hone a child into an honest person. But I think we can train her. She is of good caliber. You feel it within your bones when you are around her. I think that is what drew the bishop to her."

"So now the bishop has seen our healer for himself. What did he make of you?"

Daria laughed lightly. "I do not know what he thought of me. All I know is that he saw everything that transpired last night, from Tessa's healing to the Sorcerer's appearance . . . or should I say disappearance?"

Gianni remained curiously silent. The trio stopped outside the chapel. It was almost time for morning mass. "With each day, our battles may escalate. We must take great precautions. Did the bishop ever see your face?"

"Nay."

"Or yours, Sir Gianni?"

"My men—those of the Church guard. They knew me. I identified myself as a knight of the Church."

"If he had not, I doubt the bishop would have let us go," Daria said.

"So now we will need to hide your face as well. Let that beard grow; do not shave. See if Aldo can find an old, wide-brimmed hat for you. How about our Sorcerer? He saw you?"

"Better than I did him. His face was entirely in shadow." Gianni paced back and forth. "I almost captured him, months ago, outside Roma. He was leading a group in unspeakable ceremonies in the catacombs. We chased him out, tracked him all the way to that grove, where you found me."

"Did you get a good look at him then?"

"Nay. Again, he had his back to the light, so that his face was shadowed. Both times, all I could tell you is that he is tall, about my height or a bit taller. Dark, raven hair. Fine clothing."

"A noble?"

"Perhaps. He has a nobleman's way of speaking."

"And his men? The two others in the piazza?"

"They escaped before I drew near," Gianni said.

Daria shook her head.

"But the girl knew them as enemies?"

"Yes. Knew them before she laid eyes upon them. It was as if she could sense their approach."

Father Piero paced back and forth, chin in hand. "Very good. I would say things are progressing nicely. Let us go to mass and give the Holy One thanks!"

Daria and Gianni shared a look. If things were progressing nicely, considering the drama of the last day, what was ahead?

CHAPTER THIRTY-FOUR

HASANI helped Daria mount her horse, and she, Aldo, and Vincenzo left the courtyard. Basilio and Rune followed behind. Lucan, Vito, and Ugo remained at the house, standing guard from the towers.

Vincenzo shifted uneasily in his saddle. "Is this escort truly necessary?"

Daria leaned forward and patted her mare. "I believe it is."

"Has someone threatened you, Daria?"

"No. Not really."

"Daria d'Angelo. Who? When?"

She gave him a small smile. "Dear Uncle. A woman is allowed to have some secrets."

Vincenzo frowned. "But I can assist you, Daria. You saw that I dealt with your problem with Jacobi. Let me take care of your other troubles."

She smiled again. "I am a woman grown, Uncle. I must learn to see my own troubles through. With the aid of the Holy One, I will be fine." Her smile grew and she cocked a brow. "I am confident of this."

They rode several paces before he spoke again. "Do your troubles . . . do they have the potential of harming our shared commerce? Your troubles, after all, could become my troubles."

Daria listened to his words, swaying to the rhythm of the horse's walk. "I suppose you are correct in that."

Gianni turned in his saddle and they shared a look. What secrets were rumbling about the d'Angelo house?

"Daria," Vincenzo encouraged.

"It is nothing, Uncle. All will be well. You will see."

He sighed. "There is word on the streets," he said idly. "Of a piazza beggar being healed last night. They say she was near death, that the bishop himself was administering extreme unction rites on the Duomo steps, when the healer appeared and brought the child back to life."

"The city people love nothing more than a good tale to tell."

"You do not think it happened?"

She considered his question. "I think it happened. I think God is alive and well and working through his people in this city."

Vincenzo eyed her carefully. "Do you know who the healer is, Daria? The one from the marketplace? Or the one at the Duomo?"

"Me?" She laughed lightly. "I live a simple, monastic life, spending most of my days in either worship or reading or seeing to the documents that our business generates. There is no time to meet anyone, it seems."

It did not escape Vincenzo's notice that she had not answered the question. "I know that you minister to the ill, the poor, as your mother did before you. Surely the people speak of this woman."

"They speak of her, certainly. But they know not who she is."

Vincenzo rode on, looking up the walls of Siena's most elegant district. Abramo's fascination with the healer was most likely idle. He could learn from the man, in learning to know critical pieces of information from anyone who held power within the city's walls.

"You are angry," Daria said.

"I am frustrated," he said lowly. "It is vital that we know our enemies, our friends within this city. It is vital for the guild that we see to maximizing every single relationship we have, and determine which new ones to forge. You and I must work together, and yet you will not even tell me who threatens you."

"You bear more than enough burdens in mourning Tatiana, Uncle. Let me keep this burden to myself."

They rode in silence for a time, turning onto the busy Via di Pantaneto, which would lead them to the outskirts of Siena and the factory. When they exited the city's walls, fewer people passed by and when they crested the hill, the long, rectangular buildings came into view. People moved in and out, horses drew wagons. It always inspired him, this view. Commerce, at work. His commerce. If they were not careful, a man like Amidei would find a way to own them, using their own secrets against him. The only way to hold him off was to obtain what he sought, become an ally to him. A man like Amidei was entirely focused upon vanquishing his enemy, growing in number. Vincenzo preferred to use Amidei before Amidei got to him, or Daria. He looked over at her again and she met his glance with a question in her own. "What? What is it?"

"Nothing." They began to ride downhill, toward the guild's buildings. "It is only that we must speak of Lord Frangelico again."

"Vincenzo—"

"You will hear from the guild secretaries that output is greater than any year before it. Our storehouses are filled and we are forced to build more."

"A blessing, then. It is a blessing that our coffers are full, that we have full storehouses."

"Nay! Daria, we are in the business of sales. We must export and import at greater speed, efficiency, each and every year."

"Not if it means we work with someone of Lord Frangelico's caliber."

"Daria, you are being unreasonable. It is for the good of the guild that we must consider this. If you will not give it fair weight, then I must take it to the council. I fear they will side with me, that you will be removed as co-consul."

The knight, Gianni, dismounted and came to Daria to assist her down. Was that a look of menace in his eye? Why was he so ill at ease?

The three stood in a circle and Daria put on a false smile. She reached forward and took Vincenzo's hand. "I am certain you did not mean those words, Uncle. Grief colors your vision right now. I know how it is." She took his arm and urged him forward. "You promised my father that you would look after me, after our businesses. You know he wanted me here."

He paused as she ducked under the low doorway and into the factory, following another of her knights. He had to find some way to convince her, some way to sway her to his way of thinking. Some way. Because if he did not, he had a feeling within his gut that all would collapse about them.

CHAPTER THIRTY-FIVE

VINCENZO paced the floor of his salon, still as angry as he had been when he left Daria's side at the factory. This was why women were not allowed to lead in business; they led with their hearts instead of their heads! He had tried every angle he could, even outside as they mounted up, but Daria would not capitulate.

Even though he had wanted her in this position of power, Vincenzo was certain her father would have at least entertained the idea of working with Lord Frangelico. Giulio d'Angelo would have seen the wisdom of it, the necessary risk. Entering into partnership with Frangelico would aid their guild's business and gain them ultimate control of the city's burgeoning market. With Abramo Amidei on the move, Vincenzo could not afford setbacks like this, hesitations. He needed to take decisive action. He slammed his fist into his hand with each word. Decisive. Action.

Vincenzo hollered for four of his men. "You there, you shall see that this note is received by Lord Abramo Amidei and no one else." He turned to his desk and pulled the quill from the ink well and wrote in Latin: *I will find your healer. You deliver me the re-*

quired Lord. He blew on the ink until it was dry, folded the note, and sealed it with hot wax from the fire and a press of his ring, the family crest.

He knew not what Abramo wanted from the healer. But it mattered little to him. It was simply a stepping stone across the river he must cross . . . and if Daria blocked access from one way to Frangelico, he would gain access to him across an opposite stone.

"You," he said to the other. "Dress in dark linens. Tonight you go and find an observation point for the house of d'Angelo. I want you to follow Lady Daria, wherever she goes. I will send another to take your place at sunup. If she departs, does anything, I want you to take note of who is with her, whom she meets. If you do not recognize her companion, follow them to their abode so you can report to me their location and identity. Understood?"

"Understood, m'lord."

He turned to the others. "Someone is threatening the Duchess. I want to know whom she fears. You two ask about, listen in the taverns. Find out what is being said. See if it is Jacobi. If that fat pig has threatened her again, I want to know it. If it is someone else, I must know that too. Your second mission is this—we will discover the identity of Siena's mysterious healer."

"The one who has met in the hills?"

"Nay. He is male. I speak of the woman. The one of the marketplace and the Piazza del Duomo last night."

"Very good, m'lord. We shall carry out your orders to your satisfaction."

"Very well. Go, go," he said, frustrated that they were not immediately out of his sight.

He did not care for Daria's new independence, her secrets kept from him. Given her way with herbs and medicines, she was bound to cross paths with the mysterious healer, mayhap already knew the woman's identity. If she would not tell Vincenzo her secrets, he would learn them in other ways. It was for the good of the guild, Vincenzo's good, indeed, best for Daria herself for him to know all.

Knowledge was power. And with little else in his life, Vincenzo intended to mine every ounce from this city before Abramo Amidei beat him to it.

ᚦ ᚦ ᚦ

DARIA was resting by the hearth, rocking in a chair that Aldo had carved for her, almost dozing off when Tessa drew near.

"M'lady?"

"Yes, Tessa?" She roused and sat more upright. Hasani and Gianni lounged across from her, staring in relaxed fashion, but it appeared that everyone else had retired. Daria realized she had failed already as a foster mother—a good mother would have her children abed by now.

"M'lady, I am troubled."

Daria's eyes met Gianni's, their thoughts one. Danger? Nearby?

"What is it, Tessa?"

"It is Roberto, in the *campo*, my friend? He, he has a bad leg. It was broken when he was but a little child and healed akimbo. Roberto . . . well, he talked of going to see the other healer. The one in the hills."

Daria frowned. They could not keep all of Siena from the dark one. At least not yet.

"Roberto is like a brother to me. Nico reminds me a lot of him. . . ."

Daria sighed. "Tessa, can we see to him on the morrow? I can send you with Aldo, and you could bring him back here."

She nodded, so eager to please. But then paused. "I—I don't want him to go. The other healer is bad."

Daria sat up straighter. "You've seen him? *Know him?*"

"I have not seen him—but I know he is treacherous." She burst into tears then, falling to the ground, sobs tearing through her slender frame. Daria and Gianni both went to her. They let her cry for a moment and then Daria pulled her up, up into her lap when she sat down again, this time on the padded bench. "You must tell us, Tessa. All of it. Do not bear this burden alone. We are here to help. Trust us, child, trust us. Why do you think he is treacherous?"

The child trembled with fear. Terror raced from her eyes. "I do not know. Only that I know Roberto is likely to go to him. That healer is a bad man."

Daria and Gianni shared a look. There had been another child, one who had not survived his encounter with the Sorcerer. Were the Sorcerer and the healer of the hills one and the same?

Hasani was there, beside him in an instant, his hooded cape already across his shoulders, handing Gianni another.

"We will go after him. You shall stay here. You shall not leave this house, Duchess. Swear it, m'lady."

"Sir de Capezzana, I—"

"Swear it, Daria! Did last night teach you nothing?"

Her mouth closed slowly. Then, "I promise. I shall wake Father Piero and we will go to the chapel and pray unceasingly."

He turned from her to Contessa. "Tessa, child, I must ask you to come with me. You will know the way to the boy and I might have need of your gift. I will protect you. No harm shall come to you while I live."

The girl nodded quickly, wiping away her tears.

"Go, now, and fetch a wrap for your pretty new gown."

Gianni paused before Hasani. "I see that you wish to go. Even with the hood, someone may recognize you, recognize me with you, see the child, and tie us all to Daria. But I want you here, protecting Daria. No one is as faithful as you. Agreed?"

Hasani nodded once and Gianni clapped him on the shoulder.

"Ugo, go and fetch Vito. I want a man with us who has seen the Sorcerer before. Rouse Basilio, Lucan, and Rune; they are to be on point, in the tower and by the gate."

"Yes, Captain." Ugo ran off, pausing only to lift his heavy sword belt from beside the front gate and sling it around his hips.

In minutes they were assembled.

"Wait," Daria called. Gianni kept himself from blowing out the exasperation that built in his chest. But when she closed her eyes and knelt, lifting a hand, he genuflected and followed suit, acknowledging the wisdom.

"Lord God, we pray that you will go before these men and Tessa, that you will surround them with your angels, on all sides. Guide and protect them, Lord Jesus. Guide and protect them. Give them your wisdom. Lead them straight to Roberto and bring them swiftly home. In Jesus' holy name, amen."

"Amen," they said together. Their *amen* reverberated through Gianni's chest. He liked the feel of it as they set out through the gates on horseback. *Amen and amen and amen . . . may it be as it was said.*

They made their way to the Piazza il Campo, where Contessa once made her home. "Is he here, Tessa?" he whispered as they hovered at the entrance to the wide, shell-shaped plaza, one much bigger than the Piazza del Duomo. She was on the saddle in front of him. A wide, full moon edged over the city walls and cast long shadows out from statues and buildings.

"He has no horse; he can't be gone. He must be here, yet." Her eyes searched the places they once had slept, often huddled together. A note of fear entered her voice again. "Everyone in the *campo* was talking about it, two days past. That the hillside healer could do mightier work than even our marketplace healer. Roberto heard and believed. He said a nobleman had stopped and given him word that he was marked, marked for glory, that he was to come when the moon was high in the sky and he heard the drum. Roberto called him his angel."

"Dark angel," Vito growled.

"I did not like the man. He stared at me as if he knew me. I told Roberto he was bad, but Roberto would not listen. He wanted his leg to be right. He didn't want to believe me. And I was getting so sick. . . ."

"Did you know the man, Tessa? Did he wear any identifying mark, a coat of arms, anything?"

"Nay."

Gianni scanned the dark piazza. It was impossible to see well enough, even in the moonlight. Some city dwellers walked in groups here and there, passing by them with a question in their eyes. Across the piazza, at the bottom of the great scallop, they appeared like small mice in a great open-air cathedral, scurrying about in the dark of night.

A slow, steady, deep drumbeat sounded high above them, outside the city walls, from up in the hills. All four of them glanced upward.

"It has begun," Ugo said. "The boy is gone. Do we stand by idly, Captain, or do we go and fetch the boy?"

"It is aggravating, but the Spirit tells me to wait."

"Wait? Wait for what?" Vito asked in irritation.

Gianni shook his head. "We all must learn that our battle is on a new plane. We must learn to do battle within our minds and hearts as well as with our swords. To do so takes extreme patience."

Ugo had some retort, but Gianni was squinting his eyes, looking for some movement in the campo. *Please Lord, I beg of you, Father. Let us find this child before he reaches the Sorcerer.* His gut told him to hold even though his mind screamed at him to charge. But it was not the right time to face the Sorcerer. He wanted to capture the man. If he could vanish within the smaller Piazza del Duomo, he could certainly disappear again here in il Campo too. There were too many dark doorways leading to escape. Too many shadowed companions, perhaps willing to die for him. He had surely captured their minds. How many?

There. A small dark figure limping grotesquely, three-quarters of the way across the *campo*, moving through an avenue of moonlight, to the other side.

Tessa gasped. "There he is!" she cried.

"I see him," Gianni said lowly.

"No. Him!" He heard the terror in her voice now, saw that she pointed up, to the far side of Il Campo. Gianni's eyes instinctively flitted upward to a stone deck atop Palazzo Chigi Zondadari, the home of Leo de Loren.

The Sorcerer. He stood with arms raised, as if summoning the child.

Gianni dropped Contessa to the ground and looked to Ugo. "Remain here. Guard her with your life. Vito, with me."

"Sir Gianni, hurry," Tessa said. "You must get to Roberto before he does."

Gianni was already digging his heels into the horse's flanks.

The horses struggled to find footing on the piazza's cobblestones, finally moving into a strong canter. In thirty seconds they were across the piazza and the knights jumped from still-moving horses and ran forward. Suddenly, arrows shot past them, narrowly missing Gianni's head and Vito's arm. They wore no armor, only chain mail. And Gianni had seen what the Sorcerer's arrows did to his chain mail.

The boy, apparently afraid that they meant him harm, resumed his hurried hobble across the last few paces.

"Roberto!" Contessa called from across the *campo*, her call echoing against stone. "It is I, Tessa! It is well, Roberto. They mean you no harm! Please, Roberto. Come with us!"

The child looked over his shoulder, past the knights, squinting to try to see his friend.

"Hurry, my boy," the Sorcerer called downward, his voice welcoming and warm. "This will be the last time you need that crutch! Tonight, you become whole again!"

"I am coming!" the boy cried. "I am coming!"

"Cease your pursuit," the man yelled down to the knights. "The boy belongs with us."

"Nay," Gianni growled. He eyed the archers on either side of the Sorcerer. "No innocent belongs with you!"

"Mayhap the boy is ready to shed his innocence. He wishes to find an answer to his deformity and I shall give it to him. He will become one with the great Unknown. His prayers will be answered in full!"

Lord Jesus, protect me, Gianni prayed. *Kyrie eleison. Christe eleison. Spiritus eleison.* He moved slowly, feeling invincible, repeating the words over and over again. *Lord have mercy, Christ have mercy, Spirit have mercy.* If his life ended here, so be it. He would give his life gladly for the life of this child, a child about to be slaughtered.

He ran forward, dodging back and forth in haphazard fashion. Arrows rained down around him, but missed him. He could dimly hear the sound as they whizzed by his ear, felt the *whoosh* as another went by his neck, felt the heat of another by his side. But no arrow pierced his flesh. *Kyrie eleison. Christe eleison. Spiritus eleison. This is not a fight against flesh and blood, but against principalities and—*

Gianni reached the child and grabbed him up into his arms, just beneath the Sorcerer. The child was surprisingly strong, struggling to get away, but then became very still, looking up at him.

The Sorcerer and his archers were on their level now, having descended the stairs within. Gianni backed away, the child in his arms, warily watching the Sorcerer, his face again hidden in shadow. He continued to back up until Vito was by his side, sword drawn. The Sorcerer and his archers advanced with each step.

"You are afraid," the man said to Gianni. "I can show you the way beyond fear."

Above the Sorcerer, in the room behind where he had stood, wild shadows danced on the walls as if matching the drumbeat they could all hear, high above in the hills, louder and louder, faster and faster. Across the *campo*, Tessa was weeping. In fear? In relief?

The Sorcerer continued in a conversational, welcoming tone. "Why not come with us, knight? Why not taste freedom? Experience one of our ceremonies and know better your enemy—or discover the friends we can be."

His call niggled at Gianni. There was a pull within himself that he did not like. . . .

"Ah, yes. You feel it." The man gestured above them. "Within our sanctuary you shall experience pleasure. Power. The spiritual realm like you've never known. Come, come, my friend. You too, brother knight," he said to Vito. "Bring the boy with you and all will be well."

Gianni shook his head, pulled back as if he were physically being drawn upward. "*Apage Satanas!* I call upon the Lord Jesus Christ to protect us. You cannot harm the beloved of Christ."

The Sorcerer stepped back as if he had been hit. "Away!" he snapped. "Away from us!" he seethed. "Leave us be! The Gifted have no right to be here! This is our domain!"

Gianni raised a trembling finger to the Sorcerer. "The Gifted will one day drive you from this place, evil one. You shall be brought down, stomped out." He eyed the archers on either side of the man. "One day soon, you will be under protection of neither arrow nor magic. And then, then, you shall be mine." He repeated the words again. "Lord Jesus, protect us now from the dark one. Flood this place with your light, your life, your love. Drive away death and destruction!"

The Sorcerer whirled, his cloak glinting in the moonlight, covering his archers. The knights looked from each other back to the dark doorway.

Their enemies were gone.

The shadows among the windows of Lord de Loren were still, simple candlelight flickering in the dark.

CHAPTER THIRTY-SIX

GIANNI blew out his cheeks as he paced. Daria was examining the boy in the dining hall the following morning, atop a long table. Tessa sat by his head, holding his hand. Nico leaned against the far wall, arms crossed, clearly put out that they had brought yet another child to this house, and one that had a clear advantage for Tessa's friendship.

Daria had pulled up the boy's robe to see the deformed lower left leg. It was grotesquely twisted, his foot pointing to the right, inward. She frowned and bent low, tracing the line from knee to ankle and shaking her head. She took his ankle in hand and twisted it one way, and then the other. Daria forced a smile at the boy and offered her hand to help him rise, but he did it on his own.

"Well then," Daria said. "Tessa will tell you that the first rule in this house is that every person bathes at least once a week, if not more. Beata has drawn you a bath in the tub in the knights' quarters. See to it that you get scrubbed from the top of your head to the bottom of your feet, no?"

"Yes, m'lady," the boy said. Gianni had not heard his voice rise above a whisper since he had met him.

"Nico will bring you a set of clothes. You must burn those that came in with you and bring your bed linens down to Beata to wash."

"Yes, m'lady." He followed Tessa out of the dining hall and Nico followed him.

Daria sat down heavily. "I do not know how to fix such a terrible thing. He was a small child when it was broken. It was not set right, and the bones have healed in an odd fashion—there's actually a ball of bone where the original break was."

"You do not feel led to pray over the child, allow God to heal him?"

"Nay." She shook her head. "Nay. This one is not to be accomplished through the divine methods. My mother—my mother actually rebroke children's legs on occasion, in an effort to set them right and let them heal again."

Gianni winced. "Surely you are not considering that."

"The challenge is that if we rebreak the deformed bone, it may damage the other, or knee or ankle. Then he is worse off than when we began. And the muscles . . . that's an issue too. When we straighten his leg it might tear muscle, tendon—wounds that are oft more stubborn than bones about healing."

"Daria, if anything happens to him, we cannot seek assistance. We cannot take him to the hospital, summon a physician."

"I have some donegal and rum," she said, standing to pace now. "We could get him to a point where he will feel very little."

Gianni reached out and stilled her. She looked down at him and from this angle, with the light streaming behind her like a heavenly halo, the shape of her cheekbones and wide eyes . . . it struck him sometimes, just how lovely the Duchess was.

"Sir Gianni?"

He dropped his hand and then brushed it anxiously through his hair. What had he been saying? The boy . . . "Could it be, m'lady, that there are those you are not to heal?"

She studied him for a long moment. "Mayhap."

"Roberto has learned to cope, to live with what he has."

"But as he grows, his deformity will become even worse. Already his leg tarries in growth behind the other."

"But each of us has a deformity we must battle, be it within or without, do we not?"

Daria set her mouth in a grim line.

"All I ask is that you give it a few days, pray over your decision. Ask Father Piero to pray over it too. What you two decide, I will abide by it. But take precaution, m'lady. What you propose could very well cause Roberto greater trauma and pain than what he already suffers. Even death, should bleeding or infection set in. Given our circumstances, you cannot know you will be able to stay here to see him through."

"Baron at the gate!" called the guard, and both turned their heads to the dining hall door.

"We must hide the children," Gianni said.

Lucan and Vito entered, panting after racing from their posts, waiting for direction. "Go upstairs and guard the boy, Lucan," Gianni said. "See he takes his bath. But make sure he utters not a sound. Vito, you go and stand outside the lady's quarters. It is vital that Tessa is not discovered. The lady will see to her visitor and we will fetch you when all is well."

Beata arrived, wringing her hands, then pushing her spectacles nervously up to the bridge of her nose. "Beata," Daria said. "It is all right. It is merely the baron. Please send warm water up to the knights' quarters."

"Yes, m'lady," Beata said, calming with the task, and with a bob of a curtsey, hurried out.

Daria watched her leave, wondering at the fluttering within her belly. Why did she feel compelled to hide the children, even from Vincenzo? Mayhap all this intrigue and danger had gone to her head. If she could not trust her uncle, who then, could she trust?

"Aldo, please escort Baron del Buco to the solarium," she said, hearing the man and his knights enter the courtyard. She paced back and forth, knowing Gianni was studying her.

"Do you wish me to come with you, m'lady?"

"Nay. It would only arouse his suspicion further."

"Do not tell him of the children. No matter how much you wish to."

"Nay. I do not intend to." She continued to pace back and forth.

"M'lady?"

She ignored his query and walked out then, squaring her shoulders and forcing her face to relax. She walked up the stairs to the solarium and found Vincenzo staring out the window. He turned and gave her the customary kiss of greeting, but his actions were perfunctory, cold.

Daria watched him out of the corner of her eye as he turned to a satchel and removed a thick pile of papers, laid them on the desk, and then stood back.

"What is that, Uncle?"

"Documentation. Of what the guild will produce this year and what it could do if we had increased exportation capability. If you will not listen to me, you may study the numbers and come to your own conclusion."

Daria sighed and forced herself to walk to the desk. So they were back to this bone of contention. Again. She lifted the first sheet but did not really look at the numbers. If Vincenzo said something was, it was. "I will say it again. I am not against increasing our exportation or importation. I simply wish to find an alternate method than what you propose."

"And what method would that be?"

"Our own shipping company—"

He let out a snort of derision.

"—or another partner. Simply not Frangelico."

"Frangelico has the best connections on the seas. He has spent two decades establishing himself in ports from Constantinople to Bangkok. It must be him. We know no one greater."

Daria walked to the window, considering. "We are not the mightiest of guilds. Why must we partner with the greatest sea merchant? Why not his competitor? I'm bound to like him more."

"If we take up the yoke with someone lesser, than that is all we become, Daria!"

"If the lesser is of fine moral character, someone with whom I'd care to share a yoke, then so be it!"

Vincenzo's face was red with fury. He strode to the desk and shoved the documents back into the satchel.

"Vincenzo, why are you so agitated? This is unlike you! I—"

He held up a hand, his back to her. "Speak no more, m'lady. I fear that any further words shared at this moment may lead to irreparable harm. You are too important to me, Daria. Please. I will return in several days and we will speak of it again. Mayhap the time will give us new direction beyond this impasse."

"I will pray that it is so," she said hollowly, allowing him to depart.

He paused at the door. "I do not wish to go to the guild. But I will, if I must."

Daria shook her head. So it had come to this. She was losing Vincenzo's confidence, had no time to do her own thinking. Mayhap it was best if she left the board. She looked about the solarium. But then all of this, her home, her father and grandfather's estate, might be lost. The men, the full house, it was costing her more than she had imagined.

Below her, the gate thundered to a close behind Vincenzo.

ぐ ぐ ぐ

VINCENZO made his way through the city to the house of Amidei, where he had been invited for an evening's festivities. Abramo had sent word that there would be a surprise guest; Vincenzo knew it would be Lord Frangelico.

What troubled Vincenzo was that he had made little progress in persuading Daria to do business with Frangelico, nor had he made any headway in discovering the true identity of the healer. He had spies planted throughout the city, watching for the girl of the Piazza il Campo, who had reportedly been taken in by the healer. But Abramo was most likely thinking the same thing, may-hap knew all he himself knew already.

He sighed. The opportunity, if he was not careful, would soon slip from his hands. Abramo had asked him to discover this one thing for him; if he did not deliver, he might not gain in favor with Frangelico or the others.

He gestured for the captain of his guard to move his horse forward, to Vincenzo's side. "You had word from someone today?"

"Yes, Baron. There is word of a young girl with a knight, in-side the piazza last night. Two others with the boy. There was a battle of sorts. Arrows were launched."

"But no one was hurt."

"Nay. And the knights left the *campo*, children in tow."

Vincenzo's eyes narrowed and he glanced over to his man. "Children? The knights, you know who they are?"

The man coughed.

"Well? Out with it, man."

"They were in hoods. But m'lord, our men followed them from the d'Angelo estate."

Vincenzo pulled up on the reins and stared with unseeing eyes at his gloved hand. The company came to a halt as one. "Was Lady Daria present?"

"Nay."

"And the girl? Did your informant know who she was?"

"Nay. He could not tell if it was the beggar girl who was healed in the Duomo."

Vincenzo threw back his head and continued on. He must cover for Daria, throw his own men off this trail until he could find out the truth. He laughed. "It would not be the first time a maid was with a knight."

"It was not a maid grown, but a child, my lord. It might not have been the beggar girl; the report I heard was that she was in a noblewoman's gown."

"As I said, it would not be the first time a maid was with a knight," he ground out. "Perhaps it was a small woman with the knight, not a child. This is the word I wish passed back through the ranks."

"As you wish, m'lord," said the man slowly.

"Why the boy? Why did they take the boy?"

The knight coughed again. He understood he was on uncertain ground. "It appeared that they were intercepting the child before he reached the healer. It was that beggar boy with the twisted leg."

"Healer?"

"Yes, my lord. The hill healer was in Il Campo. He had come for the child."

"All right, then. So we are now seeking a woman, with either a boy with a deformed limb or girl child—or both—in her care. See to it that if anyone comes across her, they report to me, and no other."

"Baron, they need not bother you with minor reports. They can come to me. I can sort it out for—"

"Me and no other."

The knight's lips clamped shut for a moment. "As you wish, my lord."

They came to the Amidei house and could hear music wafting over the high walls and the laughter of women. Stable boys retrieved their horses and led them away and comely maids gestured for them to enter. Vincenzo walked out into the courtyard and slowly pulled his gloves off, surveying the scene.

Never had he seen such a heady, festive feast. A long table had been set with fresh linen and the entire center—the whole way down—was stacked with exotic fruit and flowers. Pomegranates and grapes, lemons, limes, oranges, pears. Almonds. Long, curving yellow and odd-shaped orange fruits Vincenzo had never seen. Here and there among the piles, apples had been hollowed out and candles stuck in their delicate centers. Wax dripped down across the yellow and pink skin of the fruit. Dancing flames created a warm, inviting table. On the shallow pool beyond it were water lilies, and candles had been set afloat atop it, in tiny wooden boats.

He saw Lord Damien and Lord de Loren, in one corner, cavorting with young women that Vincenzo had never seen among the elite of Siena's feasts. The women wore daringly low-cut gowns and flowers tucked behind their ears. He noticed with grim surprise Ambrogio, leaning against a post on the far side of the pool, raising his goblet in a silent toast to him, but then he was distracted by a maid at his side.

Vincenzo looked more carefully around and realized he did not recognize one of the noblewomen of Siena. Only the men. Merchants, guildsmen, and bankers of the Mercanzia. Priors and consuls. Artists and musicians. Not that women were few in number; the women outnumbered the men two to one, passing trays with goblets full of sops in wine—carnations stained pink, sitting in the red liquid. Others passed trays of pears and cheese. They did not wear their hair up, as was custom, but let it fall down their backs. All were in white, he discovered. They appeared like brides on their wedding day.

Musicians played on either side of the group, from up above, on the portico, so it sounded as if music from the heavens descended upon them. Never had he seen a finer feast. Perhaps this is how they did it in Firenze. The Sienese could learn a few fine things. . . .

"Just in time, I see," a low voice said suddenly, just behind his right shoulder, and he turned to see Abramo Amidei. He leaned forward to kiss the man on both cheeks and then do the same with the man at his side, Lord Frangelico.

He cocked an eyebrow and waved out to the table and

courtyard. "A fine feast. I feel as if I've entered a garden of the gods."

"Indeed," Lord Frangelico said, raising his goblet. "And look, there is Venus and her sister," he slurred, as two giggling young women passed by them.

Vincenzo bit his tongue when it begged to ask the fat lord where his wife might be. His goal was to strengthen ties to the man, not sever them before they were even stretched between them.

"Come, come, my friend," Abramo said, pulling Vincenzo around to the table. He gestured to the seat at his right, placing Lord Frangelico at his left. He clapped his hands twice. "Come, come, my lords. To the table. We shall eat and drink tonight as friends."

The men broke off their conversations and headed to the table. Vincenzo stole glances down the length of it and discovered that every one of the Nine were present, as was nearly every other noble of the city, twenty-four in all, with about six artisans like Ambrogio mixed in, for color, no doubt. Abramo worked quickly. He had to admire him for that.

Maidens served new goblets of wine, taking away the drained glasses with only soggy sops at the bottom. Abramo lifted his goblet and looked down the table. "To Siena's finest. Even the most noble of men need a night on occasion away from their wives, to speak of business and titillate the senses. I daresay, my friends, that you are napping through opportunity. Siena is a sleeping city. I aim to assist you in waking her from her slumber and taking her to the level of greatness she was born for. Tonight it all begins. For each of you. And for me," he said with a charming cocked brow.

"Hear, hear," Lord Damien said, raising his goblet. "May we all gain in our new endeavors in the coming year. To our host, Lord Amidei."

"To Lord Amidei," the men said as one.

The men were served one amazing course after another—first

pomegranate seeds atop melon, then fried turnips covered with diced violets. Then a rich cabbage and onion stew was ladled upon their individual trenchers and a perfectly roasted capon, stuffed with parsley and thyme, atop that.

"It is a feast for a king," said one noble from down the table. There was much laughter and discussion, and it was some time before Vincenzo noted that every time he took a sip from his goblet, a maiden was there to fill it. He glanced down the line and saw that there was a woman behind every man. Any time anyone took a drink, his goblet was refilled. His head was already a bit fuzzy; how much had he had to drink?

It mattered not. There was no clergy present here tonight, and he had no wife awaiting him at home. He was one of the few eligible men among the crowd. Ambrogio caught his eye again, but Vincenzo looked away, wishing not to think of the past, his failures with friend and foe alike. Nay, tonight he wished to think of the future, of promise, of change. He swirled the liquid within his goblet.

When he took his next sip, the maiden behind him leaned low across his shoulder to fill it, a brown coil of hair drifting over his shoulder and down to his lap. Finishing her duty, she pulled back, slowly, letting the long coil wind its way back over his shoulder and against his neck like an invitation.

"You may take her home with you if you wish," Abramo said, leaning over to him with a conspirator's voice. "She has told me she has seen you and liked you. She asked if she might serve you this night."

Vincenzo did not miss the underlying implication. He cocked a brow. "Lords cavorting with servants?"

"Ultimate freedom," Abramo said with a smile. "The finest fruits are at times those one has not yet tasted," he said, picking up a brown furry oval from the pile before them and biting it in half. He showed them the center. Tender green flesh was exposed, with a perfect ring of black seeds. He smiled.

Was there nothing this man could not do? Not touch? How

did he keep the clerics from his door? Money, no doubt. Again, Vincenzo had to admire him for his infiltration, his power already gained in this city. He wanted to work with this man, learn from him.

"So, Lord Frangelico," Abramo said. The fat lord turned from fondling his servant girl's hair, running it under his nose as if smelling it, and looked to Abramo. "Tell Baron del Buco what you were telling me before he arrived."

"Oh, yes, yes," the man said dismissively. "You see, Baron, I have been considering for some time how to export finer linens than what I am currently able to obtain. We do a little trade with the guild here, but I am considering adding additional ships to my fleet if I can count on a reasonable amount of cloth out of your warehouses."

Vincenzo fought not to give any outward sign of his pleasure. He tapped the tablecloth and eyed the lord across the table, who had picked up a capon leg and was nibbling on it. At his right, a maiden was in the lap of a nobleman feeding him grapes. Vincenzo refused to look upon them, concentrating on the man across the table. This was what he was waiting for! Abramo had delivered upon his promise!

He took a long draught of wine. "How many bolts of cloth can you move with your new ships?"

Lord Frangelico smiled and leaned back in his chair, goblet in hand. "As many as you care to send my way, my friend." His eyes flicked to Abramo, who nodded in pleasure. "We will speak of it more on the morrow, yes?" he asked Vincenzo.

"I will look forward to it," Vincenzo said.

Lord Frangelico turned back to the servant behind him and Vincenzo looked to Abramo. The man placed his elbows atop the table and leaned over in his direction. "So? Tell me what you know about our mysterious healer."

Vincenzo smiled, stalling. "Why do you wish to know her identity, Lord Amidei?"

"Abramo, call me Abramo, please. We are like brothers now, no?"

"Yes, yes, Abramo."

Abramo's eyes stilled. "Down this table is every powerful man of Siena."

Vincenzo followed his gaze and then nodded.

"I am only missing the clerics, but I am making headway with many of them. It is always easy with them, once you have the nobles in hand. It is the wealthy, after all, who feed the Church." He flicked his hand into the air dismissively. "But this healer. This healer has me intrigued. She is noble. She is veiled. My greatest satisfaction in life is unraveling secrets. I would like to unveil this one. She has power at her fingertips. As you can see, I like people with power. And a woman." He cocked his head and an eyebrow. "Mayhap I will find use for her."

"I need but a little more time," Vincenzo said as casually as he could.

"Take all the time you need, my brother," Abramo said with a smile that did not reach his eyes. "Just know that if I find her before you, Lord Frangelico might find an alternate trade vendor."

"I, I am making headway," Vincenzo said, hating his sudden nervousness, his exposure.

"Good, good," Abramo said, leaning back in his chair. "To progress," he said, lifting his goblet and drinking deeply. He turned to a beauty behind him and pulled the giggling girl into his lap, kissing her open-mouthed, right there, before them all. Vincenzo glanced guiltily down the table. No one was staring, outraged, even surprised. Abramo was not the only one behaving without decorum. Many were laughing uproariously, clinking their ceramic goblets together; others were doing as their host was, kissing, fondling. It was bacchanal. Hedonistic. Otherworldly. Free.

And Vincenzo longed for Tatiana, wished for his wife in his arms again.

Abramo eyed Vincenzo as his woman kissed his neck. "Come, brother. Your loneliness can be eased, this night. Partake, partake of the feast."

The maiden reached over to refill his goblet. He stared at the coil of hair once more across his lap, remembering Tatiana's golden hair.

When the maiden finished pouring and withdrew, Vincenzo reached for her.

CHAPTER THIRTY-SEVEN

"AND again, after the supper, our Lord Jesus took the cup, and passed it all around, saying, 'Take and eat, this is my blood, shed for you. When you eat this bread, you eat the bread of life. When you drink from this cup . . . '" Daria had never taken communion outside the Duomo, and only once a year. Every Eastertide, the highest-ranking clergymen distributed bread and wine to every baptized soul in Siena. It took three days to get them in and out of the church doors.

This was entirely different in experience. She could see herself in that upper room with Jesus himself, distributing the Last Supper to his dear ones. Knowing what was ahead, the trial of the following day, brought tears to her eyes as Father Piero came near and tore off a chunk of bread and placed it upon her tongue.

Every one of them genuflected and remained praying on their knees. Father Piero had led them in a prayer of confession, and told them his conclusion about the Sorcerer of the cave—he was the leader of the dark force, and he was here in their city because of them. It was only a matter of time before they would clash. They must prepare, prepare their hearts and minds to do battle with him. It was prophesied in the letter that this day would come, that the Gifted would do battle with those of the dark. And all felt the dark drawing near with a distinct chill.

Daria let the yeastless bread sit upon her tongue for a long moment, heavy in her mouth. Tears dripped from her eyes to her folded hands as she prayed. She washed down the bread with a swallow of wine from the chalice Father Piero offered, feeling the weight of her sins, confessing them again, confessing pride and avarice and faithlessness. . . .

"Consider this the feast of forgiveness," Father Piero said, making the sign of the cross above each of them. "You have been cleansed of your sins and freed from your bonds. Serve your Messiah well, with faith and honor. Live as freed servants, treasuring every decision you make as an honor from your Lord."

"Amen," Gianni said.

"Amen," they all said after him.

Father Piero eyed them all. "What we have done here tonight bonds us together. We are one in Christ. Draw strength from that. Come what may, draw strength from that."

They filed out of the dining hall and Gianni was at her arm. "You realize that what we just did was heresy. We could be burned at the stake for that communion meal."

"Yes, well, I suppose it is simply one of many punishable acts." She paused and turned toward him, waiting while the others filed around them and out into the rest of the house. For all his fierce words, his tone was unperturbed. "You did not put a stop to it."

"Neither did you."

"Nay, it felt right. Just. How it is supposed to be, as our Lord would have it."

Gianni smiled down at her. "Yes. Never have I felt that conjoined to the Savior than in that dining hall," he said, pointing through the doorway. "We are breaking new ground, Lady Daria.

And our new road takes us in the right direction. Though it be an untraveled path, I have a peace within me."

"Indeed," she said, smiling up at him. He was handsome, in a gruff, unkempt sort of way. Longer hair curled at his neck and sideburns. Bright green eyes smiled down upon her.

She broke away and he walked with her.

"Have you decided what to do about Roberto?"

"Yes. And no." She paused and looked up at him again. "At one moment I am certain that we must move forward, and at others I am given pause. I will take Tessa to mass on the morrow. I continue to seek the Lord's direction on what to do. Pray with me, Gianni. I cannot be alone on this. If you and Father Piero pray for confirmation too, then we *all* shall know the path to take."

꩜ ꩜ ꩜

Vincenzo awakened, again in the house of Amidei. It had been three days since he had arrived here, a blur of feast and frenzied lovemaking and heady discussion with Abramo. Each time he had attempted to leave, Abramo tempted him to stay. Finer wine. Grander feasts. More distinguished guests from as far away as Firenze. Numerous women.

Never had he experienced what he had found here. This was Roman, in stature. This was glory. At Abramo's side, he would accomplish all he desired and more. It was as if he had been waiting for this new friend, this comrade who thought like him and beyond him—something he had never encountered. He had always been smarter, faster than his competitors. To Abramo Amidei, more and more, he was willing to cede power. He had little hope of actually competing, only a hope of learning from the master, partaking of a portion of his feast.

He pulled the woman's lithe arm from across his body and came to a sitting position at the side of the bed. His head throbbed. He needed to stop drinking. It seemed from the noon meal on, they drank in this house. It would not serve him to remain thickheaded.

He had to be sharp. And he needed to leave to discover the identity of the healer.

Vincenzo had a taste of this life and he wanted the keys to keep this kingdom. Abramo would get what he wanted. The healer was not Daria, could not be Daria, but she was likely to be close to her. Perhaps Zola, that woman from the village? The healings had begun about the time she arrived at Daria's home. . . .

It might not be pleasant, he thought, but it was necessary. It was for the greater good. For the guild. For Daria. For himself. The healer must be routed out and delivered into Abramo's hands. She would likely fall in love with the charismatic man, like every other female who crossed paths with him. She would probably thank Vincenzo, down the road. Yes, thank him.

"What day is it?" he asked the girl behind him.

"What?" she asked drowsily.

"What day is it?"

"I know not. Mayhap Sunday?"

Vincenzo rose and rushed to his clothing. Sunday. Mass. His men had found a Duomo guard who had overheard the healer's promise. To bring the girl to mass at the Duomo. Every Sunday.

"Where are you going, m'lord, off in such a rush?"

He pulled on his robe and dipped his hand into a washbasin to wet down his hair. "Mass."

The girl laughed as if she thought that was the funniest thing she had ever heard. She rose up, a brazen goddess among the swirling sheets. Definitely the most enticing woman Abramo had sent his way since he arrived at this house. Vincenzo neared the bed and kissed her.

"Come. Come to my home this night." he whispered.

She laughed again and brought a hand to her chest as if shocked. "M'lord, it is not a day that the Church sanctions for marital relations," she teased.

"Nay." He laughed. "Nay, it would not be proper, were we man and wife." He took her hand and stretched it out, staring down at her. "Seek your leave from Abramo. And come to me this night."

"I shall," she said as their fingers parted. "And we shall discover new delights together. But then you must come with me," she purred.

"Where?"

"To a meeting. This has been but the beginning of your education, m'lord. Lord Amidei wishes you to come and continue your learning there."

Vincenzo swallowed hard. He wanted to know, to experience it now. If Abramo was sending it his way, he was taking it. This was like riding the most powerful of stallions. . . . It pulled at him, sucked at him, making him want nothing but more, more, more. . . . "Come to me, girl, this night. And then I will go anywhere with you."

cb cb cb

It is unwise.

Can you not sense it? The forces of evil? They lay in wait.

Why walk into their trap, Daria?

It was a foolish promise. Break it.

We cannot be beside you. Our presence will only serve to unmask your identity.

Gianni and Father Piero's words reverberated in Daria's ears, but she still stubbornly walked on. Hasani had paced back and forth, blocking her way for a time.

But she had promised the bishop she would bring Contessa to mass each Sunday. She would honor her promise. They may be behaving as heretics, but the Church still deserved respect for all that it did well. And the last thing the Gifted needed was to have the Church actively hunting them down. After Tessa's healing, the bishop had set the Church guards upon tracking the hillside healer, driving him into hiding. But they had left the Gifted alone.

Could the Gifted not see the wisdom in this? It was for their good that she did this. Their collective good.

Tessa looked up at her, fear etched across her face.

"It is all right, dear girl. You shall see. We will attend mass and then we will return home, having fulfilled our promise to your bishop."

"But your veiling, m'lady. It is not as heavy; you are not as well concealed as you were."

"I know it. But if I wear that heavy veiling, our enemies will know me for sure. This could be construed as a noblewoman's latest fashion from France."

Tessa gave her a doubtful look and peered over her shoulder, looking for the knights.

Daria pulled her back around. "Keep walking forward. Remember, we are nothing but a mother and child, hurrying to make it in the Duomo doors before they close for mass."

ॐ ॐ ॐ

THERE. Vincenzo sat atop his horse and smiled as the young girl looked over her shoulder. She was clean and her hair coiffed into a net, but she was still the beggar child who had resided in the city piazza for years. He recognized her now that he saw her.

And the woman. He could not know for sure. She was in veils and tucked her head as she walked, not looking at anyone directly. Her hair was covered in the fine cream veiling, making her hair almost appear blond. . . .

"Wait here," he said to his guard. Vincenzo handed him the reins and followed the woman and child into the cathedral. He was the last one permitted in before the priests shut the door without apology on any other latecomers.

The woman and child made their way toward the front, near the right side. Up high was where the bishop would preach to them. So . . . she was fulfilling her promise. Bringing the child to mass so that the old man could see the child was all right.

Vincenzo smiled. It was her. He could deliver on his promise. Abramo would be pleased. He made the required movements throughout the mass, genuflecting and repeating words in Latin, but he felt none of the religious fervor of his youth. Life, and moreover death, had beaten it out of him.

Still, he decided to put the time to good use, making note of various nobles in attendance. It was good to keep track of these things. In time, the bishop ended his sermon from his perch, said more words in Latin that Vincenzo did not bother to translate, and then followed his priests out the door, behind a swinging censer.

Vincenzo inhaled and smiled. It was the smell of his lover. Exotic and earthy.

He waited, near a tall marble column, while the woman and child filed out among the crowd. Still he could not make out the woman's identity.

He made his way forward, now with several people between him and the woman. For a heart-racing moment, he thought he had lost her, but then she was before him again, bent over and speaking in hushed words to the girl.

Vincenzo took several steps and grabbed her arm. He held a handkerchief in his other hand. "M'lady," he said, "I believe you dropped this."

"Nay, m'lord. It is not mine," she said, her chin still tucked.

But he knew that voice.

She had turned away, was moving forward. Vincenzo grabbed her arm again and whipped her around. "Daria," he breathed.

She raised her head then, stubbornly meeting his gaze with a defiant look.

Daria d'Angelo was not only the girl's keeper, she was the mysterious healer of the marketplace. He shook his head. "Daria. You have kept this from me. Why? *Why?*"

"Vincenzo, I will tell you but we must—"

"Your acquisition of men, your refortification of the house . . ." He glanced down at the girl, who held Daria's hand.

"To protect this? Your secret?" He stepped back, a hand going to his heart. His eyes blurred. She had betrayed him, deceived him. The one person he thought he could trust in the city and she had deceived him! Deliberately kept this secret from him! What else was she hiding?

His head whirled. She was the one Abramo wanted. He was furious with her, maddened by her deceit, but a sudden desire to protect her swept through him. It had been one thing when the healer was a nameless woman, possibly someone Daria knew; it was another when he discovered the woman Abramo sought was Daria.

"Vincenzo . . ."

"Nay," he said a hand on his head. Frantically, he fought to sort through his thoughts, their potential course of action. "Please. Do not speak. I must think."

"Vincenzo, please. Let us go to my house. Or to yours. We must seek someplace more private."

He leveled furious eyes upon her. "Nay. You stupid girl, you have forced us into a terrible corner."

"I do not know of what you speak. Really, Vincenzo, I must go. We cannot remain here."

"Oh, I hope you can tarry, at least for a moment," said a voice behind her. She turned and Vincenzo looked across her shoulder.

ഷ ഷ ഷ

"Ahh," Abramo said with ultimate satisfaction, watching as she hurriedly placed the veiling back near her eyes. "The most beguiling Duchess." He took her hand and bent to kiss it in languid fashion. "I had wondered if it might be you," he said lowly. He rose, smiling and nodding. "Vincenzo, you have kept thy promise."

She pulled away, casting a confused look toward Vincenzo.

"You have at last introduced me to the pride of Siena, the elusive Duchess d'Angelo."

"It is not a true title." Daria glanced to the child, feeling her edge away. Tessa was backing away, terror alive in her eyes. Her expression brought Daria's heart to her throat and she fought to stay where she was, to not give in to the urge to flee.

"It may not be a true title, but from what Vincenzo tells, well deserved. I could help you purchase the title, if you wish." He moved around her slowly, cutting between her and the child. "A noble title will help you accomplish what your rare business mind has not."

Daria shook her head, pretended to ignore him, while he leaned in to inhale as if he had caught a scent he enjoyed. She fought to keep her voice steady. "I have no need for empty titles. Now if you will excuse me, my lord, I must take my leave."

cb cb cb

ABRAMO could see the terror in the child's eyes, but he could also feel the power that resided within her thin frame. Daria possessed it too. And the aroma. Oranges. Cloves. So this was *their* scent, the scent of the Gifted.

Abramo hurried forward and stepped in front of them again. Daria pulled the child to an abrupt stop. She actually took a step backward and then held her position. Beautiful and courageous. He had never encountered a woman so strong. "Empty title, eh?" He cocked a brow. "What is it, then, that you have need of? I think you shall find that I am a friend to many. I can get you anything you need, anything you could want."

Vincenzo motioned with his chin and Abramo looked over his shoulder. Lady Daria's knights were making their way across the crowded *campo*, weaving between people on their way to her side. He laughed when he saw the knight of the Church, of the grove, of Il Campo, even with unshaven cheek and hat. Of course. Of course! Everything was coming together. The Gifted were here, before his very nose.

He smiled down at Daria again. "Most intriguing. It has been my most sincere pleasure, Duchess, to make your acquaintance.

And yours as well, child," he said, smiling down at her. The girl looked to be at the edge of panic. She knew him, recognized him as clearly as he did her, but he ignored it. "Your daughter, Duchess?"

"My servant," she said, edging past him again.

"Your servant," he said with a disbelieving tone. "There are not many women in the city who take their servants to mass."

"I am not like the other women of this city," she tossed over her shoulder. He watched her walk away then, her knights pulling up short of her, blending into the crowd but keeping an eye on her, casting questioning looks back to Vincenzo and Abramo.

Abramo laughed, a great belly laugh. "Nay, lady. You are not like the other women of this city," he said, more to Vincenzo than to her. He turned then to Vincenzo, clapping him on the back and leaving a hand on his shoulder as they walked. "What good fortune, Vincenzo, that our healer is your very own guild co-consul. I can tell by your face that she did not tell you of her great secret. Now I want you to tell me everything about her you *do* know."

CHAPTER THIRTY-EIGHT

CONTESSA was a bundle of nervous energy when they reached home. She was sitting, and then she was standing, then pacing, shaking her hands as if she could shake out her fear. "That man," she said for the hundredth time, "is evil."

Father Piero entered the room and narrowed his eyes when he saw Contessa in such agitation, tried to lay a hand on her shoulder in support, to cease her pacing. "He knows who we are," she said to Daria, still walking one way and then the other.

"He knows who we are," she repeated to Father Piero.

"What do you mean by that, girl?" the priest asked.

"*He* knows who *we* are."

Father Piero drew back, his mouth gaping open, eyes wide with understanding. "Who? Of whom does she speak, Daria?"

"Lord Abramo Amidei de Firenze."

"Amidei," he said blankly. He shook his head, as if he had expected to know his enemy's name. "I do not know of him."

"I do," Gianni said. "He has family from Venezia to Napoli." He rubbed his fingers together. "Money, and lots of it. Power."

Contessa was between the adults, watching as each one spoke. "He is of the dark. He is evil. He will do us harm."

"All right, all right, Contessa," Gianni said in a growl. "We understand!"

The girl drew back, eyes wide, silent.

"Look . . . forgive me," he said toward her. When she kept backing away, he turned back to Daria and Father Piero with a guttural cry of frustration. "What is next, Father? Where are we to go? What are we to do? Even my cardinal will have difficulty believing that the Sorcerer is Amidei. I am certain he has already made inroads in Avignon as well as Roma."

The priest shook his head slowly, back and forth. "You have read it many times with us. The portion of the letter we hold . . . it speaks only of our presence. Of our drawing together and effecting change at the most basic level. Of telling them of Christ's love, of his love for each of them."

"There has to be more!" Gianni cried, walking off with a further gesture of frustration.

"It is not a map, Gianni. It is prophetic, to a certain extent, but much of that is from the illuminator's vision, his understanding that we would come together to form what the author called the Gifted. It says we will teach people about the true power of God. It says we shall teach people about the true love of Christ. It says we will use our gifts to show the people that the Lord God is alive and well. It does not spell out how we are to do it."

"Then what are we to do? How am I to protect Daria, Tessa, you, the others? I do not even fully understand our mission!"

Father Piero laughed softly.

"I do not see anything amusing in this," Gianni said.

"It is just that the disciples must have felt very much like we do, right now. Hunted by politicians. Betrayed by friends. Jesus healed for some time, but specifically asked those he healed not to speak of it to others."

"The divine secret," Daria said in a whisper. "He was biding his time, holding off the inevitable as long as he could. Trying to do as much as he could before the authorities took him away." She gasped at the enormity of it. Feeling a portion of what her Savior might have felt. . . .

"But once he was known, he did not deny it."

"Nor did he claim it, exactly."

Tessa crept back to the trio, a bit calmer now. She watched each person speak. Daria looked up and noticed the rest of the household listening in too. She supposed it was good. They would all have to be told, sooner or later.

"And then Jesus became bolder. Speaking the truth, outright. Knowing he did not have much time."

"That is what we must do?" Daria asked.

"Mayhap. But my sense is that we should let out this line as long as we can . . . this middling line where people do not yet know what to make of us. In order to catch a larger fish, you know?"

"I was in error, not telling Vincenzo the truth. Now he considers me disloyal. I could see it on his face."

"You shall try to win him back, gain us time," Piero said.

"We need the rest of the manuscript," Gianni said. "There may be more clues, more prophetic visions among its illumination. Perhaps prophecy within the words themselves. Instruction on how we battle one such as Abramo Amidei."

Daria gasped then. "It is the prophecy seen on the back of the altarpiece we are now encountering. The peacock, facing the dragon."

"Nay, daughter. I fear there are even bigger battles ahead. That is the dragon."

"So then where? Obviously, we cannot remain here, in the city. They would track us to my country manor. To where do we flee? To where might we find more of what we are to discover?"

"I have considered that," Piero said. "The only place I can think of is Venezia."

"Venezia?" Daria asked.

"Venezia or Constantinople."

"Why?" Gianni asked.

"Countless sacred manuscripts and relics were housed there in the Hagia Sophia of Constantinople—and many of those were ransacked by the Venetians. Through the years I have gathered word of things that echo what we see here, in our portion of the letter. When the Iconoclasts came into power, if he was indeed prophetic, the scribe most likely knew his letter would soon be lost in the fire. The prophecy could not be lost. So mayhap he sent another copy to a friend. Or asked another to copy and send it."

"Mayhap," Gianni said. "It could be anywhere in the world, priest. You are guessing."

"But it is an educated guess," he said. "If it survives, I believe we'll find it in one of those two cities."

Hasani grunted and gestured wildly.

"The letter," Daria said. "He wants us to look at the letter. We've read it backward and forward, Hasani. There is nothing else for us to glean from it."

Hasani remained insistent and Piero went to retrieve it.

When he returned, the tall black man shoved things to the side of the table and brought several candles to the center. He stacked the sheets carefully together and then held them all to the light.

The illuminated illustrations, grouped together, and combined with the winding peacock feathers, formed a solid mass, leaving only the lower left and upper right sections to light.

"It is the boot of Italia!" Rune exclaimed.

People shifted to get a better look. All eyes scanned the pages and were drawn to the top, near Venezia. There was something beside it. Piero hurriedly turned to the third page.

Beside the painting of the priest upon the road—so clearly their own Piero now, to all—beside the swirling peacock feathers that formed the northeastern notch of Italia and denoted the map, the priest held his cross firmly. The cross literally pointed to Venezia. He set the page down silently, lost in thought.

"Backward and forward, you looked," Gianni quipped. "But apparently never *through* the thing."

Chapter Thirty-nine

DARIA left them and went to her room, suddenly wishing for nothing but a quiet evening in the sanctity of her own household. What had just been proposed felt right, right in her bones, but she did not like it. She did not want to leave her home, her city. She wanted to remain here and barricade the doors if necessary. Stand and fight where they had allies, were strongest. She did not want to continue this breathless chase for truth, for mission. It was all too enormous, too much to take in. How was she to do her portion of the business in the guild? How was she to see to business at all? And working with Vincenzo . . . he had been so hurt by the secrets she had held from him, and he already appeared tied to Abramo Amidei. Mayhap if she went to him, begged him to draw away from so dark an enemy, to see the light . . . How was she to exist without her dear uncle beside her? He was all she had left in the world.

She strode to the window and opened the heavy shutters, gazing down to the garden below and out to the city, the sun casting a warm orange glow across stucco and brick and tree. She loved this city, she loved it. *Please don't call me away from home, Lord. I just returned! Please, Holy One. Let us do as you bid, here, here among the streets and people I know best. Surely we can accomplish all that you have set out for us to do, right here. There are people here, many people who do not know of your love, your healing, your power. Right here, in Siena.*

She paced back and forth, as agitated as Tessa, feeling like an attorney before the magistrate. *Your enemy is here, now. Let us fight him here, where we are strongest.*

She paused and closed her eyes, waiting for him to answer, wishing for a voice that spoke as clearly as Father Piero's to her. But it was within, deep within, that she felt his impressions upon her heart, pushing her to submit to the Holy, to trust him.

Daria opened her eyes in frustration. "I will trust you. I will," she said, hands splayed, looking up toward the ceiling. "But please, can you not give us what I ask, Father? May we not abide here for a time?"

But there was no assurance, no internal nod. They could remain here for a time, but there was nothing to say it would not be tomorrow or the day after that they must depart. The thought of it, of leaving with no promise of return, left her bereft. Here was where she felt some connection with her parents, her kin. This was her birthplace, where she could find solace and distraction. It was where Vincenzo and she worked, or had one time worked together. And it was where Ambrogio had found her again. What other childhood friends would come to this house, eager to see her, only to find no one home but the Sciorias? How could she protect what her father and grandfather had worked so hard to attain?

Daria sat down on the edge of the bed and slumped to her back, staring up at the water spot on her ceiling that had always brought her a measure of comfort. It had been there since she was but a girl, and had appeared when her father, bathing in the knights' hall, discovered a rat on the edge of the tub. In his hurry to get away, he had jumped out of the tub, spilling the entire thing across the floor and sending water dripping down toward Daria.

It was a silly story, a family story that had grown in lore as time went on. After a few years, one rat had grown to ten. Instead of just Beata and her mother coming to see what had set Daria's room into a rainstorm from a broad circle above, the way Giulio d'Angelo told it, they went and retrieved every woman and child from the avenue below to parade through his private bath chambers.

She stared up at the water spot, laughing, laughing until she gave in to tears.

When her tears waned, she looked up to the water spot again. "Even this, Lord? You ask me to give up even this?"

She waited in the silence. Scriptures cascaded through her mind one after another. *Store up your treasures in heaven. . . . I am a jealous God. . . . You shall have no other god than me. . . . I will be with you. . . .*

Her home. Her estate. Her businesses. Were they gods to her? If he asked it of her, could she truly give them up?

Then she thought of the healings that had transpired. The boy in Contrada della Chiocciola. The old farmer's wife. Tessa. The people in the marketplace. The people, the people, absorbing her words of Christ's love like thirsty sponges. The pleasure of doing God's work, here on earth, regardless how terrifying. Never had she felt such joy. Nothing compared with it. Even this, her home, her haven.

She nodded and whispered, "All right." She splayed her arms out upon the bed, totally open, vulnerable, staring beyond the water spot. "I hear you, I understand," she whispered. "Here am I. Send me."

❧ ❧ ❧

ABRAMO Amidei sank into the sulfurous waters of the hot spring, across from Vincenzo, his olive-skinned torso as finely muscular as

Jacobi's had been fleshy and pale. "Ahh, this is magnificent, my friend. Thank you for your invitation." He leaned his head back against the stone of the spring, saying nothing more. Vincenzo had watched him take this tactic of silence time and again through the last week, giving Abramo the edge. "You are welcome," he said simply, leaning back his head too.

They sat listening to nothing but a bird upon the air, the bubbles about them, arising from deep within the earth, for some time. It was Abramo who first broke their silence, Vincenzo noted with pleasure.

"You did not expect our healer to be the Duchess," he said quietly. "She deceived you. Betrayed you."

Fury rocked through Vincenzo's veins again and he fought to keep his tone calm. "She gave me no hint that it was her. And yet, in retrospect, I was foolish for not seeing her for what she was all along."

"What she was?"

He was drawing him in. Getting him to disclose that which was dearest to his heart. "The healer," Vincenzo hedged, pulling back a little. "Her mother was always gifted with herbs, tended to the infirm. I suspected that Daria might have crossed paths with the healer, never saw that she herself was the one. I did not think her capable of such deceit."

"Deceit? Or did she merely keep a secret? Everyone has secrets."

Vincenzo shoved the warning from his heart. "Daria has never had a secret from me. I have been like a father to her since her own died. We have worked together, week in, week out. Until Marco . . ."

"Marco Adimari?"

"Yes," he said slowly, disliking how Abramo pounced upon this newest piece of information as if he had handed over a piece of gold.

"He is the one favored to take the next available seat among the Nine," Abramo said.

"If I have anything to do with it. And working with you, mayhap we can ensure that that goal is attained."

"Simple enough, simple enough. But let us get back to the Duchess. She was the one handfasted to Adimari?"

"Yes. Their union proved to be unfruitful, although there was much affection between them."

"Ahh. Very good," he said with a low chuckle. "Very good."

Vincenzo did not know to what he referred as good, but he nodded, like an altar boy before a lecturing priest. He splashed his face with the warm water, struggling for the upper hand again. Mayhap he should abandon his quest for control, submit to learning, cut his losses with Daria; move forward with Abramo, go with him wherever he opted to take him. Daria could no longer be trusted. Their business relationship had disintegrated into constant disagreement over building the guild to a greater level of commerce; their personal relationship had been eroded by her deceit. Mayhap the time was ripe for separation, a new path. "Tell me, Abramo. What is it that you want with the healer? Why the fascination?"

Abramo was studying him intently through the steam. "Because I am the other. The other who heals in the hills and caves about us." He raised his hands to the heavenlies as if the cool night air were caressing his steaming face.

"You? *You* are the hillside healer?"

"Indeed," he said with a grin, leveling a gaze back at Vincenzo. He wiggled his eyebrows. "I want power. In all forums. And I shall have it."

Vincenzo nodded, understanding at last.

"Come, my friend, to the caves when the new moon is born. We will have a ceremonial welcoming for you. Your friend, the Duchess, is of the past. We are your future. I know this—do you not?"

Vincenzo stared into his eyes across the pool, hesitating.

"All right, then. We will bring along your Duchess," he said soothingly. "You are angry with her at the moment, but you have strong feelings for her. So we will continue to pursue her. Woo her. You will be together again, as warden and ward, friends, lovers, whatever you wish. If the Duchess remains barren, we will get you babies, as many as you desire. You can adopt them, fashion them into your own heirs."

Vincenzo felt a surge of hope, as well as an odd sensation at the thought of being Daria's lover as well as warden. The idea was not as foreign as he would have expected, as if it had emerged from deep within his own heart. He had loved her, always loved her. Abramo Amidei was as wise as he was brave, in addressing subjects most would shirk.

"Bringing her alongside us . . ." Abramo raised his eyebrows. "Now that would be cause for celebration. And once we have her, all others who stand in our way will crumble. When that occurs, Baron, we will have strength beyond imagination. No one, and I mean no one, shall come against us."

CHAPTER FORTY

"I do not understand," Ambrogio said, shoving the pages back across the desk to her.

"You do," she said, eyeing him intently. "I want you to represent me as co-consul of the guild. Until I return."

"But where are you going?"

She rose and strode to the solarium window, opening the shutter and then the glass, inhaling the scents of soil and flower. "Away. I cannot tell you more."

"Daria, what is going on? What is this madness?"

She turned to look at him, and then over to Aldo, Gianni, and Father Piero.

"Are they the ones? Is it they who force your hand thus?"

Gianni stood up straighter, but held his tongue.

"Nay, nay!" She strode back to Ambrogio and took his hands in hers. "You are a fair man, an intelligent and thoughtful man, Brogi. I trust you with this task. There is no other."

"But you ask me to work with Baron del Buco!" He rose and paced himself. "I have told you that we had a falling out. How am

I to accomplish this task with that obstacle? How am I to do it at all? I am not a businessman! I am an artist!"

"I must go away for a time. The guild will not see you as a threat—"

Ambrogio guffawed at that.

"—they will not see you as trying to seize power. They will know you as their own artist, not one of the *grandi*. They will most likely immediately remove me from leadership. I expect to lose my co-consul seat beside Vincenzo, but I must hold my seat on the council. I am giving you power of attorney over my estate. Aldo will do all the work; look to him for guidance. All you do is sign the documents that come forth."

Ambrogio kept shaking his head. "Why are you so rushed? So harried? Are you in danger?"

"I cannot tell you more. Only that we must be away for a time. Please," she said, bringing his hands in hers, up, to her chest and looking into his eyes. "Please, Brogi. I beg you to do this. I will not be gone long."

He paused, wavering in the face of her intensity, and then sighed. "How long?"

"A few months, a year, no longer than two."

"Two years!" he said, pulling his hands away.

"You said yourself that you would be here, working on the paintings for the Nine anyway. You have been living in a hovel. You may abide here, in my home. It will benefit us, you having an ear in the hallways, and having you here to watch over the Sciorias and my home."

Ambrogio was shaking his head again. "There is much you are keeping from me, Daria."

She nodded, becoming angry now. "Yes. Too much. There may come a time that I can tell you. But I cannot now. Ambrogio, friend of my childhood, brother. I know what I am asking from you. Will you not do this for me?"

Ambrogio laughed in blinded wonder. "I do not know what to say."

"Say yes," Father Piero said, stepping forward. "Say yes."

"Excellent," Ambrogio said sarcastically. "Just what I needed. More pressure from a cleric." He sighed and looked at Daria. "I cannot promise that I will hold it together. When you return, it may all be in shambles. I want you to write it down, write it down that on this day, the eleventh day of August, the year of our Lord thirteen thirty-nine, you gambled all by leaving your worldly possessions to me. That you will still love me even if you find that you must abide in my hovel rather than the fine home you left to me."

Daria swallowed hard, her eyes flitting to Aldo. He gave her a reassuring look. Ambrogio would not move without Aldo's permission. "Done," she said, a smile tugging at her lips. "Pass me the quill and parchment."

♌ ♌ ♌

THE city was abuzz with preparation for the three-day Palio tournament, the annual summer celebration that included competition in jousting, sword fighting, and more. Wagon after wagon full of dirt to cover the cobblestones of the *campo* for a jousting run passed by Vincenzo as he made his way to his own home. He had spent several more nights at the house of Amidei—after assisting Abramo through the technicalities of purchasing Lord Leo's second home—finding himself absorbed in other business transactions at Abramo's side, entertaining nobles from Roma, or swept into a nubile lover's arms. It felt good, so good to keep his mind off grief, off Daria, off Tatiana. To focus on action, things he could control.

But Abramo had given him a task. *Invite her to our city's tournament on the morrow. Meet her this day and offer a way to peace between you. We will begin this night to woo her to our side. Appeal to her sense of loyalty.*

To do as he asked, Vincenzo had to return home, change clothes, review correspondence. Daria would expect him to be up on all matters pertaining to the guild when he saw her. One of the Contrada del Drago passed by him, singing, leading a high-stepping, deep-black-colored stallion—pure beauty. A knight, drunk with wine, slumped across her saddle, a *contrada* banner of purple and green wrapped around his neck. On the morrow, the city's piazza would be flooded with thousands of people as seventeen *contrade* competed for the year's honor of having won the tournament. No outsiders were allowed to compete.

Briefly, he wondered if Marco would ride in the summer tournament. He hoped he would not be so foolish. Men died in the city's *contrada* jousts and swordfights and races every year. He had his potential position with the Nine, his impending heir to consider. Vincenzo had seen him very little in the past weeks. He needed to look in on him, make sure all continued to be well with him and Francesca.

He entered his home, ignoring greetings from servants on every level. He hated being here, in this house. It reminded him of death. Of Tatiana. Of failure. He much preferred Abramo's home, filled with strangers, and people anxious to please, of fine foods and lovers and life. He almost turned and walked out. But Abramo had set him upon the task. He must do as the man bid.

Vincenzo picked up a stack of correspondence, tossing one after another back to the desk. He paused over the last, a note from Daria, turning it to the opposite side. Imprinted in the red wax was her family crest, with the peacock. He smiled. She was reaching out to him. This was as it should be.

He ran a finger under the seal and opened the page, moving toward a candle for better light.

Vincenzo,

> *I feel badly about our parting of ways. You are, and always will be, vital to me. Let us come to the table looking to*

make peace between us and discover new wisdom in leading the guild in the way it should go. Please come to my home on the morning of the tournament. I pray that we can settle our differences and move forward again as friends.

—Daria

This was good. Abramo would be more than pleased. With no effort at all he had accomplished what Amidei had asked. They would go to the tournament together, as they had for years, and on the way home, when all was well between them and in festive spirits, they would stop at Lord Amidei's home. She would be reluctant, but how could she say no, so soon after making peace with him?

Abramo could do what Vincenzo could not. He could show her the strength that lay in power. In control. In reach. In money. He would speak to her, in words that Vincenzo himself could not find—about how together they would be stronger.

Vincenzo tossed aside the note and strode to his porch, overlooking the city. He reached out his hand, seeing the city skyline cradled within it. He imagined Abramo on one side, Daria on the other. Together, the three of them had the charisma and capability of conquering Siena, Firenze, Roma, and beyond.

Vincenzo closed his fingers upon his city and looked to the hills above her. Tonight, Abramo would be pleased with him. Tonight, Abramo would show him the mysteries of his cave.

CHAPTER FORTY-ONE

"THEY think they have us. Since they know who we are, they think that they can have us," Father Piero said, looking solemnly around the group. "Let them think that. Let them think that we are here, cowering in Daria's home, trying to get our wits about us. But we will be on the move."

Daria smiled with him. As much as she hated to say farewell to her home, farewell to Siena for a time, it was now well within her, a deep, abiding peace. What mattered was that she followed her God, no matter when, no matter where, no matter at what cost. She became teary-eyed as she looked at the Sciorias, trying so hard to be supportive and true, but struggling, casting furtive, longing glances in her direction. *They are so faithful, Father. Protect them. Let no harm come to them, Lord. They are innocents!* And yet they were as brave as her knights, standing side by side with the men, intent upon the priest's words. Her parents had chosen well.

"When they come, if they come, be they of the Church or of darker forces," Gianni said, focusing on Lucan—the lone knight who would remain behind—and then glancing to the Sciorias, "you are not to fight them. If they are looking for us, hold them off for a time, pretending to have difficulty with the gate, but then allow them in, show them we are gone. The estate is fortified, but under full attack and without men, you cannot stand."

"We do not want harm to come to you. You are merely buying us time to get farther away," Basilio said.

They all nodded.

"Let them come," Lucan said. "I will do my best to protect what is yours, m'lady."

"Bless you, Lucan. May God give you wisdom and strength." She scanned the group. Who was missing? Zola. Zola had been here a moment ago.

"What about me?" Roberto asked, from his perch on the bench by the fire. He drew nearer to Daria. "I want to come with you."

Daria took his hand and smiled into his eyes. "We will return, Roberto, I promise. Or we will send for you as soon as we can. I cannot see to your healing right now. We must not be rushed, must not be harried. And we are both at this moment." She placed a hand on his cheek. "Will you trust me, child?"

Grieving, reluctant eyes held hers a moment and then he slowly nodded.

"Good." She glanced from Tessa, eyes wide with sorrow at the thought of leaving Roberto behind, back to the boy again. "The Sciorias can watch over you, help you. My friend Ambrogio is coming to live here. You'll find him very entertaining."

He gave her a tremulous smile at the thought of that. Tessa squeezed his hand.

She leaned down toward his ear. "Believe it, boy. God himself will see to your healing."

She turned to Nico. "Take care of Bormeo for me. I will send for him as soon as we are settled. Mayhap you can accompany your great-uncle to deliver him to us!"

"Yes, m'lady," he said.

Daria rose and looked around the room, smiling tenderly at the Sciorias. "We must make haste. Ambrogio will be here to meet with Baron del Buco in but an hour. The baron will arrive, expecting me to be here. We must be away by then, well away. We will escape through the crowds, flooding the city for the tournament. They will assist us to blend in, and then we will make our way out of the city.

"We will need basic provisions, Beata, Agata. Blankets, food. Several changes of clothing. Horses ready, Nico. Aldo, I'll need key documentation and money, enough for three months' provisions for our company. We will meet again in the courtyard in half an hour and Father Piero will bless us all."

Everyone rose and parted ways to get to their tasks. Piero caught Rune before he went to the stairs. "Rune, have you seen Zola?"

"No, Father. She was here this morning. I think she was with us when we began our meeting. . . ."

"And yet not at the end. She has been more oft absent than present in the last week. Ever since Tessa arrived . . ."

A shadow crossed Rune's face. "Nay. She was not present at the end. Do you fear trouble, Father?"

"Nay. Send Nico to find her and report to me when you do."

"As you wish."

章 章 章

"ZOLA," Abramo said, rising. He rounded the desk and met her across the expansive room, taking her hands in his and kissing her.

"There is no time, m'lord."

"No time?"

"They are moving out, m'lord."

"Who?"

"The Gifted! They are leaving the Duchess's estate and heading out."

"Impossible. She is to meet with the baron this morning. The Palio begins this night. . . ."

"I can only tell you what I know. They are leaving the city."

"They still have no idea that you are an interloper?"

"Not as of yet. I have avoided contact with the girl, as you requested. She watches me, anytime I am in the same room. But my absence now will be noted." She paced back and forth, in obvious agitation. "You do not intend to hurt them, m'lord, do you?"

Abramo laughed. "Hurt them? Nay. I want them with us. I only wish to sway them toward our side, our beliefs. The best ally is an enemy turned."

Zola nodded, still pacing, wringing her hands. He brought her up short. "They have gotten to you. You care for them."

"It is impossible not to! They are good people, fine people. They have treated me with nought but kindness and care."

He studied her for a long moment. "The one knight. He still has an eye for you."

"Yes," she said slowly. She met his gaze. "I believe he does."

"Good. Good, we will use that. How soon do they depart?"

"Half an hour, mayhap less."

Abramo strode to the hall and screamed for his captain. "Summon the men. I want you mounted and ready in ten minutes. Provisions for the day. Send a boy to Baron del Buco's estate with word to bring his men in haste and meet us at the home of Daria d'Angelo. Tell him the Duchess appears to be leaving." He turned back to Zola and stroked her cheek. "You have done well, my love. I have one more task for you. . . ."

✤ ✤ ✤

"It is Lady Zola! Open the gates!" Rune called from the tower.

Daria glanced from her medicinal pack, secured now on her horse, over to Piero. It was odd, that the woman had left. Mayhap she had needed something, or to say farewell.

Gianni glanced out the narrow window and, spying the woman, took off the barricade, nodded at Ugo to open the gate, and returned to helping Nico secure the last of eight packs upon the horses. Ugo began churning the giant wheel and the chain soon became taut and edged the massive door open. When it was two, then three feet open, Zola moved toward it, slowly, as if in a dream. Throngs of people were outside in the streets.

"Hurry now, woman," Gianni said from across his horse, frowning at her. "Why do you tarry? We must get the gate—"

"Enemy at the gates!" Rune cried from high above. "Shut the gate! Shut it! Men to arms! Men to—"

Three men rushed in, around Zola, with swords drawn. More were behind them. As they entered, a chill washed over Daria. Tessa began screaming. Men, men of the dark one.

Ugo was cranking the wheel again as Lucan, Basilio, and Vito met the invaders, swords drawn, shoving them backward. Gianni grabbed Daria's arm and rushed her to the stairs. "Go! Barricade yourself in the knights' hall!"

She stopped, vacillating between going to the Sciorias and Roberto and Tessa and following Gianni's orders.

"Go!" he screamed, drawing his sword and turning to meet a knight behind him, narrowly blocking the man's swing.

Daria turned and ran. She was up to the second floor when she heard Rune, moaning on the stairs above. She picked up her skirts and found him, twin arrows through his shoulder, leaning heavily against the stairwell wall, trying to make his way down.

She came behind him as he slumped to his knees. "I can get these out, Rune. But we must get into the knights' hall."

"I'm sorry, m'lady. Forgive me. It was only Zola. I thought it was safe. Then the men—they came from the crowd. It was so hard to see. . . ."

"Shh," she said, trying to block out the sounds of men in skirmish below them. Zola had been so strangely slow, as if she were allowing the men entrance. . . . "It is all right. You did your best."

"I am dying, m'lady."

"Nay, you will not die this day, Rune. You will live to sing of the day that God saved you from your wound. But you must help me, now. You must rise and go with me to the knights' hall." He nodded, and she took his heavy sword in hand, dragging it behind her, using her other arm to support the giant knight. Limping, they made it into the knights' hall. Daria helped Rune to a cot and then ran back to the door to slip the barricade bar across it.

Then she hurried back to Rune. "We must move quickly." Downstairs, she could still hear the clanging of swords, the grunts and shouts of men.

"Did they get the gate shut again?"

"I believe so."

"How many?" he groaned. "How many got through?"

"Five, mayhap six." She moved his shoulder forward so she could see the protruding arrows. Daria swallowed hard. "God answered our prayers, Rune. He protected you," she said.

"I think next time we ought to pray a bit harder," Rune quipped, wincing as she handled the ends of the arrows, pulling back fabric to study his wound.

Daria looked at the oddly formed arrowheads protruding through his shoulder. She touched one in wonder and pulled back her hand quickly, sucking at the blood. An odd, acidic taste assailed her tongue, as she stared again at the arrowhead. Razor-sharp! Like those in the forest that had cut down Gianni's comrades, Gianni himself. Gianni had said he had never seen arrows like them before. She sucked in her breath. The Sorcerer. He was here? In her house?

They both looked to the door as they heard men running up the stairs. A man slammed the door with an *ooph* and more swordfighting resounded from the other side. Daria met Rune's eyes. "I need to get these out, Rune. Now. We'll wrap your wound and then we must escape from here."

"Good. Do it." He sank to his knees on the floor, grabbing hold of the bedpost and gritting his teeth. Daria came behind him and grabbed the first arrow, pulling it farther through to get a better hold of it, making Rune cry out in agony. She took it then between her two fists and snapped off the head, wincing when it again sliced her hand, then moved on to deal with the other.

ↄ ↄ ↄ

"WHERE is she?"

"Who?" Gianni said, between gritted teeth, pushing the enemy knight from his chest and meeting his next sword as it plunged toward his neck.

"The Duchess. The master only wishes to speak to her."

Gianni whirled and slammed against the knight's sword again and again. "An odd sort of invitation, this."

"We assumed you would not welcome it."

"You assumed right." Gianni swung his sword and the knight bent backward, watching with consternation as it narrowly missed his nose.

"Who is thy master?" he asked, striking and striking again. The man was a terribly strong opponent.

The knight smiled thinly. "I hear you have met up with my master before."

Gianni leaped to a table, striking him again, this time catching him in the shoulder. The knight went down to the ground, tumbling.

Gianni glanced around, taking stock. All his men were standing. Three of the interlopers were mortally wounded or dead. Four remained. There were others, outside their door, mayhap making their way in at this moment. His eyes went to the stairs and too late, he realized his error.

The knight he was battling followed his gaze. The enemy immediately turned and ran up them, two at a time, with Gianni right behind him.

ↄ ↄ ↄ

ANOTHER man slammed into their door.

Rune slumped forward, panting. "Turn around, Rune. Turn

around," Daria said, eyeing the door. The knight turned toward her, the arrow feathers still sticking out from his chest. "Close your eyes," she commanded. He did so, knowing what she was about to do.

Placing a foot upon his chest, she reached down and grabbed the shaft of each arrow, pulling back at the same time as she pushed with her foot. The bloody arrows slid out and she tossed them aside, while the gasping knight slumped back to the cot again. She reached up to the bed linens and ripped a long strip. More men were on the landing outside their door now, battling. It was as reassuring as it was terrifying. Continued battle meant her men still lived.

She helped Rune sit up again and take off his overcoat and chain mail, then swiftly wrapped his shoulder with the linen. "We will apply my medicines when we are away from here. Do not lie back," she called from across the room. "I may not get you up again." She opened the door at the end of the hall, where water was sent to and fro, and peered down the narrow chute. There was no way Rune, with his broad shoulders, could make it down. If only they were in her quarters instead, with the secret passageway!

It was the silence that finally caught her attention. She looked back across the room and saw that Rune had noticed it too. A man rapped at the door then and Daria's hand went to her throat.

"Lady Daria! M'lady, open up!" cried Father Piero. "Hurry!"

She ran to the door and opened it, stunned at the odd sight of a priest carrying a sword.

Piero grinned at her and gave her a little bow. "The agents of the dark have attacked, and still, we stand."

She looked past him. Gianni stood, panting against the far wall, blood trickling down from his temple. Hasani was there too, seated against the other wall with knees up and panting, his great curved blade bloody and settled across this legs. But both were all right. One dead knight was at the top of the stairs. The other was down the hall.

"I thought you told us our battle was not against flesh and blood. . . ." Daria said.

"I stand corrected. It appears we must battle on both physical and spiritual fronts," Father Piero said.

"We must get out, now," Gianni said, interrupting their banter. "It is our only chance. Zola has disappeared again."

"Lady Zola," Rune said. But seeing Gianni's expression kept him from saying more. She was gone.

Daria turned and helped Rune to his feet, following behind Gianni and Father Piero down the stairs.

Gianni helped her to mount and then helped Rune. The other men appeared, nicked, bruised, winded, but well. "Aldo, Nico, bring more ropes. We will drag these bodies to the back gate. Once it is dark, you must find a way to get them away from here."

"Captain, you do not think there will be enemies waiting for us at the back gate too?"

"Most likely. But we only shut out four, mayhap five." He grinned. "If we can take down seven within our walls, we can take five more outside."

"Who are they?" Daria asked. "Did they say?"

"No. But I have a good idea," he said, tightening a strap beside his saddle. "And I have a feeling that our friend Zola was not a friend at all."

None of them dared to look at Rune. They could already feel his misery.

Daria turned to make sure Tessa was settled upon her horse and reached down to take Agata's, then Beata's hands, reminding them to encourage Roberto to stretch his leg, but not run, each day.

"Yes, yes, m'lady. We will take care of the boy. It is you we fear for. These men, they were after you. You must be off."

Daria's eyes flew to Gianni's. He nodded at her in confirmation and Daria's mouth again grew dry. She would hear more of what he knew later. "I have fine knights, all about me. We will be

all right. Simply see to the house, the boy, Ambrogio, and yourselves. And remember, I would much rather this house was taken
and burned than that any of you were injured. If attacked again,
let them in."

"Yes, m'lady."

"God be with you, m'lady."

"Aldo?"

"It will be as you say, m'lady."

Gianni was moving, through the courtyard, past the stables, to
the back gate. He climbed to the short tower and looked one way
and then the other, waving the rest of the group forward. They
could hear the steady beat of a parade drum, no doubt a troop
from a neighboring *contrada* coming through, flaunting their fine
horse and man flesh to strike terror in their neighbors' hearts. It
was the way of the Sienese during the week of tournament.

As Daria moved down the path toward the others, her eyes
scanned every stone of her beloved home. As prepared as she
thought herself, this was a physical wrenching within, even in the
midst of terror and chase and attack. Mayhap it was that that had
sent her heart scurrying backward, longing to nestle in her suite,
tucked beneath fine d'Angelo linens.

"You shall return, m'lady," Gianni said, coming alongside her.
"I will see to it, I promise. But for now we must move swiftly.
Baron del Buco will be here at any moment. Lord Ambrogio has
already arrived."

Daria looked over her shoulder and gave out a hollow laugh
when she saw Ambrogio, watching them in stunned disbelief.
Dead knights dragged behind her knights' horses on the ground,
creating a gruesome avenue of blood. Ambrogio would have to get
his explanation from Aldo.

CHAPTER FORTY-TWO

ABRAMO and Zola were waiting for Baron del Buco near the estate when he and his men arrived, horse hooves clattering over the cobblestones. "What is happening?" Vincenzo cried.

"They were trying to escape. I sent in men to waylay them."

"But Daria—"

"She is unharmed."

"And now?"

"The men have been killed or captured and her people are exiting the estate from the other side."

Vincenzo cast him a confused look. "Why do you not give chase?"

Abramo shook his head. "This is a game of cat and mouse, Baron. I only wished them to know that we could strike when we wished. If they fear we will strike again physically, if they fear we somehow know their every move, that will do us good later on. Fear is our greatest ally, Baron. You must learn to capitalize on it. Come, we will continue the hunt."

"But I thought I was to bring her to your home. That we were to turn her to our joint goals, direction."

Abramo sighed. "Plans change, Vincenzo. Those that win are those that can adapt to the changes." He moved his horse closer to the baron. "We will hunt them, drive them to fear and weakness. Cut them off before they find any more of the document that gives them foundation, strength. Then we will show the Duchess that with us, she can regain power, conquer fear. We will be her way out. In the end, she will run to us."

"What document?" Vincenzo asked. "Of what do you speak—"

"M'lord," called a man dressed in a festive *contrada* uniform, cutting through the crowd, running. He arrived at their side, out of breath. "They move, through the opposite gate."

"Our men are still in place?"

"Yes."

Abramo grinned. "It begins! I so love a good hunt. Does it not make you feel more alive, Vincenzo? As if your blood courses more cleanly through your veins?"

Vincenzo did not return his smile. This was not what they had spoken of. Not at all. And suddenly it struck him that his new-found power was not his at all. It was Abramo's, and only his.

Abramo turned and looked at him. "Are you coming, Baron? Your ward, your co-consul of the guild, appears to be departing, without as much as a by-your-leave from you. Did she not invite you to meet with her, this hour? A ploy, to be sure. Does that not irritate you? Come, let us call attention to her error."

Vincenzo looked to the d'Angelo gates, remembering times gone by, many a festival, many a celebration. Nights by the fire with Giulio d'Angelo and Marco's father. The night Daria was born, the night Giulio died, the night he agreed to work alongside Daria in leading the guild.

"Come, my friend," Abramo called. "It seems complicated now, but all will be well. Trust me."

Vincenzo tore his eyes from the gates and tossed his chin, wordlessly ordering his men to follow him. He glanced back at his captain. "We will seek out and find the Duchess. I want her unharmed, but brought to me," he said lowly. "Not Lord Amidei. Me."

The knight cast him a confused glance. "We are to capture Lady d'Angelo, m'lord?"

"Yes. Lady Daria."

ф ф ф

GIANNI cast a worried glance back toward the Duchess as they entered the busy Via di Pantaneto. With thousands of people and wagons and animals in the street, it was impossible to maintain their formation. Ciro, standing in a recessed doorway, smiled as they passed. He gave a signal down the street to a man and a group of four, dressed as villagers, moved out in front of the Duchess and the group astride horses. Five others moved in from the other side, blocking their way forward, as well as everyone else on the street heading toward the city gates.

Gianni pulled his horse to a halt. The nine men unsheathed their swords. Women screamed and men ran in the opposite direction, pushing back against others behind them. Daria cast a look over her shoulder, along with several of her men. They were turning, heading back toward the Piazza il Campo as the master had directed. *Good, good,* Ciro thought, pulling back into the shadows as they passed.

ф ф ф

"THIS way," Daria said, taking the lead. She knew the city the best and led them down one narrow back alley and then the other, Gianni right behind her, then Tessa, Vito, Rune, Basilio, Piero, Hasani, and Ugo. City dwellers cried out in disgust as they rushed by, upsetting animals and supplies. At the second gate, they were again turned away by a group of Sienese unsheathing swords.

Again, they escaped into the labyrinth of alleyways and courtyards. In a tiny piazza, when they were sure no man still followed, they circled.

"We should have rushed them, gone through," Gianni said, shaking his head. "They are herding us, like a covey of geese. They do not truly wish to take us on. Those men they sent in—they were sacrificed. If the Sorcerer had truly wanted us now, he would have sent more."

"They are trading on our fear," Father Piero said quietly, one hand atop the other. His horse pranced back and forth, still agitated by their unseemly pathway.

"Do not give in to it," Gianni said, eyeing each knight. "We are not alone. We are God's chosen, the Gifted. We must leave this city and continue to follow the Lord's calling. This is the enemy. We are stronger than the enemy."

"But we are outnumbered," said Vito. "It appears our enemy has friends in many places."

"Or people that he has paid to be so."

"Mayhap we should pray," Father Piero said. "When we feel that praying is the last thing we have time for, it is what we need to do first."

Gianni let out a great breath. "We were to pray before we set out, but did not. So, go ahead, Father. Cover us in prayer. Mayhap you can find us a way out of this city."

❧ ❧ ❧

"THEY are headed to the piazza," Abramo said, seeing the signal from one nobleman's tower sent to the next. "Excellent, excellent."

Two women rode forward, resplendent in the finest gowns and capes, each carrying an archer's bow. Vincenzo recognized them from somewhere, mayhap Abramo's estate. "Go to the next nobleman's tower and nick as many as you can. No mortal blows. Careful not to get the big German. He's already been struck."

Vincenzo frowned. It seemed an odd request. To strike but

not kill. And not to strike a wounded man. Why bother to differentiate?

Abramo laughed and looked back at him. "Relax, my friend! All is going well. My girls' arrows will send the crowd into a panic and wing those who defy us, so let us wait here, on the edge of the street until it is over."

꙼ ꙼ ꙼

FATHER Piero led the way this time, praying constantly in Latin and then their native language, one verse after another, proclaiming God's power to hold back the enemy's forces, proclaiming their faith in Christ, proclaiming their desire for God to make a way for them out of the city in safety. Daria touched her forehead, suddenly dizzy. She dropped her hand back to the saddle, and stared at the cut across her middle finger, another across her palm, from Rune's arrows.

It was odd, how the blood had congealed at the edge, unlike anything she had ever seen. Most likely because she had not cared for it immediately. She glanced over her shoulder at Rune and frowned. He swayed inordinately with each step of his steed, as if he, too, were light-headed. He had lost some blood.

She faced forward again, opening her eyes wide to try to steady her vision.

"M'lady, are you all right?" Tessa asked, beside her.

"The arrows," Daria said. "It's the arrows."

"M'lady? Sir Gianni! The lady—"

Twin arrows sliced through the air then, striking Contessa in the thigh and bouncing off Ugo's shoulder plate after denting it. Two more came rapidly after, hitting Vito's thigh guard and Basilio's back plate.

"Off, off your horses!" Gianni cried, leaping to the ground.

Contessa was screaming and her mare reared. The arrow had gone through her thigh and into the horse's flank.

Daria swayed in her saddle, trying to grab Tessa's horse's reins and still keep her seat. Dimly, she heard Gianni shouting for her to dismount, to get down.

More arrows sliced the air. Arrows. Poison arrows.

ↄ ↄ ↄ

GIANNI frowned back at Rune, Daria, and Tessa, still astride their horses. More arrows rained down upon them. Basilio helped Rune down from his saddle and then stumbled under the great man's weight, both of them going down to the cobblestone. Women were again screaming, running away from where they were. People turned at the corner and peered back at them as if watching a hanging in grim fascination.

Father Piero captured Tessa's reins and managed to calm the horse somewhat, but Daria was stretching, stretching to reach them still. Hasani, Vito, and Ugo reached up to her, urging her to dismount. What was wrong with her? She behaved like a drunkard in a tavern! Gianni ducked as more arrows whizzed by his head and arm, so close he could feel the heat. Then he ran back to Daria and unceremoniously pulled her from the saddle as still others shot by.

"The arrows," she mumbled, staring at the cut on her finger. "The arrows."

Was she going mad? "Are you wounded?" He searched her body, could find no nick or scratch beyond the cuts upon her finger and hand. She had not been pierced, merely scratched. But the wound appeared hours old, not fresh.

He took her face in his hands and stared into her eyes. "M'lady. *Daria.*"

It was then that he noticed the dilation of her eyes. Her eyes appeared almost black, so wide were the centers. Lifting a shield from his horse's side, he moved over to Basilio, who tried to speak to Rune. More arrows came his way as he moved.

"I don't know what's wrong with him, Captain," Basilio said, complete confusion washing through his face. "He's taken a bad hit before, many worse than that shoulder wound."

Gianni's eyes went to the shoulder, blood seeping through the bandage and overcoat now. More arrows came down around them, but they were protected, in this curve of the street. Daria had taken Rune's arrows out, bandaged his wound. . . . "They are poisoned. The arrows are poisoned! We must get out of this city and see to the lady and Rune. Now Tessa too." His eyes went to the girl, weeping in the priest's arms. "They haven't much time."

A high whistle blew. The city magistrate and his men were looming near, alerted by the reports of attack, battle.

Gianni shared a look with Basilio. "We cannot be waylaid. These two will be dead by sunset."

"Best be going, then," Basilio said. He motioned to Ugo and Vito and the two rushed over to them. "Poisoned arrows. Do not let one strike you."

"Right, do not allow an arrow to strike me," Vito quipped. "Did no one tell Rune?"

"Help me get this big lug atop his horse again." Together they heaved the huge German across the saddle and tied him so that he would not fall.

"On three, we will run, take a right and then the first left. We will be out of the archers' reach at the first corner, but I want some distance." Gianni raised his head to tell Hasani and Piero of their plan. But the two were already moving, Hasani behind Daria, astride her horse, Piero behind Tessa. Both held shields above and behind them as they urged their steeds to a canter and turned the corner.

♢ ♢ ♢

ABRAMO paused to speak to the city magistrate, leading a troop of twenty-four men. He told the man that a friendly argument had turned into a full-blown battle in the home of the Duchess, that the city's high tensions had obviously been ill received.

"You will not leave the city," the magistrate said to Abramo sternly.

Vincenzo remembered the man at one of Abramo's feasts, probably owed Amidei money or homage, but the small man still held onto some vestige of autonomy.

Abramo held up his hands in acquiescence. "I am not the one trying to escape. It is Lady Daria and her men who are guilty. They killed my men. See for yourself. They are the ones on the run, not us."

The magistrate furrowed his brow. "Lady d'Angelo has a spotless reputation. I find this difficult to believe." He glanced at Vincenzo. "Baron del Buco? Does this man speak the truth?"

Vincenzo nodded sadly. "The Duchess's men cut down Lord Amidei's. We have been trying to cut them off from the gates, but they continue to try and escape. Mayhap you can do what we cannot. At the very least, you will wish to question them most thoroughly."

The magistrate eyed one of them and then the other. He raised a threatening finger. "I will not have such nonsense in my city during tournament. They may put up with such things in Firenze, but not here. Sheath your swords. Put down your bows. No more weapons."

The muscle in Abramo's cheek worked in agitation. "No more," Abramo said slowly. "Of course. We do not wish anyone else to be harmed."

The magistrate turned to the two men behind him. "Seal off the gates. Stop everyone who is exiting the city. When you find her, bring Lady d'Angelo and her men to the Piazza Pubblico."

CHAPTER FORTY-THREE

EVERY new avenue they tried seemed too vulnerable or guarded. At one point, city officials gave chase, telling the Gifted that they could now not be trusted either. Hasani had led them to an empty guild warehouse near the Piazza il Campo. Wearily they had dismounted and laid Daria, Tessa, and Rune out to rest. "We wait here," Gianni said. "In darkness mayhap we can make our escape. We can split up and exit the gates separately."

"What about them?" Basilio asked, gesturing to the three on the ground.

"We should have rushed those first men," Gianni said again. "Taken our chances. It was our only opportunity."

"Do not look back, Sir Gianni," said Piero, who hovered over Daria. "Only forward. Right now, our healer is in need of healing. To say nothing of Sir Rune and Tessa. We must pray, push back this black magic that invades their bodies."

"Armanti," Gianni said. "See if she has some armanti root in her bag. If we can get some down their throats, mayhap it will make them retch, vomit up what plagues them."

"Nay," Father Piero said. "This poison is in their blood. It has moved to their hearts and back again. Their only hope is for us to pray over them. To drive back this evil with prayer."

Gianni leaned his head back against the wooden planking. "I confess I do not wish to pray. I wish to go out and do battle. Or sleep. Suddenly, I am frightfully weary."

"It has been an eventful day," quipped Vito.

Father Piero nodded. "Yes, yes, that is what our enemy hopes. Giving in to abandoned fury or running ahead of where our Savior leads!" He stood and paced, anger lighting up his face. "This is our first day of battle! Our first day! Have we not talked about this? That there would be trials, significant trials before us?"

"But Father," Ugo said. "Lady Daria. We cannot lose Lady Daria. Or Rune. Or Tessa."

"Nay! Nay we cannot. But how do we battle evil? With good! How do we fight back? With prayer! Let us drive this evil one away. He infiltrates us even now, in this haven. Do you feel him, weaving in and out between us, striving to separate us, distract us, dissuade us? You are fighting men! Fight! Fight! Fight! Fight them in a way they do not know how to battle against—with love and prayer."

Hasani was first to rise. He walked toward Father Piero, crossed himself, and then knelt beside Rune.

Gianni joined them then too, crossed himself, and said, "Bless me, Father, for I have sinned."

"Oh, my son, we all have sinned. Let us pray that Christ will drive sin away from us and lead us out of here."

"I confess not loving my enemy."

"It is difficult, man, difficult. Try to find that place within you that is of Christ." He reached out and tapped Gianni's chest. "The living Christ is within you. Right there. He is within you. Reach deep. Reach hard. Find the Christ within you and see these people for who they are. The lost. In need of our Savior. We have his power within us. Nothing can be against us for long if we are in Christ."

One after another the men came to Father Piero, for the blessing. Then each knelt, creating a circle around their wounded. And then they prayed.

ↄ ↄ ↄ

"THEY have sought refuge somewhere. We lost them," said the man to Abramo.

Abramo dismounted and walked a distance from the rest of the men, to a curve in a road that overlooked much of the city. The sun had set and a brilliant mustard and bloodred sky dominated the view. He closed his eyes to the sights and sounds around him, seeking from within a direction, a sign from his dark lord. *Show me where they are. Show me where I can find them.*

But there was only silence. His toe caught an odd cobblestone and he tripped.

"My lord," cried one of his men. "Are you hurt?" He dismounted, rushing to his aid, but Abramo was again upright, leaning with his hands on knees as if trying to catch his breath, looking to the piazza. Rage made him tremble.

Vincenzo scanned the streets before them and his eyes narrowed upon the one that led to the empty guild warehouse. "I know where they are," he said. "Come, m'lord. We can capture them if we move quickly."

ↄ ↄ ↄ

THE Gifted moved from praying for their enemies to prayers of protection for them, healing for Daria, Tessa, Rune.

"Father in heaven, in the name of Jesus Christ, we pray that you will drive out this evil poison within Daria, and Tessa and Rune. Drive it out, Lord God, and bring them to complete healing. We ask that you stay our enemies while you do this, and provide a way out of this city and to Venezia, where you have called us.

"Lord, we ask that you enter Rune's shoulder here," he said, lightly covering Rune's bloody bandage, "and suck back the poison that the enemy sent into his body. Help him to fight back against this internal attack. Thrust it from his body. Wash it away from him. Give him strength again and a sound mind.

"We ask the same for little Tessa. Suck out the poison that threatens her tiny body, Lord. Help her fight back against this. . . ."

♣ ♣ ♣

I⊤ took agonizing minutes to make their way down the curving street. Masses of people were heading into the Piazza il Campo to watch the flag throwers and flame swallowers and fireworks that always preceded tournament. They moved en masse, and there was no getting ahead of them, past them. They could only move with them.

Vincenzo ran over the details for the thousandth time. Like moving with this crowd, there was nothing to do but move forward with the tide. Abramo Amidei knew how to handle this. He did not wish to harm Daria, only bring her to their side. It was imperative now that she be swayed. If she escaped, and had so turned against him, much would be lost. He would not lose any more. He could not. How could she even think of inflicting more damage upon his heart?

Abramo looked over at him. "We will find her, my friend. Do not worry, so." He was grinning again. "Embrace this. It is life, these extremes. Embrace it, and you will find strength you did not know you had. You will become like me, thriving on it. It is the pace of the gods, man, a whole new plane. This is what it feels like to be Jupiter, Mars. Apollo has done his task, the day is done. The night, now the *night* belongs to us."

♣ ♣ ♣

DARIA sat up with a gasp, and looked around at the weeping, smiling faces around her.

"Praise God, praise the Christ," Father Piero said, stroking her head.

"Praise him," Gianni said, a tear slipping down his face.

"He is a God of wonder and might," Vito said, tears running down his as well.

"We thought we had lost you, Duchess," Basilio said, hugging her suddenly.

Daria looked from the left to the right. Tessa and Rune were beside her, sitting up as well. "What has happened? Basilio, please!"

Basilio backed up, still grinning.

"They had hold of you," Gianni said, taking her hand. "We prayed Rune and Tessa out of it, but you . . . they did not want to let you go."

"Who?" But as she asked the question, she knew of whom they spoke. A shiver ran down her spine. Outside, throngs of people were shouting, laughing. "We are near Il Campo?"

"Yes. We are still trying to make our way out of the city. It appears that every way is blocked off," Ugo said.

"Not every way," Tessa said, rising. She offered a hand to Daria. "M'lady . . . if you will follow me, I will lead you out of the city. I know a way out."

Daria cast a questioning glance to the priest. He shrugged. "And a little child shall lead them. . . ."

"Yes," Contessa said, hands on hips. She threw a long, brown braid over her shoulder. "I shall. We must make our way to the other side of Il Campo." She bent down to trace the great clamshell shape in the dust of the floor. Hasani brought a candle near. "Here is where we must reach," Tessa said, moving her braid over her shoulder again, pointing to the far corner. "There we can move aside three bricks and enter the sewer." She drew a larger circle, beyond the *campo*. "It spits us out here," she said, pointing to the northeast city wall.

"Is it not barred, there? Will we not be trapped?" Basilio asked.

"Barred, yes. But there are other loose stones that I know about."

"A child of Il Campo," Basilio said in awe. "Our God is at work."

"Indeed," Father Piero said. But his eyes were on the wall of the warehouse. Tessa's eyes followed his and stayed there.

"They are near," she whispered.

"Yes. Move," Father Piero said. "Move quickly! Everyone, move, move!"

ↂ ↂ ↂ

THE Sorcerer watched as the door to the warehouse opened and they scurried out into the crowd. "Bravo," he said in admiration. He glanced at Vincenzo; he saw them too. There were eight, plus the girl that the knight, Gianni, carried in his arms; so they had battled back the poison and healed the tall, blond knight, as well as the girl. His eyes lingered on the child, staring in their direction. "Your gift, little one, may be the most troublesome of all," he muttered.

"They are worthy adversaries," he said to Vincenzo. "As strong as we had hoped. I have seen those poisoned arrows cut down knight after knight. And there! Do you see that?" he asked in wonder. "Magnificent! Even the girl has fought against it and won! That is power, true power. We must turn them to our cause, Vincenzo, we must! If they are among us, everything, all is ours."

"They will escape into the crowd," Vincenzo said, his eyes struggling to keep track of the seven among the dark throng of people. They were perhaps twenty rows behind them. Flame throwers and torches aided them in watching, but Abramo knew he was right. And if they separated . . .

"Where will they be headed? How will they attempt to escape?"

"I do not know," Vincenzo said. "I cannot think of another way out."

Abramo's eyes followed the knight carrying the child. He laughed, suddenly. "Of course! It is the girl who will lead them out. She knows this piazza better than anyone else. We must stay close to them. And when the opportunity arises, pounce."

֍ ֍ ֍

"Where are the horses?" Daria asked.

"I paid two men to lead them out of the city," Gianni said. "They will meet us at midnight, high above the city."

"On the road to Firenze."

"On the road to Firenze," he said with a smile. "The magistrate's men will be seeking us on horseback. I figured God will smile upon us if we try this on foot. Did not Jesus walk everywhere he went?"

"Until the triumphant return to Jerusalem," Father Piero said. He glanced over his shoulder. "They still follow us. We should part company."

Gianni nodded. "Ugo, Vito, head out on your own. Make your way to the place that Tessa showed us. Make haste and wait for us there. God speed." He reached out his hand and each laid their hand atop his before departing.

"Hasani, Rune, Father, you go together." Again, he reached out his hand and each reached out to lay his atop it. "If we separate Hasani from the Duchess, she'll be less conspicuous. Again, do not be late. Godspeed." Before he said his last word, the others had faded into the crowd.

He looked to Daria and Basilio and reached out his hand to them. Tessa even leaned over and put her hand atop theirs. "Let us stay together. We will outpace our enemy. He thinks that he rules the dark. But our God, dear friends, our God is the God of light. Do not give in to shadow."

֍ ֍ ֍

ABRAMO cursed under his breath as the group divided, then divided again. He wanted them in hand by now, to use the chaos of the piazza to haul the Gifted away. But there were still twenty people between them. Up ahead, the piazza widened and there would be ways to get to them. He looked over his shoulder. "You, take five men and follow the black man, German, and priest. You, take five men and find the two brother knights. We will take the others. Bring them to me unharmed, and you will have five years' wages."

The men grinned in anticipation, patting one another on the back as they moved out, shoving aside villager and city dweller.

"Keep your eyes on that girl," Abramo said, nodding at the child in de Capezzana's arms, staring with wide, seeing eyes at them. "What do you know of her?"

"Little," Vincenzo said, shaking his head. "Only that she is that beggar child from Il Campo."

Abramo laughed. "Nay, my friend. Lady Daria is our healer. That child is important. She knows things, sees things. She knew me immediately as a threat. Which gift?"

"They all . . . they all have gifting? Like Daria?"

"Of some sort. It is how the enemy has armed them against us. I told you, worthy adversaries. And alongside us . . . we will be invincible. Come. The knight moves more slowly now, carrying the girl. And the Duchess is still struggling to get past the poison. Let us capture these four. With them in hand, the others will fall."

ъ ъ ъ

"GIANNI, they draw near," Tessa said in a high pitch, looking over his shoulder.

Basilio looked back. He broke into a run and the others followed.

They ran past bonfire after bonfire. Flame swallowers and flag throwers and sparring men, preparing for tomorrow's games.

Dancers, many dancers, circling the flames. *Contrada* boys, fighting neighboring *contrada* boys. Grandfathers, bellowing at neighboring *contrada* grandfathers. It was a heady, wild crowd and it filled the entire hollow of the piazza.

Just ahead of them, a giant appeared, flanked by two others, swords drawn.

Daria sucked in her breath. It was Ciro. Gianni narrowed his gaze at him, grabbed Daria's arm, and turned directly north, past a campfire, into a throng of dancers. They blended in with the outer circle, pushed forward to the second ring and then the third. Inside the narrowest ring in the center, they hunkered down and moved to the other side, the dancers too drunk with wine to care, thinking them a part of the festivities and nothing more.

He placed Contessa on her feet and put her hand in Basilio's. "Meet us there, Tessa. Lead him there. Do not let anything happen to Basilio, all right?"

She nodded, her expression mixed between bereft and fear and courage. He took her shoulders. "Jesus is with you. Trust in him. He is our Savior. He has brought us together. He will bring us together again."

Her expression became more resolute. "Godspeed."

"Godspeed," Daria whispered, her hand on Tessa's. But Gianni was already hauling her out from among the dancers and in a dead run for the next *contrade* circle.

A hand circled Daria's other one and hauled her backward, out of Gianni's grasp. He looked back at her, as if dumbfounded, and then cold anger quickly stilled the lines about his eyes. But Daria was turning, turning, until she came up against a huge man's chest, her arm painfully twisted behind her back.

Ciro.

He smiled down at her. "*Buona sera,* Duchess. I have dreamed of this moment."

Behind her, she could hear Gianni unsheath his sword, walking forward without pause. Ciro tossed Daria to the side, to his men, to meet Gianni's first strike. One grabbed hold of her hair and arm, while the other grabbed her waist and other arm. Daria struggled, but they were strong.

Their eyes were not on her, but on the battle before them. A crowd formed, with the tournament watchers cheering each of the knights, thinking it more of their revelry. Gianni whirled and brought his sword around in a fierce arc, slicing Ciro's thigh. Ciro stumbled backward, roared, and then ran at him, pushing against him in a powerful plunge toward the nearest towering bonfire. Gianni struggled to hold his ground, but the man had more weight, pushing Gianni across the cobblestones like a block of marble.

Ciro pushed him back and back, until Gianni's heel edged the fire. At any moment, his boot, his leggings would be aflame.

"No!" Daria screamed. "No!"

Ugo and Vito entered the clearing in a dead run, shouting in fury. Ugo plunged his sword into Ciro's side and Vito hovered in the center, brandishing his sword toward Daria's captors.

Ciro cried out and whirled from Gianni to Ugo, striking him so hard across the chest with the broad side of his sword that Ugo went flying, five, six, seven feet across the stones.

Daria's captors dropped her to the ground and unsheathed their swords, advancing on her knights.

Crying, Daria rose, swaying as she watched the men in their curious dance of swordplay in the firelight. Gianni was up, advancing fiercely, then down, rolling across the ground. Two men held Ugo and Ciro roared across the clearing, but Vito broke their grasp at the last possible moment, saving his brother's life by barely blocking Ciro's furious strike.

Daria struggled to decide. Run? Run for the meeting place? Or remain here?

She was not helping the men. Gianni glanced her way and his eyes told her what she knew all along. *Run. Run, Daria. Do not stop.*

She whirled, but there, five feet away from her, was a man in a cape, his hood hiding his face. He looked like a ghoul, an agent of the underworld with bonfire light casting eerie shadows. She had seen this one before, knew the way he moved. He turned to look over his shoulder and she caught sight of his chin, remembered a glance from the grove, on the road from Roma. His hand went to his hood and he slowly pulled it from his head.

Lord Abramo Amidei.

Gianni's Sorcerer.

"I will not fear you," she whispered, backing away. Thunder rumbled across the sky, cracking with an intensity that rumbled within their chests. The crowd roared their approval at the skies. "The Lord is my Shepherd, I shall not want. Though I walk in the valley of death, I shall not fear, for he is with me. . . ."

Abramo winced and turned his head to the side as if she had struck him, but continued his advance. She looked left and right, seeing for the first time the line of men on either side of her. They threatened to overtake her, trample her, like a herd of black stallions.

"We do not wish to harm you, m'lady," Abramo said, reaching out a hand. "We wish to show you signs and wonders. You are to be a part of us. There is glory ahead, treasures. Power."

It was then she felt Tessa at her side. She looked down to the girl and in her eyes, saw Jesus himself. Her eyes were wide and full of love, unfearing, faithful. *To love, to love thy enemy, to love others as you love yourself* . . .

Daria raised trembling hands to the sky and the men ceased their advance. "I call down the fire of heaven," she said, looking upward. "Pierce these men, Father God. Show them your love. Let them see in me and this child beside me, *you*." She whispered the last word as fervent prayer, stopped her backward steps and left one hand in the air above her, palm outstretched as if she were holding a broken dam at bay.

The crowd about them gasped. Tessa moved behind her, pushing against her waist as if she too were helping. "By the power of the Lord Jesus Christ, I command all evil ones to depart from here. We stand in the light of the Risen one, who died and rose again for us. In him we live. In us, *he lives.*"

"Stop it!" Abramo said, looking down to the ground and to the right. Men fell backward beside him as if repelled, sickened by Daria and her prayer.

"We stand in the light of the Christ, who died and rose again!"

Abramo reached up a hand like hers, but did not dare to look at her. "Stop it!"

All at once, Daria could see him, as her Father in heaven saw him. Handsome, so handsome on the outside. But inside, rotting, maggots eating at him. She could see them all. Some mostly good, just now giving into the rot. Others barely standing. Grief washed through her, a grief so thorough that it surpassed what she had suffered over Marco, over her parents, over leaving her home.

It was devastation that she felt. Separation. Exile.

Daria gasped for breath. Wavered. "I cannot heal them," she whispered. "I cannot heal you," she said through tears. "My God, the God of heaven and earth, the God who is and was and is to come . . . My God loves you! Every one of you! Only he can save you! Only he!"

Abramo wheeled back as if she had plunged a dagger into his heart.

Tessa was laughing in wonder. "Duchess. God is here. He has sent his angels. Do you see them? Do you feel them?"

Thunder rumbled across the piazza. Lightning cracked and struck the two tallest of the Nine's towers in an upside-down Y formation. Women screamed. Men shouted.

She looked down the line of men, falling to their knees, some falling to their faces, cowering in fear. In the midst of the line to the right, her eyes settled on Vincenzo.

No, no, she whispered, seeing the shell of his heart, the maggots, eating, eating away at him already.

Leave the dead to tend the dead.

"M'lady, let us be away," Tessa whispered.

"Quickly. God has made a way," Piero said lowly, suddenly beside them.

But Daria was walking toward Vincenzo, could not keep from him. She shook her head, again gasping with grief. "Not this one, Lord. Surely there is a way for him. Help me show him, Jesus. Help me show him the way. Not this one. Not this one!"

The chasm was already great between Vincenzo and her Lord. How had she not seen his weakness before now? It was Tatiana, when he lost Tatiana, he had turned his face from God. . . .

Vincenzo struggled to rise, ashen faced, and met her gaze. "You betrayed me, Daria," he said, with a rasping voice.

"I did not intend to. Please, Uncle. Come with us. We shall restore you into God's hands. You will find healing, peace there."

"I have sought peace, Daria. It is a fable. I want power. Control. That will bring me what I need."

She shook her head, tears streaming down her face. "You—you want what belongs to God."

Yes, Vincenzo said, his eyes blank. *Yes.*

Abramo had risen again, neared them, wearily drawing his sword.

"Stand back!" Piero shouted in fury. "You of the dark, stand aside for the light!"

Abramo fell again to his knees.

Leave the dead to tend the dead.

Sobbing, Daria backed away, and Gianni joined them then, his arm around her waist, his sword before them. But none came after them. Lightning flashed again, so close it blinded Daria for a moment. Thunder deafened them all. As her eyes cleared, she could dimly hear people continue to scream and run across the square to the safety of the buildings, could see the eerie bonfires ablaze and abandoned like a vision from hell.

Leave the dead to tend the dead.

"I want life, Father. Give us life. Do not abandon us, Jesus. Show us the way."

And then she turned and ran, hand in hand with Gianni and Tessa.

CHAPTER FORTY-FOUR

"DID you see it?" she asked as they entered the short alley. They followed Tessa, who limped along and watched as she began moving stones. No one appeared to be following them.

Hasani, Father Piero, and Rune emerged from the shadows, but Daria remained intent upon Contessa and Gianni. "Did you see what I saw? Could you see that? The maggots? The hollow, empty, screaming emptiness? It felt like falling." She reached out to steady herself against the wall, remembering. "Falling off a cliff when I looked into Amidei's eyes. There was nothing. Nothing of light or love or life. How can that be? How could I see that?"

Tessa nodded. Daria sought Gianni's eyes and saw the grief of the heavens in them as well. So they had all shared in her experience. She looked back to Tessa and Piero. "If that was a divine vision, I will gladly take healing as my gift."

Ugo and Vito arrived, Basilio between them, a wound bleeding at his side. The storm continued to rage, seeming to hover directly over Siena. Tessa bent and pulled out another brick. "And the angels. They were beautiful. I could have sat and watched them for all my life."

"Good heavens, m'lady," Basilio said with a shake of his head. "I've never seen anything like it."

"Angels? I did not see them," Daria said. "But I . . . I believe I felt them there, with me."

"Oh, they were on the move, all right," Father Piero said with a smile. "Magnificent. You reached out to those lost ones in love, Daria. We were watching it all nearby, praying with you when you stopped and raised your hand.

"You offered them healing. Called down the powers of heaven to reach out to them, not to control, but to love. You opened yourself up, Daria, made yourself vulnerable, and they saw the Christ within. Truth. Wisdom. Love. Power. The Christ. They could not stand against him. They could not face him. It wasn't the angels that stayed them. It was the Christ. Christ within you."

Daria sighed and gradually centered her attention on the gaping hole Tessa had created within the wall. She could hear the drip of water, the foul smell of the sewer. She backed away, grimacing.

Vito smiled. "From the brink of heaven to the soil of man. It is quite an adventure you've invited us on, Duchess." He hunkered down and dropped into the hole and the other men lowered a groaning Basilio down to him, then Contessa and Daria. The others followed.

Within the hour they had made their way through the ankle-deep sludge, to the barred gate and beyond.

They kept off the main roads, pausing briefly at a shepherd's well to tend to Basilio's wound, wash their feet, and fill their water sacks. The storm moved on, past the city, and continued to rumble in the distance like an old farmer's cart creaking away down the street. Daria's eyes scanned the city as the men rejoined them with their horses.

"You shall return," Father Piero said.

"I shall. And the others, Father? Those of the dark? Are they gone, now?"

"Nay. Temporarily dissuaded. But he is powerful, that one. The Sorcerer. He will give chase. He does not wish us to find what we seek. We threaten him, everything that he holds dear. But let us not borrow tomorrow's trouble. Let us speak of tonight's angels, and our Lord, who goes before us, beside us, behind us. . . ."

The priest nudged his mare in the flanks with his boots, soft and dripping like the rest of their feet. He began to sing, his voice raised more in a barkeep's tune than a priest's, but his words were holy, bracing. He was an odd sort of priest. But he was her priest, and she was glad he was with them.

Daria glanced backward, silently bidding Siena good-bye, even as her horse followed the others over the crest and down the other side of the hill. She watched until she could see the old city no more, and turned to consider what it was to say farewell to your home.

But as she looked before her, around her, behind her, at each of the Gifted in the dim light—at her brave Gianni and tiny Tessa; at Ugo and Vito, who made her laugh; and Basilio and Rune, so faithful and true; to Hasani, her brother, and Father Piero, who had found her as much as she had found him . . . Daria d'Angelo felt an odd sense of home.

READERS GUIDE FOR

The Begotten

DISCUSSION QUESTIONS

1. In this trilogy, characters are gifted with one prominent, spectacular gift—healing, discernment, faith, wisdom, are some of what we see so far in *The Begotten*. If you could choose one of those gifts, which would it be and why? Do you believe everyone is spiritually gifted?

2. Have you ever seen a miracle of healing or experienced it yourself? What do you think about that?

3. What about speaking in tongues? In this novel, an interloper uses it as a guise to infiltrate the group. St. Paul chastised the Corinthians for flaunting their "gift of tongues," especially when there was no one present to translate. But there are many who have a true gift, a heavenly language that is used to praise God. Discuss why St. Paul might warn us about this gift and your experience/thoughts on this subject.

4. There is biblical evidence that St. Paul wrote other letters to the Corinthians. What would you think about a new letter surfacing? Would you be apt to accept it as real? Why or why not?

5. In the medieval age, the Church was largely shepherded by men influenced by power and prestige. This is not to say that there were

not many, many holy men and women involved. But how do you think politics affects the Church today?

6. Daria is handfasted to Marco for two years and then loses him because she is unable to bear children. Did you identify with her losses in love? Why or why not?

7. Gianni is torn between two loyalties—to his Church and to the lady and her cause. Have you ever tried to serve two competing masters and felt like it was splitting you in two?

8. The culmination, or "aha moment," for the author was when Daria was in the marketplace and healing so many—and she realizes her greatest healing ministry is to share with the people the love of God . . . that if they could all understand how much Christ loved each of them, that they would find healing on a vital level (pp. 291–293). What did you think of that scene?

9. What do you think brought about Vincenzo's fall to the dark?

10. Do you think the evil one is alive and well in our world today? If so, how does he get to us?

11. Who was your favorite character in the book and why?

12. Who was your least favorite character in the book and why?

13. This is an epic quest trilogy a la *Lord of the Rings*. What do you think will threaten the Gifted? What do you think will preserve them?

14. What, ultimately, do you think the Gifted are on Earth to do?

As an ancient enemy looms near,

the Gifted's quest continues...

The Betrayed
A Novel of the Gifted

Available in hardcover from Berkley

CHAPTER ONE

October, The Year of Our Lord 1340
Siena

"SIR, we have brought the one you seek," the wiry man said from a dark hallway.

"Good. Bring her in," Vincenzo said. He glanced toward the man beside him, Abramo Amidei, staring out the window, apparently deep in thought. Or preparing for this . . .

A small, elderly woman arrived, flanked by two large guards.

Vincenzo descended the two steps downward and looked her over. Here was the last one to be questioned—the last one touched by Daria d'Angelo, healed by her. He and Abramo had wrung every detail they could from each of those healed by the "Duchess"—a title more granted out of honor than true. There had been far more than Vincenzo had realized, and each gave them more insight into Lady Daria's life with her new companions.

The city dwellers called this one Old Woman Parmo, in that there were few who reached their gray and wrinkled years, and yet she had the spirit of one who could still take on another in battle. Old eyes, rimmed in wrinkles and understanding, met his own. "Baron del Buco," she said in greeting. She did not fear. She only waited.

As with the others they had questioned, Vincenzo recognized something of Daria within this one. There was a common strength within them all. Daria had healed her. Given her height and vitality again. Vincenzo had seen this old woman himself in the marketplace, done business with her. For decades she had sold cloth, so bent over that she could not meet her customer's eye. Now here she was, before him, upright. . . . What power was that? That Daria, Daria d'Angelo, *his* Daria could do this?

Old Woman Parmo met his gaze unflinchingly, as if she already knew he had turned against Daria. Suddenly, Vincenzo's master, Lord Abramo Amidei, turned from the window and descended the stairs. With one broad stroke, he took the old woman by the neck, rushed her to the wall, slammed her against it, and held her there, struggling to breathe. "Where?" he asked between gritted teeth. "Where have they gone?"

"Who?" she said, through strangled breaths. She glanced toward Vincenzo, as if holding hope that he might assist her, and he shifted uncomfortably.

Amidei leaned closer. "You know well of whom I speak. Tell me." He leaned harder into his grip, lifting her a little higher. Her lips became blue as she desperately clawed at his big hands.

"I . . . know . . . not."

Abramo stared at her for several long moments, as if she were no more than a bug on the wall, about to be squashed. They all could hear two young men in the streets, banging on the front door of Amidei's home, shouting demands, calling for the magistrate.

Abramo released Old Woman Parmo suddenly, allowing her to drop to the floor.

Vincenzo held back, although his instinct was to rush to the old woman, assist her up. But she was not to be touched. She was not for him, not for Amidei, therefore. . . . Still, he was moved to speak. "We ought to release her. She knows nothing, Abramo."

Abramo turned upon her, writhing on the cold stone floor, still trying to catch her breath. He saw what Vincenzo saw—knees, hips, back that moved like a young woman's, not like the woman who had long suffered from rheumatism. Looking away as if in disgust for a moment, Abramo turned, bent, and grabbed her arm, hauling her upward and forward. "Very well, then, old woman. You cannot tell us where they went. But you shall tell us everything you've learned."

ය ය ය

Laguna, Northern Italia

"I do not understand," Gianni said, looking out to the lone fisherman off their island. "He has brought in his catch. Who does he think he fools, tossing and pulling on that net?"

It was late afternoon, and his knights, Basilio and Rune, stood beside him along with Hasani, Lady Daria d'Angelo's guardian and companion. They stared out to the lone fisherman. It was the same each morning. The fisherman arrived, hauled in his catch of mullet, left for Venezia, and then returned a few hours later, still fishing and yet catching nothing every afternoon, until sunset, for two days now.

"He watches us," Father Piero said, drawing near them.

"That much is obvious," Gianni scoffed, looking down at the much smaller man. "But is he friend or foe?"

They watched the big man in the small boat a while longer. "Go and fetch Tessa," Gianni said to Rune, his eyes remaining trained on the man. "She will tell us if we need fret or not."

"You still believe we are safe? Or do you believe we have been discovered?" Basilio said as Rune left.

"I know not. Tessa will."

꙰ ꙰ ꙰

THE banging on the door continued until Abramo threw it open abruptly.

"You wished to speak to me?" he said to the two young men who stood there, fear etched upon their faces.

"Nay, m'lord," the slender man said, bowing a couple of times in nervousness, obviously surprised to see him at the door. "I only wished to . . . see my grandmother home."

"And so you may," Abramo said. He gestured down the street. "Allow us to see to your safety."

"That is not necessary, m'lord," the boy tried.

"Please. It is no trouble whatsoever. An afternoon walk," he said, thumping his chest. "I always find it bracing. Don't you agree, Baron?"

"Absolutely," Vincenzo returned.

"There you have it, boy," Abramo said, turning the young man forward with a little toss toward his guards.

Abramo and Vincenzo took the lead down the street, with two guards behind them hauling along the old woman. Four others took the grandson and his friend who had banged upon Abramo Amidei's door.

The crowds split before them, cascading on either side like the wake from a boat, no eye meeting theirs. As they walked, Vincenzo thought about Daria, about how she had lied to him, refused to bring him into her confidence, failed to share with him what was happening to her as it occurred. She had taken another path. . . . It was as if he could see them on the side of a steep mountain, he on one trail, she on another. But she had chosen wrongly. As hard as this was, she must be brought around to his way of thinking, Abramo's way of thinking. This was their destiny . . . power. Strength. Passion.

They had once been like family; Daria had called him Uncle. But death had destroyed them. The death of Daria's parents, the death of her handfasting to her beloved, Marco, and their future. For Vincenzo, it had been the death of Tatiana, his third wife, pregnant at last with an heir, and then the death of his trust of Daria. That she had not confided in him, allowed him to guide her in this, enraged him for a time. Now he only felt an empty hollow within his chest when he thought of her. He wanted her with him again, beside them, making him feel alive again, whole. Abramo wanted her and hers. Together, they would leave suffering behind, cheat death, rule life.

Could she not see that his was the way to hope? Dimly, he could see her in Il Campo on that last night, tears streaming down her lovely face, a hand reaching out to him. Light surrounded her, a holy glow, her hair lifting in the wind, her eyes awash in pleading. It was as if time slowed down to a crawl, and he could see each moment with such clarity! So much was unspoken, and yet he knew what she offered—beauty, love, peace, courage. But it would take some time, work . . .

He had no time. The years were quickly advancing upon him. Now was the time to seize what was his, not wait on Daria's way. He remembered little else, other than the decision not to reach out to her when she beckoned. This was his path. This. Amidei's path. It was harsh at times, but the power made his heart surge with glory, strength. And it was immediate. Already, in taking Amidei's road, adopting his ways as doctrine, Vincenzo had doubled his wealth and holdings, lost most nights in the arms of beautiful women and other pleasures, and over the months, watched the Nine of Siena, those who held political power, cower before them. Together, Lord Abramo Amidei and Baron Vincenzo del Buco owned Siena.

They arrived at the old warehouse and reluctantly the boy turned the key in the large door, nervously nodding to them. "Thank you, my lords, for seeing us home. We will be well on our own from here."

"That is yet to be determined," Abramo said lowly. He turned the boy and shoved him through the door, into the dark warehouse. "Light some of those lamps," he said to his guards. He turned and leaned in close to the boy's friend who had accompanied him to the Amidei door. "Do not let me catch sight of you ever again," he said slowly, enunciating every word. "Do not call for help, or I shall hunt down each and every one in your family. Run home, boy. Run."

The boy's eyes grew larger and larger and with one quick, apologetic glance at the Parmo boy, he did as he had been told.

Abramo advanced upon the old woman's grandson and she cried out. The boy tried to hold his ground, fight back, but Abramo was much stronger, much larger. The boy was the key to getting to his grandmother. It was always easy, so easy, to play upon emotions. Love. It was a weakness.

Abramo turned the boy's arm around behind him and forced him to a pile of carpets. He looked upward. Good, strong beams crossed beneath the steepled roofline. "Fetch a rope and fashion a noose," he said to a guard.

Old Woman Parmo cried out, bringing one hand to her mouth, another to her forehead.

The boy dared to try to look at him from the corner of his eye. He was a strong one, this. "We know not where they went. It's been months . . . we haven't seen them!"

"I believe you speak the truth," Abramo said, handing him off to his guards. "But you know what transpired while they were here. I want to know all of it. What happened to your grandmother? How did they discover you? How did the Duchess heal her? What words were exchanged? I want every word, every moment you can remember, or I shall have your life."

"We shall not betray the Duchess," the boy said, the glint of manhood in his eyes. "You are plainly her enemies."

Abramo raised his hand and a guard slipped a noose over the boy's neck and tightened it. Another guard drew in the slack.

The grandmother cried out, "Stop! Stop!"

Abramo gestured again and the guard ceased the upward momentum of the rope. "You are willing to tell me what you know, woman?"

She nodded through her tears and watched as the noose slackened around her grandson's neck.

"Catch your breath, woman," Abramo said soothingly, taking her arm and leading her away a few paces. He sighed, as if weary. "Duchess d'Angelo obviously has uncommon gifts. She undoubtedly told you to tell no one about them. But we are not the lady's enemy, as your grandson believes. You two are merely trying to be faithful to your word. We respect that," he said with a winsome look, tossing his hands to either side. He gestured toward Vincenzo. "That man is the Duchess's trusted advisor and friend. Surely you've seen them together many a time. We fear for the lady's life, thus the necessity for our extreme actions. She left Siena under very mysterious circumstances. It is most urgent we find her, and find her quickly. You know yourself of her extensive business and holdings here." He paused to laugh under his breath. "You know who she left in charge? An artist! Things are in disarray for the Duchess. We must get word to her at once. She stands to lose everything."

Old, wise eyes followed him intently. But instead of falling toward Abramo's soothing charms as Vincenzo had seen so many do, she was edging away, visibly leaning back from him.

It was only a moment later that Abramo saw it too. He sat down on a pile of carpets as she stood against the warehouse wall, staring toward her grandson as if she were saying good-bye. Abramo rose immediately, slicing their glance with his torso.

"Tell me. Tell me everything you know." His tone had returned to cold stone. He stared at her while lifting his hand. All the old woman could see was the rope again becoming taut above Abramo's shoulder, could hear her grandson strangling.

"No. No, m'lord. Don't do this. You ask the impossible! I cannot! Not after all the lady did for me . . ."

He raised his hand again, furious eyes upon her. Now she could see her grandson's feet kicking out on either side.

"Please!" she said, hand over her heart. "Please!" She panted in desperation, shaking her head. Several moments passed. She wept, trying valiantly to hold on, failing. "All right! Release him, release him," she said through her tears. As the boy's body slumped to the ground, she turned to the wall and gave in to sobs, furious at herself for betraying her lady, unsure of what else she could do.

Abramo gave her a moment and then handed her a handkerchief. "Turn and tell me, woman," he said in a tone that belied the ferocity of his words. "If you pause for but a breath again, I will haul him to your rafters myself and leave the rope so high that you cannot cut him down for hours."

cb cb cb

"WE must move into Venezia, m'lady," Gianni said, pacing behind her.

They had taken up residence on a tiny island off Venezia, once a town, now inhabited only by the skeleton of a chapel, ruined by fire, and several families who raised vegetables and fished to feed the city. The gardens were now mostly turned over, about to release their last crop of squash and zucchini.

"Why not winter here?" Daria said, staring out a window to the sea.

She felt safe here. He understood that. But nowhere was truly safe. And here, on this tiny island, their only escape route would be to the sea. If the time came, he wanted the choice of either land or water. Their only course was forward. Their only hope was forward. "We've been here for better than two months. It is time we take our next steps, discover where the Lord is taking us."

"I thought he had brought us here," she said, looking only to Piero.

"He did," the priest put in. "We were to catch our breath, regain our strength. And we have done so. I agree with Gianni. It is time to move inland, to Venezia. We came here for a reason. Let us be about it."

Gianni moved around so that he was between her and the window. "I have found a small palazzo, m'lady. It is off the Grand Canal, the old residence of a Turkish trader. There is a warehouse on the canal level, and a floor above that. Eight, nine rooms. Two turrets, which could serve us well. It is not as nice as your home in Siena, but it is suitable. And it is for rent. I have secured it for six months' time."

She sighed and looked at the rough-hewn table beneath her hand. Gianni noticed she appeared weary. She had been through much in these months, his lady. "Very well," she said. "But before we become absorbed in city life and winter is fully upon us," she said in a voice nearly as low as a whisper, "there is something we must do."

Gianni found himself bracing as her large brown eyelashes lifted and her eyes met his. "And that is, m'lady?"

"The island of lepers. I must go there. And soon."

Gianni drew back and looked to Piero, who did not react, and then to Hasani, in the corner, who as always, seemed to have anticipated just this. Gianni shook his head. "No, Daria. Not there. Lepers! God could not be calling you there. There are hundreds upon that island. Hundreds!"

A small smile pulled at the corners of her cheeks. "Yes," she said. "Hundreds." She rose, more light and life in her eyes than there had been in some time. "We shall need to pack food. Water." She turned to Rune and Basilio, at once every inch the regal lady of Siena. "You must obtain a finely woven silk veiling. Several bolts of it. They need it for protection from the sun, and woolens to battle against the winter ahead. A hundred pair of sandals or boots. No doubt they've been left with no protection for their feet. And I need several bottles of a special oil . . ." She turned away with the knights, instructing them further.

Gianni shook his head, half in exasperation, half in glory to see the light in his lady's eyes return.

"We'll leave as soon as all is in order," she said, turning to face

Gianni from across the room. "And then, master Gianni, you shall take us to our new home in Venezia."

⚘ ⚘ ⚘

ABRAMO fingered the tapestry and lifted it closer, observing the delicate weave and detail. An old altar cloth, and at the lower right corner, a woman who bore an uncanny resemblance to Daria d'Angelo. "Fascinating, this trail of clues they have discovered," he mused. He pulled the large tapestry loose from the wall and flipped it, laying it upon a stack of linens nearby. He backed up several paces, arms crossed, and studied the image, visible among the crossed threads of the backside—a peacock, in the lower left corner. Above it, spreading across the wide expanse, towered a threatening dragon. Abramo let loose a deep, guttural laugh, arms spread wide. "Yes, yes, so my little peacock knew that I was coming."

He whirled and paced back and forth. "The Gifted are a worthy and entertaining conquest." He turned bright eyes upon Vincenzo. "This is good," he said, clapping him on the shoulder. "Good!"

"I confess it is difficult for me to see it that way," Vincenzo said. "Finding these clues only strengthens their thought that they are on some divine path. It gives them power. How is it good for us?"

Abramo waved his head back and forth. "Well, I admit, it does complicate things. But do you know how long, how long, Vincenzo, it has been since I have had a true challenge? I still consider your little Daria my greatest conquest. We must bring her and hers to our side. Many a soldier has lost a battle, but gone on to see a war won. The key is to change tactics, now. You tried to woo her, bring her along through friendly tactics, reason. You can see for yourself," he said, gesturing toward Old Woman Parmo, cradling her grandson in her arms, who still labored to breathe, "that sometimes alternate methods are needed."

He leaned closer, speaking across Vincenzo's shoulder now.

"You appealed to the Duchess out of love, out of loyalty, friend-ship, and familial ties, good God man, even as her co-consul of the guild, and she denied you. But mark my words: We shall see your Daria, Sir Gianni, even the priest, submit."

"How? How do you intend to do that?" Vincenzo whispered, still staring at the old woman, rocking her grandson back and forth, willing him to keep breathing.

"The same way I forced the old woman to talk to me," Abramo said, a smile curving his lips. "We shall make them suffer—and ex-ploit their greatest weaknesses."

"Weaknesses?"

"Come now, Vincenzo. You are quicker than that. Where is each of us the weakest? Where we are most tender, of course. The things, the people we hold most dear. Our values. Or mayhap," he said, pausing to stare out a high, narrow window, "through what they perceive is their divine call. Yes," he said with a pleased grin. "Yes. We shall find their weaknesses, every one of them. And through those slices in their armor we shall worry a hole that be-comes a gap that becomes a chasm. And then, there, Vincenzo, we shall have them."

Look for the other books in the Gifted series!

BOOK ONE
The Begotten

BOOK TWO
The Betrayed

Available now!

BOOK THREE
The Blessed

Coming from Berkley in 2008!